—LOST LEGACY BOOK TWO—

THE LAST DREAM

ALANA KAY

ISBN: 979-8-9912918-2-8 (Ebook edition)
ISBN: 979-8-9912918-3-5 (Paperback edition)

Library of Congress Control Number: 2024923179

First edition 2024

Cover by Miblart

Published by Fate Unbound Publishing LLC
Los Angeles, CA

Visit the author's website at www.alanakayauthor.com

For all the readers who unapologetically devour smut from the middle seat of the airplane. This one's for you.

To love and be loved is to feel the sun from both sides.

DAVID VISCOTT

The Last Dream

CHAPTER ONE

GIDEON

I pick up the coffee table and hurl it against the wall. It splinters into a million pieces, shards flying everywhere. It's nothing compared to the way my heart feels.

Sheena's gone. One second she was there, glowing with health, and the next she vanished in a cloud of smoke. I can't think. Pain and anger fill my chest, begging to escape. The witches betrayed us. Alina stole the person the gods meant for me. I'll make her pay in blood.

I send a chair flying after the table. It cleaves a chunk out of the drywall and falls to the ground broken. Callum flinches at the impact.

The piece that connects me to Sheena is missing. The internal compass that always points to her is gone. In its place is an aching, endless emptiness.

"Someone's watching us," Idris says, stepping in front of me.

I pause, breathing heavily through my nose as his words penetrate the haze in my brain. Slowly, I lower the only remaining chair from over my head and look outside.

A tiny flicker of movement catches my eye. That's all I need.

I hurl the chair through the window. The glass shatters a heartbeat before I jump through the jagged hole. My body becomes a whirling projectile of fur, teeth, and bone. *Speed. I need to be fast.* I leave the floor as a man and land crouched in the dirt as a cheetah, shaking bits of glass from my spotted coat.

My nose comes alive, and for a few seconds, the riot of smells is overwhelming. Until I lock in on an unusual scent. Human. Powerful. I follow it at a run, hungry for answers and desperate to make someone feel a fraction of the hurt I'm experiencing.

The trail twists and turns through a patch of trees. I have to separate the fresh human smell from smaller prey animals and older traces, but it's easy for me now that I've adjusted to this form.

The scent ends at a road isolated from the suburban neighborhood. There are fresh tire marks on the asphalt, and the acrid stench of burning rubber pollutes the air. I'm too late. Another loss, another failure, and another way I've let her down.

I sink to the ground, my stomach pressing against the warm road. A stick snaps in the woods behind me. I whip my head around. Callum jogs out of the woods, panting as he watches me warily.

His face is as hard as stone. My heart throbs painfully in my chest. I've seen this mask before. It was his go-to expression for most of our teen years. My best friend is hurting too, and there's nothing I can do about that either. I hang my head.

What good am I if I can't even protect the two people who matter the most to me?

"Gideon," Callum says. "We'll get her back. I promise you."

I growl softly at the reminder that Sheena is gone and turn my head away from him to stare down the road. He comes closer, stepping carefully around me until I see his shoes.

"Do you hate me?" Cal's voice cracks, and I lift my head just in time to see his mask slip and fall. "I'm so sorry. I made a bad call."

Even though I'd rather remain in this form, where my senses are sharp and my emotions dull, I have to try for him. Closing my eyes, I shift back and climb to my feet, naked and wrung out. Without the thrill of the hunt—gods, I can't even think about it.

"I could never hate you." My voice is a rough, painful rasp against my raw throat. "She's still alive," I assure him, kicking myself for not telling him sooner. Hope builds in his eyes, and I know what he's about to ask. I shake my head before he can open his mouth. "I can't find her. The directional pull from the bond is gone."

"Magic." He spits the word, his hands clenching at his sides.

An engine fires to life nearby, and I turn my focus back to our surroundings. If someone sees me standing out here naked, they'll call the cops. It would be even worse if a cheetah was spotted running around the suburbs; I could end up on the evening news. We don't have time for either headache. *I should have been more careful.*

Thankfully, luck is on our side—it's just Idris bringing the SUV around. His piercing blue eyes scan us both through the glass before he unlocks the doors. When I climb into the back seat, my nose is immediately flooded with Sheena's scent. I suck it in desperately, barely noticing that I'm digging holes in the seat with my claws.

"Double-crossed by a witch. How original," Idris observes to no one in particular. I growl, but my heart isn't really in it. The fae seems unfazed. "No reason to panic yet. It could certainly be worse."

"How?" I snarl, glad to have an outlet for my frustration. Callum winces as the sound echoes violently in the enclosed space of the car.

Idris looks at me through the rear view mirror, his eyes narrowing like I'm the dumbest person alive. "Alina could have killed her and fled. The fact that she healed Sheena at great cost to herself, and then abducted her, means the witches have plans for the little djinn."

His explanation makes sense, but I could do without the condescension.

"Do you think it was actually a talisman?" Callum asks.

I picture the ring and how it lit up like a Christmas tree when Sheena got close to it. That could probably be faked with magic, but the way her eyes glowed purple and her hair stood on end before she touched it . . .

"It sure as hell was something," I mutter.

I listen absently as Callum and Idris go over theories. The more they debate, the more my anger grows.

"It doesn't matter how or why they did it." I cut them both off, trying to put the lid back on my temper. "Because I will find them, and they will die. Alina stole my mate. She and everyone who helped her will pay. This is war."

Neither of them dares to argue, and we make our way back to the compound in silence.

SHEENA

POWER LIKE NOTHING I've experienced before slams into me as soon as I touch the ring. I feel myself start to disintegrate, my body breaking down into millions of tiny pieces. For one agonizingly long minute, I float there, and then I'm violently shoved back together again.

Nausea swamps me, and the next thing I know, I lose the contents of my stomach on an unfamiliar tile floor. Its pieces are black, white, and shiny, arranged in a checkered pattern like those modern diners that exist as time capsules to the 40s and 50s. I blink and imagine girls in poodle skirts sharing their milkshakes with greasers.

Where the hell am I?

A chair scrapes against the floor, and a woman clears her throat. Dizzy and disoriented, I drag the back of my hand over my mouth and lift my head slowly.

Alina is sitting at a nearby table. She's tossing the emerald ring up and down in her palm, a taunting smirk painted on her face. At least some of her confidence is for show, though. The chalky pallor of her skin and the way her hand trembles between throws gives her away.

"Well done, Alina," a smug voice says.

I lift my head further, swiveling my neck in the direction of the stranger. Standing to the side is a middle-aged woman wearing pumps, hose, and a pink pinup style dress. Not a single blonde hair is out of place, and when she turns her head, the loose barrel curls don't move at all. I'm not sure how much hair spray it took to achieve this look, but I doubt the ozone will thank her for it.

The woman's lips are painted a gaudy matte magenta, but it's the fanaticism in her eyes that stands out the most. She's looking at me with pure avarice . . . Like an art collector examining a painting they want to keep behind bulletproof glass.

"Hello, Sheena," she coos down at me, eyes flickering briefly over to the puddle of vomit. "Object-tethered travel can be disorienting for beginners. My apologies for your rocky transportation experience."

"Don't you mean my abduction?" I hiss, scrambling unsteadily to my feet. "It's not like I'm here because I want to be." I turn my back on her and focus on the one who caused all this. "You tricked us. Callum trusted you."

Alina meets my stare and laughs coldly. "Callum trusts used car salesmen more than me, babe. Of *course* I double-crossed him. Just how naive are you?"

Her eyes narrow to slits, and I feel the heat of her dislike from across the room. It's surprisingly strong considering we just met. Although, I'm finding it pretty easy to hate her, too.

"My dear, I think we're starting off on the wrong foot." The older woman cuts in, stepping back into my eye line. "Please, allow me to explain."

She gestures to a nearby booth, but I shake my head. I'm not getting any closer to this woman than I have to. Her lips purse, but she doesn't argue.

"My name is Leona Cabot. I'm the coven leader of a group of very powerful witches. Until recently, I was also one of the leaders of the enclave—you've heard of it, I believe?" She giggles with delight.

No one mentioned the witches were ever part of the enclave. I do my best to hide my shock. Sarah and Ciprian told me the witches were capricious and untrustworthy, but no one bothered to say they used to be part of the fucking enclave. My mind races, and I feel a small stab of betrayal.

"I see." Leona claps her hands together in delight, thrilled to have confused me. "Joshua and Dimitri are keeping secrets again. So prideful, those two. You see, we had a bit of a falling out. I guess you could say we disagreed about the best ways to rule." She steeples her fingers together. "This and that, incidentals and such, dear. You know how it is."

She beams at me again, waiting for a response, but I don't have a clue what she's talking about. I nod, hoping it's enough for her. Leona goes on as if I never reacted.

"When my daughter told me you were staying with those sweet boys, I just had to arrange a meeting." She gestures toward Alina, who bares her teeth at me. "I imagine you've had trouble finding any information about your history. I can help with that."

Adrenaline boils beneath my skin, but I know better than to take her words at face value. Even if my guys and their parents left some critical details out, my instincts are screaming at me to get away from this woman. I may not be tied up, but something tells me I'm going to need to rely on all of my skills to make it out of this.

Time to feel her out.

"That's so kind of you," I begin. "Although, I should warn you, I'm not really into ancient history. Callum and Gideon are a lot more interested in my powers and those dusty, old books than I am." I shoot her a smile that I hope looks vapid, then shrug. "My wishes are fun to bust out at a party." I lower my voice like I'm telling her a shameful secret. "But they aren't very practical."

Leona's magenta lips pinch into a thin line.

"She's lying," Alina hisses, standing up from the table and crossing her arms. "They wouldn't be so obsessed with her if she wasn't powerful."

I resist the urge to lunge for the bitch's throat and force myself to blink like an idiot instead. It's a lie, but her accusation is too close to some of my worst insecurities for comfort.

"I would love for that to be true, but my powers have never worked right." I try to look sad and chance a glance at the door. The edge shimmers, but I can't risk looking for long enough to figure out what I'm seeing.

"Don't sell yourself short, dear," Leona says, her creepy smile back in place. "Now that you have access to a talisman, we can help you test out your power properly."

She advances a step toward me, and my blood runs cold. If she sees what I can really do, I'll either end up chained to the wall or dead in a pool of my own blood.

"Would you really do that for me?" I clasp my hands together, internally cringing at how shrill my voice is. Thankfully, Leona is too preoccupied with the role she's playing to notice mine. She nods eagerly, and I take a chance. "That's amazing. When should I come back for lessons?"

Alina cackles like I've just told the best joke she's heard all year. Despite myself, I stiffen at the sound.

"Unfortunately, it's not really safe right now to be a djinn in this world," Leona says, her smile too wide now. There's a tiny smudge of lipstick on one of her teeth. "I'm doing everything I can to change that, but it's best if you stay here with us."

I smile and pause like I'm considering it. *Fuck. Fuck. Fuck. What should I do?*

"That's so cool," I sputter. "But I think I'd rather go back and forth. I get a little crazy when I'm cooped up."

I force a laugh, and Leona joins in. Her laughter pierces my eardrums like tons of tiny bells ringing in front of a megaphone.

By the time she stops, the hairs on the back of my neck are all standing on end.

"I understand, dear," she coos. "But I'm afraid that won't be possible. Now that your health is stable, you'll need a space to test your magic without risking exposure. Just think of this as your new home."

Leona spreads her arms out wide, and I take the opportunity to get a better look at my surroundings. A piece of the door ripples. I was right; I'm in an illusion. I'm confident of that now, but I can't tell what her magic is concealing. I let my smile fall and look at her with just a fraction of the actual concern I'm feeling. "So you are holding me prisoner," I say, letting my voice crack.

"That depends entirely on your choices, Sheena. If you want to reject my hospitality, I certainly can't stop you, but I prefer to think of you as a guest."

"A guest who can't leave," I clarify bitterly.

"Things are rarely perfect, dear."

"And if I try to walk out that door?" I ask.

Leona's smile drops, and a chill runs up my spine.

"What door, my sweet?"

I whip my head around. The door to the diner is gone—funky orange art deco wallpaper hangs in its place. It doesn't even match the rest of the room.

I guess we're both finished pretending.

"If you want to hold me here and test my powers, I'll need the talisman," I say, leveling Leona with a serious look before staring pointedly at the emerald ring in Alina's hand.

"Which talisman?" Leona asks, then winks and snaps her fingers.

The reality around us comes crashing down. Instead of a diner that's seen better days, we're in some kind of concrete basement surrounded on all sides by antiques. I'm talking about a hoarder's level mess.

I shiver at the sudden chill in the air, and for a moment, my confusion outweighs my fear. Rubbing my hands along my upper arms, I try to make sense of the clutter. There are several old pieces of furniture, tattered with age, and some broken dishes, but we're mostly at risk of being buried in ancient jewelry. Rings, necklaces, bracelets—there are even a few crowns perched haphazardly among the gilded, tarnished piles.

"You know, it's a shame you don't think much of your power levels," Leona says conversationally as her daughter hands her the ring. She looks at it for a moment without interest, then tosses it over her shoulder. I watch helplessly as it's swallowed up by a pile. "I can only hope—for both our sakes—that you just didn't have the proper resources available to you."

She looks around the room, surveying the mess fondly. "Most of the surviving djinn talismans from across the realms are right here in this room. I think you'll find my collection is quite comprehensive."

I process her words, and for the first time since I was taken, true terror sinks into my bones.

"Since you won't be going anywhere . . ." Leona reaches out and takes Alina's wrist. "You'll have plenty of time to figure out which one gives you the most juice, dear."

Before I can react, they both poof out of existence.

I sink to the ground, lean back against a dusty settee, and close my eyes. If Leona, a witch, has most of the djinn talismans in existence, it's pretty clear who is behind our near extinction. What isn't clear is what the hell I'm supposed to do about it.

IT'S HARD TO KEEP track of time. Despite there being no obvious light source, it's not completely dark in here. I guess witchcraft is the only reason I'm not sitting in complete darkness while surrounded by the spider web encrusted tokens of my murdered ancestors. That's cool and all, but it's barely keeping my panic at bay.

I've picked apart every corner of the room since they left me alone. At first, I hoped this was yet another layer of an illusion I could dismantle to find a way out. Unfortunately, it appears to be exactly what it looks like: a concrete box with no doors or windows.

Just thinking about it makes me feel claustrophobic and sweaty, but that's not the worst part. I can't feel Gideon anymore. There's no pain or buzzing, and worst of all, no tether to cling to. If I can't feel him, it stands to reason he can't feel me. He won't be able to find me.

The realization that I'm trapped and alone again almost sends me into hysterics. The only thing that stops me from letting my tears fall is the worry I could be under surveillance. There aren't any visible security cameras, but if the witches are controlling the lights with magic, then they probably have a way to watch me, too. I don't want to give them the satisfaction of seeing me break.

Maybe I'll bore them to tears.

I'm thinking of the best ways to be uninteresting when a smell catches my attention and a plate of food appears in front of me. It's a cheeseburger, complete with fries, a side salad, and a chocolate milkshake. I roll my eyes at the obvious continuation of the diner illusion. A careful sniff reveals absolutely nothing, as expected. Idris might know how to identify poisons with his fae nose, but all I smell is grease.

Eventually, pragmatism overrules my paranoia, and I take a bite. If Leona wanted me dead, she wouldn't have gone to the trouble of kidnapping me from the enclave, right? No, my gut is right about her. As weird as she is, she obviously wants access to my wishes.

What does she need me for?

Maybe the answer is in this room. The more I dig through the riches squirreled away in here, the more I worry her plans have nothing to do with money. There are more jewels here than I'd expect to find in most royal treasuries. While everything is in disrepair, nothing looks like it would turn your skin green to wear it.

When my searching causes a small avalanche of jewelry, I stop rifling through the talismans and sit back down to think. Despite the anxiety burning away at my stomach lining, I finish every bite of the food. In my experience, megalomaniacs don't keep normal eating schedules, and I don't know when I'll get another meal.

Thankfully, I still feel healthier than I have in weeks. Being surrounded by powerful magical anchors must be enough to keep me stable even if I haven't bonded with one yet.

When the lights go out abruptly, plunging the room into darkness, I can't hold back the scream that rips out of my throat. For several long minutes, I sit there, hugging my knees to my chest and waiting for an attack that doesn't come.

Once my heart rate levels off, I feel around for the edge of the settee. Curling up on top of it, I ignore the way the springs dig into my ribs and remind myself of the many places I've slept that were worse than this. Somewhere in the middle of my list, I drift off.

"SHEENA. SHEENA. LITTLE DJINN."

The voice penetrates my subconscious like wisps of smoke. It's not the first time I've dreamed about Idris, but it is the first time he's sounded this impatient.

"That is because I do not know how much time we have. Those two idiots could wake me up at any time to demand answers."

Did he just respond to my thoughts? That's new.

I crack my eyes open and take him in. The fae looks exhausted, his perfect eyebrows standing out more than usual against a face that is much too pale. He's still beautiful, but he looks like a damn ghost.

"How kind of you," Idris drawls. "But I need you to understand what is happening right now. I am visiting your dream on purpose. Can you tell me where the witches took you, Sheena?"

The fog in my brain evaporates at once.

"You're really here?" I demand, sitting up on the settee.

"In your mind, yes. I can communicate with you while you are unconscious, but I cannot alter the dreamscape in any other way. I have been waiting for you to fall asleep for hours."

He squints into the darkness, but it's hard to see two inches in front of your face.

"Where are you?"

"I don't know," I admit. "At first it was an illusion. An old, weird diner. I saw the bad edges and knew it wasn't real."

He nods, urging me to go on, but I'm pretty sure I see a hint of pride in his glowing blue eyes.

"Alina took me to some creepy lady named Leona Cabot," I say. Idris' face hardens, and I frown. "That reminds me. Why didn't anyone tell me you replaced the witches in the enclave? She ambushed me with that fun fact, and I felt like an idiot."

"Joshua does not like to talk badly about her publicly, but know Leona is dangerous and half mad. Once you're safe, we'll have time to answer all your questions. Are you hurt?"

Idris perches on the ancient couch next to me, and for the first time since I was taken, I feel a little safer.

"I'm okay," I say. "They haven't touched me, but they want me to find whichever talisman in this room makes me the strongest." I gesture around me, even though I doubt he can see much further than I can. "There are hundreds here, Idris, maybe thousands . . . Do you think she's the one who's been killing the djinn?"

"It is a distinct possibility."

"Do you think she plans to kill me?"

I haven't known him long, but my gut tells me I can trust Idris to give me the truth even if it's bad news. He reaches out hesitantly and cradles my jaw with his right hand. Even though I know it's not real, I lean in to the feeling of warmth on my skin.

"She has plans for you," he finally admits. "But I think if her primary objective was your death, you would not still be breathing. In truth, I suspect she wants to use your power to further her own."

"I won't give her anything," I insist, my anger building as it sinks in that I'm once again being held hostage to further a stranger's agenda.

Idris tilts his head to the side and studies me.

"It might be wise to play along, at least for now. We are working to find you, but the shifter cannot track your bond. He is . . . struggling."

It's obvious Idris is downplaying the situation. Gideon must be losing his shit. I understand his panic, but I don't want him taking all this on.

"Tell them, Idris. Please tell them both it isn't their fault," I urge, desperate to make sure Gideon and Callum don't blame themselves. "I'm alive, I'm not hurting anymore, and we're going to figure this out." I force confidence I don't feel into my voice, but I get the feeling he sees right through my bravado.

"I will pass on your entirely unnecessary absolution, but please keep in mind that I am not a messenger," he grumbles, a wrinkle momentarily marring the perfection of his skin before he forces his face to relax. "They do not deserve your worry, little djinn. Focus on the witches. Do not let them think you weak, but try not to reveal your full strength."

I nod, deciding to search through every talisman when I wake up.

"If I bond with a talisman, I can refuse any wishes she makes," I say. "I'm useless to her if I'm in control of my magic."

Idris considers that for a second.

"Good idea, unless she takes it from you by force."

My heart sinks. He's right, and it's not like I have anywhere to hide it. If Leona gains control of my talisman after I've bonded with it, the situation would be even worse. She could use me like a puppet. It's better to bide my time and look for another way to escape.

"Okay, so no bonding," I say. "Maybe I can find one that fits my magic well but not too well and trick her into losing interest."

He nods, but his face is starting to blur in front of me. With a spike of panic, I realize he's fading away.

"Wait, Idris, will you come back?" My voice gives my desperation away, but I can't hide it any longer.

His expression softens as he reaches for my face. I can't feel his touch at all. His lips move, but I can't hear him anymore either.

When Idris fades completely from view, I'm left sitting alone on the settee, battling exhaustion. Being here by myself makes my skin crawl, but having an ally in my dreams is better than nothing.

CHAPTER TWO

CALLUM

My father glares across the conference room table at Gideon, his expression dripping with scorn. "Don't be a fool, boy. We can't attack the witches outright. It would start a war."

"They declared war when they took her from me," Gideon roars, his voice so guttural it's hard to make out the individual words. His whole body is shaking with the effort not to shift.

As usual, my father has ignored every logical sign to shut the fuck up. Provoking an omni-shifter who is already trembling with rage is just asking for it. If Gideon's beast decides to take a bite out of him, he'll only have himself to blame. I wouldn't mind seeing my father humbled, but a physical fight won't get us any closer to getting Sheena back.

I drop my hand to Gideon's back. I can't remove his rage, but I can dull it a little bit to help him get through this meeting.

"Son, Dimitri isn't saying we do nothing," Joshua says, eying Gideon with concern. "Alina acted without honor by abducting Sheena while she was under the protection of this enclave. We cannot let that stand, or we will look weak." He looks pointedly at my father then, and I'm grateful he's speaking in a language a nightmare demon can understand.

"Of course, we'll repay the offense." My father throws up his hands. "All I'm saying is we can't start slaughtering witches because your girlfriend is missing."

"My mate," Gideon growls. "Sheena is my fated mate, not my girlfriend."

He presses his hand against his chest, and I see sadness bleed through the rage.

"She's going to be okay," I whisper, rubbing my hand on his lower back in a gentle circle. "If they hurt one hair on her head, I'll help you track down every witch in our territory. We'll see how long Alina can stay in hiding with us leading a witch hunt."

"On the bright side," Joshua cuts in with a forced smile. "Sheena bonded with a talisman. That's a relief, especially since her magic was making her so sick without one."

That's an understatement of massive proportions. Every time I close my eyes, I see the sickly pallor of her face and the excruciating pain she was in. It was so bad that I had no choice but to contact Alina for help. Sheena was dying.

"Except she has not bonded to the talisman," Idris says, walking through the door and taking the seat to my right. "I was able to reach her through her dream."

Gideon stands and stares at the fae with so much desperation it makes my stomach churn. "Where is she? Is she okay?"

"And what do you mean she's not bonded to the talisman?" I add. "We all saw it happen."

Idris looks between the two of us with one tiny line forming between his eyebrows—the only sign he's annoyed by our questions.

"She is alright. The witches have her trapped in a room filled with djinn talismans. They want her to identify which one will make her the most powerful. While there, her health should remain stable even if she does not bond with one of the objects."

Idris delivers the intel in a dull monotone, but I'm not fooled.

He's sitting six inches from me, and his energy is all over the place. It's far from the calm disinterest he's projecting.

"How would Alina get access to a room full of talismans?" I ask, narrowing my eyes at the fae. He tilts his head as though he expected better from me, and suddenly, it all clicks. "Leona. Fuck."

He nods, and Joshua and my father exchange troubled looks. I frown at them. It's time to get some answers.

"When the witches left the enclave, Gideon and I asked you why. You said that information was 'need to know.' Now, I think we can all agree, we really need to know." My voice drips with sarcasm, and Joshua winces.

My father just doubles down. "Watch yourself. You don't get to demand information from us," he hisses, slapping his palms on the wood of the table.

I stand, staring boldly into his furious black eyes. I'm not scared of him anymore, and it's time to make that clear.

"That's exactly what I'm doing, father, and you're going to deliver," I say, holding my ground. "Gideon and I have spent years working as your enforcers without asking a single question. I'm sure you prefer it that way, but when your former ally snatches my girl right out of my godsdamn hands and locks her up, things change. It seems to me, Sheena is paying the price for your power struggle with the witches, and I won't fucking stand for that."

It's the most direct thing I've said to my father in years. His face is red with fury—he's about to explode.

"You're right, Callum," Joshua interjects, and I sink back into my seat. "I'll tell you what happened, but it's not what you think. Leona's opinions had become increasingly erratic. She wanted to loosen the rules and remove protections for weaker supernaturals unless they paid a protection tax. Your father and I voted her down each time and tried to reason with her. We told her this community should be a safe place for everyone, no matter their strength."

"She accused us of conspiring against her. She was losing her fucking mind," my father grumbles. "The last straw was a council of witches she wanted to establish. Since her coven is so large, Leona thought witches should get more say. We told her it wasn't going to happen, and she packed up and left of her own volition."

"Where did she go?" I ask through clenched teeth.

"We tried to keep track of her, but she just vanished," Joshua says, rubbing his hand along his chin. "When you saw Alina at the academy, that was the first time a member of her coven had surfaced in months."

"And you didn't think that was worth mentioning?" Gideon snaps at his dad, who lifts his hands palms out.

"In hindsight, we probably should have. But with the traffickers and the hunter attacks happening, it didn't really seem like a top priority."

Joshua rubs his hand over his face again, and for the first time in my life, he doesn't look invincible to me.

"We called Alina, but she's not picking up," I say. "Since we don't even know where to attack, what's your suggestion for tracking Leona and her bitch of a daughter down?"

"I think we wait until morning," Joshua says, staving off our immediate protests. "It's late. If we call her right now, we look desperate. Leona won't be able to resist gloating, and we should avoid playing into her hands. Dimitri and I will call tomorrow."

I think it over and nod in agreement. Joshua stands, clapping me on the back as he walks by. He looks at his son like he wants to hug him but isn't sure if the affection is welcome. I don't think Gideon even notices when his dad leaves the room. He's too busy staring down at the table, lost in his own head.

My father stomps out without looking at any of us.

As soon as the door clicks shut behind him, I turn to Idris. "Is she really okay?"

"Physically, she is better than I have seen her in days. Mentally . . . Sheena is scared, but she is not letting them see. She asked me to tell you this is not your fault," Idris says, a sour look on his face.

"I was supposed to protect her," Gideon groans, covering his face with his hands. "The gods gave me a gift, and I failed her."

"It's not your fault. The witches tricked us," I argue. "If anything, blame me. I'm the one who called Alina."

"This is hardly the right moment to assign guilt," Idris snaps. "It's a waste of time. Time Sheena may not have. We have to figure out where she is and hope she can hold on until we get there. If we fail in this, the enclave could fall."

Gideon scoffs. "The witches are no match for our strength."

"The witches alone, perhaps not. But the witches with the powers of a djinn behind them . . . They would be unstoppable."

A chill rakes down my spine as Idris' blue eyes burn into me. He's right. The stakes are even higher than I realized. We cannot fail.

SHEENA

I WOULD COMMIT cold-blooded murder for a cup of coffee. Death by caffeine withdrawal is a cruel and unusual punishment.

The magical lights came back on hours ago, but no one has popped in for a visit yet. I don't know if I should be relieved or concerned by that.

I spent a while sorting the jewelry. Several pieces drew me in more than others, so I hid those the best I could. My best bet is to convince the witches I'm a dud, so they let me go home.

Home. That word has never meant much to me before. I never felt any warmth or security in my foster care placements, and the dumps I crashed in after I escaped from the traffickers were nothing more than temporary hideouts. The cabin, the enclave's compound—I like both—but home is with Gideon and Callum. Without them, I feel truly alone in a way I've never experienced.

These witches will pay.

A brief snapping sound is the only warning I get before the mother and daughter duo appears in front of me. Alina is dressed like she's about to go audition for the role of head mean girl in a high school musical, and Leona looks like an oversized bumblebee. She's covered in yellow and black stripes with the pumps to match. Her mouth is coated in a cherry red lipstick, and her eyes shine with delight as she studies me. Just looking at her makes my headache worse.

"Good morning, dear."

"Is it?" I can't help asking. Her smile creeps me out, so when it melts from her face, I congratulate myself on a job well done.

"I see you're not ready to accept my hospitality yet."

I look pointedly at the dusty basement, then back at her, raising my eyebrows. "Sorry, Leona," I simper. "I guess I didn't realize this was how you treated guests. Money must be tight."

She sucks in a breath and makes a nasty slurping sound that turns my stomach.

"I wish this room was better organized," Leona coos.

Fuck, shouldn't have provoked her, Sheena. Dread claws at my brain, but there's nothing I can do to stop her. My magic lifts me off the ground, and reality shifts as my powers warp the surrounding space to fulfill the wish.

Metal scrapes against metal as gravity loses its hold. Antiques zip through the air like projectiles, and a dozen mirrors snap into formation along the walls. They reflect the scene back to me like a tornado in a fun house.

The three of us are defenseless against the chaos. Alina raises her arms to protect her face, but I don't have that option while I'm frozen in mid-air. Leona stands in the middle of the magical storm with her hands outstretched, loud cackles exploding from her mouth. *She's unhinged.*

A few plastic tubs materialize from thin air and hit the ground with a thud. Another one whizzes so close by my head that it blows my floating hair back. Rings ping into the farthest bin, gold and silver hardware colliding with metallic screams. Bracelets, necklaces, earrings, and tiaras . . . They all find their place as my back bows under the force of the wish.

Alina ducks as a fucking war hammer sails over her head. When a jewel-encrusted dagger flies by me, the edge of the rusted blade catches my cheek. Blood wells up from the shallow cut, but I'm powerless to change the trajectory of anything. I can only hope an antique weapon runs the witches through.

Unfortunately, luck has never been on my side, and today isn't any different.

The maelstrom of flying talismans seems to last forever, but in reality, it can't be more than a minute. The wish stirs up so much dust that it's hard to see through it.

Once the last antique settles, my feet sink back to the cracked concrete. A drop of blood falls next to my right foot. It settles in among the other stains, adding an angry crimson to the dusty mess.

I brace for my usual nausea and fatigue hangover to strike. It never comes. I'm a little tired, but it's nothing like before. *Being surrounded by talismans must be preventing my magic drain.*

I pull my shirt up over my nose and mouth to avoid breathing in a lungful of vintage germs, thankful to be back in control of my body.

Alina sneezes. The sound is girly and unexpected in the silence. Her eyes water violently, and her hair looks like a bird's nest. But I don't get the chance to enjoy how rattled she looks. Leona advances toward me, rubbing her hands together. Her ruby red lips quirk up in a closemouthed smile. I'm her golden goose, and she knows it.

When her mouth opens, I brace for the worst.

"I wish this room was a little cleaner."

Gravity fades away again as anxiety settles heavily in my belly.

It's going to be a long day.

LEONA LEVITATES several talismans and summons them to her side. She grabs Alina's wrist, and they disappear with a crack, the levitating talismans vanishing with them.

I'm simply too tired to care. The basement is unrecognizable, and my body is spent after hours of granting wishes. As soon as their magic fades, my legs turn to jelly, tremors and cramps raking through my muscles.

Besides the cleaning, Leona wished for new furniture, a fully functional bathroom, and worst of all, a magenta paint job. She was so thrilled, the damn witch didn't stop wishing until my bloody nose went from leaky faucet to scarlet waterfall.

My t-shirt is plastered to my skin, stained with sweat, blood, and dirt. In all her bullshit, Leona could have at least wished for some new clothes for me, but from the looks of the new bed—a box spring and no mattress—it's clear my comfort isn't her top priority.

This is her game, and I'm still learning the rules.

A simple sandwich materializes in front of me. It's the first food I've seen all day, and I snatch it up, worried it will vanish if I'm too slow. The bread is stale, but I don't care. I devour it in less than ten bites, ignoring how dry it feels going down. Since there's nothing to drink, I drag my body to the new bathroom and focus on the positives.

It could be a lot worse. Without all these magical items surrounding me, Leona's wishes would have been my eulogy. As it is, I still feel like a stiff breeze would knock me over.

When I turn the sink on, I'm amazed to see clean, cool water pouring from the spout. I'm no plumber, but somehow my magic created a fully functional bathroom from absolutely nothing.

Using my hand, I scoop water into my mouth. Once I've had enough, I turn to the small shower. Ignoring the screaming pain in my arms and legs, I strip, tossing my dirty clothes into the corner and limping to the stall. I crank the handle and shiver as the cold water hits my exposed skin.

No pity. Trust no one. Keep it moving.

My rules rush through my head. I'm in this mess because I ignored them, but I can't bring myself to regret my choices.

As the water heats, a sigh of relief slips through my lips. The water pressure feels amazing against my sore muscles. Closing my eyes, I think of Gideon and rub my heart. I miss feeling our connection throbbing in my chest. Just a few weeks ago, it freaked me out, but now I would give anything to feel that electric current again.

If he were here, Gideon would tell me that everything is going to be fine. Callum would roll his eyes at his optimism, then get to work distracting me from my fear.

I miss them so much. A tear escapes from the inner corner of my left eye. The pounding spray of the shower consumes it. I refuse to let another one fall. I need a new plan because hiding my power from Leona isn't working.

She didn't make me hold any specific objects, and I'm thankful for that. Given the hum I feel from some of them, I know they would feed my power exponentially.

The cut on my cheek stings, and I picture the dagger sailing toward my face during the whirlwind of talismans. The dirty blade could have slit my throat or embedded itself in a vital organ, but it just grazed me . . . like a warning. I felt something more than pain when it broke my skin. Like when I touched the emerald ring for the first time, ancient power sang to me, and I tasted copper on my tongue.

I shiver with fear even though the shower is scalding hot. I didn't choose this magic, and the last thing I want to do is feed it. Power is pain, and for eight years, these abilities have done nothing but hurt me, giving cruel supernaturals a reason to play tug-of-war with my freedom.

I don't have a clue what I'm capable of, and that's what scares me the most.

QUAID

I'm risking my life to watch a witch shop.

Of all my hunches over the years, this may be the most dangerous. As I watch the young witch prance from store to store, my fingers itch to snap her neck.

She came to hunter headquarters again this morning and met with my bosses. They called her Alina, shook her hand, and even thanked her. It was disgusting.

Her intelligence dumps are still fishy as hell, but as soon as I saw her at that house with Sheena, my priorities changed. The scene has played on repeat in my brain ever since I narrowly escaped the shifter's claws. My adrenaline spikes each time I remember how close he came to catching me.

I'll find Sheena, kill her, and erase my greatest shame.

Following Alina is step one. I just wish it wasn't so damn boring. She's been shopping for two hours, and I'll have to leave soon if she doesn't get on with it. As a hunter, I'm allowed to come and go as I want, but if I'm gone for too long, someone will notice. Angus' suspicious stare at the vampire raid comes to mind. *He can't find out about my plans.*

The witch comes out of the store, arms weighed down with bags. I watch from the shadows as she looks right and left, then mutters something under her breath. Magic crackles in the air, and my fingers twitch around my blade as her arms lift several inches.

A spell to lighten the load? How pathetic.

She's a freak. An imbalance of nature putting human lives at risk. Based on the hunter code, I should strike now.

I stay where I am instead. My superiors would be livid to lose their source, but the real reason my dagger isn't buried to the hilt in her chest has nothing to do with that. If the witch dies, so does my lead to Sheena. As long as my redemption lies with Alina, she gets to live.

When she climbs into her car, I hop in mine and trail her out of town, hanging as far back as I dare. Tailing a normal person is hard enough, but it's even harder with supernaturals. Their heightened senses make them annoyingly good at self-preservation. This witch doesn't strike me as the careful type, though. She cast a spell in the middle of the street, and she hasn't checked her rear view mirror once.

When she pulls into an abandoned theme park outside of town, I drive past it. I can't follow her in there without giving myself away.

I check the time. Dammit, I've been gone for hours, definitely long enough for someone to notice. I'll just have to wait until it gets dark to come back.

AFTER DARK, I creep back toward the abandoned park. Angus didn't confront me at headquarters, but I know better than to assume that means he didn't notice my absence. I should probably lie low for a few days, but I just can't wait any longer.

Hiking the perimeter of the theme park, I suck in magic pollution. Thick and sweet, it coats my tongue and makes me want to gag. More importantly, it proves I'm in the right place.

The theme park rides cast deep, warning shadows around me, but I press on, only hesitating at the edge of the overgrown mess. I'm screwed if they put some kind of security magic in place.

I run my fingers over my favorite knife, then a pair of guns in my holsters. One shoots regular old bullets, the other a heavy tranquilizer dart. The second gun is a mandatory addition to my gear as part of the new capture directive.

It goes against everything they taught me not to kill on sight, but leadership believes we will win this war faster by taking some supernaturals hostage and grilling them for information. I'm skeptical, although I don't hate that change nearly as much as I do working with a witch.

Eying the shadows again, I take a deep breath and step forward, exhaling as my foot lands on enemy territory. No alarm goes off. No witches appear to turn me into a frog. A moment of relief is all I get because in the next breath, everything around me morphs.

The creepy park with its rusty rides and carnival games vanishes. Gone is the dilapidated, skeletal scaffolding of the mechanical swings. Tall, dry grass fades away to be replaced with neat landscaping and garden beds filled with riotous wildflowers and pungent smelling herbs.

The light of the full moon shows me what magic kept hidden: an entire living setup bathed in shadowy shades of gray. It's a cross between a suburb and an encampment. Some things look hastily constructed, while other elements—like the gardens—appear meticulously planned out and cared for.

I blink my eyes. Nothing changes.

What is this place?

Muffled voices snap me out of my stasis. I slide behind a storage shed just as two people step into view. I've never seen either of them before. The woman stands stiffly, like she's barely holding herself back from lashing out at the tall man in front of her.

"I already told you. The answer is no." Her voice rings like a bell, carrying easily to my hiding place. She taps her right heel as the man glares down at her.

"I found her first," he hisses.

I have to strain to hear him, so I sneak closer to the edge of the shed.

The man advances menacingly on the older woman. "It's only fair you return her to me."

His stance is threatening, but she doesn't give an inch. There's a moment of silence, then she laughs in his face. The sound sends a shiver down my spine.

"You're trying to call 'finder's keepers' because you snatched her out of her bed when she was a teenager? You couldn't hold on to her when she was sixteen. What makes you think you can handle her now?" She taunts.

His body twitches, a ragged, involuntary gesture that makes me nervous. Rage? Withdrawals? I can't tell, but this guy is definitely not in control of himself.

"I've been tracking her for years," he growls. "My men and I have followed that bitch all over the damn map. Do you think that was cheap?"

The woman scoffs at his argument, looking him up and down with a sneer. He's tall, almost unnaturally stretched out, but his clothes are stained and loose, hanging off of him in wrinkled, baggy folds.

"Yes, I'm sure losing the djinn is the one and only reason you're experiencing financial hardship, Lysander." He opens his mouth, but she cuts him off. "Besides, don't you know that possession is nine-tenths of the law?"

Another twitch rattles his frame as he looks around. I hold completely still, hoping he can't sense my hiding spot.

"I want a cut," Lysander snarls. "You know good and well I'm the only reason you even know she exists."

"A cut . . ." She examines her fingernails. "What cut would you like, then? An arm, a leg? With all those girls you have scattered around, I would think you were getting your pound of flesh already."

He howls. The ferocious and unnatural sound rips through the air. If I needed proof the two people in front of me were supernatural, I have it now.

"You don't have any problem with my business when it suits you."

"True," she sighs, wrinkling her nose at the man. "As disgusting as I find you and your dealings, they serve a purpose."

Faced with her disdain, he stands up straighter.

"You never were one to get your hands dirty, Leona. Afraid to ruin your manicure with a little blood under the nails?" He takes another step toward her, but his dig doesn't seem to land. If anything, the woman seems pleased.

"On the contrary." Her tone drips with amusement . . . until it doesn't. "A little blood can be a wonderful moisturizer."

Quick as a flash, Leona's good humor vanishes. She lifts her hand, and a dagger materializes, sailing through the air and pressing into the man's throat. There's enough pressure to cut but not to kill. Blood trickles down Lysander's bobbing throat, but his eyes glow yellow with excitement. He drops his head, driving the blade deeper into his own throat as he tries to sniff it.

"You will not be adding my djinn to your personal collection or your public catalogue, Lysander. Is that understood?"

More blood falls as the weapon digs in deeper. The man doesn't make a sound, but after a pause, inclines his head reluctantly. Leona spares him one last parting glance before turning her back on him.

With a flick of her wrist, the dagger leaves his throat and returns to her hand. She studies the blood coating the edge of the blade, then shakes her head. Pulling a handkerchief from her pocket, she cleans the weapon thoroughly. She doesn't bother turning around, seemingly confident he won't have the balls to attack her while her back is turned.

"If you value your life, don't come back here again." Leona delivers the threat, and I feel the hairs on the back of my neck stand on end.

Her heels click on the sidewalk as she walks away, disappearing inside an old-fashioned brick home. It's a weathered and charming storybook house—the type of place where a fairy tale witch would use candy to lure children to their death before feasting on their bones. In the middle of this abandoned theme park, it sticks out like a sore thumb.

Once the door closes behind her, I focus on Lysander. He smiles even as jerks rack through his body. He doesn't seem to notice the blood dripping down his collarbone. It adds yet another stain to his shirt.

The witch may be the apex predator in this situation, but instinct tells me he's a more traditional brand of dangerous.

When his nostrils flare and his eyes widen, adrenaline floods my veins. He looks around, peering into the darkness like he can sense me. I finger my gun, holding perfectly still. It feels like a lifetime before he finally turns and lopes off. I take my first deep breath in minutes.

I'm not sure what's going on here. My brain is full of puzzle pieces that don't fit, but this is my chance to find all the missing pieces and reveal the entire picture.

I creep toward the witch's lair. Avoiding the windows, I keep to the shadows and case the house. A door bangs in the distance, and I flinch.

When I see a cellar hatch, I stare at it, torn. If I crawl down into that enclosed space, I may never come out again. *Is killing Sheena worth my life?* The contents of my stomach sour and churn. Her death would fulfill my oath and erase my mistake. Peace could be within my reach, hovering just on the other side of that cellar door.

In the end, the temptation wins out. I work the old door open, wincing when a grinding creak from the hinge shatters the silence. It looks like a tight fit, but I think I can work my body through the hole. I step in and the wood presses against my waist. *Move; don't panic. You're not stuck.* When the squeeze ends, I pop through the other side and onto a small landing.

Feeling my way down the stairs, I descend into complete darkness. I have to duck my head to avoid the low ceiling, but I don't dare risk pulling out my phone or looking for a light switch. Instead, I squint and wait for my eyes to adjust. It looks like any other cellar that could serve as storage or a storm shelter.

I take a few steps and stumble directly into a shelving unit, barely catching a jar before it falls off the ledge. The wobbling sound is loud in the silence, but my luck holds and no one shows up to investigate.

Exploring more carefully, the pads of my fingers graze cool bricks. Crumbling mortar connects the seams. Three of the walls feel the same. When I get to the corner, my fingers tangle in a tacky spider web. It wraps around my hand. My skin crawls, and I almost lose my entire goddamn mind.

I thrash around, ripping the web from my hand and lurching away from the insect infested corner. I imagine spiders crawling up my arm and sinking their fangs into my skin. It's all I can do not to scream like a child.

My hand swings into another wall. I jump away, expecting more bugs, but quickly realize this one is different. No rough bricks meet my hand. Instead, the drywall is smooth, and I can't feel any blemishes.

Why is this wall new? Better yet, what's on the other side?

Doing my best to forget the spiders, I press my ear to the wall. At first, I hear nothing, then a muffled bang comes through the drywall, followed by a pained, feminine groan. Someone is definitely on the other side.

I check the full length of the wall from top to bottom, but there are no entry points. It seems solid. I stop to think. *Make the pieces fit.*

Lysander spoke of a djinn outside. I didn't know those were real, but I've hunted supernaturals for too long to be surprised by anything anymore. Given Leona's talk of the flesh trade, I'm willing to bet the burned out barn we found weeks back was one of his trafficking hideouts. *I should have killed that grimy fucker when I had the chance.*

I think back to the moment I saw Sheena and the witch poof out of existence. In the aftermath, the males freaked out, but I thought nothing of it. It's my job to kill supernaturals, not psychoanalyze why they do the things they do.

I assumed my ex-friend was in cahoots with Alina, but what if

I got it all wrong? I replay the conversation I just overheard. Leona taunted Lysander for abducting a djinn when she was a teenager, then letting her get away.

What's the connection?

Suddenly, the pieces click together, and I can't get enough oxygen.

Sheena disappeared when we were sixteen. One day she was there, and the next it was like she never existed. I'd been keeping my distance—a stupid kid avoiding duty out of a delusional, misplaced loyalty. When she left without a trace, I figured she had finally put together that I was a plant and taken off. But if she was taken and hunted all these years . . .

I never knew what kind of 'other' Sheena was. To me, she was just another awkward and lonely kid, desperate for friendship. I was told to get close to her, so I did. Time passed, and I became convinced that the elders were wrong about her. She was the most human person I'd ever met, so how could it all be a lie?

When I got the order to kill her during our junior year, I couldn't do it. I pulled away instead, determined to prove the hunters wrong. Except they weren't wrong, and I paid dearly for my hesitation.

So what if someone else got to her first? Just because I had part of the picture wrong doesn't mean I misjudged everything. If she's on the other side of this wall, it doesn't matter how she got there.

I grit my teeth and press my ear back to the smooth surface, but no more sounds filter through. The silence is so all-consuming my imagination takes over, and I feel a presence reaching out to me through the wall. I want to punch through it and find out for sure if I'm right, but I'm already pushing my luck here. Reluctantly, I ease back and crawl out of the cellar.

As I sneak back to my car, I feel the magic like a blade scraping against my skin. I don't look back. I already know what I would see—an abandoned amusement park, rundown and forgotten in the gloom. It's just another convincing lie, as deceptive as the shy brunette whose blushing cheeks and green eyes bewitched me as a teen.

Our reunion is coming, and it's long overdue.

CHAPTER THREE

IDRIS

I lay flat on the bed, exhaustion tugging at my brain. The full force of the enclave is focused on finding the little djinn, but all we have encountered thus far is failure after failure.

Joshua called Leona during our meeting today, and she let it ring. That refusal—while surprising—is practically an admission of guilt. Gideon is petitioning for war, but cooler heads are holding him back for now. He was so infuriated by the decision, he ripped a door from its hinges and stormed out of the room.

Even though it galled him to ask for my help, Callum stayed behind to request I check in on Sheena in her dreams. I didn't tell him I was already planning another visit.

Closing my eyes, I set my intention and activate my magic. As my reality slips away, I wake up in hers. Sheena is already dreaming, so I hover on the edge, interested to see what her subconscious is showing her.

A much younger Sheena walks along the sidewalk with a boy, laughing with each step they take. They're both hovering in that awkward space between youth and maturity.

"You said Heathcliff had it made. I think Ms. Sneade's head

almost exploded," the boy teases Sheena, and a familiar blush floods her cheeks.

"What does she know about the modern American foster care system, anyway? All I'm saying is some of my placements have made Wuthering Heights look like a fairy tale." Sheena rubs her wrist, and the boy's expression darkens.

"Is it getting bad again?" His voice is quieter now, all the humor gone.

Sheena tucks a strand of her dark hair behind her ear and stares at her feet.

"It's fine."

"Sheena—"

"I said it's fine, Quaid," she interrupts him.

He bites his bottom lip, then gently grabs her arm to stop her from walking away. "You should tell someone."

"I shouldn't have told you," she whispers.

The boy pulls back like she slapped him.

"So what's the plan, Sheena? You're just going to take it for the next three years?" His voice is loud and wobbly as it switches between two registers.

Sheena tugs her arm free and walks away. With her short legs, he catches her easily.

"Okay, Quaid," she snaps. "If I report it to my social worker, we know what will happen. It's my word against theirs. I either get labeled a liar and it gets worse, or they'll move me. That means another new start. Another school. We would never see each other again. Is that what you want?"

"No, of course not. But you don't know what would happen—"

"Yes, I do!"

"No, you don't. And if you were safe, it might be for the best."

"Just leave it alone! Please . . ." Her voice cracks, and the boy looks gutted.

The dream shifts.

Quaid holds Sheena as she cries.

It shifts again.

Open textbooks litter the carpet as they share a bag of candy. He gives her all the yellow pieces, smiling at her when she isn't looking.

When the dream shifts yet again, young Sheena stands alone.

She watches Quaid from down the school hallway, but he doesn't look at her. Other girls laugh and point. She runs to the bathroom, rushing into the stall as tears roll down her cheeks. Sheena covers her mouth, muffling her sobs as her head drops back against the graffiti covered partition.

The scene changes again.

Sheena is alone. Her bedroom is dark, and she's crying again. I can feel her broken heart.

Her pain shifts to terror as two grown men in masks burst into the room. Monsters. These aren't men, they're monsters. Magic. Fear. Darkness. My muscles tense, but I'm not a nightmare demon; I can't change this.

I'm a silent witness to this dream, watching these scenes—clearly memories of her past. These vignettes are pieces of the little djinn I've not earned. A good person would alert her to his presence, so she doesn't have to relive this. But I'm not a good person. I accepted that long ago, therefore I simply look on in fascination, unable to turn away.

Another shift.

Young Sheena wakes in a cage. She rattles the padlock, then makes herself as small as possible against the bars. Pained screeches and angry roars echo in the distance. Her heart races. She covers her ears. It's not enough.

A monster appears—the one who took her. He steps through the shadows, his yellow eyes gleaming from behind a mask. His long, lean body twitches with excitement as he nears her. Sheena whimpers, her green eyes glassy with unshed tears.

Watching from the wings, I grit my teeth. I should stop this, but . . .

I watch as the masked man makes wish after wish. Sheena

cries out for her friend. Wails. Begs her captor to stop as she writhes in pain. The wishes keep coming. Sheena fights for consciousness, but loses the battle, sinking finally to a heap on the floor of the cage. Blood pours from her nose. When the man laughs, I burn to return her suffering to him tenfold.

Time passes.

Her raw terror dulls to a conditioned sense of dread, then a partially formed longing for death. Escape. More wishes. Pain. Hope fades. The cycle repeats again and again and again. Finally, even I cannot stand to bear witness any longer.

"Little djinn," I say. My voice is hoarse and ragged; I'm as caught up in the memory as she is. "Sheena, it is me, Idris."

The scene shudders, but the bars hold.

"You are dreaming," I tell her.

Young Sheena peels her hands away from her ears, and a crack cleaves down the middle of the cage. The teen looks on in shocked hope, frozen in place. More screams sound in the distance. They jolt her into action. She scurries out and never looks back.

The dream fades.

Adult Sheena stares up at me. She looks as wrecked as I feel. It's only been twenty-four hours, but I hardly recognize the woman in front of me. Her eyes are dull, there's a cut on her face, and her cheeks seem hollower than they were last night. Her thin shirt is damp and filthy. I can see the outline of her nipples through the fabric. A good person wouldn't look.

I scan the room, blinking a few times. Gone are the haphazard piles of antique relics. The chaos has been replaced with organized columns, boxes, and stacks of talismans. There's some new furniture, but the bed in the corner has no mattress.

Sheena is curled up on the same antique settee I found her on last night. Her hair hangs in long waves over her shoulders, and the skin under her eyes is bruised. When her full lower lip trembles, the urge to offer comfort scalds me like boiling oil. I flinch away from its intensity and from her.

"I-I'm sorry . . . I just," Sheena sighs, swiping at her cheeks. "I was dreaming about . . . You know what? It doesn't matter."

I already know about her dreams, but I am strangely disappointed she doesn't want to tell me about them.

"There is no reason to apologize," I assure her, lifting one eyebrow as I observe all the changes again.

Sheena's shoulders slump. "Leona had quite the wish list," she explains, wry humor coloring her voice as she looks at the boxes and piles.

Familiar anger activates my magic, coating my skin in ice. I banish it before she notices and step closer to her.

"What happened to your face?" I point to the cut, and she snorts.

"Believe it or not, I kind of did that to myself." She touches the scab and grimaces. "In a flurry of organizational power, I was nicked by a flying dagger. Jewels, rust, the whole bit."

"She has seen your power . . ."

"She has." Sheena's face falls. "I tried to hide the talismans I'm most drawn to, and so far, she hasn't made me try them out individually. Are you any closer to finding me?"

"Not yet, but we are trying," I assure her.

The little djinn sinks deeper into herself. She hides her disappointment well, but it's still a blow. I force the ice back again.

"Idris," she begins. "Are they alright?"

I look at her incredulously. She's injured, exhausted, and trapped underground—yet she asks about those men. They do not deserve her.

"They are fine," I snap.

Sheena flinches back from my tone, and I regret my harshness.

"Your shifter is not pleased with the progress," I tell her, keeping my voice gentle. "Just this evening, he tore a door down in his impatience." Her lips twitch, the beginnings of a smile forming. "The incubus demon—" I pause, choosing my words carefully. "Callum is quite focused on your safe return."

I do not tell her his livid silence is unnerving everyone at the compound and driving all but the bravest of supernaturals away from any room he enters.

Sheena's smile grows and blooms before my eyes as she thinks of them.

I am a fool.

"If you can't find me, then I need to escape," she finally says.

The abrupt change of topic startles me, but I adjust and sink down beside her on the small sofa. Goosebumps spread along her pale arm as it grazes mine.

"How will you do that?"

"I'm not sure, but Leona is never going to let me go. Either she keeps me as her helpful slave—"

"Or she realizes the extent of your power and eliminates you," I finish her thought.

Grim lines bracket her mouth, but she squares her shoulders and says, "I would rather die trying to get away than be locked up forever."

Her words shake me to my core.

Unable to ignore the impulse any longer, I reach out and cradle her face with my hands. Her skin is warm and soft. I lean forward until my forehead rests against hers, and we breathe in unison.

"You will not take risks," I whisper. My low volume does not make the words any less of a command.

"Are you telling me what to do, Idris?"

"I would not dream of it," I tease her.

"Somehow, I doubt that."

Her face doesn't change, but some of the fire returns to her green eyes. *Gods, I envy her heat.* Clearing my throat, I pull back slightly and remove myself from temptation.

"If you see the opportunity to escape, take it. But do not give up on us, little djinn. We will not rest until we find you and the witches are dealt with."

Sheena nods, leaning back against the old couch. "Thank you for visiting again. This dream is much better than the one I was having before," she admits.

I incline my head. This is the perfect opening to tell her I saw her memories. I'm desperate to ask what happened with the boy who turned his back on her. Would she tell me about him or her captors if I asked? I don't know, so I stay silent.

As I fade from her consciousness, my thoughts are tangled with the things I saw. They linger in my mind even after I wake in my own bed. The little djinn is a weakness I cannot afford. I must distance myself from her, but I wonder if I have the strength to do it.

SHEENA

I WAKE feeling poorly rested, pissy, and sore as hell. I can't even yawn without the cut on my face tugging uncomfortably. In addition to my aches and pains, I have an emotional hangover that no amount of water or pills will solve.

I'm never in a good mood after dreaming of my captivity, but that moment I shared with Idris is tripping me up. He's impossible to read. Everything he says seems deliberate, and I can never tell if it's what he really means.

Why are you fixating on this, Sheena? I have bigger problems than Idris, and I can't forget that. Being back in captivity has stirred a lot of things up for me.

I haven't dreamed of Quaid in a long time. As a teenager, I imagined he would save me. I pictured him bursting in a thousand times, breaking me out of my cage, and destroying my enemies like the knights in the stories we read as kids.

Those thoughts got me through many hopeless days before I finally accepted he wasn't coming. That was the day I grew up and realized I needed to save myself. It made me stronger, but eight years later, the loss of my only friend still hurts. My dreams are a timely reminder: I'm Sheena May, and I don't wait to be saved.

Sitting up, I push my hair back and wince at the tangled mess. *Would it kill them to give me a brush?* I lurch to the bathroom. My muscles creak and complain with every step, but I feel a lot better than I did when I crawled into the shower stall last night.

Looking in the mirror is a kick in the ass. With my hair standing up in knots, a bloody scratch on my cheek, and stains I can't get out of my shirt, I look rabid. A manic giggle escapes me. It's pretty ironic that witches are holding me hostage but I'm the one who looks like I have a seventeenth century date with a pyre.

I swish some water around in my mouth, clearing the thick, cottony feeling. When I spit, the motion triggers a memory from just a few days ago of me brushing my teeth while Gideon showered and Callum shaved. My lips ached from smiling and fine lines crinkled around Gideon's golden eyes as he watched me throw punches in front of the mirror.

The enemies were fake then, but they're real as hell now. I stand up straighter, feeling determined. If I'm going to make it out of this, I'll need a solid plan. There's not much to work with, but that's fine. I'm used to making do with very little.

Step one: don't get killed. Step two: stay healthy enough to escape. Step three: get the fuck out of here. It's simple, but I like it.

The air in the main room crackles and pops. *They're back.* I take my time in the bathroom, doing some light stretches and pushing through the pain. When I finally come out, I'm pleased that I'm not hobbling anymore.

Leona is alone this time. She's dressed in a bright red sheath dress that clashes violently with the magenta walls she wished for yesterday. Ignoring her painted face, I focus on the bag in her hand.

"I took the liberty of bringing you some things to make your stay more comfortable," she says, smiling with delight like I'm here on some kind of all-inclusive getaway.

I grit my teeth and take the bag. The clothes I'm wearing are so filthy they make my skin crawl, so I can't afford to be petty and throw it back in her face.

Leona ignores my silence, surveying the room with satisfaction. When her eyes stop on the useless bed, she giggles. "Oh, how silly of me. Wishing for a box spring but no mattress. My mind just isn't what it used to be."

I'm not fooled. She can pretend it was an oversight, but the cunning gleam in her eyes tells a different story. This woman is calculating and cruel. She's playing chess while the rest of us throw checkers around like monkeys. It's my move now, and if I keep refusing to play, I'll lose by default.

"If there were a door in here, we could just bring one down, but the space is so limited . . ." Leona taps one ruby red nail against her chin, tilting her head to the side. "I wish that you had every object you need to live comfortably here while maintaining the structural integrity of the house, of course." She tacks the last bit on like an afterthought, and I brace myself as the depleted magic within me sputters to life.

I float.

I burn.

I ache.

And I grant the damn wish.

The space morphs and shifts. The ground shudders. I'm helpless to resist the compulsion as my power transforms this concrete prison into an oasis. I feel the dirt and rocks give way, carving out more space underground.

A kitchenette appears, then pots and pans pop into existence one by one. My stomach squeezes and churns, a grinding sound echoing out of the small bathroom space. Without even looking, I know there's a new bathtub and cabinets fully stocked with products.

My skin stings and pulls uncomfortably like I've spent too long in the sun, and then a closet materializes. It fills with clothes, but I don't have time to feel grateful for that because my back bows so violently I worry my spine might snap.

More and more objects appear, and the pain is unimaginable. A stocked bookcase, a TV, and a fully outfitted mattress complete with a lush duvet cover materialize. It feels like each one is carved from my flesh.

A framed picture of Gideon, Callum, and I appears on the wall. Despair clogs my throat. The photo is beautiful, but it's not real, and as long as I'm trapped in this basement, it never will be.

GIDEON

"LEONA WON'T ANSWER MY CALLS," my dad says.

He sounds tired, but I can't worry about that when there's a steak knife actively carving out bite-sized chunks of my heart while everyone sits on their ass. Seriously, the next person who tells me to calm down is signing their own death certificate.

"If she won't pick up the fucking phone, we should start snatching up witches until she does," I argue for the fiftieth time, ignoring my dad's scowl.

"I know you're frustrated, son, but we can't just slaughter Leona's coven. It's not right."

I roar, not giving a damn about the looks I'm getting. "What's not right is her abducting my mate while we pretend we're out of options because she screens our calls. This is bullshit. We look weak as hell."

There was a time when dad wouldn't have tolerated disrespect like this. Not from Leona, and certainly not from me. But as he stares at me now, his tight jaw is the only sign he's mad at all. Doesn't he see what this is doing to me? Sheena's absence hurts, but this inaction is deadly.

"If she took mom," I begin. His arm twitches, a sign his beast is close to the surface. It's a warning I ignore. "If that bitch stole her from you, you would paint the whole territory red. You wouldn't rest until she was home."

Dad's eyes shift from dark brown to gold, but he stays seated and holds on to his human form. One small shudder is the only sign that my words affect him at all. He puffs out a breath and leans back in his chair, watching me for a long time before responding.

"You're probably right, but your mother wouldn't want that. Have you stopped to consider how Sheena would feel if you kill a bunch of innocent women to get her back?"

He acts like I haven't thought this through, but I'm prepared to face the consequences of my actions. A tremor rocks my body. My beast is done arguing about this.

"I don't care," I spit. "I only get a chance to earn her forgiveness if she's still alive to be upset with me. The longer we wait, the less likely that becomes."

"Do you think I'm doing this to hurt you, Gideon?"

"No," I snap, my voice low and hard. "But I'm starting to think your legacy is more important to you than my future." I kick back from the table, too mad to be around him any longer. When I leave, he doesn't try to stop me.

I charge through the administrative wing, each step fueled by my anger. Shifters watch me with unease, a few fae look up with suspicion, and a demon bares his teeth as I pass.

Fuck them all.

I've known most of them for years, been groomed to lead them when the time comes, yet none of them have the balls to declare war on the witches with me. I'm surrounded by cowards. Through the haze of my rage, I feel myself growling.

When I step through the security room, I see Callum. He looks up at me with concern, but I don't stop. I shoulder past him roughly, desperate to get away. I can't be here, trapped by our fathers' decisions. My feet fall faster and faster until I'm running down the hall, bursting through the door and into the afternoon sun.

I shift, needing to feel something other than pain or anger. My senses sharpen. The stone is hot beneath my paws. I don't break stride, sprinting until the compound is just a speck in the distance and the burn in my lungs matches the one in my heart.

When I finally stop, I'm miles from home. Dropping to the ground in the shade of a craggy oak, I curl up at the base of the trunk. I'm sure this old ass tree has seen a lot of things, but it's probably never sheltered a lion before. The thought should make me smile. It doesn't.

I hear running water in the distance and realize how thirsty I am, but I don't care enough to go check it out. Instead, I focus on the grass under my coat, the light breeze, and my ragged breathing.

My ears and nose tell me Callum is coming long before he stands in front of me. I still don't move. He sinks to the ground, careful not to touch me as he leans back against the tree trunk. After a few minutes, I scoot closer, laying my head against his thigh with a huff.

"I know," Callum says, sinking his fingers into my mane.

We sit in silence. It's not uncomfortable; I still hurt, but I can think past it now.

"You're right about wasting time," he says. I lift my head with interest. Callum rolls his eyes. "Not about the mass murder. That plan is still insane." I chuff, but wait for him to get to the point. "What we really need to do is find Alina. Unless we just happen to trip over their hideout, she's the only way to get Leona's attention."

I blink and consider it, focusing on the shift back. Once I'm human again, I sit up and stare at my best friend.

"How will we find her?" I ask, my voice gravelly after being in my animal form.

"We have her phone number, so one of the tech guys may be able to track her location. If that doesn't work, we wait for her to post a picture of the best croissant she's ever eaten on social media or something, then snatch her up from the bakery," he says, snapping his fingers.

A spark of hope catches fire inside me. When I look back at Cal, I see exhaustion in the lines on his face, along with a coating of sweat.

"Did you hike all the way out here to plot a kidnapping?" I ask.

"You didn't exactly stop to talk in the compound." He looks at our surroundings, then narrows his eyes at me in annoyance. "Although, if I knew you were running halfway to Wyoming, I might have just waited for you to come back."

"I didn't plan it," I admit, scratching the back of my neck. "I just needed to be . . . anywhere else."

My words hang in the air. They're more vulnerable than I intended. The only sound comes from the water bubbling in the nearby creek and the wind rustling in the trees.

"No, I get it," Callum sighs. "I feel her everywhere and nowhere. It's driving me insane that Idris can talk to her and I can't."

I frown. That is infuriating. It's also brand new information. "He visited her dreams again?" I ask.

"Last night."

"Is she okay? What did she say?"

Callum runs his fingers through his hair and sighs. "She was exhausted. Leona has been testing lots of wishes on her, and Idris said she had a cut on her face." Most of my calm evaporates, replaced by white-hot anger. "She asked about us again. She's worried."

Just like that, my anger slips away.

"We've got to get her back," I insist.

"We will," Callum says, squeezing my shoulder. "We'll find Alina, then negotiate her release. After she's back with us and safe, we'll get revenge."

He looks at me, and I sense his determination. Together. We can do this together.

I stand, reaching down to help him up. Callum grips my palm, and I yank him into a bone-crushing hug. He sinks into it, and for a full minute, we just rest in the understanding that this sucks, but neither of us is alone.

"Dude, this is nice, but you're butt ass naked," Callum jokes.

I pull back with a laugh. "Yeah? I don't hear you complaining."

He doesn't deny it, so I grip the back of his neck and pull him in for a kiss. There's passion between us, but it's banked. This is about comfort right now.

As we hike back to the compound, we talk about strategy, timing, and catching Alina before it's too late.

It's the first time I've felt hope in days.

CHAPTER
FOUR

CALLUM

Our tech guy, a demon named Albert, laughs as he types away behind a mega desk of four computer screens. "She's a fucking idiot."

"Thank the gods for that," I say, blood roaring between my ears as I rock my weight back and forth beside him.

"Not only does Alina have her location services enabled, but she also just checked in at a trendy restaurant."

Albert turns a screen toward me, and I'm suddenly staring at 'the most epic, amazing, adorable vegan starter salad' Alina has ever seen. It's just lettuce and seeds, so I don't get the appeal, but if that pile of dry vegetables helps me get Sheena back, I'll eat salad with no complaint for the next year.

Finally, something is going right for us.

Thanking Albert, I leave the tech room at a brisk walk. By the time I get to the courtyard, I'm jogging, terrified we'll be too late. I didn't take Gideon with me to talk with the nerds for two reasons. First, I didn't want him to get his hopes up. Second, he's been kind of a dick to everyone this week, and I didn't want him to scare them off. I need him now, though, and he's not picking up.

"What?" Gideon finally answers, voice snappy.

"I've got a location on Alina. Meet me at the car."

"On my way."

The line goes dead. I yank open the car door, hopping in on the driver's side. I'm not even finished buckling my seatbelt when Gideon hurtles into the passenger seat with enough force to make the entire SUV rock.

"I want to drive," he growls.

I shake my head. "No way. You can barely speak right now. I'm not letting you behind the wheel when you're this keyed up."

Gideon's snarl rips through the enclosed space, proving my point and rattling the windows ominously. I refuse to budge, thrumming my fingers against the steering wheel.

"The longer you argue, the longer it will take for us to get there," I reason.

"Fuck, fine. Go," he demands. He snaps his seatbelt into place, eyes glowing gold.

I throw the car in reverse, and we peel out. For a few minutes, all I hear is Gideon's heavy breathing. Once he gets that under control, I pass him my phone.

"It's open to an app Albert downloaded. The blue dot is her phone's location. Let me know if it leaves the restaurant," I tell him. He takes the phone, and from the corner of my eye, I watch him stare obsessively at the dot. "You can't kill her," I remind him.

While I trust Gideon with my life, this witch stole his fated mate. Even if he doesn't mean to, he could do some serious damage. If he destroys our only lead, I know it will gut him.

"I know," he mutters, voice vibrating with tension.

"We'll bring her back to the compound and use her as leverage."

"I understand the plan," he snaps, then takes a deep breath. "I'm not okay, but I'm fine."

That actually makes perfect sense, so I quit pushing and clap him on the knee with my right hand. "We're going to get our girl back."

"Damn straight," he agrees, his eyes never leaving the blue dot.

As we pull up near the restaurant, I notice it has an old speakeasy design. With no obvious entrance, diners are coming and going through a small alleyway at irregular intervals. I find a parking spot nearby.

"Let's find a place to hide in there," I say, pointing to the alley. "As soon as Alina pops out, I'll hit her with a dose of my power. Once we get her hands secured, she won't be able to use her magic."

I bounce in my seat as Gideon grunts in agreement and pulls a pair of handcuffs out of the glove box. When he turns to look at me, his eyes are gold. I hold his stare, but neither of us says a word. There's no need to. We both know this is our best shot, and we can't afford to waste it.

After waiting a few minutes, there's a lull in customers, so we make our move. We sneak into the alley, hiding behind a large industrial dumpster. From this vantage point, we can see everyone coming and going through the door.

An hour passes with no sign of her. *How many courses is this damn meal?* I check my phone for the fifteenth time, but Alina's dot hasn't moved. Just as I'm beginning to wonder if she isn't quite as careless as we thought, the door opens with an audible whine.

I see blonde hair and high heels, and even in the dark, I know it's her. Unfortunately, she's not alone. There's a guy with her, and she's talking his ear off. They stop just a few feet from our hiding place.

The man goes in for a kiss. *Wow, right next to the dumpster. Really?*

Gideon snaps into action, bashing him over the head with his fist. The stranger sinks to the ground like a wet noodle. I grab Alina's head with both hands, slamming my magic into her as quickly as I can. She staggers, pupils dilating as I flood her with sensations.

Alina's hand moves toward me, disoriented and sluggish, but I know better than to underestimate her. She's had as much training as Gideon and I. Heat singes my cheek as I dodge the green fireball she aims at my face. I force more of my power into her, shoving her back against the concrete wall.

Gideon returns from stowing Alina's date in the dumpster. He wrenches her glowing hands behind her back and cuffs them. She won't get another shot off with her hands secured. I release my hold on her head, stuffing a rag into her mouth just before she can let out what I'm sure was going to be a blood-curdling scream.

After all that, it's easy to muscle Alina into the backseat. Less than ninety seconds after she exited the restaurant, she's in our control. Ignoring the grunts and muffled squawks coming from behind the gag, I throw the SUV in reverse.

Once we're out of the city, I nod to Gideon, and he pulls the gag out of her mouth.

"Have you lost your fucking minds?" Alina screams. The pitch combined with the volume hurts my ears, but one homicidal glare from Gideon shuts her up.

"How was your salad?" I ask, enjoying the flash of dismayed understanding that floods her face when she realizes how we found her.

"You may think you're smart, Callum Casanell, but my mother won't let this stand."

"Oh, we're counting on that," I tell her.

Alina narrows her eyes, and there's a bitterness there I've never noticed before. "You're too late," she spits. "The djinn is already dead. She was so weak. Her heart stopped just attempting some little party tricks."

"If I wasn't one hundred percent sure that was a lie, I would let Gideon crack your skull open like a walnut," I say conversationally. "Let me be perfectly clear, Alina. You betrayed me. Therefore, you are dead to us. The only reason you aren't rotting in that dumpster with a bunch of vegan leftovers is because your life is now a bargaining chip. You better pray to all the gods that your mother agrees."

Alina sinks back against the seat, malice in her eyes.

"Where is Sheena?" I ask, even though I don't expect an answer.

She huffs, crossing her arms and turning to look out the window. She's stubborn, but no matter how mad I am, I'm not really comfortable interrogating a woman. Hopefully it won't come to that.

When I pull into the compound, the gate closes behind us with a metallic clang. My father, Joshua, and Idris are waiting in the courtyard.

We climb out of the car, and as soon as Alina catches sight of them, she starts the waterworks. "Joshua, please help me," she wails. "Gideon and Callum brutally attacked me."

I roll my eyes and snap a photo of her blotchy, tearstained face with my phone. "Thanks for saving me the trouble of making those real."

Alina takes a step back, lips trembling. She looks at our dads. They don't budge. They're probably mad as hell that we acted without their approval, but they won't show any dissension in front of an enemy—not even one they watched grow up.

"No harm will come to you if your mother makes the right choice," father hisses at her, and the remaining color fades from her cheeks.

"You're making a mistake." Alina sobs, and some of her hysteria sounds genuine now. "Mom won't give her up . . . Not even for me."

If I gave a shit, that would strike me as sad. It's too bad for Alina that my empathy is limited to a very select handful of people at the moment.

"For your sake, I hope you're wrong." Gideon speaks to her for the first time, and Alina cringes away from him. She's put on a hell of a performance so far, but now she really seems scared.

We march her to a holding room in silence, leaving her hands bound and locking the door behind her. Idris looks at us both, but I hold up my hand. I don't want her overhearing anything. This conversation can wait until we're somewhere private.

Together, we walk to the conference room. As soon as the door closes behind all of us, I face the fae.

"She claims Sheena's dead."

"I can assure you, that is untrue," Idris says, and I nod.

"Alina lies as easily as breathing. She always has." I sink down into the chair. "The only part of her bullshit that might be true is the bit about her mom not giving a damn."

A shared look goes around the table. We all remember what Leona was like.

"Whether she cares or not, failing to protect her own daughter shows tremendous weakness," Idris reasons. "Even if she's desperate to keep Sheena in her clutches, this will force her to act."

"You know we have to talk about this." Joshua sighs. "You two went completely rogue."

"And I would do it again," I say firmly.

"You do not run this enclave," my father hisses, then darts a worried glance at the way Gideon's arms shake. The only reason we're avoiding another one of his wall-rattling, vein-pulsing rage fits is his fear that Gideon might shift and tear him to pieces.

I sigh. I stopped caring about Dimitri Casanell's opinion a long time ago. "No, I don't. But you ordered me to protect this community, and that's what I did," I argue.

My father opens his mouth, but Idris beats him to it.

"We cannot underestimate the witches again. If Leona goes unchecked . . ."

I look at Idris in surprise. He just subtly deflected the attention away from me. It's obvious he's into Sheena, but surely that doesn't mean he's looking for an ally in me.

"We should have taken action against her months ago," Joshua admits. My father twists his mouth like he just swallowed a lemon. "But she was once an ally and friend. Neither Dimitri nor I wanted to believe she was capable of this." Joshua looks to my father, who nods, the motion so brittle I wonder if his neck might snap in half.

"I understand we've strained your trust," Joshua says, turning to Gideon and me, deep lines of fatigue carved into his face. "I wouldn't have stopped you. Neither of us would. But we could have backed you up. I hate that you thought you wouldn't have our full support in this."

I can't hold his eyes any longer, so I look down. Gideon—who's been quietly holding himself together in the corner—steps up to his father. They share a tense look, then Joshua wraps his arms around his son. The hug looks painfully tight, but it's genuine. Tears burn the backs of my eyes unexpectedly.

"We'll help you get your mate back," Joshua promises, his tone fierce.

I glance at my father, only to find his black eyes locked on me already. There's a world of emotions staring back at me, but I'll be damned if I can identify a single one.

Idris scrapes his chair back from the table, pulling us all out of the moment. When I look at him, he's smiling. It's a disturbing expression, cutthroat and malicious. For the first time, I'm glad he's on my side.

QUAID

I SNEAK BACK to the abandoned amusement park and make my way to the cellar's entrance. Shouts of rage reach me as soon as I pass through the magical barrier. My first instinct is to assume I've been spotted and take cover. Then I realize the sounds are coming from the house.

"How dare they take my daughter? I'll peel the skin from their bones for this insolence." The voice is piercing. There's no response.

"And make no mistake . . . When I get my hands on Alina, she will pay for her foolishness too. She puts our entire operation at risk."

Now that the woman is speaking at a more normal volume, I recognize the voice. It's Leona, the older witch from before, and someone has made her furious.

Creeping closer, I keep to the shadows until I can peek inside. There's a fire burning in the hearth. A drop of sweat rolls down the bridge of my nose. It's an incredibly hot summer; I don't know how anyone inside that house is handling the heat.

Inside, Leona stands alone, gripping her phone and staring at the screen like it personally offended her. The flames roar behind her, painting sinister orange streaks across her face.

"Your daughter may be a foolish witch, but she did deliver the djinn," a new voice says.

Maybe her phone is on speaker?

Leona whips her head around to stare at the fire. "Don't bother telling me what I already know," she hisses. The flames shrink like the fire itself is intimidated.

"I wouldn't dream of it. Alina allowed herself to be caught. You have every reason to be disappointed."

As the disembodied voice speaks again, I can tell it's not coming from the phone. I blink, confused and unnerved.

"I'll deal with my daughter in due time, but Joshua and Dimitri cannot be allowed to think they've bested me." Leona starts to pace. "I have their djinn, and it's time they learned not to mess with me."

She grins directly into the flames, and despite the heat, a chill rolls down my spine.

"Will you kill the girl?"

"Of course not," Leona scoffs. "Then my years of searching would be for nothing."

A jeweled dagger appears, hovering in the air and spinning in place as the witch stares down at a table covered in antiques. Wary of the floating blade, I inch to the side to get a better look.

It's packed with old, expensive rings, necklaces, crowns, and weapons.

"The djinn is powerful. That much is clear." Leona turns back to the fire. "But the question remains—just how powerful is she? Tomorrow, we'll find out. And if we're lucky, we'll send a message to the enclave in the process."

The fire shrinks to embers, the unnatural flames dying down so quickly I question whether they were ever really there to begin with. My heart pounds. The witch paces. The dagger spins.

What is going on here?

Gritting my teeth, I slip back into the darkness and head to the car, ignoring the cellar for now. Sheena is probably in there, and I'll find out for sure tomorrow night. If the enclave is involved too, her power is something to fight over. That means I need to remove it from the playing field.

SHEENA

"You are hurt." When Idris appears in my dreams for the third time, those three words are the first out of his mouth. I want to argue with him, but truthfully, I feel like I got hit by a train.

This dream magic of his is interesting. I know I'm actually asleep, but everything feels so real, including my very legitimate exhaustion.

Sitting up gingerly, I brace myself against the tufted headboard. "I hurt, but I don't think I'm actually injured." I trail off as a massive yawn breaks free.

Leona only left after I fell to my knees in the middle of the basement turned luxury apartment she forced me to create. The many shades of pink are disturbing, but I will say the mattress is a nice improvement.

Idris takes in the changes slowly, then looks back at me, a question in his eyes.

"Impressive, right? Do you think I have a future in interior design?" I bow at the waist dramatically, flinching when it feels like my abs are coming apart at the seams.

"Your men captured the witch."

"Leona?" I gasp.

"No, the younger one," he says. Burning hatred replaces my hope. It takes up all the space and replaces the softer emotion with something more noxious. Idris studies my face, but continues his explanation without commenting on whatever he sees there. "You will need to be careful. When we called to negotiate a trade, Leona reacted . . . poorly."

I huff. Somehow, I'm willing to bet that's an understatement.

"She's going to be out for blood tomorrow," I groan, sliding back against the pillows and curling in on myself. I feel so sore, so tired. My eyes will barely stay open, but I know once Idris leaves I'll be one moment closer to waking up to more of Leona's tests.

"Will you tell me something?" I ask.

"What do you want to know?" He sounds hesitant, but I'm desperate for a distraction.

"I don't know. Anything. Tell me about your realm," I choke out, hating how my voice sounds thick and watery from the tears I'm fighting. It makes me feel weak. Any moment now, Idris will leave me to my misery; he won't tolerate my weakness. I turn my head toward the pillow and feel the bed dip.

"Close your eyes," Idris whispers. My eyelids flutter shut at the melodic sound of his voice. "My kingdom—it is beautiful, little djinn. With skies so blue that all other colors pale in comparison. You would run barefoot through the thick grass, a breeze tossing your hair and sunbeams caressing your face as the birds sing an endless song of joy. With each breath you took, the rich scent of the flowers would captivate your senses."

I sink into his descriptions, doing my best to imagine something so beautiful.

"What do the flowers look like?"

"More delicate than lace, they look like joy and come in every color you can imagine. The deepest of reds and palest of yellows. Some bloom as large as your head—rich, bright, and bursting with health. Roses and violets cannot compare to the flowers of the fae."

His voice sounds far away but filled with longing—I don't want to lose this moment. "Would anything look familiar to me?" I ask.

"Some things would feel similar. The fae realm shares many characteristics with Earth, but it is more vibrant, more alive," Idris says. "The streams that trickle down from the mountains are colder than ice. If you dipped even one toe in, the chill would steal the breath from your lungs."

The deep, melodic timbre of his voice lulls my fears and aches away. Despite already being in a dream, I'm falling asleep. I struggle to voice my final question. "Why do you picture me running through the grass?"

"Because you would have to run. Or die."

I sink into unconsciousness, thinking I must have misheard him.

WHEN I WAKE, Leona hovers over me like an evil spirit, her beady eyes studying me in the silence.

I jerk fully awake, eying the witch carefully. She looks especially deranged today. Her bright red lipstick is smeared at the corners, and her earrings are mismatched. This can't be a good sign for her current mental health or my future physical wellbeing.

Leona grabs my upper arm, sinking her bony fingers into the soft skin hard enough to bruise. I want to pull away, but I have nowhere to go.

"I wish you would come with me quietly and make no attempt to escape." There's a new bite to her voice. She's stripped away all of her fake, sticky sweetness. In its place, I see the real Leona: a scary, power hungry woman who will do anything to get what she wants.

If she's finished with the games, what does that mean for me?

I go limp as the magic takes hold. Her grip on my arm tightens, but I can't fight back, no matter how hard I try.

When I hear that unmistakable crackling sound again, I'm shocked. If she's taking me out of here with magic, maybe I'll have a chance to escape. The squeezing feeling intensifies as I'm dismantled and reassembled again. It feels just as awful as when Alina captured me, but I don't throw up this time.

The sun beats down on my face, momentarily blinding me. Once the spots fade from my eyes, I'm surprised to see it's actually closer to sunset than sunrise. After all this time in the basement, my schedule is off.

I'm so grateful to be out of the concrete box, all I can do is stare at my surroundings in wonder. There's a house, an assortment of trailers and RVs, and some garden beds. It looks like a community, but there's no one around.

Where the hell is everyone?

I hear a sound and notice a rusted out trailer used for transporting horses to my right. Two faces look back at me through the dirty window, but they're too far away for me to tell anything about them. *Other hostages?* The tires on the trailer are flat, and with the late afternoon heat at full blast, it's got to feel like an oven in there.

I look away quickly as my mind takes me back to another time I heard others suffering and chose to save only myself. The sounds I heard from that cage . . . Sometimes, I wake up in a cold sweat and wonder what happened to the people I left behind. Are they survivors like me or nameless victims who never got a chance? Nausea churns in my gut, worse than the magic transportation sickness.

My instincts tell me to ignore the faces in the window. If I get the chance to save myself again, I need to take it. *No, not this time,*

Sheena. The angry part of me wants to sprint up to that trailer, rip the lock away, and help whoever is inside escape.

That idea is a death sentence. It's foolish. Impossible. It would only slow me down. I may know how to run, but that doesn't mean I know the first thing about how to be a hero.

"I sent everyone important away, so we have some privacy." Leona's voice rips me out of my head, and I realize none of this matters because I'm still her prisoner.

"Let's find out what you're capable of," Leona says, excited.

I shiver with dread despite the heat.

Leona yanks me over to a plastic folding table. I'm still bound by her wish, so she doesn't need to be so rough. But I think the power imbalance makes her happy.

The table is covered in scrapbooks. Leona has made architectural plans for an entire village of pastel homes. I blink a few times, trying to make sense of the explosion of colors I'm looking at. It's like she tried to fuse retro maximalism and modern day witchy aesthetic.

To my right, there are designs for massive gardens, a lake, and an open space labeled 'moon ceremony arena.' Beside them are half a dozen talismans. All of them are ones I felt a strong connection to.

I was so careful. How did she know?

Fear digs its claws into me. I know why she sent everyone else away and brought me outside alone: she doesn't expect me to survive another day.

When Leona grips my chin and pulls my face up, she makes no attempt to hide her mania. "I wish you would create my witch's paradise exactly how I've always dreamed of it," she croons.

There's no power in this universe that could stop what happens next. I feel the now familiar sensation of magic being siphoned from me. For every piece of her dream I fulfill, there's a dozen more waiting in line. The pastel houses, the lake, and the gardens—they all take shape, carved from my very essence, sucking the life from me until I'm gasping for breath.

My skin grows cold, my vision tunnels. I long to sink into the waiting oblivion and make the pain end. *Gideon, Callum . . .* They would want me to fight. Hovering over the ground, I tremble like a leaf as I cling to consciousness with slippery fingers.

Leona looks surprised and elated as her paradise comes to life around her. Gone are the makeshift buildings. Even the table turns into an outdoor seating area, complete with a beaded gazebo and wicker egg chairs.

It's a freak show, a twisted oasis, and I'm paying the bill with my body.

Like a switch being flipped, the drain ends. I fall to the ground but barely notice the impact as cavernous, terrifying emptiness consumes me. This staggering hunger is somehow worse than when my magic was eating away at my body.

Leona stands over me and watches my face like a movie playing out on the big screen. I grit my teeth. If I had my free will, I would tear her to pieces.

"You think I'm a monster," she says. "But we aren't so different, you and I. My kind were hunted, hated, and persecuted as well." Leona looks down at her wrist, and for the first time, I see thick, white scarring circling her pale skin. "The fae, angels, demons, and shifters came from other realms and invaded Earth."

She spins around in a slow circle to survey the village. Blood runs down my face, and I taste copper. I close my eyes and silently beg for help as tremors rack my body. *There. Something is there.* It starts with a tickle along my ankle. That turns into a tingle along my back. I open my eyes, and when Leona turns back around, I give her my full attention.

"This world—my home—didn't belong to them, but they took it anyway. By whatever means necessary, they moved in and stole it." Her eyes shine with tears, and she sucks in a breath. "The original code of my coven prevented violence, so we welcomed them. They turned that hospitality against us time and time again, and now we fight for what was ours all along."

All this time, I've been imagining tearing Leona to shreds for the pain she's put me through, but I understand her anger and bitterness. I'm just a means to an end for her. Somewhere along the way, her desire for justice soured into something darker.

"What did my kind ever do to you?" I ask, my voice coming out raspy.

"Nothing, my dear," Leona says, tugging her sleeve back down over the ruined skin of her wrist. She smiles at me brightly. "You are a tool. In fact, you're the most valuable tool to surface in my lifetime. I can regret your fate, but it won't change the past or sway my plans for the future."

She sits down in one of the chairs and gestures for me to do the same. I drag myself into it with trembling arms. The tingle in my spine starts to sting.

"We've tested your object manipulation, which is truly remarkable." She looks around at the transformed community, then winks at me. "Now, let's see what kind of weapon you are."

I recoil, but there's nothing I can do to stop her.

"I wish Joshua would free my daughter, then slaughter everyone in the compound," Leona trills the words, her voice a childish singsong. I feared she was going to use the hostages in the trailer as test dummies, but this is so much worse.

As I hover over the ground again, the last dredges of my magic shoot out. My vision blurs, and then the sting spreads like an electric current through my entire body. I embrace it, latching on with everything I have left. I can only hope I'm not the weapon Leona wished for.

CHAPTER FIVE

GIDEON

After years of yapping nonstop, Alina refuses to talk. It's annoying, but at least her crocodile tears have run dry. When we told her we contacted her mom, she just rolled her eyes and settled back in her seat. It's a waiting game now.

I hate waiting.

Footsteps echo down the hall, and I look up, confused to see dad rounding the corner. He's not supposed to try reasoning with her until later tonight.

"Did something happen?" I ask, hoping for good news.

He ignores me, shouldering by and heading straight for the holding room. *Maybe he's still upset about our argument.*

"Dad, what's going on?" I try again, but he acts like I'm not there. When he reaches for his keys, I run my hand down the back of my neck. "Look, I know things have been heated, but I'd like to talk it through."

I wait a beat, but he doesn't react at all. I frown. It's not like dad to get mad and pull the silent treatment. When I put my hand on his shoulder, he pivots, and I barely see the punch coming. The hit lands directly on the bridge of my nose. I hear it crunch as I stumble backwards. Outside of combat training exercises, my father has never once hit me.

"Dad, stop," I say, feeling a little panicked as he immediately tries to unlock the door again.

When I grab his shoulder this time, I'm able to dodge the wild punch he throws at me. My dad is strong, and he's got more experience fighting than I do, but I'm taller and outweigh him by at least twenty pounds. I yank him back from the door, and his keys clatter to the ground.

I narrowly dodge another punch to the face. While I'm trying not to hurt him, he fights like his life depends on it. It takes all my skill and concentration to protect myself and keep him away from the door.

I glance in the cell window. Alina watches us through the glass with her lips pulled back in a creepy smile. That's when it clicks. Whatever is turning my dad into a mindless lunatic is magical.

How can I break this spell?

Dad charges again, reaching for me and partially shifting his hands into talons. I try to get out of the way, but one digs deeply into my bicep, leaving behind a nasty puncture wound. When he tries to rip out my throat, I start to panic.

"Dad, fight this! You're possessed," I shout.

He lunges at me again like he can't hear anything except whatever the magic is telling him. I grab his wrists and slam them into the wall. He pushes against me, driving his knee up. I twist at the last second and the blow hits my hip.

Desperate, I scream for help. A moment later, the door bursts open, and Dimitri and Callum run through. I turn my attention to them, but that's a mistake. Dad takes advantage of my distraction and slams his head into mine. My vision goes spotty, but I hear their shocked gasps.

"What the hell is going on?" Dimitri demands.

"The witches," I sputter, dodging another wild haymaker. "They've hypnotized him or something."

That gets a reaction. Callum grabs my dad's back and takes a nasty elbow to the gut for his trouble. It gives me some breathing room, though. Then, as abruptly as it began, dad freezes.

I look around, confused by the change until I see Dimitri's eyes. They're unfocused. He's placed an illusion on dad.

"This would never work if he wasn't out of it." Dimitri's voice is strained. "Quick, put him in the other holding room. I doubt my illusion will block the compulsion for long."

Callum and I muscle him into the room. It doesn't take much effort. After trying to kill me a minute ago, dad is as docile as a kitten now. Blood drips from my shattered nose, and I cringe. In the heat of the moment, I didn't feel it too much. Now, fucking ouch.

We lock the door, and Dimitri drops the illusion. Immediately, dad barrels into the door like a bullet shot out of a gun. He roars with rage, and I stumble back. Seeing my father like this . . . Shit, he's terrifying.

A muffled laugh echoes into the hallway. Alina is cackling like she's at a comedy show, and it makes my blood boil. I take a step in her direction, but Callum holds me back.

"No. That's what she wants," he tells me. "We don't know how this is happening, so until we do, both doors stay closed."

I nod, then glance at Dimitri. He's watching his friend slam into the door repeatedly, a look of unease on his face.

"Father, have you ever seen magic like this?" Callum asks.

Dimitri hesitates, then shakes his head. "Not from a distance. Alina can't cast from that cell—it's insulated against magic." He looks back at Joshua, and my worry builds. "He shouldn't still be fighting. The room should cancel out the spell."

Blood splatters on the window as dad's fist splits from the force of his punches.

"He's hurting himself," I say. "What should we do?"

Before anyone can respond, dad abruptly stops. His golden eyes go back to the rich brown I'm so used to seeing, and he shakes his head like he's waking up from a nightmare. I step up to the door, and he stares at me through the window with confusion and horror.

"I don't think it was witch magic," Callum murmurs. "I think it was a wish."

I look at him, stunned—and that's when I feel her. *Sheena.* The mate bond roars back to life in my chest, and I stumble toward the door.

It's time to get our girl.

SHEENA

I SLUMP BACK into the chair. *Why am I so cold?*

Power shoots out of my skin like needles stabbing from the inside out. More magic sinks into me, but it's not enough to offset the drain. Leona watches me as if I'm a science experiment defying her original hypothesis. I'm dying, but she's entertained.

Run. You've got to run, Sheena.

I try, but when my brain tells my body to stand, I slide off the chair and slump to the ground instead. Leona laughs. I see her mouth open in that familiar mocking way, but I can't hear the sound over the roaring in my ears.

I don't want Leona's face to be the last thing I see, and yet, I can't seem to look away.

I'm so fixated on her that I notice the moment her laughter morphs to outrage. Leona flinches, her eyes focusing on something behind me as she reaches for her neck. There's a dart sticking out of it. She pulls it free, and magic sputters in her palms before she falls to the ground beside me. Her eyes are glassy. She reaches for the table, dragging something over the edge. I feel a jolt in my gut. Then, she's gone.

Keep it moving.

This is my chance to get away, but my vision tunnels. A face appears above mine; and I must be dead because Quaid is standing over me, looking at me like I'm a ghost. I smile and reach for his face. He slaps my hand away.

Wait, that can't be right.

If I'm dead, he should be nice to me. I open my mouth to tell him so, but no sound comes out. My pain spikes again when he hoists me up and throws me over his shoulder. The little blood that was still functioning in my body runs to my head. His black combat boots are the last thing I see.

When I come to, I see the boots again. And ass. It's a nice ass, but I don't have time to appreciate it. I'm rocking back and forth, and the sensation gives me violent motion sickness. Nausea swamps me, and I vomit all over the ass and boots. The rocking stops.

"For fuck's sake," a male voice mutters. My vision swims as I'm swung upright. I wobble and blink up at a man I haven't seen in eight years. "Really, you're just going to yack all over me with no warning?" Quaid rubs one boot against a clump of grass, then the other.

"It's not my fault," I say. "You know I get carsick."

"So you do recognize me. I wasn't sure." Quaid's voice is cold and detached. He sounds nothing like the friend I remember, but everything like the teenager who turned his back on me. The pain of the old betrayal flares to life in my chest.

"Of course I recognize you," I snap. "I was held hostage, Quaid; I don't have amnesia."

He narrows his eyes and stares at me. I stare back, but my legs choose this moment to buckle and betray me. I fall on my butt in the grass, trying to make the move look deliberate by scanning our surroundings. It's not dark, so I assume I wasn't unconscious for long.

"Where are we?" I ask, taking in the unfamiliar field.

"Doesn't matter," he grunts, and I glare at him.

"Umm, yes, it does. I'm grateful you saved me—although I

have a really long list of questions about what the hell happened —but I've been living in a crazy lady's garage, so I would really like to go home," I explain, clinging to my patience by a thread. "And I can't do that if you don't tell me where we are."

Quaid keeps up the intense stare, and it's starting to get on my nerves. Another annoyance: how fucking hot he is. Sure, he was always good looking in a stretched out, gangly kind of way, but he's filled out now. The wicked scar stretching from his temple to his lip makes him look even more rugged. My heart thumps erratically. Nothing is as frustrating as the ridiculous fact that his brown eyes flecked with amber still make me feel safe.

"You don't need to go home."

"Excuse me. Yes, I do," I argue, blinking up at him rapidly.

He purses his lips in a very familiar gesture. Good, I'm annoying him, too. That's comforting at least.

"You won't be going home because I didn't come to rescue you, Sheena. I came to kill you."

My jaw drops, and I look him over with confusion. *He came to kill me?* I know our friendship didn't end on the best of terms, but murder seems a bit much. Honestly, I can't deal with this right now. I'm exhausted, sore, and still half nauseous. If this is his idea of a joke, it's not funny. This is hardly the time to experiment with risky dark humor.

"What? Why would you even say that?" I ask. Unexpected tears burn behind my eyes, and the feeling of betrayal triples in size.

"Because you shouldn't exist," Quaid hisses. "Your kind are an abomination."

"Well, I don't know how you could possibly know that because as far as I know, I'm the only one of my *kind* that exists."

He ignores me. I try to catch his eye, but he's focused on a patch of ground to the side of me. When he pulls a gun out of a holster on his hip, I realize he's serious. I've escaped from a maniacal witch only to fall into the hands of another psycho. Could he have suffered a mental break in high school that I missed?

"Is this why you ditched me before my birthday?" I demand. Maybe it's a dumb thing to ask, but if I'm about to die at the hands of my ex-best friend, I deserve to know why at least.

"They told me to kill you then, and I refused. I assured them you were human," Quaid says, looking at me like I betrayed him.

None of this makes sense. I shake my head, hoping to clear it, and hold up my hand before he can say anything else. "We'll get around to who the mysterious 'they' are in a second. Can we start with how 'they' knew I wasn't human in the first place? Because I sure as hell didn't."

Quaid scoffs at me, his right eyebrow quivering. It's a sure sign he's getting mad, and goddammit, that makes me madder. *What right does he have to be pissed at me? I'm not the one threatening murder.* I narrow my eyes at him, and he flips the safety off the pistol.

"You don't have to lie, Sheena. I'm going to kill you anyway."

"I'm not lying, you jackass," I shout, angry tears spilling from the corners of my eyes. "I just found out what I am, and I didn't even know I wasn't human until I turned sixteen." I sniffle, shooting a glare up at him. "I was laying in my bed, crying because you didn't wish me a happy birthday, then two guys put a bag over my head."

His eyebrow twitches again.

"Tell me who the fuck 'they' are," I demand. "Is someone blackmailing you or something?"

Quaid lowers his gun slightly and has the audacity to look at me like I'm insane. "Blackmailing me? Why would you think that?" He asks, his voice indignant.

I swipe angrily at my tears, but the waterworks won't stop. It's ruining the tough persona I'm trying to preserve.

"For starters, you said 'my kind' and called me an 'abomination.'" I put air quotes around the words, but all the sniffling takes the edge off my sarcasm. "And last I checked, my best friend wasn't a brainwashed bigot!"

Quaid lifts the gun again, aiming it straight for my chest.

"We were never best friends."

His words are quiet, but they cut me just as deeply as his abandonment did in school.

"I see that now. My mistake," I whisper bitterly. He avoids making eye contact, but I can't have that. "If you're going to kill me, at least have the courage to look me in the face when you pull the trigger," I spit the words out.

Quaid raises his eyes to mine, and his stoicism falls away. I see pain, anger, and determination staring back at me. It's the final emotion that convinces me he means it.

I'm really about to die.

"No. You absolutely are not."

The new voice startles me, and I realize I said my last thought out loud.

As I look around, my heart tugs violently in my chest. The bond is back. I catch sight of tattooed arms and messy curls and smile through my tears. They came for me.

Then all hell breaks loose.

IDRIS

MOMENTS AGO, Gideon yanked me out of my office like a rag doll and demanded I create a portal using the coordinates from his heart. Absurd. Yet, somehow—and I am still not sure I understand how—it actually worked.

We step out of my portal and see a hunter pointing a gun at the little djinn. Adrenaline rips through my body with the might of a raging river.

Unacceptable. I throw a glamour over Sheena, making it look to the hunter like she has vanished. At the same time, Gideon body slams him. The gun goes off. I feel a stab of panic, but a quick glance through my magic shows me the bullet missed her.

Sheena tries to stand, swaying on her feet, and Callum catches her.

The pistol goes off again. Gideon growls, and the weapon flies through the air. Grunts, groans, and thuds punctuate the brutal fistfight, which is lasting much longer than I expected. The hunter fights with surprising skill, but he's still a human. He won't be able to match an omni-shifter's rage and strength for long.

"Don't kill him," Sheena says, her lips trembling.

"He can't beat Gideon, sweetheart," Callum reassures her. "Just look away. It will be over soon." He pulls her head into his chest, but she struggles against his hold.

"No," Sheena sobs. "Don't let Gideon kill Quaid."

Callum stares at her in shock, and my face must reflect the same surprise. *Why is she protecting him?* That name . . . It's familiar. I squint at the hunter's face, but it's difficult to make out his features beneath the blood.

"He was pointing a gun at you, little djinn," I remind her. It must be the shock making her talk this way. Perhaps she will see reason if I appeal to her rationality. "He is a hunter."

"I don't care who he is or what he says," Sheena wails, trying once again to pull away from Callum. "I don't care about any of it. He's my friend."

Her voice is raw and scratchy, and I flinch away from her. Gods. I loathe her tears.

I'm not the only one.

Even in the middle of his murderous rage, her obvious pain is enough to stop Gideon mid-punch. He holds the hunter at arm's length, one giant hand wrapped around his throat. The human's face turns purple, and his body twitches from the lack of oxygen. As Gideon holds him still, I tilt my head to take a better look at his face, and everything snaps into place.

The friend. The one from her nightmares. I'm not sure how to interpret this new information, but from Sheena's obvious distress, it changes everything for her. She sobs harder, covering her face with her hands. Gideon's scowl turns homicidal.

"It's okay, baby," he says, his voice soft, gentle, and entirely at odds with the look in his eyes. "I won't kill him if you don't want me to."

Without another word, Gideon turns back to the hunter and punches him hard in the temple. The human drops to the ground like a sack of old grain, and Gideon leaves him unconscious in the dirt.

He sprints across the field so quickly that my eyes barely track the movement. I expect him to take Sheena from Callum, but he surprises me by wrapping his bloody arms around both of them.

"Please, don't cry," he mutters gruffly, even though his voice sounds suspiciously close to tears as well. "You're safe."

The three of them cling to each other. It's so painfully intimate, I have to look away. Never again will I have that. I don't deserve it, but more than that, I won't take the risk.

Standing alone, I give them another minute before I clear my throat and say, "We need to get back to the compound."

Sheena lifts her head and frowns. "The hostages. I have to go back," she insists.

Immediately, I shake my head. "Absolutely not. We cannot put you right back in Leona's hands. How did you get here, anyway?"

"Quaid," she murmurs, glancing at the hunter's limp body. "I thought I was dreaming. He came out of nowhere, shot her with some kind of dart, and grabbed me. I just came to a few minutes ago."

Her explanation covers how she escaped the witches, but I still have questions about how a human with limited resources found where Sheena was being held before the enclave could manage it.

"I know what's coming next." Gideon groans and kicks a tree stump. "You're going to demand we wake that motherfucker up so he can show us where the lair is, aren't you?"

"That is risky—" I begin.

"But necessary," Sheena interrupts. "Especially because I think I bonded with a talisman, and it might still be there."

Her words send a spike of relief running through me. If she is bound to a magical anchor, her power cannot continue to eat her alive. I can only hope Leona did not abscond with the item, as that would create a whole host of new problems for us.

"Shit, baby." Gideon scratches some flakes of dried blood off his face, then grins. Perhaps he is excited for a chance to kill someone, since his last prey was spared.

When he sucks in a deep breath, his nose twitches in excitement. Gideon whoops loudly.

"What now?" Callum asks, narrowing his eyes.

"My nose just healed. We don't have to wake him up because I can track their scent." Without waiting for further input, Gideon's body morphs into a bloodhound. Tail wagging with anticipation, he sniffs at the grass a few times, then lets loose an obnoxious baying howl.

I take a step toward him, but he disappears into the woods before I can formulate a proper word of caution. *No strategy. No contingencies. Does he not realize his eagerness makes him vulnerable?*

Callum mutters under his breath and sighs, hoisting the hunter's unconscious body over his shoulder. He drops a kiss to Sheena's cheek, then trails after the dog, leaving me alone with an exhausted and overwhelmed little djinn.

"If I offered to take you back to the compound, would you listen? Or would I just be wasting my breath?" I ask her, my voice betraying my irritation with the impulsive shifter.

Her tired grin surprises me. I'm even more stunned when she closes the distance between us and wraps her arms around me. "Thank you, Idris," Sheena whispers. "The dreams . . . Well, let's just say they kept me sane and reminded me why I had to fight."

Sheena's words penetrate my armor, touching something inside me I would rather she fail to reach. We're allies. Nothing more. Nothing less. I should tell her so, but something holds me back. Instead, I return her embrace, keeping my mouth closed and ignoring the way she fits perfectly in my arms.

"Also, in answer to your earlier question—yes," she says, a twinkle in her green eyes. "You'd be wasting your breath."

She wobbles on her feet, and I sweep her into my arms with an exaggerated sigh that makes her giggle.

"Very well, then, little djinn," I drawl as we follow Gideon's howls. "Let us rescue some hostages and secure your talisman."

"No one is here," I say.

Gideon shifts back into his human form. He sniffs at the air, unfazed by his own nudity. "But they were," he says. "Recently, too."

I scan the pristine village in front of us with some surprise. *How could Leona establish such a robust community without our knowledge?* Sheena pats my chest, pulling me from my thoughts. I set her down cautiously.

"That's where the trailer with the hostages was," she says, pointing at a small purple cottage.

"Do you think they drove it away?" Callum asks.

"Not exactly." Sheena shudders. "More like it doesn't exist anymore because I turned it into a house when I granted Leona's wish."

She squares her shoulders and takes off, leaving the rest of us gaping after her. By the time we catch up, she's reaching for the doorknob. I dart around her and grab it myself. I rattle the handle, and someone inside squeaks.

"I told you there were hostages," Sheena says, elbowing me in the ribs.

I look at Gideon with annoyance. "So someone is still here."

The shifter shrugs, then plows his shoulder into the cheerfully painted white wood. The door splinters and falls open with a bang so loud I can only assume people in the neighboring county also heard it. His break first and ask questions later attitude would be the death of us all if we were attempting stealth.

"Gideon, you can't go in there," Sheena insists, wedging her body between him and the door.

"Why not?" He sniffs the air again. "I don't smell any witches."

"Because you're naked. You're going to scare them."

Her expression is so scandalized that I cannot help but laugh. The other three stare at me in shock. Gods, just because they've never amused me before doesn't mean I lack the ability to appreciate humor. Foolish. All of them.

Gideon blinks at me a few times, then looks down at his body like he's never seen it before. He puts on a faux shocked expression that makes Sheena laugh.

"I'll be on hunter watch, then," he says. "They may need your skill set anyway, Cal." Gideon winks at his friend, and Sheena turns red in the face. But it's not from laughter this time.

"Absolutely not," she hisses, glaring at the incubus.

Callum looks her over possessively, heat burning in his dark eyes. "Not *that* skill set, Sheena. You know I save that for you."

Their subsequent eye contact is not suited for public consumption. Feeling uncomfortable once more, I navigate through the wreckage Gideon made of the door.

When my eyes adjust to the low lighting, I see two women huddled in the corner. I raise my hands in a nonthreatening manner, then my nostrils flare in shock. *It cannot be.* I take in the pointed ears, the delicate, sharp features. *They are fae.*

"What's going on?" Sheena follows me inside, and the women flinch back again. "Oh my god, are they—"

"Fae? So it would seem," I grit the words out through clenched teeth, frustrated by my own ignorance. *How did they get here? Why is Leona holding the folk hostage?* I would have paid a hearty ransom for their safe return, and the witch must have known that.

"Your majesty, you came for us." One woman bursts into tears, which sets off the one behind her. Within seconds, they are both wailing.

"Stop crying," I demand. "You are safe now."

The sobs cut off with a few abrupt hiccups, and Sheena glares at me. My order may seem harsh, but she does not know my people like I do. Their tears will be a great source of shame for them when they think back on this interaction later. I am simply sparing them from the sting that comes after your own feelings betray you.

Callum steps up beside me, and a numbing energy wafts off of him. As their tears dry, they climb to their feet and bow to me with renewed confidence. The sight brings me so much comfort and pain that I have to look away.

"I am not your king here," I say. "Just your leader." The distinction is of critical importance, but they both seem confused by it. "Follow us. I want to know how you ended up here, but that story can wait until after we have sorted out a place for you to stay."

One dips her head to acknowledge my words, and the other falls into an awkward curtsy. I hide my grimace, determined not to embarrass either of them further. It will have to do for now.

When we all step back out into the sun, Gideon is peering in windows with the hunter draped over his shoulder. The fae woman gasps at the sight of his bare buttocks, and Sheena snickers. *Children. I am surrounded by children.*

"Where is the item you left behind?" I ask, choosing a vague description on purpose. Sheena's secrets belong to her, after all.

My eyes narrow when I notice the folk are staring at the little djinn. "Rawob gu kiyaaumas," they whisper in our native tongue. *Granter of wishes, or simply, genie.* While I know Sheena does not speak fae, the grimace on her face tells me she is reading the context clues well enough.

"They might have, uh, been watching as Leona made me create all this," Sheena admits, waving her hands around at the village.

I take in the pastel buildings, lush gardens, and rippling lake. The sheer enormity of magic needed to create something like this boggles my mind.

"That's amazing, Sheena," Callum says. "You're amazing."

"Yeah?" She looks over at him. "You aren't scared of me?"

Callum takes her hand in his. "Your strength will never frighten me." He presses a kiss to her knuckles, and Sheena's cheeks tinge pink as a wicked grin spreads across his face.

The demon is a shameless flirt. I clear my throat to draw her attention.

"Yeah, umm, it was on the table over there." She points to an outdoor seating area, a frown on her face. "But—"

"Hey," Gideon shouts. "The hunter is waking up."

As the human comes to, he looks around, blinking rapidly until he spots Sheena. His eyes drill into her with a hatred so visceral it's impossible to mistake. Gideon bludgeons him in the head again, and the hunter slumps down to the dirt.

"Jesus," Sheena says. "Be careful with his head. Humans get CTE and all kinds of shit from brain trauma."

"I'm pretty sure that thing inside his skull is already broken, baby. He's a murderous lunatic." Gideon's words are gentle, but I don't miss the little djinn's flinch.

"He's brainwashed, but maybe we can help him see supernaturals aren't all monsters." She looks between us hopefully.

None of us have the heart to tell her that we certainly are monsters to him.

"We can worry about that later," I say. "First, we need to locate the talisman." I desperately try to bring her back to task.

Sheena sighs. "It isn't here."

"How can you tell?" Callum asks.

"Ever since I bonded with it, I've been able to sense it. Almost like the mate bond." Sheena touches her chest and looks at Gideon. "I was slipping away," she admits. "Leona didn't expect me to survive all this." She points around at the village and cringes. "But the talisman—I know this sounds crazy—it practically begged me to bond with it. I felt like it wanted to save me. I wasn't ready to go, so I reached out and grabbed it with my magic. It changed everything."

"That was smart," I tell her. "You made the right decision."

"Thankfully, my power ran out when she wished for Joshua to go on a rampage." Sheena shudders.

Gideon rubs the puncture marks on his arms, then scratches the back of his neck. "About that . . ."

"What?"

"The good news is you're really strong. Even from a distance."

"Oh, shit."

"Yeah, that's what I said when my dad headbutted me," Gideon jokes.

"I'm so sorry." Sheena covers her face with her hands. "He must hate me. Is everyone okay?"

Gideon stares at her in concern. "Everyone is totally fine. He stopped fighting, probably as soon as you lost consciousness. It's just a few bumps and bruises; nothing a few hours of rest won't take care of." He steps closer to her. "Baby, no one, and I mean no one, thinks this is your fault. We're just glad to have you back safe."

"And on that note," I interject. "If the talisman is not here, we should return to the compound and regroup. None of us want to be here if Leona returns with a coven of angry witches."

Sheena shudders, and then Callum and Gideon look to me expectantly.

"Another portal, I presume?" I ask drily. "You know I cannot just create these out of thin air whenever you are too lazy to drive."

"I don't know. It seems to me that's exactly how it goes," Gideon says. He grins, knocking his shoulder into mine. I blast him with frost, and he jumps back, looking to the others for backup.

"I don't want to walk home, so I'm not pissing the fae off," Callum says, slipping his hand into Sheena's.

This one is not as foolish as he appears.

Closing my eyes, I focus on our destination and weave threads of magic in with my intent. The portal takes form in my mind, and when I open my eyes, there's a circle of blue light swirling in front of me. Sheena gestures for the freed fae to go through first. Once they are gone, she and Callum step through. Gideon tosses the hunter back over his shoulder and follows them. I hold the portal open, my magic unspooling rapidly from the strain.

As I step into my portal, I sense another presence. By the time I spot him, it's too late to back out; my magic is already transporting me to a new destination.

I decide to tell no one about the man watching from behind the lavender house.

CHAPTER
SIX

LYSANDER

I can barely hold my bones together as she slips away again. Her scent dances on the wind. I suck it in, tasting it on my tongue. Another deep breath traps the djinn's distinct flavor in my nose and mouth.

They say I imagine things, that no one can smell power, but that's only because they aren't me. Each person carries a different essence, a personal signature. The weak always smell like stagnant water with a hint of something else. Maybe it's rotting mushrooms. Maybe it's a honeysuckle blossom crushed beneath a boot.

The djinn smells like freshly spilled blood and naughty dreams. Coppery, succulent, and ripe for the taking. She's a juicy steak just waiting for me to sink my teeth in and tear her to pieces.

Haven't I waited long enough?

I glance at the stupid purple house and spit on the freshly painted wood. What a waste. Leona has no vision or taste. She's a bossy, self-important bitch.

My boys and me might not be a match for the witches right now, but we're patient. I'll let the enclave and Leona's coven take each other out. While the victor licks their wounds, I'll swoop in and take what's mine.

Stomping through the garden, I trample over Leona's herbs and flowers, imagining all the riches my djinn will give me. As her smell begins to fade, I go ahead and light a cigarette. No matter where she goes, I'll find her.

Taking a drag, I remember the moment I stumbled upon her in that foster home. I've carried her scent in my nose ever since, and I'll carry it with me for as long as she lives. I need to breathe that magic in each and every day. More than that, I need to be the one who controls it. Real power isn't the magic running through your veins. Real power is having the balls to take what you want by any means necessary.

QUAID

I COME TO SLOWLY, my head pounding in time with my heart. I keep my eyes closed, though I wouldn't be surprised if I open them to find my brain leaking out of my ears. The last time I woke up, I was only lucid long enough to realize the shifter was carrying me over his shoulder. It was almost a relief when his meaty fist slammed into my head and put me back under.

As revolting as that was, it isn't as bad as the fact that I failed. Again.

I've squandered every single one of my chances to kill Sheena. I should have shot her and left her to rot next to the witch. There was no reason to carry her away or talk to her when she woke up. Now, I've been taken hostage. That puts the lives of every single one of my brothers and sisters at risk. If I follow my training, I'll end myself before that happens.

That noble thought isn't sitting right with me, though. Is it cowardice or curiosity?

Sheena called me a bigot. Her green eyes stared up at me,

brimming with judgment. She thought I was the monster, and when I pointed my gun at her . . . Dammit, I felt like one.

Maybe all the blows to my head are clouding my thinking because I'm feeling a disturbing amount of guilt. I don't like it, but I can't stop the thoughts from spilling out one after the other, each one faster than the last. My head throbs harder.

She claimed to have no idea what she was when we were in school and accused me of abandoning her. It didn't appear that she was faking her feelings of betrayal. She's wrong, of course, but seeing that look on her face made me feel sick to my stomach.

Harden your heart. She's one of them. It's a brutal truth. One I've never wanted to accept but desperately need to. No matter what Sheena says, I know what supernaturals are like. I've fought them for years. Now that our roles are reversed and she has me at her mercy, she'll show her true nature.

If I get another chance to kill her, I have to take it. No moping. No hesitation.

I crack one eye open to get my bearings. I'm lying on a twin bed. It's not big or fancy, but it's clean and comfortable enough. The lights are dim, which is a blessing for my pounding skull. Through an open door I see a toilet, a sink, and a small shower cubicle. This might be the nicest holding cell I've ever seen.

Why keep someone you plan to kill comfortable?

Maybe they're trying to trick me with kindness so that I'll give away the hunters. It's an interesting tactic. I can't underestimate them. Supernaturals aren't dumb; they're dangerous, crafty, and care nothing for the value of human life. They may talk a good game, but they can't change who they are any more than I can.

I'm drawn out of my head by the sound of hushed voices arguing. Although if I can hear them, they aren't as hushed as they might think.

"You can't go in there, sweetheart. It's dangerous."

"He's my prisoner."

"That's funny. I don't remember you taking him into custody. What I do remember is him pointing a gun at you."

"You don't know him."

"And you do?"

After that, the voices become too quiet to make out. Eventually, the door clicks open and Sheena steps through. The dark-eyed demon follows so closely behind her that he's practically attached to her back. I don't like it.

"Quaid," Sheena says carefully.

I stay quiet. She waits a few minutes, but I know for a fact I can outlast her. She's never been able to stand silence between us for long. Even now, I can actively feel her annoyance building. Higher and higher it climbs until she's simmering like a tea kettle left on the stove too long.

Three. Two. One.

"Don't you have anything to say?" She snaps.

I look up at her, pretending to be surprised. "I think we said all there was to say in that field."

"Don't spew clichés at me, Quaid Hoover." Sheena stomps her foot. "You sound like some jock doing an interview after the big game."

The demon blinks at her in surprise, but I've seen her temper a million times before. If she's still anything like the Sheena I knew, she's just getting started.

"You said we were never friends," she begins again, and my eyebrow lifts. This line of questioning genuinely surprises me. I expected her to ask about the hunter headquarters and maybe offer to spare my life in exchange for coordinates.

This has to be part of her strategy, which means my play is clear. Goad her until she admits the truth.

"And?"

"And? I want you to admit that was bullshit," Sheena hisses, her eyes sparking with rage.

"Why would I do that?" I drawl. "It's the truth, isn't it?"

Hurt clouds her green eyes, but I don't care. I can't.

"I see," Sheena says coolly. "So I was a target. Just a job from the start?" I shrug my shoulders, but she's not done. "Sorry, I'm not familiar with the process, but is it standard procedure to wipe away tears and buy tampons for someone you've been hired to kill?"

The demon flinches at her words and glares at me. When he puts his hand on her back, I frown and stand. The hunters aren't mercenaries. He knows that. I know that. *Why doesn't she?*

"I wasn't getting paid to kill you." As soon as the words are out of my mouth, her eyes flash with triumph, and I realize my error. I've just gobbled up her bait—hook, line, and sinker.

"Yes." Sheena snaps her fingers. "My mistake. It wasn't a job, which would at least make sense. You planned to kill me for free. Your only friend. The only person who actually loved you." Her voice breaks, and she turns away from me.

I'm growing tired of her acting.

"I'm a human, Sheena," I say drily. "You don't have to pretend like you care."

She whips her head around, staring at me in disbelief. Her eyes are bright with unshed tears, but she doesn't let them fall. Stubborn to a fault, even in her fury. I used to admire that about her.

"You have no right to tell me who or what I can care about," Sheena spits. "I might have just been a target to you, but like it or not, you were my friend. My only friend. The one person I thought had my back. You don't get to tell me how I mourn that loss."

Her eyes ripple to purple before settling back to their usual emerald green. I take an instinctual step back. It's the sign I need to regain my equilibrium. For a second there, her words were getting to me.

Sheena notes my reaction and wipes all emotion from her face. Her complete lack of expression reminds me of how she looked when she faced her bullies in school. That emotional wall kept all the people who wanted to hurt her out. It was practically impenetrable, but I've never been on this side of it before. Maybe it's for the best.

"Aren't you going to ask about the hunters?" I finally ask the question for her, unable to stand the tense atmosphere any longer.

The demon looks at me like he wants to peel the skin from my bones and use it to make an umbrella. I wonder what's stopping him.

Sheena scoffs, drawing my attention back to her. The sound is bitter and raw. "Listen carefully to this, Quaid, because I'm only going to say it once." She takes a step toward me. "I don't give a single, solitary, flying *fuck* about your cult."

My eyebrow twitches. "It's not a cult."

"Oh? So it's not a secret group of isolated people with beliefs and obsessive ideals that others find sinister and threatening?"

"That's not fair. It's secret for safety reasons," I say, unsure why I'm even bothering to argue with her. My teachings are clear. She's never going to understand because she's the problem.

"Whose safety?" Sheena asks.

"Humankind."

"Ahh, because everyone who doesn't look and act exactly like you should be eradicated. History always paints groups with ideologies like that in a positive light, right?" She taps her chin, eyes narrowed.

"It's not like that," I snap. "You're dangerous."

I step toward her, and the demon takes a step toward me.

"If you come any closer or say another hateful word about the love of my life, you're going to find out exactly how dangerous *I* can be," he snarls.

It's a clear threat, but that's not the part that sends me reeling. I ignore him and stare at Sheena.

"You're dating a demon? You aren't—"

"A demon? No, I'm not. I'm a djinn," Sheena interrupts me. "Why would that matter, anyway? You're black. I'm white. Although both of our heritages are *clearly* more complicated than that. Are you going to tell me our differences should have kept us from being friends?"

"Of course not. That's obviously not the same thing," I say, rolling my eyes at her twisted logic.

"Is it? You're brainwashed, Quaid."

Bigot. Cult. Brainwashed. She's got it all wrong.

"I'm not brainwashed," I yell, then force myself to lower my voice and reason with her. "I understand why you wouldn't want to accept my beliefs, but that doesn't make them untrue."

"How kind of you to see things from my perspective. You're so magnanimous, Quaid." Her tone is thick with sarcasm and brittle with anger. "If I step closer, are you going to wrap your hands around my neck and squeeze for the greater good?"

Sheena pantomimes the movement, and I barely bite back the urge to tell her it's the best idea she's had all day. She makes me feel sixteen again in the worst ways. I forgot how impossible it is to argue with her. Against my better judgment, I'm drawn into it like always.

"If I did, would that get you to shut the fuck up?" I snap.

Sheena laughs coldly as she crowds my space. With barely an inch between us, she has to crane her neck to stare up at me. Although the demon's face is tight with tension, he doesn't pull her back. I'm not fooled by his restraint. I'm sure he's preparing to intervene if I so much as lay a finger on her.

"Are you sure you're allowed to say fuck? Would your overlords like that kind of language?"

"Get fucked, Sheena."

"Oh, believe me, I do," she hisses, her chest heaving.

I stiffen, shocked by the turn the argument has taken. Teenage Sheena had no boundaries in a fight either, but she also didn't have sexual conquests to throw in my face back then. My words should cut her deeply. Maybe she has changed in the years we've been apart.

"You're bragging about sleeping around? How classy."

She snorts. "If I'm already evil, I don't know why I would bother with classy. Seems like a waste of time to me."

I sigh. She always twists my words like this. If I keep talking, it's just going to get worse. "I don't have anything else to say to you."

Sheena searches my face. I want to retreat and recover in privacy, but I have nowhere to go. I lock eyes with her. I can't show weakness.

"I'm not going to let you go," she admits. An unknown emotion flickers through her eyes, but it's gone too quickly for me to identify.

She's referring to my captivity, but for a second, I swear she means it differently. *Do I want her to mean it differently?* If she trusted me again, it would certainly be easier to kill her. Maybe I'm going about this the wrong way.

Sheena looks back at the demon, and he nods. They're having some kind of silent conversation that I can't track. That used to be us.

"I can't set you loose to continue killing the most vulnerable members of our community," Sheena says, her tone all business now. "Even the 'abominations' deserve to rest easy without having to worry about being murdered in their beds."

I open my mouth to tell her I've never killed anyone in bed before, but vampire screams echo in my mind. I press my lips together tightly.

"I also can't risk you running your mouth about me and putting more opportunistic assholes on our tail."

"So you're going to kill me," I say matter-of-factly.

I almost feel relieved. It would solve a lot of her problems, but also force Sheena to own up to her own hypocrisy. It would make things simpler for me, too. I wouldn't have to kill her.

"No," she murmurs, quietly dashing my hopes. "I'm not going to do that either."

"Why not?" I demand before I can think better of it.

Sheena tilts her head and some of the cold indifference melts away. "Because, unlike you, I have no interest in pretending any part of me is capable of ending your life." She studies my face; I can't look away. "While I might not have been your best friend, you were mine. That means something to me, and until it doesn't, you'll be my hostage."

She spins on her heels, then strides out of the room with the demon. I hear the door lock behind them emphatically, the period at the end of her statement.

No one beat me. I wasn't tortured for intel, and I'm still alive. I should be happy, but I want to scream instead. Sheena made her opinion of me crystal clear, so much so that my heart is damn near beating out of my chest.

She always did have to have the last word.

CALLUM

THE SECOND WE LEAVE the holding cell, I press Sheena up against the wall and kiss her with all the pent up tension I've been feeling for weeks. It spiraled out of control during her abduction, but even before that, it was killing me to watch her magic consume her.

Her lips are soft, and even though I took her off guard, she doesn't hesitate. Sheena kisses me back just as fiercely, and it calms the anxiety inside me. I need to feel her safe and healthy in my arms more than I need to breathe.

When I pull back, we're both panting. Her eyes flash purple as she smiles up at me, and I can't help myself. I press another tiny kiss to the corner of her mouth.

"Not that I'm complaining, but what was that for?" Sheena asks.

I smirk and fan my face. "Sweetheart, when the sexual tension is that thick, you can hardly expect an incubus to come out unbothered," I tease.

"What do you mean?" Her brows furrow.

She knows exactly what I mean, but I'm more than happy to

spell it out for her. "You and that hunter. There's enough passion there to set us all on fire."

"Me and Quaid?" She frowns. "Absolutely not. You're reading that all wrong."

"Am I? It's not like I'm a walking lust detector or something."

"No, I mean, we were mad," Sheena sputters. "That was anger."

I know what I felt between them in that room, but I didn't realize mentioning it would bother her this much. She looks worried, and I regret teasing her about it.

"Maybe I made a mistake," I whisper, tucking a loose strand of her hair behind her ear.

"We were never more than friends," Sheena says, then laughs bitterly. "And apparently I misread our friendship, too."

I kiss her again, desperate to wipe the hurt off her face.

"He's a fool, Sheena, but his mistake is my reward," I purr.

"Callum . . ." A deep blush spreads over her cheeks and down her neck. "I want to do something reckless," Sheena says.

Her words are music to my ears.

"Like get fucked by a demon in a hallway," I whisper as I kiss her neck. "That's just so out in the open." I nibble on her earlobe. "Where anyone could walk by."

I slip my hand inside her shorts. She grinds down on my fingers, her heavy breathing the only sound in the deserted hallway.

"And see you taking my cock like you were born to do nothing else," I say, grazing my lips against hers. "Something like that?"

"Yes," she gasps.

I shove her shorts down her hips, wedging my thigh between her legs. Sheena rubs shamelessly against the denim of my jeans, her lips parted in pleasure as I stoke her banked lust to a boiling point.

There's only one thing that could make this moment more perfect. I slide Sheena over until her back is wedged between the holding room door and my body. Every time I grind against her, the door rattles in its frame. I grin.

I mostly kept my mouth shut while she argued with the human, and he got off easy in my opinion. The best way to punish him now isn't to kick his ass. No, I'm going to force him to listen to the woman he discarded being satisfied by someone else.

I pull back from our kiss and look Sheena in the eye. Consent is more than just enthusiastic sex or permission to use my powers in bed. "Are you okay with this?" I ask, tilting my head toward the loud door, the room, and the obvious message we'll be sending if we go through with this here.

Sheena's eyes morph to purple, and the devious look on her face makes me hard as a rock. When she cups my dick and bites her lip, I'm a goner.

"I want you to fuck me like I'm as evil as he thinks I am," she says.

A shiver rakes down my body. In two quick moves, my dick is out, and I'm inside her. With barely any foreplay, it's a tight squeeze. We both groan as I work my cock in and out in shallow strokes until she can take the whole thing. Once I'm buried inside her, Sheena clenches around me like a vise. It's a deliberate move, and I smirk.

"Are you trying to rush me, sweetheart?"

"I would never," she lies, squeezing my cock even harder.

Her message comes through loud and clear, and I go to work. I fuck her like we aren't standing up in a hallway. I fuck her like I might never get the chance to again. I fuck her with all the pent up fear, anger, and worry I've felt since she was taken.

The cell door rattles until I worry the hinges won't hold, but Sheena comes more alive with every rough thrust. She's never looked stronger or more beautiful to me. So I tell her. I tell her how perfect she is and how good she takes my cock. I describe the way she makes me feel in explicit detail until her head thumps back against the door and her clenching around me is no longer a choice.

Sheena asked me to fuck her like she was actually evil, but that's so far from the truth, I can't even pretend. Instead, I fuck her like she's the reason I wake up every morning. My thrusts begin to slow, and I drive into her as far as I can, bringing a shadow up to play with her clit.

"Sweetheart, look at me," I beg.

She opens her eyes. They're a solid and majestic purple—proof that I'm making her feel really damn good right now. I keep my movements deliberately unhurried because I want her to remember what I say next forever.

"You're strong, but it has nothing to do with your magic. You're beautiful, but I would want you even if you weren't. Your passion, your wit, your kindness, the way it feels like I'm coming home every time I'm inside you—I love it all. Just a moment of your attention is worth any risk in the universe. Anyone who thinks otherwise is a fool."

I kiss her, and when she shatters around my cock, she tells me how much she loves me. The feeling of her losing control paired with her words is more than I can take. My rhythm falters and I explode inside her, stealing secondhand oxygen directly from her mouth.

In the aftermath, we fix our clothes quietly, stopping from time to time to kiss. I can sense lust that doesn't belong to either of us coming from the other side of the door. I would rub it in, but I no longer give a shit about the sad human or his terrible choices.

"I missed you so much," I admit, dropping my forehead against Sheena's. "I'm sorry I trusted Alina with your safety."

The guilt has been eating me alive, but Sheena just shakes her head and reaches up to tangle her fingers in my hair. I lean into her hand. I love it when she touches me like she's as desperate for the physical connection as I am.

"If you hadn't, I would be dead," she argues. "Maybe it didn't go exactly like we hoped, but I'm still alive, aren't I? We get another day together, and that makes it all worth it."

I nod, and we leave the miserable hunter behind. Maybe he

learned a lesson, maybe he didn't. All I know is my girl is going to hear how incredible she is until she's sick of it. No one gets to make her feel like she doesn't belong.

QUAID

THE DOOR RATTLES, and I eye it suspiciously. Maybe Sheena isn't satisfied with getting the last word. If she wants to fight more, I'm fucking ready. I brace myself to put her in her place, and the door rattles again.

A feminine moan. Another rattle. *Surely she's not—*

"You feel perfect, Sheena."

I see red. She's fucking that demon against my cell door. Rage floods my body, and before I can think better of it, my palms are pressed against the door. I'll knock it down with my bare hands. Kill them both.

The demon groans.

Jesus Christ. My hands fall to my side, fists clenched, but I can't make my feet move. Fragments of nasty talk drift through the door, and there's nowhere for me to go to get away from it. I could hide in the bathroom, but that reeks of cowardice. She's doing this on purpose. I can't back down to her. Not now. Not ever.

"Callum, please." The sound of Sheena's voice reaches my ears. It's needy, desperate, filthy . . . . With horror, I feel my cock responding. The door rattles in the frame, jostling my body.

He can't give it to her right. I would make her scream the building down. Teach her exactly what happens when bad girls turn their back on—

Fuck. What the hell is wrong with me?

She's a freak, an abomination. The only fantasy I should have with Sheena on her knees in front of me is the one where I put a bullet in her head. My erection wilts as my imagination provides me with the image of her lifeless body falling to the ground.

"I love you," she moans, and for a minute, it's like she's talking to me. I imagined those very words coming from her lips so many times in high school. Fantasized about what it would feel like to distract her from studying and drive her wild beneath me.

"Callum." His name on her lips yanks me back to the present, and I grind my teeth.

These fantasies got me in trouble when we were sixteen. My assignment was to kill her. I wasn't supposed to fall for her. She's not mine, and I don't want her to be.

A strangled moan comes through the door. I close my eyes and listen to Sheena's heavy breathing. The door smacks my forehead with every stroke. My dick pops back to attention, even as disgust curls in my gut. With any luck, it will give me a concussion and I'll forget this ever happened.

"Yes, yes, yes, Callum!" His name is muffled, and I imagine her biting down on his hand to keep quiet. The rattling stops, and I hold completely still. Two inches of metal is the only thing separating us. I don't dare breathe and give myself away.

I stay frozen against the door, muscles locked rigidly in place until they're both long gone. Bile builds up in the back of my throat. My plans haven't changed. They can't. But—*goddammit*.

My erection isn't going anywhere, and I can't resist any longer. With my eyes firmly closed, I slide my hand down to my pants and unzip them, replaying the sounds of her gasps and moans as I tug my cock in rough, angry strokes. Rolling my thumb over the tip, I imagine her begging me to fuck her harder, green eyes sparking with defiance as I take her apart thrust by thrust. When I come in my hand, it's to the thought of Sheena telling me she loves me.

I'm not sure who I hate the most: her or myself.

LEONA

My daughter captured, my prisoner set free, and my brand new home infiltrated by a cultist. I throw my head back and laugh. Fate is a fickle fiend, but this war is just beginning.

If I'm to take back my home from this never-ending horde of invaders, it will cost more than a few new houses. They're just kindling in the pile, more fuel for the enclave's funeral pyre. When the time is right, I'll light the match and burn them all to ash. Imagining their screams as I vanquish them from their stolen territory is music to my ears.

I twirl the jeweled dagger around in the light, examining it from all angles. Each facet shines now, brilliant in the firelight, casting fragmented prisms of color against the wall.

The djinn may think I don't know what she did, but I saw her magic take hold of the talisman, watched the rust fall away from the blade like sand as she writhed in pain. Sheena believes this dagger is her salvation, but I intend to use it as a leash around her pretty neck.

Since I'm not without mercy, I'll let her have this victory. She can hold tight to those fools she thinks she loves. But soon, yes, very soon, I'll reel in the slack, and she'll come crawling back to me.

CHAPTER SEVEN

SHEENA

How dare Quaid burst back into my life and stir everything up? I should be happy to be home with Callum and Gideon, and I truly am, but this is a lot to unpack. When we were kids, I thought Quaid abandoned me for some childish reason, not because he thought I didn't deserve to live.

Did my best friend ever even exist, or was it all a lie?

With one hand wrapped around Cal's, I shove through the swinging door ahead of us much harder than necessary. It smacks against the opposite wall. Dozens of startled eyes turn to stare. Heat floods my face. I just entered the security room like the Kool-Aid Man.

"Hi, good morning," I mutter, executing what might be the most awkward wave of all time. Callum's lips twitch, but he keeps his mouth closed.

A tall and wiry guy I've never met before joins us. "Good morning, Miss Sheena. I'm Albert. We're so glad you're back safe." He addresses me like I'm important, which is both nice and kind of strange. He turns to Callum, and his expression becomes serious. "No sightings of Leona yet, but she pulled an enormous sum of cash from one of her accounts this morning."

"If she made a withdrawal, why couldn't you see her?" Callum asks.

"She executed the withdrawal simultaneously from multiple ATMs around the state. But when we access the cameras at each location, we see the same thing."

"And what's that?" Callum taps his foot against the ground.

Albert shrugs. "Not a damn thing."

"She can turn invisible now? That feels so unnecessary." I groan and throw my head back. "If she's taking money out of her accounts, then she's not going back to the village. She's on the run with my talisman. Should we assume she knows I bonded with it?"

Callum considers my question. His handsome face is grim, even though our romp in the hallway erased even the tiniest of imperfections from his skin.

"I don't know," he admits. "Most of those antiques were valuable, even without their magical properties. Maybe she just didn't want to lose it."

Callum is trying to think on the bright side, but I can tell he doesn't believe his own words. While I appreciate the effort, I don't think we can afford optimism right now, not when it keeps biting us in the ass.

I'm opening my mouth to tell him that when every computer monitor in the room turns white. Bold magenta text scrolls on a loop across every screen.

The key to our dreams, the witches' greatest wish.
Cat, mouse, or corpse, which will this djinn become?
Make your move, but victory will be mine.
XOXO Leona

Albert's fingers fly across the keys, but the scroll of text continues.

"Turn it off," Callum roars.

Against my will, my feet inch toward the door. I try to yell to Callum for help, but I can't pry my mouth open. His eyes are glued to the screens like everyone else as invisible strings yank at me. They might as well be chains for all the success I'm having at breaking them.

She's trying to take me back. Someone. Please, anyone notice.

Panic threatens to drag me under. My skin burns as though all my nerve endings are on the outside of my body, each one hooked to a magical tether. Nausea churns in my stomach. I try to force myself to get sick to catch someone's attention, but I can't even do that.

My head snaps toward the door, and I can't see them anymore. The chatter in the room morphs to a roaring in my ears.

A touch on my back.

Fingers gripping my arm.

Callum spins me around. His face fades in and out of my vision. It's colorless, but I can't tell if it's real or my perception. When he wraps his tattooed arms tightly around me and pulls me away from the door, I want to sob with relief.

The roaring grows louder. Blurry figures dart in all directions. Pink words. Cat. Mouse. *I have to go somewhere. Now. I've got to get to her, no matter what it takes.* It's important, the only thing that matters.

A sharp stabbing pain digs into my heart like a harpoon. It overrides every other sensation, yanking me back from the edge and clearing my mind.

The mate bond. Gideon. Callum.

I fight with everything I have, but I can't so much as twitch my fingers. Leona may have control of my body, but I'll be damned if she gets in my head again. *Focus, Sheena, focus.* Bit by bit, I sift through the roaring sounds until I can make out individual words.

"She's being summoned."

"Everyone, shut up and calm down."

"It's going to be okay, sweetheart. I've got you, and I'm never letting go."

I cling to the last one, replaying Callum's words over and over. The blur around my vision drifts away like smoke. I see his handsome face inches from mine. His black eyes are wild, but he's entirely focused on me.

"She's not stronger than you." Callum's voice is fierce. "Come back to me, Sheena."

He presses a kiss to my cheek.

Every muscle in my body tries to pull away, but my mind clings to Callum. He's strong enough to hold me back for now, but what about when he starts to get tired and I can't stop? Will I have to go back in a cage for my own safety?

"Don't spiral," he grunts. "We'll figure this out. I promise."

There's a massive crash behind me, then I sense Gideon. A second later, his strong arms curl around us both, and I can feel his rumbling growls vibrating against my back. The pain in my heart fades as I catch a whiff of his familiar scent.

"Are you okay, baby?" Gideon demands, his voice quivering with anger. I'd give anything to answer him, but I'm still magically muzzled. "How is Leona doing this from a distance?"

"I think she's using the talisman to summon Sheena. She can't seem to speak or move unless it's to leave," Callum responds.

Gideon tightens his grip. "Well, how long will it fucking last?"

"There is no way to calculate that with any real precision." It's not Callum but Idris who answers. "But it will eventually stop. Even with the talisman, Leona must be expending tremendous energy on this. She cannot keep it up forever."

A rush of relief washes over me. I don't have the capacity to figure out if it's his presence or his words that make me feel safer.

I still can't turn my head, but from the corner of my eye, I see Idris studying me. He notices my struggle at once and steps into my line of sight. "I am sorry I could not check in with you sooner, little djinn. I needed to get the two fae we rescued settled."

I'd like to nod, but since I can't, I have to settle for staring back at him like a creepy doll.

"I imagine this is quite frustrating," Idris murmurs.

That's the understatement of a lifetime, and I plan to tell him so as soon as this witch gets out of my head.

Involuntarily, my foot kicks out and slams into Gideon's shin. It has to hurt, but he doesn't even flinch. He drops a kiss to my cheek before turning to his dad and Dimitri as they join us in the now crowded room. Joshua looks a little worse for wear. There's faint bruising on his face, and I remember with shame how Leona's wish possessed him.

"I'm sorry," Joshua says quietly. "I know how awful it feels to lose control of your body." Even though my magic put him in a similar position just hours ago, he looks at me with genuine compassion. A single tear trickles down my cheek.

"Thank you," I whisper.

Excited faces whip toward me, and I realize with a jolt that I actually managed to say the words out loud.

"Did it wear off?" Gideon asks.

"If you do not let her go, we will never know," Idris drawls.

Gideon growls, but he does pry his arms away. Slowly, Callum follows his lead until I'm left standing on my own power. I eye the door nervously, then squeak like an idiot when I spot a head of platinum blonde hair standing in the back of the crowd.

"Give it to us straight, Sheena. Any more urges to join the dark side?" Ciprian jokes, but I'm already on the move. I throw myself into his arms with an embarrassing hiccupping sound somewhere between a laugh and a sob. "Gods," he groans. "Have you been working out? That was quite a hit."

"Where have you been?" I demand.

"Vegas, but I would have come back sooner if anyone had bothered to mention that the witches were using you as their personal voodoo doll."

Ciprian glares at the room at large.

"Catch me up to speed. The witches are bitches, and your

former best friend is a hunky homicidal hunter? Am I missing anything? Add any more dicks to the roster?" Ciprian tilts his head obnoxiously toward Idris.

I should be mortified, but I burst out laughing instead. Giggles escape from my mouth as my eyes leak a ridiculous amount of tears. Maybe I'm going into shock. If so, I don't have time for that.

"How long did you workshop that line?" I swipe my tears away, horrified to be having this breakdown with an audience.

"It's called wit, Sheena." Ciprian taps his temple, but there's worry in his eyes as he looks at me. "No pre-pro required. Now, stop crying. It's making Gideon scarier."

I glance over at my mate, and sure enough, Gideon's face looks like a thundercloud. Both of his hands are clenched into fists, and the remaining tech guys eye him nervously. Peeling myself away from Ciprian, I drag my friend fully into the room. Then I grab Gideon's hand. He sighs, and the bond in my chest hums contentedly.

"You're pretty much caught up, but Leona has my talisman. She's trying to use it to pull me back. It almost worked," I admit, my voice trailing off with shame.

"You obviously have to leave," Ciprian says.

I'm a little shocked by the suggestion, but it sends Callum and Gideon over the edge and they both start bellowing.

Ciprian closes his eyes like he's praying for patience. "Gods, I didn't miss you two," he says. "Did I suggest you run her off like Ole Yeller? No, I didn't."

"They shot Ole Yeller," I say, confused by where he's going with this.

"Oh shit, really? What about The Yearling?"

"Also shot."

"Fuck, mom told me they all went to live somewhere else."

"I hate for you to find out like this, but she definitely lied to you."

"Ciprian, you're thinking of White Fang," Joshua says, sounding bemused by this entire conversation.

"That's the one!" Ciprian snaps his fingers and grins. "Anyway, I'm not saying we drive you away. I'm trying to send you on a quest with your posse like Homeward Bound."

"Are you on something?" Callum narrows his eyes at his brother. "That metaphor doesn't work either. You're telling her to leave home, not find it."

Ciprian sighs. "No, I'm telling her to leave this home and go to someone else's."

"Whose?" Gideon asks.

Ciprian points at Idris, who, for the first time since I've met him, looks completely flabbergasted.

"My homeland is a war-torn hellscape, demon." Idris bites the words out through clenched teeth. "Why would I be here if being there was a possibility?"

"It's either that or one of the other realms." Ciprian shrugs.

Everyone goes silent like they're desperate to come up with something better but are drawing a blank. I'm surprised when Dimitri steps forward and clears his throat. He hasn't said a word so far, and I almost forgot he was here.

"Despite the convoluted delivery, my son's plan has merit," he says. "If you go to another realm, Leona won't be able to summon you from here. Magic spells cannot cross the boundaries between worlds, but your bond with your talisman is permanent and should still allow you to control your wishes from wherever you are."

"That doesn't fix anything except the immediate issue," I argue.

"But it buys time," Dimitri insists, looking to Joshua who nods reluctantly.

"Yes, he's right. We can keep using Alina as leverage while negotiating on your behalf. And who knows, maybe you find a solution during your—"

"Quest," Ciprian interrupts, crossing his arms with a smug grin.

I glance at Gideon and Callum. They both seem to be considering the idea seriously. Meanwhile, Idris is standing so still he could be carved from stone. I remember the things he's shared about the fae realm and want to kick myself. *Of course this plan has shaken him. No one is considering his feelings at all.* That ends now.

"May I have the room to speak to Idris?" I ask, keeping my eyes on him.

There's a pause and a few grunts. Callum and Gideon exchange looks, then shuffle toward the door and everyone else follows. They have to wrestle the broken door to get it to close, but eventually, it sits almost how it should.

I study Idris. His face is completely blank. The guys don't trust him, but I've seen a different side to the stoic fae. He's the one who kept me sane while Leona held me in that concrete basement. I won't be part of any plan that does the opposite for him.

"You don't have to do it," I whisper.

IDRIS

THE LITTLE DJINN looks up at me, her eyes as vividly green as crushed clover, the skin underneath bruised with fatigue. She's giving me permission to walk away, and there's a host of reasons I should.

There's a bounty on my head.

I'm one of the most recognizable people in the realm.

The folk need my leadership here.

Each of these reasons is more valid than the last. I should pick one and be done with it, but I cannot. Because there is a burning emotion in her green eyes I have scarcely felt in decades: hope.

If Sheena ventures into my homeland without my protection, she will not last a day. She'll be torn to pieces alongside that pair of well-meaning fools. The little djinn would be better off living under Leona's thumb in a gilded cage.

"I meant what I said, Idris. You don't have to do it." Sheena shifts her weight from foot to foot.

Her discomfort with silence is a surprising trait for someone who has spent so much time in her own company, but I suppose silence while in the presence of others can feel threatening. Especially if you don't know if a person is considering something that could put you at risk.

"I know thinking of your homeland pains you. I won't ask you to face that again for me," she says.

I lift my eyebrows. I assumed she thought I didn't want to go back because of the danger, but I should have known better. The little djinn found the heart of the issue with no trouble at all: I miss my home. Seeing it again will feel like a blade sliding between my ribs. Her being in on my secret makes it so much worse. I'm left vulnerable and disarmed by her perception.

"Please, say something," Sheena begs. "I feel like you're fucking with me."

"I am not, as you so elegantly put it, fucking with you," I say. "Some of us like to actually think things through before speaking. It is a habit your generation would do well to cultivate."

"Okay, grandpa, sure." She scoffs, but the sound is relieved. "Have you had enough time to plan your carefully crafted response? Fair warning, at this point, I expect nothing less than a masterpiece."

Despite her needling, I take my time formulating an answer, though I already know what I must do. I cannot in good conscience let either her hope or her life be snuffed out. Not while I know I could prevent it. Sheena's fate in the fae realm shall be mine as well.

"Thinking of my homeland does pain me," I admit. "This will be a dangerous trip, but I will escort you." I drop into a formal bow, and her eyes widen in surprise.

Sheena opens her mouth, but before she can speak, the constant scroll of pink text vanishes, and the monitors turn black around us. We both stiffen, and I step closer to her. I'm not sure if

I expect the magic boxes to grow arms and attack her or for the summoning magic to take hold again. When neither happens, we both relax infinitesimally.

"In any case, we should hurry." I glance at the broken door. "I expect Leona will not let us rest for long. We need to cover some ground, so we can finally be a step ahead of that insufferable witch."

Sheena nods, although she still seems apprehensive. When we try the door, we find it wedged tightly shut. Gideon is to blame for breaking the flimsy thing, and then for fixing it so tightly back into the frame that it can't be moved. I have to kick the mangled hunk of wood completely down for us to get out—an undignified action that I would have preferred to avoid.

After I step through the splinters, I take Sheena's hand to lead her through the mess. A surprised blush spreads up her neck, and the sight of it both frustrates and leaves me transfixed. *Has the poor girl never experienced common courtesy?*

When we enter the hall leading to the shifter wing, I continue walking at her side. She regards me with a questioning expression, and I wait for her to piece together the reason I'm escorting her.

"Oh, right, because she could summon me at any time." Sheena sighs. "I'd love to stop being the big liability and be the big badass instead."

"Impossible," I say. Sheena stops and stares at me with hurt, but I'm not finished. "It is impossible for you to be a *big* anything. You are the little djinn for a reason, after all."

She rolls her eyes and groans, but the hurt look is gone from her face.

As we walk down the hallway, I imagine someone else co-opting my nickname for her. The very idea fills me with possessive rage. *She is my little djinn.* The thought is troubling, so I let her walk the remaining few steps to the Therion residence alone, watching as she disappears through the door.

"BABY, I REALLY DON'T THINK this is a good idea." Gideon walks down the stone stairs bearing a look of disgust and a bag that likely outweighs the djinn. Sheena trails behind him carrying a much smaller pack on her back, stubborn lines bracketing her mouth.

I sigh. It's far too early in the morning for bickering. Leona attempted to summon Sheena twice more during the night. Gideon and Callum were able to stop her each time, but I don't think anyone got much sleep.

"He's coming with us," Sheena insists. "It's not up for negotiation."

"I hear you, but we're kind of on the run here. Is this really the best trip to bring a captive as your carry on?"

When Callum joins them, leading the hunter down the stairs, it suddenly becomes clear what they're arguing about. I step up to the group, dropping my bag onto the gravel with a thump.

"Explain," I say, pointing at the human.

Sheena has the grace to look a little more conciliatory when she meets my eyes, but her crossed arms tell me she's not backing down. "He's my prisoner. Where I go, he goes," she explains her rationale defiantly, chin set at a stubborn tilt, practically daring any of us to argue.

"I hope you realize this is not a vacation, little djinn. If you are concerned about feeling homesick in a realm where no one is trying to kill you, I can assure you there will be plenty of enemies among the fae. You do not need to bring your own."

I glare at the hunter, remembering the moment we popped into that clearing to see him pointing a gun at Sheena's face. The human watches the current proceedings carefully, saying nothing. I give him my back and focus on Sheena.

"I like it when you make jokes." She drops her bag and looks up at me. "But do they always have to be at my expense?"

"I was not joking."

"Neither was I. He's coming."

With that edict delivered, she tosses her hair over her shoulder and stomps back into the house. Though it galls me to no end, I look to the others for help. Callum just sighs, adjusting his grip on the hunter.

"Look, we've been arguing about this for hours. She's not going to budge."

"Why does she want to bring him?" I ask. "Does she think she needs a human shield?" I eye the hunter again, but this time speculatively. He is large enough, but he would be difficult to maneuver if we find ourselves in a tight spot.

"I think she's worried about his safety if she leaves him here," Gideon says, rubbing his hand over his face.

Since I'm already watching the human, I see several emotions dart through the man's eyes. They are gone too quickly to identify, and quite frankly, I have no interest in what he's feeling.

"Why would she care what your fathers decide to do with him?" I ask.

Gideon tosses up his hands, and Callum shrugs. "He's her friend, I guess."

"I beg your pardon. He held her at gunpoint, his finger primed and poised on the trigger." I squint at the human as he stares at the ground. "That sounds like something a fae friend would do. Did anyone check?"

The hunter's head whips up, and he narrows his eyes at me like he's daring me to come closer. I'm almost tempted.

"It's not that," Callum says, hesitating. "I say we let her bring him."

"Are you going soft?" I demand. "He will only slow us down. If you are worried that telling the little djinn no will jeopardize your place in her bed, I am happy to do it."

"Happy to take my place in her bed or tell her no?" Callum takes a threatening step toward me, and I let loose a mocking laugh.

"Watch it," Gideon growls. He frowns at me, then looks at his friend. "Actually, Callum, you haven't been arguing against this very hard at all. What do you know that you aren't saying?"

Callum looks down at the ground, moving some pebbles around with the toe of his heavy-duty boot. When he glances over at the hunter, he must reach some sort of decision because he stands up straight. "Look, it's not my place to say," he mutters.

"But there is something to say?" Gideon prods, and Callum dips his head in acknowledgment. "That's good enough for me."

Of course, that kind of insipid reasoning would work on him. He's all loyalty and no logic. I might find it endearing if it wasn't so maddening.

The front door opens and Sheena returns, followed by the blonde nightmare demon.

"All I'm saying is you should take some lube. You don't know what the shopping conditions are like in this realm."

"Ciprian, please." Sheena sighs, then shoulders past the hunter to stand next to Gideon.

"Just because you don't want to talk about this doesn't mean it should go unsaid. Did any of you pack lube?" Ciprian scans our entire contingent, but I'm not entertaining his antics. After a moment of silence, Callum nods at his brother. Even though he's the one who brought it up, Ciprian cringes and mutters under his breath.

He turns his attention to the hunter, looking at him with the disgust most people reserve for something abhorrent they find on the bottom of their shoe. "So you're the former best friend . . ." Ciprian circles the hunter, malice radiating from every pore.

"You've got it all wrong," Sheena corrects him. "He was my friend, but it wasn't real on his end."

"Oh, I see, so he's an idiot?"

Some of the stoicism drops from the hunter's face, but he still doesn't speak. Ciprian crowds his space, studies him from head to toe, and sneers like he finds nothing but fault.

"Look here, hunter. Whatever your bullshit is—I don't care. Sheena is my best friend now. The best one I've ever had. If you hurt one hair on her head, you'll wish she had let me kill you last night when I begged her for the honor."

If the hunter is intimidated, he doesn't show it. Instead, he looks around the demon at Sheena with a question in his eyes. It's the wrong move. Even I know Ciprian doesn't enjoy being ignored. In the next second, the hunter's gaze goes glassy and unfocused, and his entire body tenses. A nightmare. The demon doesn't pull us in, but we all know what's happening.

Sheena loses it.

"Stop it! Stop, right now!"

She yanks on Ciprian's shoulder, but he ignores her, his black eyes boring holes into the side of the human's face. When Sheena looks back at Gideon with desperation, he steps forward and picks Ciprian up like a child. He shakes him hard until the illusion lifts and the demon's skin turns slightly green.

"Fuck, Gideon. I'm not a protein shake," Ciprian groans.

When he gags, we all take a step back, except for Sheena.

"What the hell, Ciprian?" She shoves him in the chest, her eyes flashing purple. "What did you show him?"

"Something he needed to see." Ciprian's tone is gentle, despite her aggression. When she reaches out to push him again, he captures both her wrists and looks down at her. "It's okay, Sheena. He's okay. Look at him."

She does, and besides being a little sweaty and confused, the human appears no worse for the wear.

"I didn't scare him or show him anything like what I showed you before," Ciprian promises her, regret shining in his eyes.

"Why won't you tell me then?"

Sheena's breaths are coming in short little gasps, each one faster than the last. It reminds me of the time she found herself trapped in one of his nightmares with no warning.

"Because that's his story to tell now, not mine." Ciprian presses a kiss to her forehead and hugs her tightly. "Trust me, Sheena. I promise I'm looking out for you."

When she finally relaxes and returns his hug, his relief is obvious.

"My phone won't work in this realm?" She asks, looking to me. I shake my head. "I'm sorry I shoved you, Ciprian. Good luck with the wings while I'm gone."

Sheena smiles deviously, and the demon groans, but neither bother to explain to the rest of us. When she turns to me, the stubborn glint is back in her eyes.

"Should we go?" She asks.

Every eye turns to me expectantly, and I can't help snapping, "I suppose you all just expect me to whip up another portal on no sleep. Of course. Coming right up."

I tune them out and close my eyes, thinking of the home I left behind. Meadows filled with wildflowers, mushrooms as tall as a house, and an endless stream of blood. The thoughts hurt, but my connection to the fae realm makes my magic stronger. I feel the air whirring around me. It whips my hair against my face, and when I open my eyes, I'm looking through a portal into the place I never thought I'd set foot again.

I grit my teeth and step through. Only the gods know what is waiting for us on the other side.

CHAPTER
EIGHT

SHEENA

We step into the swirling blue lights, and I cling tightly to Gideon's hand. I feel Callum at my back, his chest a warm, comforting pressure as the magic picks us up and throws us out of the portal's other side.

I can't believe I'm visiting another world.

I blink a few times, and my jaw drops. I've never seen anything so beautiful. This is a lot to take in. Idris brought us to a meadow. It's bursting with wildflowers in colors I can't even describe, the fragrant smells so bold, bright, and inviting that I inhale deeply, eager for more. In a flash, Idris is on me, pinching my nose between two fingers.

"If you smell with such reckless abandon in these lands, it could be the last thing you do," he whispers, his blue eyes darting left and right before they settle back on me. "The first lesson of fae: if it is beautiful, it probably wants to kill you."

He releases my nose and steps back, settling into a slight crouch as he looks across the meadow at the edges of a forest. I take a small, cautious breath, my lips barely parting, and wonder if Idris is being paranoid or if things really are this dangerous.

"How does time work here?" Callum asks, staring up at the sky.

I follow his eyes up, and my jaw drops. There are two suns. *Two.* I gape at them while doing my best not to stare directly into the light. One is a vibrant orange, the other a blinding white so bright I'm not sure it's even safe to look at it indirectly. They're facing off in the sky like mortal enemies.

"Both the days and nights are longer here." Idris points to the orange sun. "Sipsi sets first, initiating a two-hour twilight period." He glances at our group, his posture rigid. "If something separates us, that is your chance to find shelter for the night. If you are exposed when Ahnsid drops below the horizon, you will not last more than a few minutes."

How ominous.

I blink a few times to clear the dark spots from my vision. Quaid is staring at his feet, completely ignoring the fact that his body is casting two shadows. I roll my eyes. He can pretend his boots are the most interesting thing here, but he's not fooling me. I watched him devour fantasy novels around the clock, so I know this is blowing his mind, even if he doesn't want to admit it.

Gideon makes up for Quaid's lack of a reaction by studying everything around us with an acute intensity. "What comes in the night?" Gideon asks. His golden eyes narrow, pupils slitted like a cat, as he scans the field and woods.

"Monsters," Idris says, taking off across the field at an intimidatingly fast clip. He looks over his shoulder at me pointedly. "Keep up. Only about two hours of Sipsi's light remains."

I'm determined to make him eat those words, but I have to catch him first. Once we start hiking, it doesn't take long for me to realize that's never going to happen. *Keep up, he said. Well, I say, fuck him.* Not everyone is gliding around this realm on horse-sized legs. There's imbalance in this herd, and it's pretty infuriating to be the only mini pony in a procession of Clydesdales.

Sweat trickles down my neck, and I hoist my bag higher on my back. Gideon's mouth opens. I silence him with a glare. He's offered to carry it about seventeen times so far, but I survived eight years on the run by myself. I don't need a man to carry my shit.

Callum glances back at me, holding a wide-leafed plant carefully out of my path. Its leaves are a vivid purple, shaped like a palm tree's frond, with veins that glitter in the light and edges as sharp as a fucking machete. I found that last part out the hard way, but at least the slice in my t-shirt is acting like a vent and allowing the breeze to dance along the bare skin of my stomach.

Meanwhile, Idris is blazing ahead with a single-minded drive that's a little unnerving. He never looks back, leaving it up to us to keep up, and I'm finding it really difficult not to throw something at him. Unfortunately, I've yet to see any pebbles.

"Do they not have rocks here?" I grunt, scuffing my foot through the dirt, but feeling only coarse silt beneath the soles of my shoes.

Callum is walking a few steps ahead with Quaid, while Gideon, as he so eloquently described it earlier, is 'guarding my rear.' Ciprian would have a field day with that one.

"Now that you mention it, I haven't seen any," Callum says, tugging his t-shirt up to wipe sweat from his face. The move exposes his abs, and I can't help staring at the defined ridges of muscle on display.

"You've got a little drool, baby." Gideon taps the corner of my mouth.

I waggle my eyebrows. "Can you blame me?"

"No, I guess I can't," Gideon growls, the words a low, sexy rumble that makes me shiver despite the heat.

We both look at the sexy demon ahead of us as he deliberately flexes his abdominal muscles and shoots us a smoldering look. Gideon bites his bottom lip. Clearly, I'm not the only one feeling a little hot and bothered.

My eyes drift away from Callum and settle on my former best friend. Quaid is marching along silently, staring straight ahead. *Stubborn ass.* I'm getting tired of his disinterested super soldier act.

If he's too brainwashed to enjoy visiting a brand new realm, that's his problem.

"Keep up," Idris calls back to us, his voice snapping with impatience.

I throw my head back and groan. "I thought Sipsi's light was supposed to be gone by now. That bitch has been making me sweat for way longer than two hours."

"Idris did say time moved differently." Gideon shrugs.

"If he meant hours in a different way, maybe he should have explained that," I grumble.

As we crest a slight hill, I look ahead and the colors of the forest seem a little darker. New shadows dance around us as we weave carefully between the sharp palm-like trees.

"I think Sipsi heard you," Callum whispers.

I follow his gaze and, sure enough, the orange star that has been baking us in heat since we got here is nowhere in sight. A chill settles over me, and the change in temperature is so abrupt it puts my body on high alert. We pick up the pace as our collective urgency starts to match Idris' own. There's no more lagging behind, and no one complains.

The minutes stretch to hours. My breath comes in ragged gasps, but I don't even consider asking for a break. Not when I can barely see my feet anymore. Darkness is falling over the land, and with each step we take, my heart beats faster in my chest.

Idris said the monsters come at night. I swear I can sense them —creatures hiding in the woods, waiting for the second sun to set so the moon can illuminate their hunting ground.

Gideon puts his hand on my shoulder, and I almost jump out of my skin. He squeezes me silently in apology. I don't blame him for seeking the physical contact. We're all on edge, and the unsealed mate bond always makes tense moments more visceral.

I barrel straight into Callum's back. It's grown so dark that I didn't even notice him stopping. Following Gideon's lead with the hand on my shoulder, I slide my finger into Callum's belt loop so we don't lose contact.

"We've reached our stopping point for the night," Callum whispers.

The relief I feel is staggering.

There's no sign of the white sun at all anymore, and when I glance up, three moons wink down at me from a loose triangular configuration. Each one is in a different phase. One waxing, one waning, and one full and round like a giant eye in the sky staring down at us. I shiver. I have no interest in sticking around to find out if the gaze is friendly.

Up ahead, I hear a scraping sound, followed by shuffling and a thud. I peer around Callum to where I last saw Idris, but he and Quaid are gone.

"We're going to climb down a little, then drop," Callum says, turning to face me. It's so dark, I can barely make out his features. "Gideon will lower you down to me." Before I can ask any follow up questions, he takes my bag and drops it, then disappears into what I now realize is a jagged hole in the ground.

"Your turn, baby." Gideon nudges my back, and I look into the dark recess below. There's a glimmer of light, but it's too faint to tell how far down it is.

I'm nervous, but every instinct in my body is telling me it's not safe to linger up here. Gideon grabs hold of my forearms and lowers me into the hole, inch by inch. We lurch slightly when he drops to his knees, then again when he lies down. *Jesus, this is deep.* Before I can worry that Callum won't be able to reach me, hands wrap around my ankles and slide up my thighs.

"He's got me. You can let go," I tell Gideon, raising my voice slightly to make sure he can hear. He releases me, and I brace myself against the rock to avoid getting a face full of scrapes.

The hands on my thighs crawl up to bracket my waist, steadying me as I land in the underground chamber. I step forward to get a better look at the cavern, and it's a good thing I do, because Gideon's bag comes sailing through the hole, hitting the ground with a thud. Seconds later, he climbs down the rough, stone wall and lands beside us.

"I pulled the rock back over the hole," he says. "It wasn't a perfect fit, but the angle was awkward."

"That should be fine," Idris says. "Unless someone with thumbs braves these woods at night, we will be safe." He's still tense, but he seems more at ease now that we've reached our stopping place for the night.

And what a place it is. This cavern is like nothing I've ever seen before. It's made of rock, so I guess that answers my earlier question about the absence of pebbles. Still, it's not shale or granite, or anything else I'm familiar with. The stone is bright blue with milky crystal swirls throughout. I reach out and run my fingers along the surface. Instead of the rough texture I expect, it's smooth like glass and cool to the touch.

"Is this place natural?" I ask, unable to hold back my curiosity.

"Yes." Idris points to the hole we came in through. "Except for the entrance, which was added as a safety precaution for night travel." He gestures around the space with the solar powered lantern we brought from home. "We are standing in a pocket cavern. This particular section runs underground for miles."

"Are there other entrances?"

Quaid's question shocks us all. It's the first time he's spoken since I pulled him from the holding cell this morning. Judging from the sour look on his face, he's annoyed with himself for opening his mouth.

"Why? Are you thinking of escaping?" Idris drawls. "If so, you will be doing us all a favor by putting yourself down and sparing the little djinn that decision."

"Idris," I hiss, shocked by his sudden aggression. When his sharp blue eyes cut to me in the artificial light, there's no remorse to be seen. I take a step back from his cold stare, my heart pounding in my chest.

"This human is a liability none of us asked to be saddled with. I will do no one the disservice of pretending otherwise." Idris holds his arms wide to include our surroundings. "As I stated earlier, we must remain alert to stay alive here. Now, thanks to him, we also have to guard against backstabbing." His eyes narrow back on me, pinning me in place. "Your sentiment will be the death of us all."

"That's enough," Gideon growls, stepping slightly in front of me.

As much as I appreciate his protection, this is my battle to fight. I square my shoulders and move back into the line of fire. I need to make Idris understand. "My sentiment may be a risk, but if I lose it, I'm no better than Quaid believes I am," I say the words quietly, locking eyes with Idris.

For a long moment, I hold his stare. No one speaks. Finally, Idris dips his chin and turns away. I release the breath I didn't realize I was holding, and my shoulders slump with relief. He might not agree, but at least he's respecting my decision.

"There are hot springs down the corridor. I will be back shortly." Idris shatters the silence. All emotion, even his earlier frustration, is gone from his voice. I know better than to think he has lost interest in the topic, though.

His footsteps echo along the cavern floor. I don't try to stop him. The argument is as resolved as it's going to get right now. Although I would love to see the underground water feature, Idris needs space.

I turn to face the nearest wall of the cave. The white, iridescent swirls are all unique, and they continue in every direction. I'm captivated by how random they seem. I search for patterns, but don't find any.

Only when I feel a pang in my chest, do I turn away from the wall. Gideon is sitting on the ground, digging through his enormous bag. He looks perfectly content, but we share a magical connection that tells me otherwise, and that uncertain stinging in my heart didn't come from me.

When I walk over to him, Gideon looks up with a dazzling smile. He's so beautiful. I sink into his lap, butterflies dancing in my stomach. He exhales and pulls me into his chest, and I feel the tension seep out of his body. My heart thuds contentedly.

"I'm just giving the connection what it wants," I echo the words he said to me weeks ago in his kitchen in Colorado, and he laughs. It feels like a lifetime has passed since then.

Callum plops down beside us and grins. "Do you have anything tasty in there?" He points at the duffle, and Gideon narrows his eyes.

"Didn't you bring your own food?"

"Yeah, but my mommy didn't pack my lunch, and I know for a fact I smell chocolate coming from somewhere over here."

"Hands off my shit."

As they banter back and forth, the last piece of stress I carried from the hike slips away.

"Look, you either have to share your treats or share Sheena. It's not fair that you get everything." Callum pouts, and Gideon's arms tighten around my waist.

"You're thinking really hard about this decision," I tease, and he nips playfully at my neck.

"Fine," Gideon growls. "Inside pocket. Right side. The code is 72724."

For a split second, his declaration is met with silence, then both Callum and I burst out laughing.

"You locked the sweets up?" Cal wheezes, pulling out a small lockbox from the zippered compartment.

I think about the numbers he chose for the combination and snort. "And the code is your mom's name?"

"What?" Gideon mutters defensively. "Those cookies are valuable."

"I can't argue with that," Callum says, sinking his teeth into the chocolate chip masterpiece with a satisfied moan.

The sound makes me squirm in Gideon's lap. He inhales sharply by my ear. "If you keep wiggling around like that, you're going to have to do something about the results, baby."

"Promises, promises," I whisper, twisting in his lap to press a kiss to his lips.

I mean for it to be a gentle caress, but that flies out the window as soon as our mouths meet. As always, Gideon's kisses are a language of their own. I feel his joy at having me back in his arms, the lingering fear from when we were apart, and his need to have me close.

I do my best to soothe him, sinking my fingers into his curls and holding tight. With my kisses, I reassure him that I'm here, that I don't plan to disappear again, and most importantly, that I love him.

We pull apart, and I sense eyes on me. Quaid is watching. I'm somewhat embarrassed, but when I feel how content Gideon is, even that twinge of self-consciousness fades. The universe, the ancient gods, or some mystical combination of the two matched us down to a cellular level. I never want to feel shame for showing Gideon how much he means to me.

"Do you like chocolate chip?" Callum's question pulls me out of my head, and I'm surprised to see him offer half of his cookie to Quaid.

My former best friend hesitates, then reaches out and accepts the dessert. "Thank you." His voice is unsure, but he eats the broken cookie, devouring it in two large bites.

My stomach chooses this moment to growl loudly. Gideon passes me a cookie of my own, and I pop it into my mouth. Flavors explode on my tongue. *Holy shit.* These are so damn good. I can't even be mad that Gideon hesitated before picking me over them. Dammit, I'm proud to even be in the running.

I lick my fingers, careful to make sure no melted chocolaty goodness gets left behind. When I look up, all three men are staring at me like I'm the meal. Even Quaid is looking at me with unmistakable hunger, although his expression is more pained than the others.

I'm about to say something about it when I notice the biggest centipede I've ever seen crawling up the wall of the cave by Quaid's head. It's bright orange with fuzzy black antennas, and—are those fangs? I squeak, grabbing a flashlight from the bag in front of me and scrambling out of Gideon's lap.

The terrifying insect is only an inch from Quaid's ear. I ignore everyone's panicked questions and swing the flashlight at the bug's horrifyingly segmented body. My aim is true, and the creature lets out a grisly, high-pitched wail as I crush its midsection into the cavern wall. Guts spill out. Part of its body stays stuck to the stone, but two pieces, including the head, fall to the ground by Quaid's hip.

I kick the pieces away from him, then sink down into a crouch. Quaid trembles, staring at the bug's head in terror. Gently, I turn his chin toward me, forcing him to look away from the corpse. Quaid has a fear of insects, especially ones that bite, although I doubt he would ever admit his phobia out loud.

"It's dead. You're okay," I murmur.

Quaid's pupils are huge, swallowing up the rich mahogany color I'm used to. He's also holding his breath, so I suck in an exaggerated gulp of air, hold it for a few seconds, and then blow it out slowly.

"Follow my breathing. You're okay," I whisper.

He inhales and exhales along with me, and I'm pleased to see his pupils returning to a normal size.

Only when his right thumb grazes my hip do I realize he's gripping my waist tightly between his calloused hands. Goosebumps spread across my skin, starting with the points of contact. When I look down, his fingers fall away from my body like I'm radioactive.

I stand abruptly, pretending his reaction isn't another slice to my scarred heart.

"Everything is fine," I say, turning back to Gideon and Callum who are gaping at me. "It's totally okay. We don't even know if it's poisonous. It could be a nice bug."

"Actually, it is highly poisonous and carnivorous." Idris saunters back in, his wet black hair tucked behind his pointed ears. "The human's death would have been painful and slow as the 'nice bug' waited for his meat to rot and fall off the bone."

Quaid's rich complexion fades to an unnatural waxy color.

Gideon mutters a curse under his breath as he eyes the centipede warily.

I frown at Idris, my earlier irritation returning. "Good to know," I hiss, snatching a set of sweats from my bag, then meeting his icy gaze. "Are there directions to these hot springs or should I just wander around in the dark until I get wet?"

I hear my mistake immediately, but it's too late to take the words back. Callum and Gideon roar with laughter, and a choked sound escapes from Quaid's mouth. Idris keeps his cool, but I see the beginnings of a smile on his face.

"Little djinn," Idris croons. "I am confident there are plenty of men here eager to ensure your pleasure. No darkness necessary."

That's it. I've officially had it with his mood swings. Tossing my hands up, I stomp away, still carrying the flashlight I used to bludgeon the murder bug.

GIDEON

I MUFFLE MY LAUGHTER as Sheena storms off. A moment later, I realize I'm wasting a golden opportunity. Reaching into my bag, I grab a change of clothes and see Cal racing to do the same out of the corner of my eye. *It's on.* I rush to beat him out of here. When he lobs a travel shampoo at my head to slow me down, I growl and nail him in the chest with a bar of soap.

"So eager," Idris drawls as he towels off his hair lazily. "Embarrassing."

I stop what I'm doing to stare at him in disbelief. "Have you seen her?" I ask, pointing in the direction Sheena just disappeared. Idris raises one arched black brow and shrugs, but I'm not fooled.

"You can pretend all you want, fae," Callum says. "But we all know if given half the chance, you'd trip over your own feet to follow her into the dark."

"Perhaps," Idris sniffs. "But I would not need a sidekick to get the job done satisfactorily."

I chuckle and shake my head, not offended by the dig in the slightest. "That's your loss." I muss Idris' hair as I walk past him, enjoying how his eyes snap with anger.

"Also, Idris, if you're thinking of it like a job, you're going about it all wrong," Callum teases, his features sharpening in anticipation. A shiver runs down my back.

The hunter watches our sparring, his eyes darting back and forth like a pendulum, only stopping a few times to stare at the centipede's body. He's definitely got a bug thing, but this isn't the time to mess with him about it.

I charge into the dark, my body screaming at me to follow my girl. Cal is right on my heels, only pausing long enough to order Idris to babysit the hunter while we're gone.

I shift my eyes into my lion's, so I can see better. The walls aren't much wider than me. *This is going to be a tight squeeze.* When Callum bumps into my back, I grab his free hand and tug him along after me. He can't see as well in the dark, and I don't want to slow down. I hear running water ahead and pick up my pace. Absolutely nothing will come between my mate and me tonight.

Gradually, the cavern walls grow farther apart until the cave opens up to a large underground lake. Sheena's pale silhouette draws my gaze like a magnet. The water ripples as she steps in. Her soft, gentle curves slowly disappear below the surface.

I stop at the edge just to watch her. The unfulfilled mate bond buzzes with excitement, and a whine builds in my chest. Sheena turns to face us, and the top swells of her breasts peak out of the water, a teasing glimpse of skin I can't wait to get my hands and mouth on. Callum's breathing tickles the back of my ear.

The flashlight Sheena wielded as a weapon earlier is propped against a stalagmite. Cal and I drop our bath supplies beside it. Its yellow glow barely pushes back the darkness.

"You laughed at me," Sheena says, sinking down into the water until only her head is visible.

"I'm sorry, baby—"

"We'll make it up to you—"

Callum and I talk over the top of each other, but I have to say, I like what he's thinking. When his hands snake around my body and tackle the buttons on my flannel shirt, a shiver runs down my spine. Callum takes his time, scraping his blunt nails over my torso as he works the buttons loose. I shudder as my nerves come alive.

Sheena stands up straight and watches him undress me quietly, her bottom lip trapped between her teeth. The water laps at her rosy nipples. I groan, and they visibly tighten. My shirt falls to the ground, and Callum's fingers drop to the button of my pants.

"What do you think, Sheena? Should I send Gideon in after you?" Cal's voice is liquid smoke—deep, thick, and teasing as he toys with my waistband, sliding one finger under the material to trace my hipbone.

I want to make a witty comeback, but all my blood is rushing south. If he doesn't hurry up and take my godsdamn pants off, they may be stuck there.

"Only if he plans to make up for laughing when he gets to me," Sheena says.

She's issuing a challenge, but the anticipation and our extended time apart means my body is in no condition to be teased. Callum must sense my desperation because he stops waiting. His fingers make quick work of the clasp of my pants. My breathing is ragged by the time he pulls my zipper down.

"Is he hard for us, Callum?" Sheena asks, her voice husky and low.

Cal's hand crawls back around to my lower stomach, pausing long enough that I have time to stop him if I want to. He sucks in a sharp breath when I grab his hand, but I have no intention of shoving him away. Instead, I push his fingers down, groaning when he grips my cock and strokes it with the perfect amount of pressure.

"He's hard as a rock," Callum rasps, running his thumb over the sensitive head of my dick.

Shit. It feels so good. I tremble as he grinds against my back.

"I can't see," Sheena complains, taking a step toward us and revealing more of her skin.

"Well, we can't have that," Callum says, then yanks my pants and boxers down until I'm standing completely naked in front of my mate while he strokes me.

If he keeps this up, I'm going to explode all over the cave floor. Since I don't plan for that to happen until I've rung at least a handful of orgasms out of Sheena, I grab Callum's hand and pull him around in front of me. My lips crash into his, and I devour his mouth as I hold both of his hands still.

When we pull back for air, Callum's lips are puffy and pink, and he looks like he's starving. I feel a momentary rush of pride that I did that to him, then I get down to business, tugging his clothes off until he's as naked as I am.

We turn together to face the water. Sheena looks like she's five seconds away from pouncing on us. As she licks her lips, I snatch up the flashlight and take it into the water with me.

The water is warm as it laps around my ankles. It creeps up my legs the deeper I go until I'm standing directly in front of my mate. Sheena launches herself at me, and I catch her, loving the jolt of electricity I feel when her naked body collides with mine.

Sheena's skin is slick and soft as it brushes mine in the water. Gods, I could spend the rest of my life wrapped around her. I'm dying to kiss her, but I hold back. I don't want to lose this view of her face yet. Big green eyes, freckles, the way her damp hair clings to her neck . . . A wave of emotion hits me. I blink, hoping somehow I can save this moment forever.

The water moves behind me, then Callum pops up on my right. Heat radiates off of his body, and goose bumps spread across my skin.

"What's the flashlight for?"

"I thought we could play a game," I say.

Callum's teeth flash as he smiles. "What kind of game?"

"Sheena said she was worried about fumbling around in the dark, so we need to make sure she's clean. No spots missed. I'll hold the light," I suggest.

Sheena shivers with excitement. "Sounds like fun . . . as long as I win."

"Oh, baby, I promise you'll come out on top."

I slide her down my body and walk us deeper into the pool until it's up to her chest. Then, I take the flashlight and shine the beam of light on her neck. Callum slides his finger along the spot and drops his lips to her skin.

I move the light to her mouth and smile as my best friend drops a heated kiss to her soft, pink lips. Next, I slide the light down to her left breast, which is partially underwater. The light penetrates the water, casting patterns on her skin. Callum's fingers dance along her curves, touching, cupping, and lightly pinching her nipple. Sheena arches her back with a gasp, and he takes the hint, replacing his hand with his mouth.

Her purple eyes lock onto me, and the desire I see there makes me want to tell the world that this woman is mine. Powers, no powers—I don't give a damn. If I can spend the rest of my life putting this look on her face, I'll never need anything else.

"Gideon, please," Sheena whispers.

I know what she's asking for. Since I'm unable to deny her anything, I shine the light up one of her inner thighs, and then the other. Callum follows the path with his fingertips, stopping exactly where she needs him: right between her legs. He and I stare at her pussy through the water, but that's not enough for me. I haven't tasted her in days. That changes now.

I toss the flashlight back toward solid ground, and it bounces off the wall. The light sputters out, and we're plunged into complete, inky darkness.

Sheena gasps, and I smile, diving face first into the water. I grab her hips to anchor myself and slide my tongue out to taste her. She jerks at the first touch, but I pull her in closer, fucking her thoroughly with my tongue.

When my air runs out, I initiate a partial shift to breathe underwater. It's not something I've done often, and never so that I could eat someone out without wasting time to come up for air, but it may be the best idea I've ever had.

Sheena yanks on my hair, and I feel a stab of panic through our bond. She's worried about my oxygen. Callum's fingers graze my neck where small gills have formed, then he goes right back to fingering our girl. I hear his voice, muffled by the water, and Sheena's panic fades. I pat her hand and get back to business.

Her legs tighten around my head. With both of us working her over, it doesn't take much time at all for her to come. Her moans of pleasure reach me even underwater, and I kiss my way up her body slowly, enjoying the smooth texture of her skin and the bite of pain from her tight grip on my hair.

When I resurface, I shift my airways back to normal. It's still pitch black. Sheena's panting is music to my ears.

"Show-off." Callum chuckles.

"Not all of us can be sex demons," I say.

"Gideon," Sheena whines. "Please, I need you."

I don't have a lot of experience with pretty words, but I think that's got to be the best sentence in the world.

Lust makes me reach for her with both hands. Love makes those same hands tremble as I slam her down on my cock. We both groan the second I sink home, and I just hold her there for a moment, savoring the feeling of her body wrapped around mine.

My heart jumps in my chest. I can't go through another separation. The phantom ache in my chest remembers how empty I was when the witch magic concealed Sheena from me. It's just an echo of what I would have felt if she was really gone, but it was enough to prove to me I don't want to be in this world, or any other, without her.

Sheena finds my lips with hers in the dark and kisses me desperately. "I missed you so much," she whispers.

"I missed you too," I say, thrusting into her fiercely.

Callum wraps one hand around her neck and the other around mine. It's a gentle touch—a test for us both. He's barely using any pressure, but just seeing his hand on her throat and feeling his fingers on mine makes my temperature rise.

My rhythm falters as Callum tightens his hold. Sheena whimpers. She's close too. Each time I bury myself inside her, she grips me tighter. When she cries out, I muffle the sound with a kiss and spill inside her. The soul deep relaxation that floods my body in the aftermath of my orgasm makes my knees weak, and we sink under the water until I lift us up again.

Vaguely, I hear Callum sloshing around, but before I can ask where he's going, he comes back with the soap and shampoo. He lathers us both up, and soon we're laughing and playing in the water.

After everyone is clean, Sheena and I sandwich Callum between us and give him our full attention. I trail biting kisses down his neck as Sheena rides him. When he comes, his magic flares out and drags us both over the edge with him.

Once I can make my muscles work again, I wade out of the water and grope around in the darkness until I find the fallen flashlight. It doesn't work at first, but luck is on my side because it turns on just fine after I knock it against the wall a few times.

We leave the underground lake together, exhausted but smiling. I haven't felt this good in days, and I never want it to end. As soon as we're done running for our lives, I'm asking her to make the mate bond permanent.

CHAPTER NINE

QUAID

I almost met my end at the fucked up hands of a meat-eating centipede. I glance down at the severed head, imagining dozens of tiny legs crawling up my back. No matter how many times I remind myself the bug is dead, I can't seem to make myself believe it.

Looking around the cave, I scratch at my forearm and consider the facts. I'm in another realm with Sheena, surrounded by enemies. If someone had predicted this two days ago, I would have called them a liar and probably snapped their neck for emphasis. But there's no point in denying reality. Shit, there are two damn suns in the sky. They beat down on me for hours. That was no illusion.

I'm probably the only human in this entire realm.

I scratch my arm again, ignoring the fae's stony stare from the other side of the cavern. Sheena returns to the forefront of my brain, not that she ever really left it to begin with. I clench my fists at my side. My hands felt so good on her waist, but I shouldn't have touched her. I would have been better off serving myself up to that bug on a platter.

Sheena killed it without hesitation even though she's my captor. Why would she do that? *She knew I would freeze up; she was protecting me.* No. That can't be it. She has a plan for me, so it would be a bad move to let me die. *But the males want me dead.*

Maybe they planted the bug to get a reaction out of me. I suspect that earlier argument between her and the fae was staged. It's all an elaborate scheme to trick me into trusting her again.

I won't fall for it. Not when I know what she's doing with those two guys in the dark. My stomach flips and twists angrily. She's proving every negative thing I ever thought about her is nothing but the truth.

"You are a man of violence," the fae says.

I flinch at the sudden sound of his voice and meet his eyes warily in the light of the lantern. His expression is unreadable. Maybe he's planning to kill me while Sheena is occupied.

"I do what must be done," I tell him, not seeing much point in staying silent.

"Ah, a man of violence and principles," he clarifies, and I dip my head in acknowledgment.

The fae's eyes glitter in the darkness as he looks at the walls of the cave. When he glances back at me, the bitterness I see there startles me. "Many years ago, I was the same," he says. "I fought, bled, and slaughtered with conviction. I clung to those principles more than anything else in my life, yet they forsook me when I needed them most. I lost everything I cared for."

"And what does that leave you with now?" I ask, caught up in the story despite myself.

"Violence." He stares at the dead bug, then turns toward the sound of laughter echoing off the walls. "You would do well to remember that, hunter."

The only thing I need to remember is how easily supernaturals lie.

Sheena comes back while I'm still focused on the fae. His expression doesn't change, but some of the ice melts from his eyes as he watches her. The compulsion to do the same feels like some kind of dark magic. I can't wait to be rid of it. Rid of her.

The huge shifter has his arm tossed over Sheena's shoulder, his fingers playing with the wet ends of her hair. I shift my gaze to the demon and blink. He looks like a fucking painting.

"He feeds on lust," the fae explains as his lips curl up into a cruel smirk. "An incubus demon only looks like that after he has been well fed."

The demon shoots him a warning look even though Sheena doesn't seem offended. She blushes bright red like always, but when she looks at the dark-haired freak, she seems proud of what she sees.

The shifter drops down next to me, digging around in his bag and tossing things in all directions as he searches for god knows what.

"How is it possible to make such an enormous mess with the contents of only one bag?" The fae asks, staring in horror.

"Oh, I'm sorry." The shifter grins, pointing at the scattered clothes. "Does this bother you?"

The fae bares his teeth. "It should bother any civilized person."

"Don't," the demon sighs. "If he knows it gets to you, it will only get worse."

"He only had one towel in his bathroom," Sheena adds with a laugh.

"That's not fair, baby. If I had known I would have company—"

"I doubt advanced notice would have changed things, dude," the demon interrupts, dodging the balled up shirt the shifter lobs at his head.

"Yeah, do you even own a second towel?" Sheena slides down beside him. Her ass barely touches the ground before he pulls her into his lap.

"If you want me to, baby, I'll buy a towel for each day of the year," he assures her, smacking a kiss to her cheek.

Sheena blinks a few times. “Where would we possibly store that many towels?”

“I’ll get you a bigger house. Imagine it.” He spreads his hands wide. “Built-in cabinets stuffed from floor to ceiling with . . . Fresh. Clean. Linens.”

“How romantic,” the demon says drily, dropping himself down next to the bigger guy.

“I am, aren’t I?”

The shifter continues digging around in his bag, looking pleased with himself. When he finds a blanket in the mess, he wraps it around a yawning Sheena. I watch out of the corner of my eye, refusing to show overt interest in her nasty little threesome.

“A bigger house would just give you more room to make a mess,” Sheena teases, pushing her wet hair behind her ear. “What’s the plan for tomorrow, Idris?”

“First, we need to kill the hunter.” The fae points at me, and I go completely still. “We can leave his body for the centipedes to eat.”

The phantom itch crawls up my arm again. It’s all I can do not to scratch myself raw.

“Be serious,” Sheena snaps.

“But I am,” he drawls. “You know I never joke.”

“Oh, you joke, it’s just always at my expense.”

“Can you explain to me exactly how it is at your expense, darling?” The fae’s creepy blue eyes sparkle with delight. “After all, I did not suggest we leave your body for the centipedes to find.”

He looks her over with interest. It makes me want to plant my fist in the middle of his smug face. I scratch my arm instead.

“Because he’s my . . .” Sheena hesitates.

“Your what?” He presses.

“My hostage, dammit. I already told you that.” Sheena crosses her arms over her chest. The demon and shifter glare at the fae, their joking from earlier completely forgotten.

"Stop looking at me like that," the fae snaps at them. "If she could answer that question honestly, we would all be a lot better off."

"Just leave her alone about it," the shifter growls. "She already told you her decision."

"This human is beyond hope." The fae points at me again, his lips pressed in a tight line. "He will snap her neck the first second one of us turns our back." He whips his head around to Sheena, his expression softening slightly. "Some people are beyond redemption, little djinn. Your determination is admirable, but you cannot save him."

Fury builds in my chest, but I make no move to speak. They're talking about me like I'm not even here, but there's no point in defending myself. The fae is right. I have to kill her, no matter what it takes.

Sheena sinks further back against the shifter, a shadow falling across her face as she watches the fae. "I hear your opinion, Idris," she says quietly. "Please understand that I don't like putting any of you at risk." Her voice wobbles as she looks at me, and I feel sick. "But I haven't given up on him yet."

Maybe that costs her something to admit, but it costs me everything to hear. I slump further against the wall.

"So you will continue to protect a man who wants you dead?" The fae asks. Sheena nods, her jaw clenched tight even as her lips tremble. "Very well, I will take first watch. Tomorrow, we will attempt to discover what is left of my kingdom. If our luck holds, we might actually make it there alive."

In the wake of that ominous declaration, he extinguishes the lantern. Both the darkness and silence in the cave are absolute. I try to sleep, but the combination of the fae's eyes on me and Sheena's stubborn words won't let me rest.

I don't believe her.

I can't.

IDRIS

I WAKE IN THE COOL DARKNESS of the cavern, my body tense and sore. My mind is in even worse shape. The moment I set foot back in my realm, long dormant feelings began to tear at me like wolves. Some soft, some sharp. After years of being ignored, they are all out for my blood. My mind—the weapon I've honed to be sharp and logical at all costs—has proven ill-equipped to hold the attack at bay.

My homeland. Beautiful, bold, and dangerous—she wraps around my heart and squeezes until I beg for relief. No one hears my plea. There is no relief to be had.

Today, I will again feel the warmth of Sipsi's gaze on my face. Bitterness will overshadow that simple pleasure because I cannot stay. I must die or leave, and until that happens, each step I take will be haunted in equal measure by the beauties and perils of this realm.

Despite the perpetual darkness of the cavern, I sense dawn approaching. My eyes adjust to the gloom, and I see the little djinn sleeps on. She looks peaceful, her head tucked securely under Gideon's chin as he keeps watch. The lion and the lamb.

The hunter is already awake. He watches me warily, the scar on his face standing out in the dim light. A foreboding chill runs down my back. This man radiates violence from every pore. If Sheena persists in protecting him, he will be her ruin. I am certain of it, but perhaps I should not have tried to convince her so aggressively.

My regret tastes bitter and sharp on my tongue. The same tongue I used to berate her last night. Internally, I sigh. I've lived far too long to believe I have the right to say every truth that pops into my mind. Emotion ruled us both last night. Mine demanded I lash out, and hers told her to protect the human. We both would be better off locking these feelings away. If I'm to keep us alive, I cannot afford distraction.

I flip the switch on the lantern. The light reflects off the crystallized minerals of the cavern wall, and I avert my eyes. "Time to get up," I say.

Gideon and Callum snap to attention at once, but it appears the little djinn is far from home in the fleeting epoch of dawn's rebirth. Sheena cracks one emerald eye open, then curls further into the shifter.

"Are you sure?" She grumbles. "It's still dark."

"Indeed," I say, calling on my renewed patience to avoid snapping at her. "And it will remain dark all day because we are underground."

"Oh, right." She yawns and sits up, stretching her arms over her head as she scans the space. "Quaid, do you want to wash up?"

Sheena looks at him like a snake she wants wrapped around her. As though she knows perfectly well he could bite her at any point, but she can't resist the urge to tempt his nature. *Damned foolish sentiment.*

"Make it quick," I say after the human nods. "I want to be on the move in half an hour."

Sheena gives me a thumbs up in response, grabbing the flashlight and a wad of men's clothes from her bag. I shake my head. Of course she thought to pack something for him to wear.

"Let's go, then," she tells him. The hunter stands and follows her silently out of the chamber. Callum rushes after them.

When I look back, Gideon is staring at me pointedly. "What?" I demand, unable to hide my exasperation any longer.

"She can't help it," he says, sifting through the mess at his feet.

"I know that."

"Then why did you push so hard last night?"

There's no judgment in his voice, only curiosity. It's for that reason alone I humor his question. "Because he has the power to hurt her," I say.

"We'll protect her." Gideon's face turns serious in a blink. "Maybe it doesn't seem like it to you, but Callum and I aren't letting him out of our sight."

"Not all pain is physical."

Gideon stops rifling through that chaotic duffle of his for a moment and furrows his brow as he works out my meaning. "You think she loves him?"

I shrug, tossing him a prepackaged pastry. "Do you not?"

"Maybe," Gideon admits. "But it's different. He's her best friend."

"That is true, but Callum is also your best friend." I eye him carefully, determined not to overstep in this. "Is your love for him different?"

I've seen Gideon's omni-shifter fly off the handle in a heartbeat for less impertinent questions, but his hands remain steady. He takes his time answering, biting into his pastry and chewing slowly as he thinks.

"I don't know," he says, sounding troubled by his own answer.

He does not like being unsure.

I prop my elbows on my knees and lean forward, intrigued by this illuminating glimpse into his psyche. If I can't have clarity myself, perhaps I can help him muddle through a little better.

"If the hunter snaps out of it and comes running back to her begging for forgiveness, what would you do?" I ask, tearing off a hunk of my own breakfast.

Gideon leans back against the wall, staring down the dark corridor they disappeared into.

"I don't know," he repeats his earlier answer. He polishes off the pastry, then rubs the palm of one hand over his heart. "But Sheena and I would work it out no matter what. I didn't imagine sharing my girl, but now I can't see myself denying her anything that makes her smile."

"You are in luck then."

I dust off my hands as Gideon balls up his pastry wrapper and stuffs it into the main compartment of his bag. I wince. He's a slob, but the shifter is growing on me.

"How do you figure that?" He finally asks.

"Well, he certainly is not making her smile right now, is he?"

Gideon chuckles at that, then begins haphazardly stuffing all the things he tossed on the ground last night back into his bag. Nothing is organized or folded, and there's no way it's going to zip at this rate. Groaning, I cross the chamber and slap at his hands.

"Please. Let me," I hiss.

Gideon shrugs, and for the next few minutes, I sort and organize the contents of the bag. Setting order to the chaos soothes some of my jagged edges. It's not until I catch him grinning out of the corner of my eye that I realize I may have fallen for a trap. I rock back on my heels and narrow my eyes.

"Did you trick me into repacking your bag?" I demand.

Gideon loses it, laughter exploding out of him. The sound booms off the natural stone walls with a boisterous abandon that reminds me of his father. I maintain my blank stare, surprised when I have to resist the urge to join in.

"You looked like you needed something to occupy your mind," Gideon admits with a shrug. "Plus, you can tell I'm no good at it."

I tilt my head. For the first time since meeting him, I realize he's more than just a pretty face perched atop a mountain of muscles.

"You are far more perceptive than I ever realized," I admit.

"Mom always said it was my greatest strength . . . besides breaking things."

"She is a smart woman," I say.

Gideon grins at me, and I see Sarah in his expression. Usually, he looks like a direct copy of Joshua, but now that I'm looking for it, I see her emotional intelligence staring back at me.

I turn back to my task, and by the time the others return, I've finished putting Gideon's bag in order. They are all in one piece, though Callum seems stressed, and the tension between the little djinn and the hunter is so thick it has practically taken physical form.

"Should we head out?" Sheena asks, tapping her foot against the rock.

"There is time to eat," I respond.

Sheena scarfs down the pastry Gideon passes her and packs her bag in record time while the other two hurry to catch up. Once everyone is ready, I climb the handholds in the wall and shove the heavy rock to the side.

After so long underground, the light from the dueling suns momentarily blinds me. I blink to clear the spots and wait, straining my ears for any sign of danger. All I hear is a faint breeze rustling through the trees and the whimsical trill of birds greeting the dawn.

Satisfied, I push my way out of the hole. I expected to stumble upon any number of enemies the moment we set foot in this realm, but we've been here almost a full day, and the worst thing we've encountered is a ravenous centipede.

I signal for the others to follow. The hunter is the first to hoist himself up and out of the way. Then I hear scuffling and the muffled sounds of an argument. Frustrated with the holdup, I look down the hole.

"What is taking so long? I demand.

"Tell them I can climb out just fine," Sheena hisses. Her hands are on her hips and she looks exasperated.

"You might fall," Gideon argues.

"I assume you'll catch me," she snaps back.

I understand her frustration, but they just got her back. I'm not surprised Gideon is feeling overprotective. Getting him to realize it without an explosion is the real trick.

"My apologies, little djinn," I say. "I did not realize your hands were hurt so badly."

Gideon's head snaps down to Sheena's balled up hands. He pries them open and examines each of her fingers, then frowns up at me. "There's nothing wrong with her hands."

"Exactly," I say. "Now, quit smothering her and get up here. We do not have time for your nonsense."

I retract my head before he can decide to argue, amused by the way his expression changes from baffled to irritated.

Even though I just advocated for her independence, I lift Sheena to safety as soon as her head crests the lip of the opening. The handholds run out near the top, and I don't want her to lose her balance and hit the side.

Pulling her to my chest, I hold her body against my own for much longer than she needs to steady herself. The hunter narrows his eyes, but Sheena's sharp intake of breath is a balm to my blackened soul. I spin her around to face the most beautiful phenomenon my realm offers.

In the cool morning light, Sheena surveys the scenic vista, her green eyes sparkling with curiosity and pleasure. The vivid orange ball of light burns through the cloak of night, painting streaks of burnished ruby and swirls of the purest lilac across the morning sky. The gods only know how much I've missed the view of Sipsi rising to meet Ahnsid, but it's Sheena who captures my attention. In this moment, I think I'd do just about anything for her to look at me the way she stares at the second sunrise.

The shuffling noise of several bags being shoved out through the hole brings me back to the task at hand. Gideon and Callum appear next. Callum narrows his eyes as he takes in our closeness, but he bites back whatever scathing remark he was preparing for me when he sees how captivated Sheena is by the sunrise. I have no doubt I'll be treated to a full recounting of his jealous displeasure later, though.

Gideon, meanwhile, slides the heavy rock back into place like it's nothing, then marches over and tugs Sheena out of my arms without hesitation. The abrupt movement jars her focus, and she looks up at him, her chin set at a stubborn tilt.

"I told you I could do it," she says, having clearly not forgotten their earlier argument.

Gideon nuzzles her neck obnoxiously, teasing a giggle out of her. "I knew you could. I just wanted my hands on you, baby," he purrs in her ear, bringing that pretty blush blazing to life on her cheeks.

Sheena melts in his arms, and I shake my head at his calculated move. I certainly misjudged him earlier. That's twice this morning he has shown me the error of relying solely on my first impression of him.

"Which sun is that again?" Callum asks, pointing to the bright orange star as it completes its ascent.

"Sipsi," I say. "Ahnsid rises first and sets last, but nothing compares to the colors Sipsi casts."

I hear the reverence in my voice, and I don't bother masking it. If they know how I love these views, how I miss them like an ache in my bones, well, maybe that isn't the worst thing in the world.

"Time to go." I adjust my pack until it hangs evenly on my back, then set forth into the forest. The others follow with no complaint.

Here and now, bathed in buttery light as the new day dawns bright and wondrous around us, I fight a smile. Perhaps we won't die after all.

IT ONLY TAKES THREE HOURS and one ambush for my morning optimism to drift away like smoke.

We are definitely about to die.

An arrow sails through the air. It makes a faint whistling sound before it imbeds in the purple bark of a weathered tree, missing Callum's head by mere inches. We all freeze.

Then a chorus of whistling whines breaks our collective trance. A dozen arrows pierce the thick, humid air, but my magic is strong here. Stronger than it has been in years. It swirls in my chest, eager to act. With a wave of my arms, I cast a wide glamour over our group, making us all as close to invisible as possible. It won't stop an arrow, but it's difficult to aim at something you can't see.

"Take cover," I order, pointing to a large boulder. Everyone scrambles toward it.

Sheena huffs out a sigh of relief. "Is anyone hurt?" She asks, looking sharply at each of us.

One of the archers had better aim than the others. Gideon's body is rigid with pain, an arrowhead buried in the back of his bicep. It's not a life-threatening wound by any means, but his shifter healing can't start until the projectile is removed.

He grits his teeth and reaches awkwardly around to pull the arrow out of his arm, but I stop him. Before I realize what I'm doing, I slide both hands to Gideon's temple and take his pain.

After I've siphoned it all away, I nod to Callum. Even though he is visibly shaken, he grasps the arrow and pulls it out in one sharp yank. Blood spurts from the puncture, but Sheena is ready with a makeshift bandage. She ties the shirt around Gideon's arm and presses a quick kiss to his cheek.

Another arrow pings harmlessly off the boulder. We are only safe until our attackers decide to circle around.

"Why are they so quiet?" Sheena asks.

I raise my brows. I am surprised she noticed the silence at all. In a battle, most people can't hear anything over the roaring in their own ears. It takes years to develop coolness during combat, yet Sheena is already thinking past her own surging adrenaline.

"They do not want to identify themselves," I tell her, a grim suspicion forming in my mind.

Sheena shoves a strand of dark hair behind her ear, her frown deepening. "How the fuck would we recognize them?"

"The fae realm is fragmented. Any accents would be a dead giveaway."

I pick up the discarded arrow and wipe away Gideon's blood so that I can examine its construction. As I expected, the wood is rare and easy to identify. The shaft comes from the trunk of a pale pink lynsom tree. This variation grows icy crystalline strands of hanging plant matter instead of leaves, and the wood is known for being nearly indestructible.

"This arrow," I say. "It was not made anywhere near this territory." The nearest grove of lynsom trees grows hundreds of miles from here, but that fact is less important than the implication behind it.

"It's a frame job," Callum mutters. "Whoever is attacking us wants to pin this on someone else."

I nod. "Unless a contingent from the Court of Ice somehow knew we were coming before we did."

I chance a glance around the corner of the rock, feeling my own magic grow cold within me. There's still no sign of our attackers, but I can sense them on the wind. They remain hidden among the wild plants we've been navigating all morning.

"Could a seer be involved?" Gideon asks, his lips pale with blood loss.

I think his theory over, then shake my head. "It is unlikely. There has not been a fae born with that gift in centuries, and the folk do not trust outsiders."

I glance at the hunter, but he's crouched motionlessly, scanning the trees on our unguarded side with military precision. He's completely unfazed by our brush with death.

"That sounds hostile," Sheena mutters.

"It is the fae way." I shrug.

"Well," she says, cracking her knuckles and smiling nervously at the rest of us. "Let's show them how a djinn does things."

QUAID

"That's a terrible idea," the demon hisses. "The last thing we need is everyone in this realm lusting after your powers, too."

"I'm not weak anymore," Sheena snaps.

I tilt my head. Her tone is sharp, but I hear doubt, too. Her confidence often wobbled when we were kids—like a newborn deer, she would run one second, unstoppable and eager, then tumble ass over tits after crushing self-doubt got the best of her.

Like me, she's the product of an unstable upbringing. She learned quickly that obvious weakness made her more vulnerable to attack. I lost count of how many times I told her to 'fake it until you make it.' It looks like she's still following my old advice.

"You were never weak," the demon says. His black eyes are like bottomless pits as he looks back at her.

His stare is so focused, I wonder if he's hypnotizing Sheena or doing some kind of mind control. I tense to throw my body between them, then stop myself. *Why would I risk my life for her?* It's not my job to protect her. It never was. I don't need to pretend anymore, so I don't know why everything still feels so tangled.

In high school, Sheena's resilience and compassion inspired and confused me. Now I know the truth. She's a selfish creature, just like the others, designed to survive no matter the odds. The nuance they are all exhibiting right now won't last.

Even primitive birds learn to mimic human emotions, but that doesn't mean they're capable of truly feeling them. These four will show me their true colors eventually, and when the time is right, I'll end them. Until then, my best option is to observe.

"I'm not suggesting I stroll out into the middle of the clearing and show them the whole song and dance," Sheena grumbles.

The fae watches her carefully, a calculating look on his face. "Then what exactly are you suggesting, little djinn?"

That nickname again. I hide my grimace at the infantilizing endearment. I don't know how she stomachs it. It's another sign that she's not the same girl I imagined.

"Recon, intel, I don't know. Maybe a distraction that gives us time to get away."

"You will grow tired."

"Not like I used to." She emphasizes each word, directing sharp, pointed looks at the three males around her as she speaks. Whatever she was trying to remind them of clearly hits hard because the demon looks haunted, the shifter irate, and the fae thoughtful.

"Okay." He scratches behind one pointy ear and narrows his eyes at Sheena. "But we do nothing that could reveal your gifts."

She nods before the fae even finishes his thought, then turns to look at the demon. "You better hold me down, Callum."

Sheena looks at him with enough banked heat to start a forest fire. I want to roll my eyes because she's clearly trying to distract him. The demon shakes his head and pulls her between his thighs, wrapping his arms around her like restraints.

She closes her eyes for a moment, then looks up at the fae. "I'm ready."

"I wish our enemies would reveal themselves." One second he's whispering the words as if they're the world's deadliest secret. In the next, I feel magic against my skin, and the Sheena I know vanishes. In her place sits a dangerous creature with glowing purple eyes, angular features, and floating hair.

It's exactly how she looked when I found her with Alina, except that time she was hovering above the ground. I suspect the only reason she isn't tossing aside the rules of gravity now is because the demon is holding her down.

Sharp, guttural words drift over to our hiding place. It's nothing I can make out, but the fae's expression turns grim as he listens.

Sheena's appearance returns to normal, yet the tiny hairs on my neck remain standing on end. *She's one of the monsters.* I can't forget it.

"I wish they would turn on each other with no mercy," the fae says. I stiffen but nothing happens.

"Yeah, I'm obviously not going to fulfill that one, Idris," Sheena says, swatting at his chest.

Her words seem to affect all the men profoundly. The demon presses a kiss to her cheek, and the shifter squeezes her hand.

The fae shrugs, his lips curling into a smirk. "Very well. It was worth a shot. I wish for a nonlethal distraction that sends our enemies scurrying in the opposite direction," he says, voice dripping with sarcasm. "Thereby giving us sufficient time to escape and find shelter."

Sheena's green eyes change to purple mid-roll. It's damn unsettling, but not nearly as disturbing as the horrific roar of god knows what coming from the distance. Panicked shouts follow, along with the sounds of a disorganized retreat.

The fae's eyes widen, and he mouths the word run. No one questions him, although I see the shifter glance in the direction of the roaring with a curious glint in his eye. Only after his friend kicks him in the shins does he sigh and nod. They take off at a jog, the shifter's giant body serving as a buffer between the enemies and the demon carrying Sheena.

Since I have no interest in being left behind to find out what made that monstrous sound, I sprint after them, my heart pounding. We run for at least a mile before stopping in the shade of an enormous tree. For several minutes, we listen carefully for sounds of pursuit but hear only our own heavy breathing.

"Baby," the shifter gasps. "Whatever that was, it didn't sound nonlethal." He rubs his injured arm with a wince.

"I don't even know what it was," Sheena says, pushing on the demon's shoulder until he takes the hint and puts her down. "It's not like I have creative control over how I grant the wishes. My choices are red or green, stop or go. Also, you didn't have to carry me all that way, Callum. I was fine to run after like ten seconds."

"But how do you feel?" He demands, looking at her as if he expects her to collapse at any moment.

"I honestly feel okay," Sheena says, shaking her arms out. "Maybe a little sluggish, but I don't think my nose is about to gush blood."

She's so caught up in her own excitement about not having a nosebleed that she doesn't notice how the others flinch at her words. *I'm definitely missing something here.*

"So?" The demon looks expectantly at the fae. "Who were those guys?"

"Stupid question." He waves his hand dismissively. "Our attackers are utterly insignificant. What you should be asking is who they report to."

If looks could kill, we'd be burying the fae right now. The demon's obsidian stare is truly chilling, but the pointy-eared asshole doesn't seem to care.

As for the shifter, he just sighs like the entire exchange is wearing him out. "C'mon, Idris, just tell us," he grunts.

"I expect I should," the fae finally admits, pursing his lips and staring off into the distance.

We wait expectantly, but when he starts walking without saying anything else, even I want to smack him in the back of the head for his coy bullshit. The demon hisses under his breath, but Sheena shushes him, then takes off after the fae. We trail after her, watching as she jogs to catch up with him. The bastard ignores her, letting her hover at his side like a gnat.

With each step she takes, I see her temper building. Does the fae not realize he's playing with fire? Sheena grabs his arm, and I stand back to watch the show. At least I'm not her target this time around.

He stops and looks down at her, one black eyebrow raised arrogantly like he's the king of the fucking world. Sheena's eyes spark. *Wrong move, asshole.*

"Do you need something, little djinn?" He purrs.

"Yeah," she spits. "Some communication would be fucking nice."

The fae takes hold of the hand gripping his arm and brings it slowly up to his mouth. He presses a kiss to her wrist, his blue eyes never leaving her face.

"Such a dirty mouth." The smug prick leaves his lips against her skin as he speaks. "If you need something from me, you know you only have to ask."

Sheena pulls her wrist away from his mouth and stares up at him like he has disappointed her. "If you really mean that, then stop trying to provoke them," she says.

The fae widens his eyes and feigns confusion. I glance at the others and see the demon practically bristling with annoyance.

"Darling, I cannot imagine what you mean." He rubs his thumb across her wrist, and she snatches it completely away from him.

"That." She points at him. "That's what I'm talking about. The wrist kisses, the pet names, the damn sunrise."

"My apologies. I did not realize Sipsi's light would upset you." He dips his head, and the demon growls.

"It's got nothing to do with the sun, Idris, and you know it," Sheena says.

"I am afraid I do not. You are going to have to spell it out for me."

The fae seems amused now, like he's enjoying the conflict, but I'm not fooled. Have none of them realized it's just another of his diversions to avoid answering the original question?

"You're hitting on her, dude," the shifter says, running a hand through his curls before sitting down heavily on a log. "Don't play dumb."

Sheena's face turns red, but I can't tell if it's from embarrassment or anger.

The fae bows stiffly to her. "I apologize. I did not realize my attentions offended you."

"You didn't offend me," Sheena sighs and looks back at the other two men. "I just sometimes feel like you want to get a rise out of them and you use me to do it."

The fae's head snaps up, and his cold eyes drift over her. "Believe me, Sheena, bothering them is only a fortunate side effect." He gestures to her face. "Perhaps I just like being the one to make you blush for a change."

Sheena ducks her head, and the fae turns his attention back to the other two.

"You have both been blessed with the affection of an extraordinary woman. I would advise you to prepare yourselves for future frustration because I will hardly be the last to notice what a treasure the gods have blessed you with."

That was the furthest thing from an apology I've ever heard, and he still hasn't answered the question. I'm almost impressed.

When he starts walking again, Sheena reaches her limit. "Idris, tell me where we're going. Right now," she demands, her voice hard and strained. "Or I won't take another step."

"To visit my sister, of course."

The fae doesn't turn around or break stride, and Sheena has to hurry after him yet again.

"Oh. That's . . . great?" She sounds unsure, her brow pinching with worry. "Do you think she will know who attacked us?"

His lips peel back in a menacing smile. "I certainly expect so, considering she hired them."

CHAPTER TEN

SHEENA

We follow after Idris in silence while my mind races. I didn't even know he had a sister, but now that I think about it, there's a lot I don't know about him. He told me he left his home for safety reasons, but that's common knowledge around the enclave. I consider him a friend, but would he say the same?

Idris' vivid blue eyes shift toward me. "Your thoughts are quite loud, little djinn." He smiles. "Do you care to voice any of them aloud?"

"That depends." I keep my voice low. "Are you in the mood to answer my questions or play more mind games?"

Idris thumps his palm against his chest and groans. "You both wound and tease me. Do you not believe me capable of doing both simultaneously?"

There's a rustling sound in the woods to my right. I shudder, and Idris takes a half step closer to me. We're walking so close together that our arms occasionally brush.

I'm tempted to resume the banter, but maybe if I approach this more like a battering ram, I'll be able to knock a hole in his defenses. "Your relationship with you sister," I begin. "What's that like?"

"Do you remember the sandwich you made me weeks ago?"

I remember his lips on my wrist and how his blue eyes seemed to see right through me.

"Yeah." I furrow my brow. "What about it?"

"As we dined, you may recall I told you a little about the familial relationships between the fae aristocracy."

I think back to that lunch. It was chaotic and loud, and it feels like a lifetime ago, but we talked about our mealtimes as kids. I mentioned foster care, and Idris said the fae realm lacked warmth.

"What I failed to mention at the time was the constant, obligatory assassination and poisoning attempts."

"Oh," I mutter, a bit horrified.

"Indeed." He keeps walking. I expect that to be the end of the conversation, but Idris surprises me when he clears his throat. "My sister is a unique woman, but she lacks a certain thirst for blood that the folk particularly value."

I consider that for a moment, thinking of the group that ambushed us without warning and the arrow buried in Gideon's shoulder. If his sister hired those guys . . .

"It looks like she got over that while you were gone," I observe.

Idris' lips curve up slightly on one side. It's not exactly a smile, but his eyes are amused.

"So it would seem."

We walk on in silence.

Sipsi's orange glow fades away, which means we need to find shelter for the night. The sooner, the better. Every muscle in my body hurts. If my brain wasn't replaying the sound of that monster's roar on a loop, I think I would have thrown myself down on the trail a few hours ago and refused to take another step.

"Will we make it to your sister's place before dark?" I ask, wincing as the blister on my big toe chafes roughly against my old boot.

"I suspect that would be foolish," Idris says. He's only a few feet ahead of me, but his voice sounds a million miles away. He looks up at the position of the remaining sun, then scans our surroundings again. "Not much further. No caves tonight."

My joints are glad to hear that, and from Callum and Gideon's relieved sighs, we're on the same page.

It's starting to get cold. I'm not sure how much ground we've actually covered, but it's enough for the biome and climate to change. We started our journey dripping sweat, and now I can see my breath on each heavy exhale.

After escaping our attackers, we spent the rest of the day climbing, tromping through miles of exotic underbrush. The plants and terrain morphed from the colorful, leafy forest we started the day in to craggy hills with branchless trees that stretch so tall I can't see the tops. The trunks are as slender as my wrist with iridescent silver veins that sparkle in the light. With each gust of wind, they sway like ribbons, bending but never breaking.

My stomach grumbles, and I try to embody the strength of those trunks as I trudge across the cold, rocky ground. Aside from the trees, there's no other plant life, only rocks, and each step we take echoes endlessly no matter how lightly we tread.

A screech joins the clatter of our footsteps, and a bird the size of a large dog swoops in front of me. It's pure white, and the feathers are almost metallic, reflecting the light like scales. The brightness stings my eyes, but it's so beautiful I can't look away. The bird lands on one of the slender, silver trees and watches us with unnerving intelligence.

"Are there shifters here?" I ask.

"No. Why would you . . ." Idris looks at the bird, then smiles. "That is a qamarion."

"Let me guess, it eats meat," Gideon jokes, snapping his teeth playfully at the bird.

"Only fish. Unless you transform into a trout, there is no need to worry."

"It's watching us," Callum says, eying the bird warily.

"Qamarion are smart and nosy."

"Now that you've seen it, could you shift into one of those?" I ask Gideon.

He looks the bird over, challenge sparking in his eyes. When my mate kicks off his boots and drops his pants, I realize I've made a mistake.

"Wait, I didn't mean—"

Gideon tosses his shirt at me, and then the giant, blonde man disappears. In his place stands an enormous bird. I sigh, then frown when I notice one of his wings hanging a bit awkwardly. Dark blood stands out against his white, reflective feathers.

"Gideon, you're going to make it bleed again. Change back," Callum grumbles, exasperated by his antics.

I'm not sure how I can tell, but I swear I see Gideon's smirk on the bird's face. It's unnatural and hilarious, and a giggle bubbles out of my mouth before I can stop it. The bird nips at Cal's ass playfully, and my laughter grows.

"Stop encouraging him," Callum says, dodging Gideon's sharp beak and shooting a disgruntled look my way.

When Gideon saunters over to me, I'm stunned by his size. His head reaches my chest, an angle he takes advantage of by nuzzling me with his beak. I pet the sleek feathers gently, stunned to find them cool and glassy but lightweight beneath my fingertips.

"You're a beautiful bird," I tell him. "Now, turn back into my mate before you give Callum a heart attack."

Gideon makes a warbling sound, which the bird in the tree immediately mimics before flapping its shiny wings and taking off. The force of the launch makes the tree bend, and I watch as it gradually returns to its original position instead of snapping back up once the bird's weight is gone.

"Damn, did you see how far it—" I look over my shoulder at the group and forget everything I was about to say.

Gideon stands naked, grinning at me with both dimples on display. My cheeks burn as I toss him his t-shirt, annoyed that the sight of his body still has the power to make me blush. From his smirk, he's pleased with the effect he has on me.

While Gideon dresses himself, I sit down on the cold rock and take inventory of our ragtag group. For once, Idris isn't rushing us. He actually seems marginally impressed by Gideon's transformation. But Quaid watches my mate with an indecipherable look on his face. Maybe he's changing his mind about supernaturals . . .

"It's pretty cool, isn't it?" I look directly at him, but he doesn't acknowledge me. He's barely spoken since I told him he was coming with us to this realm. As a teen, Quaid was always more comfortable with quiet than me, but this silent treatment is extreme, even for him.

Sadness sinks in as I study Quaid. He's tall, handsome, and aloof in a way that makes me want to cry. Scars of all sizes cover his body. Most of them are new to me. I used to know the story behind every bruise or minor inconvenience in his life, but now I'm left wondering if he's as marked up on the inside as he is on the outside.

"Is this how it's going to be?" I demand, clinging to my helpless anger. "We experience a new realm with odd trees and crazy birds, and you don't say shit."

"What do you want me to say?" His voice is a low, dark rumble, gravelly from disuse.

I roll my eyes, unimpressed with his apathetic act. "There's not a script, Quaid. You say whatever you're thinking."

"The last time I did that, you called me a bigot," he snaps.

I feel a small sense of satisfaction in knowing that my words did have some effect on him.

"You really expect me to believe the only thoughts left in your head are about 'exterminating abominations?'" I put air quotes around the last two words, and he narrows his eyes. "Because, if so, that's incredibly boring."

Quaid takes a step toward me, and I stand so he can't tower over me as much.

"The skinny trees . . ." He points at the dancing trunks. "Their elasticity is remarkable."

His voice is still detached and robotic, but I'm so relieved to hear him show an interest in anything not murder related that a huge smile spreads across my face.

"I know! I keep waiting for one to snap, but they seem unbreakable," I say, chafing my chilled arms with my hands.

"It is not impossible, but they are deceptively strong. Much like you." Idris tosses the remark my way with no warning, then readjusts the straps of his bag.

The pleasure of the compliment makes my cheeks warm, but I don't know how to respond.

"Time to head out," Idris says, tilting his head north.

Gideon slips his hand in mine, and I tuck myself into his side, grateful for his body heat. When I sneak a look at Quaid, I find he's already watching me. Our eye contact drags on, but we've been apart too long for me to read him like I used to. He breaks the connection and looks away, but I can't help feeling a sliver of hope.

Maybe he will gain a new perspective in this strange world.

CALLUM

THIS ENTIRE EXPERIENCE feels like I gobbled up a handful of shrooms and let my anxiety fuel a fever dream. There's a secret sister, former friend betrayal, and a never-ending hike through a creepy realm filled with hidden enemies. Everywhere I look, there's a new mess for me to clean up.

My best friend—boyfriend, whatever he is now—got shot with an arrow, then transformed into an ostrich's paler, shinier cousin. To top it all off, the bendy trees make me nervous. They're too tall, too skinny, and—dammit, now I feel guilty for body shaming a godsdamn tree.

Gideon slides his hand into mine. He's always been a tactile person, but this casual affection is new. *Does he realize I'm falling apart?* When he squeezes my hand, I remember the pressure I had to put on the arrow to pull it out.

There was so much blood. Gideon's blood. Coating my fingers and dripping onto the forest floor. Gods, he could have been killed. There's still a risk of infection, and we're stuck out here in the middle of—

"I'm here. Sheena's here," Gideon says. "We're all walking together. Just breathe, Callum."

Absently, I hear my breath escaping in ragged puffs. Gideon inhales deeply next to me, then blows out the air slowly. I do my best to match his cadence as Sheena darts a worried glance my way. Shame clogs my throat. It's thick, bitter, and just as corrosive as the anxiety crushing my lungs.

"I'm sorry," I gasp. I feel helpless. Trapped.

Gideon frowns, eyebrows pulling together as he looks over at me. His thumb strokes mine, and Sheena moves to my other side to claim my other hand.

"You don't have to feel sorry," Sheena whispers, tightening her hold. The stimulation is almost too much to handle, but I don't want her to let go either. "There's a lot going on, a lot that's out of our control. Your brain doesn't like that," she murmurs.

The cold, sharp air slices through my anxiety and I manage several long, deep breaths. Some of the pressure on my chest eases. As the worst passes, I want to retreat and process this alone, but sandwiched between the two of them, I have nowhere to go.

"I'm letting you both down," I finally admit.

Gideon snorts. "Says the guy who never lets anyone down."

I dredge up my time-tested, perfectly curated list of failures and prepare to argue, but Sheena distracts me before I can. She pulls our clasped hands to her lips and kisses my knuckles, then holds them against her cheek.

"You don't always have to be strong," Sheena says.

Her words hit me like a punch to the gut. *Don't I?* I'm a supernatural. A high-level incubus demon. Strength is both a biological prerequisite and a social imperative. Weakness paints a target on my back. Weakness is death.

"Not when you're part of a team," Sheena insists.

My stomach flips as I realize I just aired my fears out loud where anyone could hear. Idris is walking a few paces ahead, the hunter following closely behind him. Even if the human can't hear us, the fae certainly can.

I shake my head, hoping that will be the end of the conversation, but Sheena's jaw is clenched tight. She's going to be stubborn about this.

"Per your logic, then, I guess I should be ashamed of the days I was dying and too weak to walk down the hall," she says.

I shiver, remembering how small she looked laying in Gideon's bed, and how I lived in fear of the moment I would go to wake her and those beautiful green eyes wouldn't open. I cling to her fingers now, her body heat assuring me she's still here.

"That's different," I insist. "You couldn't control your body."

"Oh, my bad. I didn't realize you were feeling this way on purpose. Better snap out of it, then." Her voice drips with sarcasm, and I roll my eyes.

"The arrow. That creepy bird. Even the trees weird me out," I mutter.

"Right?" Gideon chuckles. "I keep waiting for the tops to snap off and skewer us."

"Don't think I didn't notice the subject change." Sheena sighs. "I suppose I'll allow it. For now."

She's so cute. I can't help messing with her. I send a tiny zap of lust out from each of my hands, enjoying the way they both gasp. Sheena swats at my chest, but her free hand lingers on my left pec to cop a feel.

"Just what this hike was missing—a boner to rub against my cargo pants," Gideon complains, releasing my hand to adjust himself. "You just sent the little blood I had left in my body straight to my cock."

Sheena giggles, and I feel the last bit of my anxiety disappear. I take another deep breath.

Up ahead, Idris stops and pulls aside a thick, tangled curtain of gray, fuzzy vines, holding them back as we approach.

"Now that we have all been forcibly immersed in your private arousal experience, I suppose this is as good a time as any to tell you we have reached our destination." Idris' tone is dry, but Gideon just grins at him.

"Thank goodness," Sheena says, releasing my hand to hurry on ahead. From the stiff way she walks, I can tell she's sore. I'm in a similar situation myself. Sheena gasps, and I push past Idris, looking for the cause of her shock.

My jaw drops.

In front of us is a seemingly unending sea. The stone we've been walking on for hours slopes down right into it. There's a sharp wind blowing, yet not even a ripple disturbs the glassy surface. It's pure blue, oddly translucent, and I'm not positive it's water. Dark shapes zip around below the surface, moving faster than my eyes can track.

"They are hundreds of feet down. No cause for alarm," Idris says when he notices what I'm staring at.

"And if I decide to go for a swim?" I ask.

"That would be cause for alarm."

"Let me guess. The fish are carnivorous?" Sheena asks, finding her voice after her initial shock. She watches the water with a healthy dose of suspicion, but Gideon's eyes flash gold as he fixates on the dark shapes. I slip a finger in his belt loop and tug him back in case he decides to add another creature to his shifting arsenal.

"Honestly, I do not think you would classify them as fish at all." Idris raises one dark eyebrow.

Gideon takes another step toward the water.

I've heard enough. "Monsters, fish, whatever. It's getting dark. How are we crossing this thing?" I ask.

"We are not."

Idris walks directly off the edge of the rock and onto the water with no hesitation. Instead of falling, he hovers just above the surface. I watch his feet carefully, noticing tiny ripples below his boots.

"Fucking fae glamour," I mutter.

Idris laughs and flicks his wrist casually. The ripples disappear and a stone pier takes shape. It's only wide enough for one person to cross at a time and leads to a massive boat.

Of course. This rich, entitled prick has a secret fairy yacht, because why not? I squint at the vessel, but it's too dark to make out any details.

"Do they even have gasoline here?" I ask Gideon. He shrugs. "I wonder what makes the boat go."

"Who knows?" Sheena laughs. "Magic, good vibes, fairy dust?"

The remaining sun sinks lower in the sky. The black shapes loom even larger under the surface.

"Let's talk about it inside."

I brace myself and step out on the narrow gangplank. There are no handrails, but thankfully, it's firm under my feet. The wind is the real problem, and I panic when I imagine it picking Sheena up and tossing her straight into the water.

I twist my head around to check and see Gideon carrying her. From the look on her face, he didn't give her a choice. The hunter plods along behind them, face expressionless as his braids whip in the wind.

I look down and regret it immediately.

The water is still calm, but the creatures more than make up for it. The dark shapes are thrashing around in a frenzy like they can sense it's dinnertime. I tear my eyes away and hustle across the remaining twenty feet to the edge of the boat.

The yacht is silver, gleaming in the light of the three moons. The boat lurches beneath my feet as I step onto the deck. I grip the railing to stay upright. Pain rips through my fingers, and I recoil so quickly I almost fall overboard. By the time I'm steady enough to pull my hand back, the skin is bright red and burning.

"Idris, you motherfucker," I shout. "Your fucking boat just attacked me."

The fae appears in the doorway, an intrigued look on his face. "I am shocked that the ward still works. It has been years."

He beams down at my hand with genuine delight as I cradle it. I glare back at him. "It would be nice if you looked a little less impressed with yourself and a little more apologetic that your boat set me on fire."

"She did not set you on fire. She froze you."

"Oh, what a fucking relief," I snarl as the other three come up behind me.

"What's going on?" Sheena asks.

"Don't touch anything," I hiss. "This boat is a bitch."

"She is not!" Idris seems greatly offended on behalf of his floating palace, which shouldn't surprise me one bit. There isn't much risk in loving a pile of wood and metal.

"One moment," he says. His eyes go vacant as he waves his arms. A blue film appears, coating the boat like a second skin, then it pops. Idris grins. "The ward is down. The rest of you may board."

He disappears into the cockpit, and I reach out with my undamaged pinky finger to graze the railing. When I don't feel any pain, I exhale and follow the damned fae inside.

While the boat has not been used for some time, it's not in bad condition. Besides some dust and a faint musty smell, it's all buttery leather and soft, luxurious textures. Gideon, Sheena, and the hunter step in behind me, all three looking around in wonder.

Idris is more animated than I've ever seen him. He darts around to inspect everything, then pulls on a series of levers that pop out of the walls. Given his usual stoic, constipated expression, this enthusiasm creeps me the fuck out. I rub my throbbing palm as I track his every move.

"If you could please stand in the center of the room," Idris demands, gesturing impatiently for us to tighten up the loose circle we're standing in.

We all shuffle forward. After my earlier encounter, I'm not taking any chances.

Idris pulls down on a small, silver lever.

I stiffen as a hissing noise fills the air, followed by a clean floral scent. Before my eyes, the coating of grime vanishes as if it was never there. Windows sparkle, chrome gleams, leather shines, and the energy of the boat itself seems to hum happily. If Idris' excitement was creepy before, a happy boat is ten times creepier.

I gulp. "Is this damn boat singing?"

As soon as I ask, the floor dips violently to the side and throws me off my feet. I land painfully on my hip and look up to see Idris smirking deviously down at me.

"Did that answer your question?"

IDRIS

When the demon tumbles to the floor, I let my smile truly spread. *Oh, how I missed this.*

"Her name is Safina," I tell them, eying the gleaming interior of my yacht with pride. Callum struggles back to his feet, and I can't resist a little dig. "It seems she is not an admirer of yours, either."

"What? How did—" Sheena sputters, gaping in amazement at the clean furnishings, the chrome lever I pulled, and finally me.

A tingle runs down my spine. Gods above and below, I like how she watches me. I run my fingers along the lever, pleased to see the metal shining like new again. "Some incredibly advanced spells."

Sheena steps back into Gideon's body. "Are there witches here?"

"Not all magic belongs to those capricious covens, little djinn." I frown. When she relaxes, I continue my explanation. "Sorcery is its own form of currency in the fae realm. Those who have powerful gifts profit greatly from anyone willing to pay."

"Like you," she says.

I dip my head in acknowledgement.

"Did you pay extra for the attitude?" Callum rubs his hip, then winces when his ice chapped palm comes into contact with his clothes.

I turn back to the panel of levers to hide my smile, flicking a small golden switch into the upright position. The windows become opaque, giving us privacy and blocking our view of the eerily still waters of Shard Lake.

"Complex fae magic leaves a mark—a signature of sorts from its creator," I say, sitting down on the wraparound couch and resting my head against the cool leather. "The woman who did Safina's spell work is obstinate, tempestuous, and cunning. The boat reflects that."

"Of course it does," Callum mutters, easing himself down gingerly in the seat across from me. "What did you tell Sheena when we arrived: everything pretty in this realm wants us dead? I guess this boat fits the bill."

The deck moves under us again, but in a gentle rolling pattern this time. Callum narrows his eyes. "What was that about?"

"She likes that you called her pretty," I translate.

He cringes, and Sheena sinks down in his lap to inspect his red palm.

"Is she sentient?" The human's voice is unfamiliar and unexpected. I glance up to study him and see he's inspecting Safina's luxurious interior, head crooked to the side.

"Not in the sense that you and I are," I answer him, holding his gaze when it falls on me. "Safina's personality is more of a lingering echo of the magic used to animate her. I admit that I am surprised to see how well she still functions."

Gideon throws himself down next to me on the couch, his weight nearly bouncing me off the seat. I slide several inches away from him, but if he's offended by my need for space, he doesn't show it.

"The woman who cast these spells . . . . Will she sense we're here?" Sheena asks, looking up from Callum's hand.

Satisfaction hums in my chest. As her intuition grows, so too does my pride in her abilities. "Your reasoning is impressive," I say.

She snorts. "Don't you mean paranoia?"

"Thinking like that can mean the difference between life and death in this realm," I say, shrugging. I don't care how she wants to characterize her cunning, as long as she doesn't stifle it.

"Then you'll be happy to know I'm fully aware you didn't answer my question. I'm also not going to let it go," she tells me, challenge sparking in her green eyes. Sheena digs her hands into her quads, wincing as she massages the tension away from her sore muscles.

I lean forward and hold her stare, unable to resist the urge to goad her. It doesn't take long for her to toss her hands up in the air.

"Come on, Idris," she groans. "It's obvious you're cooking up some grandiose scheme. But I think we deserve to be in on it. Our lives are on the line here, too."

She makes a valid point, but it'll be a snowy day in the demonic realm before I admit it.

"What if the success of my plan hinges on your ignorance?" I ask. "What if telling you all would practically ensure our imminent demise?" I shape each word like a barb, sharp and dripping with accusation.

The others shift uneasily in their seats, but the little djinn simply studies my face.

"Does it?" Sheena finally demands, questioning the authenticity of every word out of my mouth with two simple words.

I bare my teeth to mask my secret delight.

"Not at all," I hiss. I'm not sure what I'm expecting in response to my admission—maybe for her to curse or throw something at me—but when Sheena tosses her head back and laughs, I'm tempted to join in.

"Idris, don't take this the wrong way, but your riddles fucking suck," Gideon says.

"Seriously, we've had the world's longest day, and the second we sit down, you bust out the mind games," Callum snarls.

Sheena's laughter trails off. She wipes a tear away from the corner of one eye. "I didn't think anyone could make me more paranoid, but then I met you. If I passed your test, does that mean you're ready to tell us what the hell is going on?"

"Certainly, darling." I bow my head to her and ignore the glares from the others. "Tomorrow morning, we will sail to the Court of Stars. We will navigate through the moat, stopping only when we reach the gate. Once there, we will demand entry to my palace, which will be granted."

"How can you be so sure?" Sheena asks.

"Because the only thing the folk like more than uncontested power is a challenge. When we are spotted onboard this boat, which was enchanted by my sister, Zara, many years ago, rumors will spread faster than flames through dry grass. She will demand an explanation for my return, and in exchange, we will demand a safe place at court."

"And why would she give us that? She put an arrow in my shoulder like three hours ago," Gideon grumbles.

"For one, I gave her that throne. She sits on it thanks to me and me alone—"

Sheena holds up her hand to stop me. "You told me yourself there was no loyalty among fae, especially not family. What if you go in for a hug and she buries a knife in your back?"

"She will not be able to reach it," I say.

"Be serious." Sheena rolls her eyes. "That feels like hubris or assumption."

"It is not an assumption." I shake my head, thrumming my fingers against the supple leather. "As I said, Zara will not be able to reach my back."

"How can you be so sure?"

"Because you will be there to guard it, little djinn," I purr, basking in the hot flush that spreads down Sheena's cheeks. I've unnerved her, scoring a point in our sparring match.

From the other side of the couch, Callum's eyes flare with jealousy. Riling him up is quickly becoming one of my most easily accessible joys.

A rough smack on my shoulder pulls my attention to Gideon. He looks at me in the way one might stare at a distant and particularly tiresome relative. "Save the lines for later, dude. Is there a place to clean up and rest in this beautiful—not even a little bit melodramatic—boat?"

I brace my hands on my thighs and stand. "Of course, if you will all be so good as to follow me, I will show you to your quarters."

A chorus of groans sound out as they all force their exhausted muscles back into action. Sheena's low moan sends a bolt of electricity down my spine, but I ignore it. As long as I remember nothing can come of this flirtation, nothing will.

CHAPTER ELEVEN

QUAID

The enemy surrounds me.

As I stand on the top deck of this strange boat, lit by three moons and countless stars, I feel oddly numb. No matter how long I stare down at the dark depths, there's not a single ripple to be seen. Maybe this lake is just a lake, or maybe it's actually a silent predator in disguise, brimming with insidious intent, waiting for its prey to slip up.

Just like the supernaturals.

If I jump into this water, would it boil me alive or suck the marrow from my bones? Could I even make it to shore before those black shapes reach me? Even if I could outswim them, I can't get home without access to a portal. That means access to magic, which I don't have without my jailers.

The inescapable truth is Sheena and her band of deadly boyfriends have me exactly where they want me: a captive audience to their long con. They're putting on a hell of a performance, but I won't fall for it. Not this time. I can't soften for her.

As if I summoned her with my thoughts, Sheena steps up to

my side, leaving several feet of space between our bodies. "Are you okay?" Her voice is uncharacteristically uncertain.

"Do you ever wish things were different?" I blurt the words before I can think better of them.

"In general? Or between us?"

I can feel her looking at me, but I keep my focus on the odd shapes in front of us and simply shrug in response. Sheena sighs. The wind tries to steal the familiar sound, but I know her mannerisms so well that my mind fills in the blanks.

"For almost as long as I can remember, I wished everything was different," she murmurs. "I wished I had a family. I wished to be loved and safe. I wished you would have stuck by me."

I glance at her, but she's the one staring out into the distance now.

"I wished for so many damn things . . ." Sheena laughs, sharp and bitter. It's a sound I've never heard from her before. "Just imagine my shock when I realized I could grant everyone's wishes but my own."

"You really didn't know," I say. It changes nothing in the grand scheme of things, but I can believe her about this at least.

"No. How could I? Most supernaturals don't come into their powers until they're sixteen, and it's not like I had parents to give me a heads up."

I look over at her, years of memories tearing through my mind like razor wire.

"When you found out," Sheena says, wrapping her arms around herself and turning to face me. "Did you consider telling me the truth?"

Her tone is neutral, but I hear the pain of that old betrayal shining through. It reopens the ugly wound in my chest. God knows it's never fully healed.

"You're upset I didn't tell you, but I saved your life," I snap. "They told me to kill you, and I disobeyed a direct order. I had to ignore you to keep the target off your back. I thought if I could prove them wrong—"

"That things could go back to the way they were," she says, finishing my sentence.

I nod. Sheena brushes a tear off her cheek, but another takes its place. My hands curl to fists as she silently cries under the moonlight.

"I assume you found out I wasn't quite as human as I appeared after I was abducted."

"Yes. My superiors made sure I knew that." Bitterness coats my voice, and I clear my throat to get rid of the feeling.

Sheena sniffles, and every muscle in my body aches to comfort her. I hold myself back. It's safer for us both.

"What if . . ." She pauses and rolls her bottom lip between her teeth. "Did you ever think about running away with me?"

Her voice breaks, and an enormous fissure inside me cracks wide open.

"Every fucking minute of every miserable goddamn day."

"Even now?" Sheena's voice is thick with tears, her shoulders trembling.

I stare at the moisture clinging to her eyelashes and groan. "Especially now."

My admission sets off an avalanche inside me. Regret, anger, fear, hope, and joy tear loose in chunks and crash into each other. In the cataclysmic tumble that follows, I feel the softer emotions grind to dust inside me.

Sheena and I face off in the cold, the expanse of pain between us vaster than this damn lake. The laughter. The tears. All the memories and moments that brought us here are wedged between us. Neither of us is willing to let go, but holding on is destroying us both.

We collide violently in the dark, and it's goddamn brutal. I yank her against me, lifting her feet off the ground so there's no space between us. Sheena wraps her legs around my waist, her heels digging angrily into my lower back. When I press my lips to hers, I taste the salt of her tears.

The kiss is a betrayal of everything I stand for. I'm out of control. With my brain sinking to the bottom of the murky lake, I lick at the seam of her mouth, tasting her pain on my tongue. Sheena trembles in my arms, but she has one hand wrapped around my throat in warning.

Touching her is better than my wildest dreams. It hurts more than my worst nightmares. I prop her on the boat's railing and nibble on her lower lip. I should kill her right now while she's vulnerable. All it would take is one good shove to put her at the mercy of the monsters below. *If they consume her while I watch, will I finally be free of her?*

My arms clench around her instead, my body rebelling against my own thoughts. Sucking in a breath, I pull back. Sheena is so heartbreakingly beautiful with her lips swollen from my kisses. Tears stream down her face; seeing her pain feels like justice in a way. It's not enough, but at least I don't hurt alone.

"And now?" I demand, my voice jagged and raw. "If you could, would you still change everything?"

Sheena looks up at me. The shape of her face is achingly familiar, yet it's somehow as foreign to me as this entire fucking realm.

"I wouldn't change a thing," she says, holding my gaze. "If I had lived a different life, I wouldn't be who I am today." She tucks a strand of hair behind her ear. "I'm finding my happiness one day at a time."

"Even now?" I whisper her earlier question back to her.

She smiles. The expression lights up the dark and sends another wave of pain through my battered heart. She rubs her thumb across my bottom lip.

"Especially now."

Sheena slides down from the railing, and I let her go, watching until she vanishes into the shadowy interior of the boat.

I stare down at the waters until the cold and my thoughts become too much to endure. Sheena is everything I've ever wanted, and I can never have her.

SHEENA

I STUMBLE DOWN the narrow stairs, my thoughts so tangled I doubt I'll ever make sense of them. I can still taste Quaid on my lips. Sugar, heat, and bitterness—a unique flavor seared forever in my brain. It was a kiss of contradictions. Healing but destructive. Delicious but toxic. Everything and nothing.

As a girl, I longed to be his. I dreamed each night that he would ride up on a white horse, climb through my window, and carry me away to our happily ever after. It's impossible to know how much time I wasted imagining our first kiss, but I never pictured this grim reality. I was dumb then, and I'm even dumber now. Seriously, what kind of idiot follows a man who has sworn to kill her into the dark alone?

Quaid has made it perfectly clear I'm the villain in his story, but I still tumbled straight into his arms. I'm lucky he didn't snap my neck or toss me overboard. On top of that, I just put two wonderful relationships at risk all for one taste of a fantasy.

I groan. *What will Callum and Gideon say about this?*

I tiptoe toward our bedroom. Idris was gracious enough to give the bigger room to the three of us for the night while he shares the smaller bunkroom with Quaid. I'm surprised my former friend managed to sneak out without waking Idris.

Except, apparently, he didn't.

I flinch as I spot Idris standing in his doorway. He watches me silently, and I press my hand to my heart as it races with fear.

"You scared me," I whisper.

Idris studies my face, head cocked slightly to the side. "My apologies. Did you find what you were looking for?"

My stomach sinks. *He knows.* I'm not sure how, but I'm absolutely certain. I open my mouth, close it again, and finally decide on the simplest truth.

"I couldn't sleep."

"The search for closure keeps many people up at night," Idris says.

"Have you found it yet?" I ask. I turn the conversation back toward him, suddenly desperate to know who put the shadows in Idris' eyes—anything to distract me from how my bruised and greedy heart beats painfully in my chest.

Why do I suddenly want so much?

The pull toward Gideon never fades. My fated mate always senses exactly how to make me smile when all I want to do is cry. Then there's Callum. He knows my body better than I do, and his heart fits with mine like two halves of one whole. They are more than enough.

I shouldn't have kissed Quaid. He broke my heart at sixteen, and I've been guarding it ever since. A concept I'm sure the gorgeous fae in front of me is perfectly familiar with.

We watch each other in silence. His black hair almost looks blue in the dark. When Idris reaches for me, I suck in a breath. It's only when he brushes away my tear that I realize I'm crying again. Oddly, I don't feel ashamed. Maybe it's because he has already seen me in some of my lowest lows.

"I no longer believe closure is an actual destination, darling. But since you still have the courage to seek it, I can only offer you my envy and best wishes," Idris says, his voice hollow and bleak. His hand lingers on my cheek for a heartbeat, then slowly drops to his side.

We both turn to face our respective rooms.

"It's not too late for you," I tell him, pausing with my hand on the doorknob. "You have time to keep looking."

"Good night, little djinn."

His door closes behind him with a soft click.

I follow his lead and enter my shared room, groping around in the darkness until my shin grazes the edge of the bed. As soon as I slide beneath the covers, strong arms wrap around me. Gideon pulls me into his chest, his hands rubbing soothing circles on my back. I'm sure I feel like an icicle, but he doesn't seem to mind.

Guilt gnaws at me. My heart feels like it's trying to claw its way out of my chest. I can tell the minute Gideon notices my distress, because his body curls around mine even tighter.

"What's wrong, baby?"

"I kissed Quaid." I blurt the words, desperate to get them out in the open and face the consequences. Lying about it was never an option. The very idea of deceiving Gideon or Callum like that makes me feel sick.

"Did he hurt you?" Gideon demands, his hands resuming their circuit on my back.

"No. I mean—the talk was brutal, but he didn't physically attack me." I trail off, surprised by this reaction. "Aren't you mad?"

"I'm a little upset you went off by yourself," Gideon grunts. "That hunter's brain is still a fucked up mess. He's not ready for you."

"What do you mean? I'm yours," I insist, my words coming out in choked gasps as my confusion turns into panic. "Yours and Callum's."

"Whoa, calm down, baby," Gideon whispers. "Everything is okay, I promise."

"I don't understand."

Gideon curses. "Callum would be better for this conversation."

"No, no. By all means, keep going," Callum drawls from Gideon's other side. His sleepy voice is sexier than anyone's has a right to be. "You're both doing such a good job."

"Did you hear?" I ask, determined not to have any miscommunication between us.

The sheets rustle, and Callum's hand reaches over Gideon's body to cradle my face. "Yeah, I heard," he says. There's a hard note in his voice that's directly at odds with the gentle way he's touching me.

"I'm so sorry." My voice cracks as the emotions I've been trying to bottle up since my conversation with Quaid break free.

"Don't cry," Callum demands, but it only makes my tears fall faster.

"Dude, fuck you. You're making it worse," Gideon growls.

"Godsdammit, Sheena. Neither of us is upset. We saw it coming."

"What?" I hiccup, brushing my tears away.

"It was obvious, sweetheart," Callum says. "You've been in love with him since you were a kid."

"But I'm with both of you," I insist. *Does he think I would give up everything we've built for a chance with Quaid?*

"Have you stopped loving us?" Callum asks. "We can take off and give you space if you've changed your mind."

"Of course not," I say, horrified he could even think that. *I've ruined everything.*

"Sweetheart, I fucked you against that door so he could listen. Why do you think I did that?"

"I don't know," I sputter, my cheeks heating. "To get off. To help me get even."

"I mean, sure. Those were both perks, but I'm not an exhibitionist. I would have fucked you just as hard against any other door in the compound."

Gideon groans, and I feel his erection poking against my lower belly. A shocked gasp escapes my mouth.

"Please, ignore me. My body doesn't understand that this is a serious conversation."

"Really, man?" Callum scolds, but I hear the smile in his voice.

"Give me a break." Gideon groans again. "You're both rubbing all over me while talking about fucking against doors. I'm only human."

"No, you're not."

"It's an expression," Gideon snaps, sounding pained now. "Stop grinding against my ass."

I press a kiss to his neck, burying my face in his warmth with a sigh. His growl is the only warning I get before he rolls us both, flipping me on my back to hover over me. Gideon's golden eyes slice through the darkness. The hunger I see there takes my breath away.

"This is taking too long, and he's fucking it up worse than I did," Gideon grumbles, ignoring Callum's protests.

I bite my bottom lip, and Gideon crashes his mouth down on mine, nipping ferociously at my lip like he's jealous of my teeth. When he pulls back, I'm panting for him, desperately wishing he would relax his forearms so I can feel his full weight on top of me.

"I'm going to tell you a few things, Sheena, and you're going to listen," Gideon says, his voice demanding. "Got it?"

Usually, I would argue with a tone like that out of principle, but this doesn't seem like the time, so I nod instead.

"You kissed your childhood best friend. That's not a problem for Callum or me. Not because we have plans to give you up, but because it's painfully obvious there's still something between you two. All I ask is that you're more careful. Whether you want to admit it or not, Quaid is dangerous."

Gideon dips his hips, grinding his hard dick directly between my legs. I arch into him, my breathing coming in short gasps. It feels so good. I can barely focus on what he's saying.

"If you want to claim the human, the shady fae fucker, or both, go right ahead. But do you feel my cock right now?" Gideon rubs it against me again, and I moan at the delicious friction. "It's yours. It belongs buried balls deep inside of you. You may have confused me and my cock with someone a whole hell of a lot more noble earlier, but neither of us is interested in stepping aside for your first love."

Gideon sucks a hard, bruising kiss against my neck, and I feel the scrape of his teeth against my skin. The slight pain is exquisite, and in this moment, I would do absolutely anything to make him keep rocking against me.

"If we need a bigger bed to accommodate all these dicks, I'll have one made. But, baby, I'm not going anywhere unless you drive me away. Is that clear?" Gideon says, his golden eyes piercing into me.

"Yes, I've got it," I moan. "Please, touch me."

Before the last syllable leaves my lips, he claims them with his own. Gideon's kiss is like an antidote for every toxic emotion inside me. He siphons away my fear, hurt, and anxiety, replacing each worry with desire and love.

When he slides down my body, I bury my fingers in his hair and yank hard on the curls. He growls, annoyed that I stopped him. As a rule, I generally don't discourage him from going down on me. This is a first. But I can't wait any longer.

"Not now," I hiss. "All that talk about burying your cock deep inside me—I want that."

I'm desperate for him, my arousal soaking my panties and turning me into a writhing mess. Callum groans. The sound brushes across my skin like a caress.

"Do you have anything to add?" Gideon turns to look at him, and I squirm. Without shifting his focus away from Callum, he drops his weight onto me and traps me beneath him.

"To your speech or the impending sex?" Cal teases, then curses under his breath at Gideon's demanding snarl. "Damn. Nope, you covered it. I think I'll just watch tonight if that's alright."

Gideon grunts in agreement, but I'm not paying attention. My brain is too busy short-circuiting every time he rubs against me. I blink once, and my clothes vanish. They're gone so quickly I would think he used magic if I didn't hear seams ripping under his fingers.

"Careful, I've only got two spare sets of—"

Gideon thrusts inside me, and I moan. There's no warm-up stroke, no easing me in, not this time. He bottoms out, and the burning stretch makes my eyes roll back in my head. I plant my feet against the mattress, aching for more of him.

He kneels in front of me, muscles bunching as he drives in and out. I can't look away. From his wild curls to the burning need in his eyes, every part of Gideon is beautiful. I want to kiss him more than I want my next breath. We're so connected that he knows. Rocking back on his heels, Gideon pulls me up to straddle his thick thighs. The position spreads me wide open, and after two days of hiking, I feel the sting in my muscles.

It's worth it.

I bury my hands in his hair and stroke his tongue with mine. He tastes possessive, demanding, and perfect. I lose myself in his flavor. With his hands gripping my ass, Gideon pulls me down on him again and again. Each time, he hits that spot inside me—the one that sets me on fire. When my orgasm starts building, it's so intense that I'm almost afraid of it.

Gideon doesn't let me hide. He pulls back from our kiss, staring at me with brutal satisfaction as I come apart. With nothing left to muffle my pleasure, I gasp and moan, helpless little squeaks escaping my mouth with each thrust.

When he slides his thick fingers between us and pinches my clit, I can't hold back any longer. I explode. My body fractures into a million pieces. Completely undone, I ride the waves, floating in the hazy aftermath for god knows how long until I sink back to reality.

As soon as Gideon sees my eyes focus back on him, he loses his tight grip on his control. His rhythm becomes erratic until he finally lets go and spills inside of me with a grunt. Dimly, I hear Callum's groan through the roaring in my ears, and I glance to the side to see him coming in his own hand. To my exhausted body, our panting breaths sound like a dirty lullaby.

Gideon presses a gentle kiss to my neck and chuckles.

"What?" I ask, slumping against his body and letting his muscles support me.

"Do you think Safina has any spare sheets?"

The bed beneath us trembles, and crisp clean linen and blankets wrap around us within seconds.

"Holy fuck," Callum says, his mouth dropping open.

Gideon looks down at the sheets with a calculating gleam in his eyes. "I wonder if Idris would consider taking the yacht home with us."

"I cannot make portals of that size, you fool." Idris' irritated voice comes through the shared wall clear as fucking day.

Oh no. If he can hear Gideon, and we can hear him . . . I collapse back onto the bed, pull a pillow over my face, and wait for embarrassment to devour me whole.

This is a problem for tomorrow.

CHAPTER
TWELVE

GIDEON

I step out on the deck, rolling out the stiffness in my arm. Thanks to my enhanced healing, the arrow wound is all but gone, and with both sunbeams shining down on me, I feel cheerful as hell.

Until I spot the hunter.

Fury boils in my gut. My insides twist, my vision flickers, and my muscles twitch angrily. Every single part of me demands I shift and rip into this idiot. I lock my animal urge down and lean into my more human desire: punching this bastard in the face.

Four long steps bring me to the hunter. I latch onto his arm, spinning him around to face me. My fist cracks into his jaw, and I lay him out. He catches himself on the railing with a grunt, rage flashing in his eyes.

"Listen to me carefully because I'll only say this once," I snarl. "If you ever make her cry again, you'll be getting up close and personal with the monster fishes."

Quaid looks over his shoulder, eying the irregular shapes as they dart toward the boat and circle beneath us. Thrumming my fingers along the railing, I weigh exactly how pissed off Callum will be if I get a closer look. *Maybe I can take a dip and check them out.*

"She kissed me back," Quaid says, dragging my attention away from the fish. He crosses his arms over his chest, smug triumph lighting up his eyes. He leans back against the rail like he planned to be shoved there.

"I don't give a damn about that," I snap. "Sheena cares about you, but you're so blinded by hatred that you can't see anything else. Are you ready to face the day you drive her away for good?"

The hunter narrows his eyes at me, but not before I see pain flash through them. I take a step back.

"I pity you," I say quietly, meeting his glare. "No, seriously. You know her in a way none of us ever will, and you're throwing it away for nothing."

"It's not nothing. It's everything," he hisses.

I roll my eyes. "You wanted me dead before we met. Make that make sense."

"Your kind killed my parents." The words spill out of him, then he slams his mouth shut. He squeezes his lips into such a thin line that blood can't pass through them anymore. They turn white around the edges, and the boat lurches beneath us.

"I'm sorry for your loss," I begin, pausing to run a hand through my hair. I can't imagine losing my parents. His loathing makes a lot more sense, but if his parents were also in the cult . . . I need to know. "Were they hunting?"

It's the wrong thing to say.

"Does it matter?" Quaid roars, pushing off the railing and taking a step toward me.

His aggression sets my beast off again. My shifter instincts long to taste his blood on my tongue. I'm used to reining in my dual nature, but part of me doesn't want to. Maybe beneath all his twisted logic, the hunter is right to fear us.

"No, I guess it doesn't," I admit.

Quaid's shoulders sag at my honesty, and I watch the anger drain out of him. Without it, he seems smaller. When he looks out across the lake and turns his back on me, I let that be the end of the conversation.

I head inside and spot Sheena standing in the main cockpit. She's not visible from the deck, but she's definitely within earshot.

"You didn't have to do that," she whispers.

I'm relieved she's not mad, but I hate hearing the sadness in her voice. "Yeah, I did, baby," I say, wrapping my arms around her. I tuck her into my body until all I can feel are her soft curves.

Sheena is the one part of me I can't live without. I don't even want to try. When we met, I was shocked to learn I had a fated mate. While I lusted after her immediately, loving her snuck up on me. She's been through so much, but as long as I'm breathing, she'll never have to face anything alone again.

I kiss her cheek. "Did you know about his parents?"

"I knew they were dead, but I didn't know why." Sheena sighs. "I guess I should have pieced that together by now."

"Don't beat yourself up about it. He didn't tell you, so that's not on you," I say. She hums in acknowledgment, pulling back from my hug.

"Angus—his guardian—always gave me the creeps." She furrows her brow. "I didn't like how he looked at me."

I add another name to the list of people from her past that I need to track down. It's getting pretty damn long. "Like he wanted you or wanted you dead?"

Sheena shudders, and I drag her down to the leather couch, putting my body between her and the door.

"I don't know, really. I just knew he didn't feel safe," she whispers, glancing over my shoulder at the door. The hunter still stands at the rail, body rigid as the wind whips through his braids. "I never told Quaid. It felt silly," she admits.

I shake my head. "Your instincts gave you a warning. Trusting them kept you alive for a long time," I remind her.

"What about when they told me to shimmy down the gutter of your cabin?" Sheena teases with a smile.

I grin and pin her against the couch, rubbing my stubble

against her neck until all I can hear are her crazed giggles. "They were full of shit that time, baby."

I kiss the creamy skin where her neck meets her jaw, and she relaxes against me.

"Yeah, they were." Sheena presses a soft kiss to my lips, and my heart pounds with satisfaction. I can't wait to make her mine forever.

IDRIS

Love. So unapologetically complex. So irrepressibly dangerous.

I watch Gideon interact with Sheena on my couch. He's so painfully gentle in the way he holds her, ever conscious of his greater size and strength. The shifter positions himself as her feral protector one moment, then turns and bends his very nature to meet her emotional needs in the next.

I wonder if she sees it. I wonder if he fears it.

I remember the vacant rage in his eyes while Leona held her hostage. Weaker beings cowered away from him in fear. Doors were torn from their hinges. His emotions slipped away until anger was the only thing that kept him going. Gideon knows quite well the pain of losing her, yet still, he risks it.

I once believed the thirst for power was the most dangerous force in all the realms. Now I know that for the lie it is. Love is the most deadly desire of all, and gods help anyone caught in its grasp.

Turning my back on the two lovers, I grip the smooth collection of levers and infuse my magic directly into the navigation system. Safina hums with satisfaction as the enchantment takes hold. My intent is the only fuel the vessel needs to reach the Court of Stars.

My sister and I will meet face-to-face today. I will look into her eyes and wonder if she plots my death.

So many of our shared bloodline lay beneath the ground, their bones white and gnarled by time. One by one, they fell victim to the very deceit, plots, and assassinations they themselves once orchestrated. Forgotten even by the fae who bested them—the only connection they share with each other is that none of them reached old age.

It's likely I will never know if the child I protected tirelessly in our youth works just as hard now to send me into the afterlife. My sister may not have engineered the betrayal that sent me crawling to another realm to lick my wounds, but power corrupts and I've been gone a long time.

I told the little djinn I no longer believed in closure, but part of me still longs for it. *Impossible. Not in this realm, not ever.* I cannot allow these thoughts to distract me.

I slam the throttle forward, and Safina glides across the water. New resolve steels my spine. I am nothing like this boat, traveling silently and leaving no wake in her path. Fountains of blood and legions of splintered bone litter my past. I give no mercy and expect none in return. I am Idris, King of Stars . . . Or, at least, I used to be.

A knock on the wall next to me rips me out of my reverie. When I turn to see who is disturbing me, I find Callum studying me with a wry grin.

"Sorry to interrupt," he says, looking anything but apologetic. "You seemed deep in thought, but I can't help but notice we're on the move."

I shelve my irritation and focus back on the instruments in front of me. "We will arrive at the palace within the hour," I tell him, my tone clipped. He has no right to my thoughts, and even less to my feelings.

Callum studies me for an uncomfortable length of time before turning his attention first to his paramours and then to the hunter.

The human remains on the bow. While my Safina is spacious, I don't think anyone on board missed the confrontation between him and Gideon. I heard the crack of that punch from my narrow bed below deck. Add in the midnight kiss, and I have no doubt the hunter's limited processing capabilities are severely overtaxed.

"Sounded like a good hit," Callum observes, keeping his voice low and one eye on Sheena.

"Indeed." I allow a cruel smile to take over my face. "I only regret that no splash followed."

Callum snorts, his amusement cutting off abruptly as Sheena joins us. "What are you guys talking about?" She asks, noting my smile with suspicion.

"Fish food," Callum quips.

Sheena narrows her eyes at him, letting the silence drag on uncomfortably. I make myself busy with the levers and avoid eye contact. While I have no problem waiting her out, the incubus is the weak link here. It's only a matter of time before he cracks under the—

"Dammit, it was a good hit. That's all I'm saying," he says. I sigh, noting less than a minute passed before he crumbled like stale bread. "Even you have to admit, he had it coming, sweetheart."

"If we want to show him every supernatural isn't a monster, making jokes at his expense isn't the way to do it," Sheena says, crossing her arms.

"Yeah, but there's a difference between monsters and pussies." Callum trails off, realizing his mistake far too late. I focus on the horizon to maintain my composure. "I just mean—we can't show weakness to a hunter."

"Are you trying to tell me pussies are weak?" Sheena demands.

Callum groans in dismay. I feel him look to me for help—a fool's errand. He's neck deep in sinking sand of his own making, and I don't care nearly enough about his wellbeing to toss him a rope, metaphorical or otherwise.

"No. Of course not," he insists.

"Callum loves pussy, baby," Gideon asserts from the corner in his booming voice.

I close my eyes for a few seconds to block them out. If only I could impede my ears as easily. *Gods, I have killed hundreds, but do I truly deserve this torment?*

Callum groans. "Thanks for the help."

Out of the corner of my eye, I watch him step into Sheena's space and whisper in her ear. It's a ridiculously transparent tactic, but with the way a blush creeps up her neck, it appears to be working. Callum presses a scorching kiss to Sheena's lips and backs her into the control panel, not six inches from where I stand.

"Pardon me for being in your way," I drawl. "After all, I am just navigating the vessel."

Sheena breaks away from her demon, pushing at his chest insistently, but it's too late—their display has completely disturbed my solitude.

"Go bother Gideon," she tells him.

She pastes a pitiful attempt at a stern look on her face, but the effect is ruined when her frown flips to a rosy-cheeked smile three seconds later. Callum saunters away, confident he's no longer on her bad side.

"I'm sorry about that," Sheena says, angling her body near the open window to take advantage of the morning breeze. "I can't imagine what possessed him to do that."

I look at her, tilting my head to the side. "Can you really not?"

"I'm not a pushover," she argues, looking at me with heat of a different kind burning in her eyes.

I dip my chin, then turn to observe the other two. They're sprawled on the couch, talking with an ease that only comes from long acquaintance. It's unnatural to observe a relationship with no obvious artifice. It's surprisingly intriguing. *What would it be like to interact with others without layers of hidden intent?*

"Are you worried about seeing your sister again?" Sheena's soft voice pierces through every layer of my defenses in one strike. She draws blood with her sincerity alone, and I fear if I look down, I'll see a gaping hole in my chest.

"I am not sure what makes you think you have earned the right to ask me a question like that," I snap at her, watching her face fall.

"Sorry I asked." Sheena knocks her shoulder against mine as she leaves my side.

"You would do well to remember, little djinn, that I am not one of the desperate puppies who loll along behind you, panting for a crumb of your attention. We are working together toward a common goal. Nothing more, nothing less."

The distance between us is for the best. She won't agree, but we can hardly march into a den of enemies on friendly terms. The target would be obvious for all to see, and we'd be dead before nightfall.

Sheena turns her back to me and raises two middle fingers over her shoulders. I hide my smile and engage Safina's throttle. I would allow no one else in this universe an opportunity to show me such disrespect, but there's no need to tell her that.

"Message received," she snaps. "There's no need to ramble on, Idris."

Sheena tosses a cruel smile over her shoulder, and desire floods my body. That calculating look, designed to cut me down to size, turns my cock to stone instead.

I wonder if she has any idea.

SHEENA

Idris is so obvious. Every morning, no matter how many suns happen to rise, he wakes up and puts on his emotional armor. He locks himself behind layers of aloof energy, then goes through each day acting like nothing can touch him. If anyone does manage to get too close, he hurls a verbal barb in their direction and shores up his defenses.

He's not fooling me. Not any longer.

Sometime between seeing his discomfort over the construction mess at the compound and his dream visits during my captivity, I figured him out. Idris is a survivor. Running wasn't an option for him, so in order to survive, he became a guarded, devious strategist. Now that he's back in the fae realm, the spikes he grew to protect himself are too.

I asked if he's worried about seeing his sister, but I already know he is. Sometimes, Idris broadcasts his pain so clearly, I feel like I'm watching one of Ciprian's illusions. Trusting me. Caring if I live or die. These are unforgivable chinks in his armor that his clever mind can't allow.

So I stomp away and give him the space he needs to feel safe. I toss my hair angrily to make the act extra convincing. It's the least I can do after all the times he took my pain and asked for nothing in return. Idris can keep his armor on today, but eventually, I'm going to prove that he doesn't need it. At least, not with me.

Peering out the window, I consider my second problem. Quaid. Even looking at him stirs up a nasty combination of complicated emotions in my chest. What we have . . . I'm not sure if it's a rare delicacy or lethal poison, but I can't stop stealing little tastes.

"Someone bring the human inside," Idris demands. "We are nearing our destination."

I grunt in response. The cowardly part of me wants to send Callum or Gideon out to grab him, but I'm working hard to deny my instinct to run. That means fighting some battles, even if I'm not sure I can win.

When I walk out onto the deck, I brace against the force of the wind, stopping a few feet behind my old friend. "It's time to come in. We're almost to the palace," I say.

Quaid doesn't move. He doesn't react to my words at all. He's probably waiting me out, expecting a detonation. As a teenager, I wouldn't have been able to resist reacting to his silent treatment, but today . . . Today, I'm too tired for this shit.

I pivot to leave. The wind picks up at the exact moment I lift my foot off the deck. The gust propels me forward several steps, but my legs are too stiff and sore from all the hiking to adapt to the sudden change. They buckle beneath me, and I close my eyes, putting my hands out to break my fall.

A toned arm catches me around my waist before I can make contact with the hard deck. Quaid's familiar smell coats my nose, but I don't get to enjoy it for long.

"Be careful," he growls, shoving me away from his chest.

I shake my head at him, then stomp into the spacious interior. He follows me inside, and I catch his reflection in the gleaming glass. There's a vicious scowl on his face.

"Baby, are you okay?" Gideon rubs my upper arms, concern and anger warring for dominance in his warm brown eyes.

"I'm fine. We're fine," I grumble. "Isn't that right, Quaid?"

"Super." He grits the word out.

I feel a small sense of satisfaction. I won't let him hide inside his stubborn head any longer. The stupid ideals festering in there are changeable, but only if I can force them out into the open and challenge them. My insecurities tell me it won't be enough. I might not be enough. But I promised myself I would pick some battles, and this one is my top priority.

A gurgling stomach breaks the silence, and Gideon pats his belly. "About eating," he says. "It needs to happen soon. Are we thinking at your sister's place, or do we want more leftovers?"

"It depends," Idris responds.

"On what?"

"Your poison tolerance," he says coolly.

Gideon sighs, then leaves the room. When he returns, he's holding an armload of snacks. It's more than enough for all of us, but he stares down at the pile like it kicked his puppy.

"What's wrong?" I ask, selecting a prepackaged blueberry muffin from the assortment.

"I'm just hungry," he murmurs.

Callum shakes his head. "Gideon's not a big fan of leftovers. He's seen all this food before, so he doesn't want it."

I snort a laugh. Now that I think about it, I don't know that I've ever seen him eat the same thing twice in a row. "Are you picky, babe?" I tease him.

Gideon tucks an unruly blonde curl behind one ear and shrugs. "Food is important."

I think about the way his mom prioritizes family dinners—and even lunches—at the compound. When the three of us were at the cabin, he always made sure we ate breakfast together, too. Maybe Gideon is missing more than just the variety of food.

"It's nice to share, too," I say, tearing off a chunk of my muffin and offering it to him.

Gideon's eyes light up, and he accepts the bite with a big smile. Quaid stares, but I ignore him. I don't like the way he judges every move I make. It's like he's waiting for me to turn into a rabid dog and give him an excuse to put me down.

Gideon tosses mini cereal boxes to the others. Idris isn't facing him, so I wait for the little cardboard projectile to smack him in the back of the head. He spins around at the last second and catches it one-handed. I roll my eyes. *Of course.*

Idris glares at him, but Gideon has arranged his face into an innocent mask. I'm not fooled. My mate pays close attention, and he doesn't like it when anyone treats me poorly. This is his way of paying Idris back for his earlier dig at me.

We eat mostly in silence, the tension building more by the minute.

When the boat comes to a smooth stop, Idris turns to face us all. "We have arrived."

CHAPTER THIRTEEN

QUAID

It's a literal castle. I feel sheepish noticing this, but it sparkles, too. I've never even left the country before, and now I'm in the fae realm staring at an enchanted palace that looks like it was dunked in magic. If I squint, I can just make out tiny figures—guards, probably—staring down at us from the tops of the high stone walls.

We sail up to the front gate like we own the place. The castle is so beautiful; I'm itching for a weapon. While our scheming fae tour guide obviously picks and chooses his moments to tell the truth, I've seen enough to know he wasn't lying about the pretty equals deadly equation.

I glance at Sheena to see how she's reacting to the palace. Her mouth hangs open as she stares in wonder. "It's mesmerizing," she whispers.

I almost tell her I feel the same way, but I keep my mouth closed. No good can come from drumming up our old camaraderie.

Kissing her last night was a mistake, and I shouldn't have caught her when she fell this morning. A rush of adrenaline and panic swamped me when I thought she might tumble overboard. Internally, I sigh. I've had plenty of opportunities to kill her, yet something holds me back every time.

I'm kidding myself. It's the same problem I had before—Sheena just doesn't feel evil to me. But that doesn't mean the hunters are wrong about the others.

When my parents were killed, the hunter community provided for me and kept me safe. More important than that, they gave me a purpose and the means to execute it. I can't turn my back on them.

"What's the play, Idris?" The demon asks, staring up at the looming castle walls with concern.

"Quiet," he hisses.

"Halt!" A voice echoes down from the parapet.

"What a cliché," the shifter says with a snort. "A hundred bucks says the next words out of this guy's mouth are 'who goes there?'"

"Who goes there?"

"Pay up," he chuckles.

"Shut up," the fae snaps. He turns back to the gate, blue eyes blazing. "Open the gates. The King of Stars has returned."

He doesn't raise his voice, but the sound echoes across the water of the moat unnaturally. I shiver. I guess you don't have to yell if magic does the job for you.

We hold perfectly still, the silence tightening its bony grip on us by the second. When the gates finally move, they let out a deafening screech. Each half is almost as wide as a football field, and I have to squint to see the tops shifting among the clouds.

Idris adjusts a lever, and the boat glides forward. After hours on still waters, the sudden waves take me off guard. I stumble. The boat lurches violently to the right and the left. *Jesus Christ.* I widen my stance to keep from falling. The underwater movement of the gates is sending tidal waves surging down on us from both sides.

We're about to get crushed.

The water rises up higher and higher in the air. Around me, the others suck in terrified breaths. I brace for impact. Before the twin walls of water can crash down on us, they freeze in place.

What? Why did it stop?

I look back and forth between the waves, then notice Idris' hands spread wide. His left thumb twitches, and a trickle of water cascades down from our left. It hits Safina's hull with the force of a boulder. Sheena steadies the demon as the boat shudders, rocking violently before it rights itself.

My fists clench at my sides. The water obeys the fae for now, but sweat drips down the side of his face. This is taking a toll on him. Even as his cold blue eyes sizzle with determination, I know he won't be able to hold it back forever.

Sheena cautiously lays her hand on his back. *No, don't wreck his concentration.* Magic crawls across my skin. I reach out to pull her away, but the fae's arms lock in the air, and the boat glides forward without him touching the levers. The demon glances at the shifter, then they place their hands on his shoulders.

Our speed triples, and the hairs on my arm stand on end. *Are they lending him their strength?* I stand perfectly still as we pass between the towering columns of water. Trapped in an enclosed space with four activated supernaturals, I find myself hoping they're powerful enough together to hold the water back.

I can taste their magic. Even as wonder sparks in my chest, their powers make my skin crawl. Blue, purple, gold, and black—their eyes lack even a sliver of humanity. On a normal day, they all pass as humans in their twenties, but these eyes are a dead giveaway.

The boat comes to a stop at a shimmering, silver dock. The massive gates shut, and the water recedes. Sheena breathes a shuddering sigh, her shoulders slumping as her eyes shift back to green.

"That was—" she begins.

"A test." The fae finishes her sentence. "My sister is fond of games." He yanks a lever into a neutral position, anger making his movements jerky. It's a far cry from his usual creepy, stoic grace. "Get your bags. I am sure she has more planned for us."

For once, no one argues.

We step out on the dock in formation. Sheena stands in the middle, surrounded on all sides, with me at her back. If anyone tries to get to her from behind, I could step aside, but I can admit to myself that I have no intention of letting that happen. If she dies, it will be at my hands.

When Sheena notices our positions, she grits her teeth. "Idris is the damn king. Shouldn't he be in the middle?"

"No," the fae snaps.

I'm sure she wants to argue more, but there's no time. A dozen armed guards march toward us, a deadly display of muscle. Their swords gleam in the direct sunlight. After the massive waves, the armed goons feel a little anticlimactic.

When they reach us, a hulking fae in the front line steps aside to reveal a woman. She's tall and slender with straight black hair hanging to her hips. Some of the strands are pulled back to reveal her pointed ears and highlight the delicate silver crown on her head. She doesn't need the hairstyle. No one could miss that thing.

"My long lost brother, returned at last." Her voice is low and melodic. The queen eyes him, then the boat behind us, affection showing only when she looks at the vessel. "You have no idea how long I've looked for Safina," she says, warmth infusing her voice.

"Safina is my boat," he hisses.

"Yes, but with you gallivanting off to only the gods know where . . ."

"The Earth realm is hardly uncharted territory, sister," he drawls.

She looks back at him, scoffing at his clothes. "Perhaps, but it's so provincial. So crowded with humans." She sneers at each of us, her eerie blue eyes stopping on me. "Do you have any plans to introduce me to your friends?"

"It depends. Do you intend to keep us standing on the dock until nightfall?"

The fae queen rolls her eyes, then turns on her heels and saunters away. With a flick of her wrist, the guards file in around us. Since we're still alive, I guess that means we're supposed to follow her.

No one says a word.

IDRIS

THE PALACE SMELLS the same. It reminds me of the kind of visceral betrayal that brings you to your knees. Memories I have no interest in revisiting force their way to the front of my mind. Ice tingles at my fingertips.

Zara leads us into her private parlor and dismisses her personal guard. *Something is wrong.* As soon as the door closes, she drops her mask. Gone is the confident queen. In her place stands my scared little sister.

"Zara, why would you dismiss your guard?" I throw my hands up in frustration. "I could be here to kill you."

She snorts inelegantly, reminding me yet again of the wild hellion who chased after me through the forest in her youth.

"If that's your intention, brother, by all means, proceed. If not, we have many more important things to discuss."

"Is it hubris or a newfound malaise that incites your reckless exposure to danger?" I demand. *How dare she lecture me about priorities?*

"Hypocrisy," Zara says, narrowing her eyes at me. "As nothing compares to the way you exposed me to all of our enemies when you crawled to another realm to lick your wounds."

Her accusation lands as intended. I pretend to engross myself in an examination of the wall as I regain my composure.

I frown as I take in the art. Nude sprites dance along a grove of enormous celise mushrooms. *Good gods.* Many are engaged in a different dance—fornicating in a variety of configurations atop the house-sized, iridescent caps. I blink. If memory serves, the murals in this room used to depict the Great Fractal Deception—a strategic maneuver that resulted in a grand slaughter and victory over our rivals in the Court of Suns.

"Redecorating?" I prod at the corner of the painting with my thumbnail, where two women are depicted in a passionate embrace. "Bit lascivious, is it not?"

"Don't touch it," Zara hisses, yanking my arm back. "Fresco is as much delicate science as art. The plaster must be allowed to bond with the pigment and dry unmolested by magic or boorish louts. If disturbed before the time is right, all is lost."

There's a double meaning there, but I no longer have time to waste. I turn my head sharply, provocative painting forgotten in my desire to get to the bottom of this mystery. "Who threatens you, sister?"

"All in good time, Idris."

Zara sinks down on a velvet chase, and I notice the telltale signs of fatigue at the corners of her eyes. She's taken great pains to hide them, but the longer I observe her, it's easy to see my sister is fraying at the seams.

"Tell me why you thought it was a good idea to come back with no warning," she says.

"There was no time to send word," I admit.

She sighs. "You must know your unannounced arrival made my rule appear weak. I was forced to order aggressions to prove otherwise."

"Yes, we received your warm welcome," I drawl. "It was not to our liking."

Zara sniffs with disdain. "It was merely a warning. If I wanted you dead, you wouldn't be standing here to defile my favorite fresco, brother."

"Perhaps your favorite fresco defiles me." It would be better commissioned in a brothel than our ancestral palace, and she knows it. I turn my back on the randy mural and drop into a chair. "And if I wanted you dead, you would never have seen me coming," I retort, annoyed that I'm letting her get to me enough to argue like children.

"Enough of this." Zara waves her hand at me dismissively, then looks at the rest of my party. "You still haven't introduced me to your friends."

Most of my so-called friends are hovering at the edge of the room, looking varying degrees of uncomfortable and amused, while Gideon is trying to get a closer look at the damned mural. Zara studies them one by one, noting Sheena with particular interest.

"They are members of the enclave I am a part of." I drag her attention back to me, then introduce everyone.

"I see . . . You gave up one kingdom only to pursue another? How curious."

"I grow bored of your jabs, sister."

"And your time away has changed you, brother." Deep lines mar Zara's forehead as she studies me, cataloguing my differences and weighing their threat potential. I wait in silence until her shoulders slump, and she sighs heavily.

"Admittedly, I am finding it difficult to speak plainly. You see, there are so few whom I can trust."

She sounds tired. Another stab of worry hits me.

"The folk seem stable," I begin.

"They are as they always were," Zara says, waving her hand. "Sexist swine who would rather see you rule, but we've had no uprisings in your absence."

"Lunar or solar, then?" I suggest, mentioning the courts of our two nearest rivals.

She shakes her head, studying the rings on her fingers. I wait for her to continue, but Zara seems lost in troubled thoughts.

"In the interest of time, maybe you should just tell me, so we can dispense with this tedious guessing game," I tell her, my tone dripping with deliberate condescension. Years ago, the same goading would have driven her to violence. Now, the only sign I see that it affects her at all is a miniscule tick in the lean muscle of her jaw.

"The land is dying," Zara whispers, her voice catching on the words.

"Dying how?" I shift in my chair uncomfortably.

"It's difficult to explain, brother—truly, everything seems normal—but the fields produce a strange, inedible yield."

"Did you question the boundary guards? The fields could have been poisoned."

She's shaking her head before I even finish talking. "There have been no known breaches. What's worse, my alchemists cannot detect any toxins in the soil or streams." Zara slides her fingers along the velvet armrest, her eyes fixed on the silver fabric as it subtly changes shades beneath her hand.

I frown into the crackling flames in the fireplace. Our land has been fertile for generations. I've never heard of anything like this in our histories. This necessitates careful consideration and planning. We must consult first with the network of spies and—the fire dies, a thin sheet of ice encasing the logs. I look away.

"You said there have been no recent attacks. Is that normal?" Sheena asks, disrupting my musings.

My sister startles slightly as though she'd forgotten we weren't alone. I relight the fire with my magic, hoping no one noticed the brief lapse in heat.

"No, it is unprecedented. In truth, the prolonged peace is making my troops uneasy." She narrows her eyes at the little djinn. "Why do you ask?"

Sheena shrugs, but holds my sister's eye contact. "If your enemies are also acting weird, maybe your land isn't the only one with problems."

I consider her idea impassively. If the other courts are dealing with similar struggles, it makes sense that their focus isn't on the normal border skirmishes that typically occupy their time. A chill crawls up my spine as heaviness falls upon my shoulders.

I have no idea how to heal a realm.

I LEAD OUR DISHEVELED GROUP down sinuous corridors, falling back into the route I tread for more than a century with ease. Cold air slinks up my legs, the chill slipping through the thick walls. The brutality of this realm is everywhere I look. My father died in this hallway. I watched his blood stain the silver mortar just there. I—

"I have a lot of questions," Sheena whispers, her teeth faintly chattering.

I silence her with a sharp look. Anyone could overhear us in these halls. Even now, I have no doubt that Zara has a spy or two lurking in the shadows, watching from holes in the paintings or listening behind the many tapestries that detail my ancestors' prowess in battle.

Before we left her private parlor, my sister informed me she ordered for my old rooms to be aired out as soon as she heard I was back in this realm. Zara hired mercenaries to kill me even while preparing the staff for my arrival. What a traditional fae greeting. My lips twitch and my eyes burn as I turn down a narrower hallway.

The sconces are older here, tarnished with age and neglect. Something unpleasant stirs in my gut at the sight. During my time on the throne, the metal casings shone brighter than the fae lights they housed. Their poor condition is a tangible mark of my lengthy absence.

At least someone had the decency to dust off my portrait. Commissioned after my coronation, it hangs to the right of the entrance to my quarters. I look regal, poised, and defiant. In reality, I feared for my life. With assassins lurking, even sitting for that painting put me at great risk. But the message it sent—complete and utter control—was worth the danger.

"Is that you?" Gideon asks, reaching for the canvas.

"Stop," I order, smacking his hand down. "You will get oil on it."

"You and your sister take your art very seriously." Gideon grins at me, then looks back at the portrait. "Do you still have that sword?"

"If you cease your chatter, we can leave this drafty hallway and find out."

"It's in here?" Gideon points to my quarters. "Nice, I've always wanted to learn to fence."

Without waiting for permission, he throws open the door and disappears into my room. The others follow him without a word. The peace doesn't last. As soon as I close the door, they all turn as one and bombard me with the questions and observations they've been holding in since we arrived.

I hear nothing but a dull roaring in my head.

Gideon vanishes into my closet. I don't want him poking around in my things, but he returns before I can drag him out. His lips move, and I focus on what's he's saying.

"Were you serious about the risk of eating here? Because my breakfast is long gone," Gideon complains, rubbing his stomach.

He plops down in an ornate pedestal chair. It's a delicate antique that groans under his weight. I open my mouth to tell him to be careful, then close it again, my eyes prickling unexpectedly.

"I think you should sit down, man." Callum grabs my arm, his grip surprisingly gentle as he leads me to the sitting area.

I sink down in the familiar space, memory and reality interlacing in a painful but familiar chain mail pattern. Armor is suffocating. I told my father so when he commissioned my first set. His response to a toddler's discomfort taught me my first lesson in why I needed it.

Breathing deeply, I focus on anything other than the overwhelming feelings in my chest. If even one tear should fall, I'll be forced to gut the lot of them and toss their bodies from the turrets.

SHEENA

IDRIS CLINGS to his composure by a thread. His shoulders are rounded and tight as he hunches over the couch, chest heaving, feelings on display in a way I know he must hate. Privacy. He deserves his privacy.

"Everyone out," I demand.

I jiggle door handles until I find an unlocked one that opens into another bedroom. I point inside, and Gideon, Callum, and Quaid reluctantly file through. Closing the door behind them, I turn to Idris.

My friend—whether he wants to admit to any attachment or not—is fighting an invisible battle. Blue eyes wide and unseeing, he's clenching and unclenching one hand rhythmically while the other clings desperately to the arm of the fainting couch. I don't know how to help, but he's been there for me. The least I can do is return the favor.

I tiptoe over to the sofa, sinking down beside him. His hand opens and closes again. Open. Close. Open. Close. When his fist unclenches next, I slip my hand in his, twining our fingers together. Instead of pulling away, he clutches me like a lifeline.

"You're safe, Idris," I whisper. "I'm guarding your back, remember? You can let go."

After a pause that seems to drag on forever, I feel his body shake against mine, racking with silent sobs. A bitter cold settles in the room. I scan our surroundings diligently, focusing on the doors and windows.

I'm not sure how long it's been since he's allowed all the tension inside him to unravel, but I won't let him down, not while he trusts me with something so monumental. By the time he sags against me, my eyes feel gritty and raw, the fatigue of the last few weeks catching up to me.

"I did not expect this," Idris murmurs.

"Emotions are sneaky like that." I squeeze his hand gently.

"This kingdom, the folk, this palace . . ." He gestures to our surroundings, and I see his breath in the air. "They hold so many memories for me. Some I treasure, some I cannot bear to face."

"I've got a few reminders like that hanging around myself," I admit, looking at the closed door between Quaid and me.

"These agonies from the past draw blood so easily. Do you think they ever dull?" Idris' voice is raspy, nothing like the silky, suave melody I've grown so used to from him.

I take my time forming a response. "I'm not sure the sharpness or time actually matter," I say, remembering some of the questionable choices I made in the interest of self-preservation after meeting Gideon and Callum. "I think we have two choices: allow our past to inform our future or destroy it."

He hums in response, and the air heats noticeably. My exposed skin stings, but the rising temperature is a relief. Idris' hand slides across the back of mine. He strokes the delicate skin of my wrist with his thumb, and I can barely focus on the subtleties of the conversation. My nerve endings buzz as I lean into his body.

"What if you can no longer tell the difference?" He asks.

Each syllable caresses my skin, sending tingles down my spine. If Idris feels the same distracting pull to me, he doesn't show it. I have to replay his question three times in my head to make sense of it.

"Then I'm afraid you're like everyone else." I laugh, turning my head to face him.

Only inches separate us, and when his blue eyes dip to my mouth, I lick my lips. It's an involuntary gesture, but it snaps the tension between us like a rubber band. Suddenly desperate for air, I suck in a breath. I don't know if I'm relieved or devastated when Idris stands and pulls me to my feet.

His hand cups my cheek. "Darling, when I kiss you for the first time, we will both be able to tell the difference."

My heart races and heat rushes to my face. I want to ask him what he means, but I fear I already know. I rub my hands against my upper arms and try to pull myself together.

When we rejoin the others, there's a heavy blanket of exhaustion in the air. No one brings up Idris' moment from earlier, but I think it put the seriousness of the situation in perspective for us all.

Much to Gideon's relief, the queen sends a member of the staff to deliver food for us all. I'm horrified when Idris snaps his fingers and demands the fae woman try each dish first. After she's still standing several moments later, he dismisses her with another negligent wave of his hand. She curtsies and quietly backs out of the room.

"That was incredibly rude," I tell him.

Idris looks over at me with his mouth open, fork poised in mid-air like I just suggested we go skinny dipping in the moat.

"That is her job," he says.

He chews on his aborted bite, then spreads butter onto a warm roll and tears off a chunk. When he offers the piece to me, I take the opportunity to decline with an imperious wave of my hand. His lips twitch.

"Point taken, little djinn."

After that, we fall on the food like animals. This home cooked dinner tastes even better than I expected after days with only prepackaged, processed foods. Some of the spices are unfamiliar, and I'm pretty sure I've never had this meat before, but it melts in my mouth. Each bite delivers a rich explosion of flavor directly to my taste buds.

When I look up from my plate, all four men are staring at me hungrily, their own food lying forgotten in front of them. I dab at the corner of my mouth with a napkin.

"What?" My tone warns them to behave.

Callum shovels a piece of fruit off his own plate onto mine, a devious smirk on his face. “Nothing, sweetheart. We’re just happy to see you enjoying your meal.”

His words are innocent, but the look in his eyes is anything but. At least he didn’t say anything overtly dirty. I’ll just pretend they aren’t looking at me like I’m the next course.

“Holy shit, baby. I’m almost there. Can you bite into the fruit real slow?” Gideon groans.

I drop my fork to cover my face with my hands. As always, his teasing makes me feel both sexy and mortified. I hear a muffled oof, but I’m not sure who just smacked him.

“Gideon,” Idris says, clearing his throat. “I grow tired of hearing of your untimely erections.”

“You could always mix things up and start telling us about yours,” Gideon tosses back.

A wild giggle escapes me. If I’ve started finding boner jokes funny, I’m clearly overtired. I take it as my cue that it’s past time for bed.

I push back from the table, snagging the piece of vividly pink fruit and snapping it in half. I toss both pieces into my mouth and leave all four of them at the table. Quaid’s laughter follows me out of the room. It’s the best sound I’ve heard in years.

CHAPTER **FOURTEEN**

LEONA

Frustration churns inside me as I weigh the best way forward.

"But to pursue the djinn all the way to another realm . . ."

I turn my back on the flames and tune out the grating voice. It's true. The risk is great, but my dream of having Earth back under the witches' control outweighs every possible danger.

"The fae will not protect an outsider," I interrupt the droning of my old ally.

Gladytha was once my mentor—a task the mother coven assigned her many decades past. She was old when she accepted the role, and the goddess only knows what she would look like if I released her from the flames now.

I look at the jeweled dagger in my hand. Another relic from a different time, much like Gladytha, except this one is far more useful to me. I face the fire once more.

"The fae don't even protect each other," I remind her. "I'm sure they will be only too happy to turn her over to us. After all, she's a foreigner encroaching on their lands."

"As you will be as well," Gladytha ventures, her voice paper thin and reedy in the flickering flames.

I detest the very sound of her. Even after all this time. Even after I surpassed her strength and banished her to the fireplace, she seeks to undermine me.

"Their magic is nothing compared to mine." I grit my teeth, focusing on the tension in my jaw instead of my mounting anger. "Perhaps you've forgotten your place . . ." I let my threat hang in the silence. If Gladytha would rather exist in the water of my toilet, I would be happy to make that happen.

I open my mouth to tell her as much, but she's already beating a hasty retreat. "Of course, dear. I am sure that you are right," Gladytha says.

The flames bank as she cowers away from me. The sight does more to cool my temper than any words possibly could. My former mentor, a once powerful witch, fears my strength. The knowledge zips through my veins, and my magic hums with delight.

It's a balm to my soul after the djinn slipped from my grasp. It took days for my spies to figure out where she went. I never considered that the enclave's tenuous alliance with the fae would pay dividends for them this quickly. That's my mistake, but now it's my time to act.

I snap my fingers, and the flames flinch once more. So predictable. So invigorating. I tilt my head back and laugh.

"Summon the others. We have an invasion to plan."

CALLUM

"Tell me why everything looks so soft, but then I touch it and end up bloody?"

Gideon wipes his injured finger on the leg of my pants, then slips it into his mouth. I shake my head and shove him away.

"I think most people assume groping artwork is bad," I say.

"Come on, I didn't grope it. I barely touched it," Gideon says, pointing at the fully functional diorama with narrowed eyes.

A series of interconnected clouds in muted colors hover over a miniature waterfall, complete with mist and the faint sound of water crashing along the rocks. The display is full of magic and whimsy, and as soon as Gideon saw it, I knew he would want to see what was holding the clouds up. Now the pink one is stained with his blood.

"Do you think every sculpture here comes with its own built-in security?"

"For your sake, I hope not," Sheena teases.

Idris is late. He told us to meet him here this morning, but we've been waiting in the fancy receiving room for half an hour with no sign of him. This room is part of his quarters, which I've come to realize is a massive maze of interconnected doors. I opened six of them this morning trying to find the bathroom.

"Maybe we went to the wrong room," I suggest, leaning back in a surprisingly comfortable wing-backed chair. Sheena is curled up in my lap, right where she belongs.

"Maybe he enjoys making you wait," Quaid says. I'm still not used to the hunter's voice, but at least he's finally speaking. The silent, never-ending bitch face was equal parts unnerving and infuriating.

"Or he simply had more important things to attend to," Idris says, prowling into the room and eying us each critically.

Gideon sidesteps in front of the diorama, trying to hide the bloodstained cloud from Idris. I can't decide if I want him to pull it off or get caught.

"None of you are wearing the clothes I sent you," Idris snaps.

"Yeah, honestly, we couldn't figure them out." Sheena speaks up for us all, laughter in her voice.

"Plus, Gideon couldn't get those tight ass pants over his thighs," I add, grinning as I remember him hopping around like a jackass while trying to pull the pants up. He refused to give up until the fabric split under the pressure, and I nearly died laughing.

"You are going to stand out," Idris hisses, scowling at us.

"I'm pretty sure that's not because of our pants," I say.

"Very well." He turns to leave with no warning. "Follow me. We have much to discuss."

We shuffle to our feet reluctantly and trail after him. *Demanding fucker.*

"Have you talked to your sister this morning?" Sheena asks Idris, hurrying to catch up with him.

"I have."

"And?"

"And the witches know we are here," he says.

Sheena comes to a screeching halt. In a flash, Gideon is by her side, all mischief forgotten. I grab Idris' opposite arm, pulling him to a stop. His blue eyes glitter with irritation as he faces me.

"Are you telling us Leona reached out?" I ask, clinging to my patience by a thread.

Idris sighs and drops some of his obnoxious formality. "She wishes to negotiate the return of her property."

The last word has barely left his mouth when a ferocious growl tears through the room. It rattles the tea set laid out on the sideboard and makes my heart race. Sheena lays a hand on Gideon's trembling chest and the sound stops.

"What are the terms?" Sheena asks. Her green eyes are wide but guarded. I hate the shadows I see returning to her eyes at the mention of that fucking witch.

"Per the report, the message appears to be something along the lines of 'deliver the djinn to me or else.'"

Idris' face is expressionless and hard as he looks down at Sheena. He might as well be carved from granite for all the emotion he shows her. While it seems cold to me, Sheena becomes more relaxed the longer she looks at him.

"I take it your sister wasn't a fan of that?"

"Certainly not," Idris says, his lips curling up on one side. "The other fae rulers will not like her tone either."

"Why are you worried then?" Sheena cocks her head to the side.

"Witch or not, no fae will cower before a human."

"But?" Sheena asks, and Idris sighs.

"I fear their reaction when they learn you are under the protection of the Court of Stars."

"Because I'm an opportunity," Sheena says, resigned.

Idris dips his chin. "After centuries of feuding, the rival courts are always looking for a new advantage in their war games."

The tension in the room builds exponentially.

"Fuck fae politics," Gideon snarls. "What can we do about Leona?"

Idris looks over at him, a cruel smile curving up his lips. "We let her come. And when she arrives, we secure the talisman and deal with her once and for all."

I THRUM MY FINGERS along the enormous round table as boredom threatens to drag me under. We've been in this strategy meeting all day. At first, I was fully invested. I would do anything to keep Sheena safe, and I like having a plan, but so far, the royals won't listen to a word any of us say.

It's just Idris and Zara going back and forth trying to outsmart the other. They've argued the merits of half a dozen plans, but don't seem to be any closer to actually choosing one. Both of them seem genuinely content to run scenario after scenario ad nauseam, reacting to each one with so many hypotheticals that my head hurts.

When my mind starts to wander for the fifteenth time, I let it. I imagine Sheena sinking her teeth into that tasty pink fruit from last night, juice escaping the corners of her mouth as her tongue darts out to capture every drop. I picture shoving Gideon down on this ancient table and making him beg to come as they hammer out battle plans around us.

It's way past time for lunch, and my incubus is hungry.

My own devious plan takes shape in my head, but do I dare execute it? I glance to my right. Sheena is chewing on her bottom lip, her green eyes glazed with boredom.

Hell yes, I'm doing this.

Excitement curls low in my belly as I drag my right hand off the table and into my lap. No one glances my way.

I slide my hand over to Sheena's knee. She smiles at me, then focuses back on the opposite side of the table where Idris and Zara are having yet another heated debate in the fae language. This happens whenever they get particularly agitated, but since none of us understand, it gets old pretty fast. To Sheena's right, Gideon might actually be asleep, and on my left, Quaid is staring at the wall like it's Rosetta's fucking Stone.

So far, so good.

A mask of faux focus slips over my face as I pretend to listen to the bickering fae. Under the table, I inch my fingers up Sheena's leg, stop halfway to my goal, and massage her tense thigh muscle. As she relaxes into my touch, her lust comes roaring to life. I breathe it in eagerly. When her hand settles over mine and drags it up to her pussy, I want to cheer.

She's wearing her favorite pair of frayed jeans. I slip the button from the loop and wait until the fae siblings are having a particularly loud disagreement to slide the zipper down. Then, I make Sheena wait.

With my hand curled around her thigh, I let her dwell on the fact that her pants are undone in a room full of magical beings. Anyone could see. How would she explain? I let her worry, I let her plan, and most of all, I let her think about what I might do to her. Anticipation, nerves, a dusting of shame—each second I hesitate, her feelings grow more intense. I let her sink into the chaos until her body is thrumming with tension.

I slip my index finger between her legs and tease her pussy

over her panties, feeling nothing but wet silk. With her pants still on, my movement is limited, but that just makes the setting hotter. She has no escape. Not from me, and not from the sensations I give her.

When I move the soaked fabric to the side and touch her delicate skin with no barrier, Sheena's entire body jerks. Gideon's eyes snap open, his nostrils flare, and his golden stare freezes us both. He knows exactly what I'm doing to her.

I expect Sheena to panic, but she surprises me by winking at her mate and opening her legs wider beneath the table. With Gideon watching, I ramp up my movements. The stream of lust I've been snacking on becomes a flood.

"What do you think, Sheena?" Zara asks. "You've spent the most time with this witch."

The queen looks at my girl, who clearly doesn't have a clue what's going on. Sheena's mouth opens and closes, and I slip two fingers inside her. Her eyes flutter shut. I almost take pity on her, but—

"The witches shouldn't be underestimated. Leona has a dangerous, sizable following and commands others through a series of mutually beneficial allegiances," Quaid says from my left, drawing their attention.

I freeze for a second, truly shocked. The hunter just deflected for Sheena, knowing full well it would lead to an interrogation. I focus on the lust I'm feeling, and sure enough, some of it is coming from him. Quaid knows what I'm doing to her, and he's helping us hide it. I don't know what his play is here, but we might as well give him a show.

"How do you know that?" Idris asks him.

I resume my movements between Sheena's legs, feeling her tremble. Quaid drags his eyes away from my girl and glares at the fae.

"Because I followed Alina for weeks."

"Your marching orders are to kill on sight, are they not?"

"Yes," he admits.

"Then why did you let her live?" Idris demands.

"Drop it." Quaid's tone is low and lethal. Everything about it screams 'fuck off.'

A muscle in Quaid's jaw ticks, and I feel Sheena clench around my finger. *She likes him mad.* I curl my finger inside her, tapping on the spot that never fails to make her go wild. Her lust spikes, but I sense her holding back. She's afraid to come in here. *Too bad it's no longer up to you, sweetheart.*

"Why?" Idris repeats, raising his voice and pushing back from the table roughly. His chair topples over with a clatter.

I grind the heel of my hand against Sheena's clit. I can feel her clinging to the edge. It won't take much to push her over.

Quaid stands to face Idris, slamming both palms down against the wood in anger. "Because I knew she had Sheena," he roars. "And if I killed that fucking witch, I wouldn't have been able to get her back."

Quaid turns to stare at Sheena, and that's when I strike, pumping my fingers inside her with abandon. She shatters with the hunter's eyes glued to her and his chest heaving with rage. She makes no sound, but lavender consumes the green of her irises, and I feel the intensity of her orgasm throughout my entire body.

Holy. Shit. So much energy is flowing into me, I feel like the entire realm is spinning. I'm so drunk on Sheena's lust that I barely remember to refasten her jeans. She slumps down low in her seat and sucks in a shaky breath.

Quaid's eyes burn into the side of my head, anger and lust pouring off of him in waves. Technically, I got away with my game, and I'm certainly not bored anymore, but I can't help worrying that I might have just stirred something up that was better left alone.

CHAPTER FIFTEEN

SHEENA

I don't remember the end of the meeting. The walk back to Idris' rooms is a blur. All I can think about is how Callum just gave me one of the best orgasms of my life in a crowded room while my first love shouted that he disobeyed orders to find me.

Quaid claims it was all so he could kill me himself. But, if that's the case, why hasn't he gone through with it? In the grand scheme of things, I'm not that hard to murder, and he has yet to make a serious attempt.

Idris stayed behind to talk more strategy with his sister, but the rest of us trudge back to his rooms in tense silence. I'd be lying if I said I wasn't on edge. I rub my hands along my upper arms, using the friction to clear my head. It doesn't help.

We step past the life-sized painting of Idris, filing into the chilly room slowly. When the door closes behind us, I spin to face my former friend. Quaid stands just inside the door, his expression shuttered. My heart sinks to the bottom of my stomach. I don't know what I expected. Maybe some honesty after everything we've been through. But his mask is back up, his defenses fortified. Those dead eyes, his apathy . . . I hate them so much.

For days, I've locked my anger down, scared to drive him further away. Why the fuck am I doing that, though? Everything I've bottled up is still trapped inside me, begging for release as I tiptoe around Quaid's issues. I'm a Sheena-shaped glass house filled with pressurized gas—overfull and primed to blow.

"Do you have anything to say?" I ask, my voice tight.

Quaid stares, silent and passive. My fingers twitch.

"I asked you a question."

Nothing.

Callum shuffles nervously by my side, but there's not even a flicker of emotion from the man who was once my everything. Reality sinks in. *My voice doesn't matter to him. Not anymore.*

I did this to myself. I created my own purgatory. Unblinking, his blank eyes watch me hold myself together with shaking fingers. I want to stew in the unfairness of it all, but fuck that. *Fuck him.* I've made this too easy for him. Quaid needs to face what he's done to us.

I charge at him. He backs into the door.

"Don't look at me like that," I hiss.

He stares back at me with that same guarded look firmly in place. I have to get rid of it, so I shove at his chest. Callum tries to pull me back, but I shrug him off. When I go to push Quaid a second time, he grabs my wrists, a sliver of anger flickering past the shields in his brown eyes.

Gideon clears his throat. "Maybe we should all take a minute to calm—"

"Down?" I demand. "No. Not this time. I'm not calm, and I won't be until he stops fucking looking at me like that."

"Finally dropping the act?" Quaid sneers down at me. "Bravo, Sheena, you played the role longer than I thought you could."

"Oh, I'm the one playing a role? That's rich coming from you," I snarl, my voice thick with unshed tears. "The only things I'm done pretending about are you and the pain you cause."

The judgment in his eyes fades back to nothing, and his grip on my wrists loosens. But I'm not talking about physical pain, and he fucking knows it. I study his face, breathing past the enormous lump in my throat.

"You look at me from his eyes, speak with his voice, but you're not the Quaid I remember. I'm done acting like it doesn't hurt."

The more I vent, the less pressure I feel. But in place of my anger and bitterness is a liquid pool of sadness that threatens to drown me.

"That Quaid was never real."

He says the five words I fear most. More than all the death threats and cult bullshit put together. He was my savior, but if that person was all a lie . . . The pool inside me ripples, water licking at my ankles.

"Don't look at me like that." My voice is barely more than a whisper.

"Don't look at you like what, Sheena?"

The water climbs to my knees, and the first tear trickles down my cheek.

"Like I'm nothing to you."

"Is that how I'm looking at you?" Quaid demands. I try to pull my arms free from his hold, but he won't let go. "Did I look at you like you were nothing when you came all over the demon's fingers?"

The mask slips from his eyes, revealing an bottomless pit of anger. It's as unfamiliar as his indifference. This is what I wanted, what I demanded from him, but now it's too much. I need to retreat, but Quaid won't let me go.

"Why does it matter how I look at you, Sheena?"

The water is to my chest now. It's too late to wall it off.

"Because when you look at me like that, part of me dies."

"Oh my god, you're so dramatic." Quaid advances on me, tipping his head at Callum and Gideon. "You already have two boyfriends. Don't you get enough attention?"

"You don't get to talk about them," I hiss. "Not now. Not

ever." I push my body into his, forcing him back against the door once more.

"Okay. Then I'll look at you however I damn well please."

"No, you won't," I sob, my chest heaving with every shuddering breath I take. The water bobs against my chin and trickles into my mouth and nose. "You can't look at me like I'm your enemy while I'm in love with you."

Quaid makes a choking sound. Tears roll down my cheeks, soaking the neck of my shirt. He pushes his forehead against mine and closes his eyes.

"Would you rather I look at you like this?" He whispers, eyes opening. His mask shatters, and suddenly, I'm staring through a window into his soul. The sixteen-year-old boy I knew is trapped. Tortured. Screaming. Banging against the walls of a tunnel with no light at the end. His hopeless agony matches my own.

The water fills my lungs.

"I just want the truth." My voice breaks.

He flinches, but holds my eye contact with grim determination. "The truth is: I'm in love with you, too. But you are my enemy."

Quaid presses a brittle kiss to my lips that I'm too numb to feel. There's no oxygen left inside me. No room to come up for air. He pulls away and walks jerkily from the room. When he closes the door behind him, I sink to the floor. I'm losing him all over again, and there's nothing I can do about it.

I've drowned, but stubbornness keeps my heart pumping blood to my body. It beats out of sync. With a piece missing, maybe it always will.

I wipe my eyes with my sleeve and climb shakily back to my feet, letting the numbness coat my entire nervous system. Callum and Gideon stare at me. They don't know what to do or say, but I'm grateful for their silence. There's no fixing this, and wishing won't change a damn thing. I'm done hoping my best friend comes back to me. It's time to let him go. I have to move on.

"Baby, I'm so sorry."

I nod to acknowledge Gideon's comment, but I don't need his pity or anyone else's right now. I force a smile.

"How can I send him back?"

Gideon freezes, and Callum shoots me a wary look. My eyes feel gritty and raw. I can't get rid of my sadness, but I can do what I do best: survive.

We're in another realm, but I'm the one who's been living in a fantasy world. Quaid made his priorities clear from the start, but I was too stubborn to listen.

It's time to make changes. That's become clear to me. They all tried to tell me it was a bad idea to bring Quaid along, but I made decisions that impacted us all based on my childish feelings. Trusting my stupid emotions put us all at risk, and Idris was right to be mad at me. I'm mad at myself.

"How can I send him back?" I repeat.

Callum shifts uncomfortably on his feet, darting a loaded glance at Gideon. They're waiting for me to change my mind. Based on my track record, I can't blame them for the assumption, but that's not going to happen.

"Just spit it out," I say. "I'm standing right here." *And I'm not made of glass.*

Callum runs his fingers through his dark, shaggy hair and sighs deeply. "It's just . . . Is that what you really want?"

Isn't he listening? I can't have what I want. Callum was here. He witnessed the entire ugly scene. Why is he making this harder than it has to be?

"Obviously," I hiss. "I've said it twice now."

"If you send him home . . ." Callum braces himself and looks me dead in the eye. "Sheena, that's it. He'll be gone forever. Are you going to tell me the woman who was just crying buckets on the floor is really done?"

I flinch, but at least he's not trying to tiptoe around my feelings anymore.

"It's past time for me to be done," I insist. "Bringing him here was a mistake. You all tried to tell me, and I didn't listen."

"Baby, you were following your heart." Gideon reaches for my hand. "We didn't get it at first, but we do now."

My fingers hang limply in his warm grip. He's trying to comfort me, but all I feel is disgust with myself. "Yeah, and when has following my heart ever been the right call?" I pull my hand back and wrap my arms around myself.

Gideon's face falls, hurt shining in his brown eyes. "I thought it worked out pretty well for us," he mutters, turning to walk away.

I feel sick. A slice of panic gets past my barrier of numb, but when I open my mouth, I struggle to find the right words. "Gideon," I croak, half stretching my arms out toward him.

He turns back around, and whatever he sees on my face must be pathetic enough to absolve me. Gideon erases the distance between us and pulls me against his chest.

"I'm not going anywhere," he assures me. "Your heart is safe with me."

The battered organ in question thuds erratically in my chest. Gideon kisses me gently, and I feel him, warm and reassuring against me, melting the barrier I worked so hard to build. I kiss him one more time, then carefully pull back from his hold.

"If you really want to send him back, we can make that happen," Callum says. When I lift my head to read his expression, I see tension in the tight set of his mouth.

"You still think I'm making a mistake," I say.

"I think you're understandably upset." Callum watches me closely as he considers his words. "But I also think if you send him away today, there's a strong chance you'll regret it tomorrow."

"I won't," I groan, annoyed that I'm being forced to justify my feelings about this again.

Another man might back down from the frustration in my tone, but not Callum. He steps closer to me. "You will," he says, soft but insistent in a way that's infuriating. "Maybe not tomorrow, but someday you'll regret it, and I don't want that for you."

Does he really think regret is worse than constant rejection?

"It's not your choice, Callum." I stand my ground and try to appeal to his logic. "If I send him away, one mess will be solved. Once we deal with Leona, we can start our lives together with no drama."

Callum snorts and points at the lavish, fae decor all around us. I narrow my eyes at him, and he holds his hands up in surrender.

"All I'm saying is, there's always going to be drama, sweetheart. That's just the way things go, but what's between you and the hunter . . . That's the kind of thing that's never over."

"Don't fucking say that," I snap.

He's wrong. He has to be because I can't hold this pain back forever.

Callum doesn't push anymore, but I know him well enough to see this conversation isn't over for him. He'll try again, and I'll have to make him see my decision is final. I'm removing Quaid from my life as soon as Idris gets back and makes me a portal. My mind is made up.

QUAID

I'm in love with you, too. But you are my enemy.
I'm in love with you, too. But you are my enemy.
I'm in love with you, too. But you are my enemy.

THOSE ELEVEN WORDS play on repeat in my head until they lose all meaning. Just letters, sounds, and syllables squeezed together. Thousands of years ago our ancestors breathed life and meaning into a series of grunts, and now, any given sequence of disembodied noises has the power to destroy worlds.

Breaking hearts? That's light work.

I slam my fist into the stupid tile mosaic covering the surface of the bathroom. My knuckles split and blood runs down the white grout. Another punch. Another. I don't stop until I paint every groove red with my blood. My knuckles are shredded, but this pain is nothing compared to how I felt putting that devastated look on Sheena's face.

She's no more evil than the homecoming king at our high school, or the cashier at the corner store who looked the other way when we shoplifted snacks after school. I can see that now, but it makes everything so much worse for me.

If only those eleven words were the whole truth. But they're not. If only I could love her without the hate. But I can't. My oaths are driving us apart, and I'm not doing either of us any good pretending otherwise.

I don't belong in her world.

Sinking down to the floor, I close my eyes and let the chill of the tile wall soothe my heated skin. Familiar images creep into my head, but I didn't put them there. The nightmare demon planted these pictures against my will back on Earth, and they've tortured my every waking moment since we stepped through the swirling blue portal.

Sheena laughing in the kitchen at something I said. Her arms draped over my neck as we dance to imaginary music. Her lips pressing against my scarred cheek as she whispers she loves me. A ring on her finger, a cuddle on the couch, a perfect kiss. Each moment is beautiful.

There's only one problem: they're fucking fake.

I've never seen that kitchen. The ring doesn't exist. And I can't remember the last time I made Sheena smile, much less laugh. It's a cruel, cheap affectation of a life I'll never get to have. I would kill to preserve every single phony second.

I've considered the demon's motives for planting the illusions in my mind more than I care to admit. While I hiked through the fae jungle, I played the visions over and over, fixating on his intent and searching each image for clues. My obsession with the fantasy, paired with our reality in the fae realm, painted an entirely new picture of the woman I thought I knew.

Sheena became more than my former friend, more than my nemesis, more than a mistake on my spotless record. Like a parasite, she latched on again without even trying. But I can't belong to her—not when I don't even belong to myself.

I sacrificed myself on the altar of revenge when my parents were killed. I still owe the hunters my life. Sheena is following a different path, and I don't belong on it. Even though she's not a killer, I can't have her. No matter how much I wish I could, that dream is out of reach.

Our fight was ugly, different from our sparring in the past. I pushed her too far, and deep in my soul, I know Sheena won't ever forgive me for it. I don't deserve another chance, and I won't ask for one.

She might hold me captive forever, but I won't give either of us another thing to regret. Now that I've burned the bridge, she'll forget about me. It's for the best.

I look at my shredded knuckles and wince. Sheena told me she loved me. The words tore her to pieces, but she gave them to me anyway.

As a kid, that would have changed everything for me. I would have risked it all if I'd known how she felt, but time is both our greatest gift and the cruelest curse. It taught her to fight for the things she never had: a brighter future, a fuller life, and epic love. Those hopes were stolen from me long before I met her. Time taught me to pursue justice, vengeance, and retribution. All I have left is my honor.

Of all the lies I told Sheena and the things I held back, at least the final blow I dealt to her was completely true. *I'm in love with you, too. But you are my enemy.*

IDRIS

"I NEED TO TALK TO YOU," Sheena demands.

The sudden sound of her voice startles me. I find her standing as still as a statue in the back corner, hidden in shadow. Given that I've only just darkened the door of my personal bedroom, she must have been waiting to ambush me.

These young supernaturals have become so demanding and entitled. They really ought to learn something about patience. I take my time unbuttoning my coat before I answer her.

"By all means then, darling, allow me to drop everything at once," I croon, dipping into a low bow. I expect a scoff or a rude gesture in response, but I get neither. She doesn't mention the delay or my attitude at all. It's the first sign I have that something has gone terribly wrong.

"I need you to grant Quaid clemency and send him home."

Her demand is shocking enough on its own, but the tone she delivers it in . . . Good gods. It's so lifeless that I briefly consider the possibility that someone is impersonating her.

Pulling her into the light to assess her aura, I sense no outside magic or glamours at work. The cold chill coming from her frightens me even more. I drape my coat over her shoulders, but I'm not sure she even notices.

"What happened?" I ask, looking around for her cohorts. There's no sign of them or a struggle, but if someone dared come into my rooms and hurt her—

"Nothing happened, Idris. I've just finally realized you were right."

"Indubitably, but to what specifically are you referring?"

"The hunter," Sheena says, referring to him by his allegiance and not his name for the first time since he appeared. "He doesn't belong here, and I never should have insisted we bring him."

Her face doesn't change at all throughout the recitation. I might be proud of her stoicism if it didn't make me so damned uneasy. I've been telling her this all along, but now that she agrees . . .

Sheena stares impassively back at me. I open my mouth to respond, then think better of it. Turning on my heel, I shove through the door to the adjacent bedroom. It's apparent at once that Callum and Gideon have been listening in. Both of them look concerned.

"What is going on?" I ask.

"Oh, so my words aren't enough for you?" Sheena chases after me, each step crackling with an anger that I'm frankly relieved to see. It's a welcome change after the peculiar display I was just subjected to. "What kind of patriarchal horseshit is this?" She stops at my side, her glare spilling from me to the other two and back.

I tilt my head and observe Sheena closely. Her eyes are bloodshot, and the skin around her right thumb is raw like she's been scraping at it. Someone has clearly distressed her, but that's not exactly new. It happens often and almost always because of the human, who is notably absent.

"What did the hunter do this time?"

"Send him back," Sheena demands. "It needs to happen."

"Darling, on that point, you and I are now in perfect tandem," I say. She nods triumphantly, but I'm not finished, so I hold up my index finger. "But I will not be creating a portal to send that worthless man to the bathroom or anywhere else until I know exactly what brought this on."

Gideon's shoulders dip to a reasonable level, and Callum ceases tormenting his hair. Their obvious relief makes me even more determined to get to the bottom of this.

Sheena stomps her foot, and an angry growl escapes her lips. "Dammit. Why not?"

"Because I no longer make portals on demand," I tell her wearily. "In fact, I have decided it is high time I imposed some demands of my own. The price for this particular portal is the truth. Your truth."

"I already told you," she snaps.

Her words are laced with frustration, but I can tell she's losing her grip on her anger. Beneath it, I sense the same unbearable cold from before. I pull my coat tighter around her shoulders and fasten the top button gently.

"Try again," I suggest.

She clears her throat, her green eyes shooting daggers at me. "I'm giving up. There. Is that what you wanted to hear?"

"Certainly not," I say, my tone gentle.

Sheena backs up a step, and her index finger scrapes against the sensitive skin of her thumb.

"You told me my sentimentality was dangerous. I agree," she says, tossing up her hands. "I'm admitting that I made a mistake, and I'm asking for your help to fix it. Why are you making this so hard?"

I'll never admit this to another soul, but denying her right now is one of the most difficult things I've ever done. Sheena's resilience is so deeply ingrained in her being. Watching it falter is deeply unsettling. I've seen her tired, irritable, stubborn, and hurt, but I've never once seen her shut down. This defeated look on her face means we've all failed her, and that simply won't do.

I hold out my hand. She stares at it suspiciously.

"Come with me, little djinn," I say. Sheena opens her mouth to argue, so I sweeten the deal. "Come with me. We will talk it over, and then I promise I will make your portal."

She takes my hand. I draw on my magic until Callum and Gideon's concerned faces and the lush rooms of my former life in the Court of Stars fade away to nothing. Around us, the meadow we first arrived in materializes. I take in the rich smell of the flowers, the gentle glow of the suns, and the brittle shell of the woman I know.

Sheena doesn't even look twice at the beauty of her surroundings. "Why did you bring me here?"

"For an honest conversation," I say, surprised to realize I truly mean it. If her scoff is anything to go by, she's not impressed by my forthright intent.

"And we couldn't have one of those back at the palace?" She looks down at her shoes. "If you plan to make me walk all the way back, you should have at least let me put on my boots."

She makes these kinds of quips often, but this one lacks the playful bite that always makes me want to laugh.

I sit down among the flowers and tap the spot next to me. "You know very well neither of us will be walking back," I say. Sheena sinks down at my side, staring blankly at the horizon. "Now, tell me what happened with Quaid."

The hunter's name feels sour on my tongue, and I don't miss her flinch when I use it.

"You know what happened." Sheena sighs. "It's the same thing that's happened half a dozen times."

"You argued?" I press, and she nods. "What made it worse this time?" I've often observed her enjoy their squabbling, but there's a piece she's not telling me. I don't like that.

Sheena shrugs. "He says I'm his enemy, so I decided to believe him."

Except, the human has been telling her this since the beginning, and each time, she's refused to give up on him. She is still holding back.

"What else did he say, darling?"

Her eyebrows squeeze together, and I catch her sharp intake of breath. Sheena stays silent for so long, I worry she doesn't intend to answer. When she finally speaks, it's with a dull monotone.

"He said he was in love with me, but that it didn't change anything," she admits, her body sagging ever so slightly next to mine.

White, hot rage fills me. For weeks, Sheena has been steadfast in her affection. She has borne the hunter's every cruel word—his continuous apathy—all while staunchly defending his life. She did all this as she fled from a madwoman. And now . . . he has the audacity to hand her this burden? This twisted approximation of love poisoned by his hatred? No wonder she's shutting down. It should have been his to carry alone.

"I will kill him," I whisper, moving to stand.

Sheena grips my pant leg, tugging me back to the ground. "Why do you even care? You've made it perfectly clear we're allies, not friends."

Ridiculous. I turn to watch her, but she's staring ahead vacantly. She doesn't look at the beauty all around us. She doesn't look at anything.

"You cannot believe that," I speak the words through gritted teeth. *She must know the truth.* I allowed her to see my most vulnerable moment in decades. I've given her trust I've offered no other since—

"Idris, you told me on the boat less than a week ago. I don't know why I would think anything else."

Sheena pulls a blade of lavender grass from the ground, rolling it between her fingers until it's nothing but pulp. Once it's battered and bruised, she tosses it aside. We both stare at the mutilated plant. It's much the same color as her djinn eyes.

"You know . . ." Sheena sighs, but there's no feeling in the sound. "I've developed a terrible habit recently. When a guy tells me to fuck off, or that it's never going to happen, I decide I know better. I tell myself he'll come around, that I can change his mind, or that he doesn't really mean it. But really, I'm just an arrogant idiot who believes my feelings matter more than someone else's choices."

Sheena laughs, a hollow grating noise I hope to never hear again. "Seriously, Idris, just think about how disgusted my ancestors would be with me."

"Little djinn—"

"I mean, they were hunted to the brink of extinction, and here I am whining because some guy—"

"Sheena, please," I try again.

"That all stops now. I'm done hearing only what I want to hear."

"Perhaps you can delay this new practice until tomorrow," I suggest, urgency overwhelming my practiced charm.

"Nope." Sheena shakes her head. "I'm putting sentimentality behind me, and there's no time like the present. You had the right idea all along."

"Do not ever listen to me, darling. I am the greatest fool in all the realms."

I infuse every drop of charm at my disposal into my smile, but Sheena ignores it and reaches for another blade of grass. I catch her hand before she can pluck it. Fear makes my heart bump erratically in my chest.

"I was in love once," I admit. Sheena abandons the grass and looks up at me. "It ended . . . poorly."

I can do this. Being honest with her—it is different.

"Kirsi was a princess of the Court of Ice. They were the closest thing to allies my kingdom had, and our marriage was meant to strengthen that partnership. At first, it was only politics on my end, but Kirsi was so different, so free with her emotions and affections. Her laugh . . . It turned heads, made me forget . . ."

The chill in my body spreads from my heart to the tips of my toes.

"What did you forget?" Sheena asks, her grip on my hand tightening. It's the only point on my entire body that still feels warm.

"That all fae, no matter the court, have one thing in common."

Sheena hums deep in her throat. "She betrayed you."

I nod, feeling some of the weight ease at the admission. "It was all a plot to get close to me, find my weaknesses, and destabilize my rule. Her father intended to annex my court into his territory."

"But you found out."

I shake my head. "Zara suspected it first, but I refused to listen. I accused my sister of seeking to spoil my happiness. We quarreled bitterly. It was not until I woke in the night to find Kirsi poised to plunge a knife of ice in my chest that I believed the truth."

A shudder runs through my body.

"The look on her face haunts me still. Severe, emotionless—she was a stranger to me in that moment. I was so wrong about her, and my people nearly paid the price for my naivety."

"What did you do?" Sheena asks.

I consider lying to her, but it doesn't feel right. Bracing myself for her judgment, I clear my throat and lift my head. "I simply reminded her that I, too, was a bloodthirsty fae noble at heart."

The memory flashes through my mind. Driving Kirsi's own knife between her ribs. It melted there, soaking her nightgown along with my tears, while blood trickled from her lips. I blink the image away, turning to Sheena, desperate to read her face.

"What happened that night—"

"You did the right thing," she interrupts.

"Yes, darling, but that is not—"

"And you learned from your mistake. You didn't give her a second chance to betray you."

"Little djinn, what I am trying to tell you . . ." I suck in a deep breath. "Is that I know the difference now."

The woman in front of me is nothing like Kirsi, and I've done us both a disservice by trying to hold her at arm's length.

Sheena *is* the difference for me.

Here in this meadow, surrounded by flowers, bathed in sunlight, and deafened by the sound of my own racing heart, I make what may go down in history as the most foolish decision of my life.

Gripping Sheena's chin in my hand, I kiss her like I've been longing to since she handed me her sandwich. For the first time in a decade, I taste the lips of a woman I truly care for. They're as soft as I imagined them to be, perfectly sweet, and completely . . . still.

The chill spreads to my lips. I pull back to find Sheena staring at me, unmoved, unaffected, and if I'm reading her correctly, entirely without remorse. The weight of her rejection hits me while I'm at my most vulnerable.

Her lips curl, and she lifts one dark, delicate eyebrow.

"Now, about that portal you promised me."

CHAPTER
SIXTEEN

GIDEON

He made Sheena cry. Again. My worry and anger are going to blow, and I know just the target. Cracking my trembling knuckles, I head toward the door.

"Don't do it, Gideon," Callum groans without lifting his head. He hasn't moved from the chair he dropped into after Idris and Sheena stepped through the portal.

"I need to. He hurt her," I growl, but it sounds more like a whine. I have to get relief from this violent mess inside me.

"And I've hurt her, and she's hurt you. This isn't the first time, and it won't be the last," Callum argues.

"What's your point?"

"You can't fight all her battles."

"Fucking watch me," I grunt, the animal inside me insulted he would even suggest we aren't up to the task.

Callum stands and puts his hand on my shoulder. When I growl this time, it's more beast than man. My hands tremble.

"You could kill him if you go in there like this."

He's right, but if the alternative is to sit here and do nothing, that might kill me.

"I can't. I need—"

Words. I can't explain the issue, and the more I try, the more jumbled everything gets. The shaking spreads from my hands to my arms.

"Whoa, it's okay, Gideon. What's going on?" Callum asks.

"We haven't sealed the bond. The time hasn't been right. As a man, I understand. As a beast . . ."

"He's losing his patience." Callum finishes the thought for me, and I nod. "How can I help?" There's worry in his voice, but no fear or judgment, just understanding and a reminder that I'm not in any of this alone.

I spin and pull him into my arms. He's solid, strong, and as much mine as the woman we both love. When I kiss him, I don't hold back. I can't.

There's usually a tussle over dominance between us, but Callum can read my body better than I can. He knows that's not what I need.

Callum lets me control the pace of the kiss and pull his head where I want it. I take, he gives, and the layers of anger and frustration fall away, leaving raw want and need in their place.

"Cal," I gasp.

He bites down on my earlobe. "Relax. I'm not going to leave you hanging," he whispers directly into my ear. Goosebumps spread along my neck.

He slips his fingers into my belt loops, then uses that grip to tug me along as he walks backward. When his back bumps against the wall, he grins up at me and sinks down to his knees.

I weave my fingers into his messy hair and yank his head up. I need to see his face. Callum isn't just some random guy I'm hooking up with. He's my best friend, the person I've counted on for my entire life. He's my person, and I need to know he's okay with this.

His black eyes lock with mine, and the hunger I see staring back at me takes my breath away. *He wants this. Wants me.*

When Callum bites down on his bottom lip, I tug it out and replace it with my thumb. He sucks my finger into his mouth, reaching for my fly with both hands. Cal doesn't drag things out or tease me. He tugs my pants open with no hesitation and pulls my dick out. It twitches in his hand as he runs his thumb over the head.

He strokes me from base to tip, and I shudder. His grip is tighter than I'm used to from a partner, more like how I handle myself, and I'm already so worked up. I know it's not going to take much. I pull my thumb from his mouth, enjoying how his teeth scrape against my skin, and arch into his palm.

"Callum," I repeat, unsure what exactly I'm asking for.

"Don't break me," he hisses.

Before I can make sense of his words, Callum takes me into his mouth. I'm pretty sure my best friend has never sucked a cock, but—*holy fuck*—you would never know it. He works me over like it's his damn job. When I feel myself bump against the back of his throat, I almost lose it. Every time I get control of myself and find a comfortable rhythm, he finds a new way to torment me with the warm, wet glide of his tongue.

Callum lashes at a sensitive spot. I moan. His eyes whip up to mine, and the satisfaction I see swirling in the dark depths leaves me gasping. Combined with the tight fit and pressure, I'm already on the edge. He eases off, giving me more time to enjoy how amazing it feels for him to play with me like this.

After a few minutes, the animal inside me perks up and watches with interest. It wants out. It wants to dominate. I hold back, but Callum senses the change. He slides his mouth away, his breath coming in quick, raspy pants.

"Let go, Gideon. I can take it." He lets his head fall back against the wall, then opens his mouth and waits, one eyebrow raised arrogantly.

It's the spark of challenge in his eyes that breaks me. I surge forward, shoving my dick into his mouth roughly. Callum takes every inch, and before I realize what's happening, I'm slamming into him in fast, deep strokes. With his head against the wall, he has no choice but to take it.

Seeing him at my mercy is so fucking hot. Whenever I bottom out, his throat moves. *I want to feel it.* I snarl and wrap my right hand around his neck. He gags beneath my fingertips.

I grunt and pick up the pace. Pressure builds at the base of my spine, and there's nothing I can do to hold it back any longer. When my orgasm slams into me, I pull out, spilling half in his mouth and half on his face.

Callum licks his lips.

"Holy fuck," I groan.

He lets out a raspy chuckle, and I help him stand. *I just fucked my best friend's face.* I'm not exactly embarrassed, but I was so rough . . .

"Shhh, you're thinking too loud," Callum says. When he looks at me, though, he's the one who seems unsure. "Was that okay for you?"

"Are you fucking kidding?" I growl. "I'm going to be thinking about that when I jack off for the next ten years."

"Maybe you won't need to use that same memory for the entire decade." He grins, then wipes the come off his face, sucking his fingers clean one by one.

I stare at his mouth, completely mesmerized.

"You know Sheena's going to be pissed she missed this," Callum says.

As soon as I think about my mate in this context, my limp cock takes interest in the conversation again. Cal notices and holds both hands up.

"Nope, put that away. I have to actually breathe oxygen sometimes or I'll have brain damage," he teases.

I realize now that I never even touched him, much less returned the favor. My face burns, and I rub at the back of my neck. "I'm sorry. I didn't," I begin, pointing loosely at him. "I can . . ."

Callum throws his head back and laughs.

"Gideon, I'm good," he assures me, the humor dropping out of his tone. "There's no pressure. This is our pace. No one else's. It's not like we're ready to announce it to the enclave."

I nod, sinking down into a chair, unsure about which part of what he said isn't sitting right with me. I'll figure it out later. There's already enough going on.

We snuggled with Sheena under the covers last night, trading ridiculous what ifs until all three of us were desperately trying to muffle our laughter. Sheena's giggles were so real, but that was before everything got so twisted up.

"Do you think she's okay?" I ask.

"Probably not," Callum admits. "But we can help her through it no matter what happens with the hunter."

I open my mouth to respond, and the air hums with the sound of an incoming portal.

SHEENA

IDRIS BRINGS ME BACK to the palace without a word. I can still taste his lips on mine, but I don't have the energy to deal with that. It's too much too soon after Quaid's bombshell.

The timing is just a little too convenient. Idris is crafty—he made a move because he's working an angle. I know better than to assume he's changed his mind and decided to pursue something with me. Especially after that story he told me in the meadow.

As we step into the bedroom I share with Callum and Gideon, both men greet me with worried looks on their faces. I want to run into their arms and let them tell me everything is going to be okay, but I can't. If I drop my guard and let myself be comforted, I know I'll fall apart again.

Idris keeps an arm's length between us. He doesn't want to be anywhere near me. That's fine. I don't need him. All I need is his portal. I bargained for it fair and square, and it's time for him to pay up.

"Where's Quaid?"

My guys exchange glances, then Callum clears his throat. "His room, I guess."

"I'll go find him." I give them a brisk nod and pull my shoulders back.

"I can get him, baby, but are you sure you're ready to talk again?" Gideon asks, worry shining in his warm brown eyes.

My heart flutters for a brief moment. I breathe in and blink, then exhale through my nose slowly. "We won't be talking," I explain, fixing my gaze on both of them. "Idris agreed to send him back."

"Umm, shit." Callum runs his fingers through his hair. "I'm just going to come out and say it. This feels like a bad move."

"I hear you, but it's my decision," I insist, rolling my shoulders back.

"So you're just going to unleash him on everyone back home? He'll start hunting down other supernaturals first thing," Callum argues.

I force a shrug. The tension pulls against my skin, making it feel too tight. I'm sick of this responsibility. I didn't ask for it. I've never even wanted to be part of this brutal, bloodthirsty community. I'm an outcast among humans and only an asset to supernaturals. *Why should I protect strangers?*

"That's not my problem," I say briskly, wanting nothing more than to scream it from the turrets until my throat is as raw as my heart.

Callum puffs out his cheeks, releasing the air audibly as he watches me. He doesn't understand, but why should he? He was born and raised within the safety of the enclave. I know it wasn't always easy for him, but our problems aren't the same.

"Baby, if he attacks the compound, they will have no choice but to kill him," Gideon says, trying a new tactic.

My heart skips a beat. I imagine Quaid going on some kind of suicide mission. We all know how it would end.

"Again, that sounds like it's still not my problem."

"Sheena," Callum says, a touch of judgment in his voice.

"Callum," I say, sarcasm coating my tone.

He sits down on the edge of the bed beside Gideon. They don't know how to deal with me like this. *Good.* It's about time I grew a backbone. I love both of them, but I can't allow those feelings to weaken me. I'm no one's goddamn wishing well. If that means more people decide to call me an enemy, so be it.

Tapping my foot against the floor, I look between the three very different men in front of me. They're all staring at me with an eerily similar expression.

"Are we done here?" I demand. I'm finished debating this. The sooner they run out of things to say, the sooner I can get rid of Quaid and move on with my life.

"I'm not."

Speak of the fucking devil and he shall appear.

"That's tough shit," I say, keeping my voice brisk. "Idris is going to send you home."

Quaid circles around to face me. Even though he's getting what he wants, he apparently needs to twist the knife one more time. My pride won't let me back down, so I raise my eyes to his and immediately regret it.

He hides nothing from me, but I'm not sure if that's by design or necessity. Every second I look at him is like staring through a window into our own personal hell.

I wrench my eyes away, but Quaid crowds my space, cupping my face in both of his hands. His knuckles are split and bloody. "If I could be different, Sheena, I would do it for you."

"Excuses," I hiss.

He drops his forehead to mine, stealing some of my precious air supply and surrounding me with his familiar scent.

"Does it even matter that I love you?" Quaid asks.

There it is. The twist of the knife. Hearing him say it again threatens to tear my careful composure to pieces, so I scoff and shove him back a step.

"Because my love made such a difference." I hear the bitterness in my voice. Why should I bother hiding it?

I look at Idris, and he steps forward with a grim expression. "Do try not to go on a murderous rampage any time soon, human," he says.

Quaid shifts his focus off of me, and I can breathe again.

"I won't," he says. "I'll leave the enclave alone."

No one responds. Those are just words, after all. It remains to be seen if he'll stick to them.

Idris activates the portal, his eyes fixed politely on the opposite wall. Only my resolve holds me still as Quaid walks toward the blue swirling lights. My childhood friend stops by the portal, his shoulders slumped.

"Loving you destroyed me, Sheena. For your sake, I wish we'd never met."

Magic rises within me. I can't change the past, even if I wanted to, so it fizzles out. Quaid steps into the portal, and it closes with a pop.

The hateful bastard stole the last word. I focus on that, letting the irritation fuel me. If I don't, I might worry that his love destroyed me, too.

I look away from the fading blue sparkles to find all three men staring at me like you might look at a beloved pet that recently started foaming at the mouth.

I roll my eyes and brush my hair back over my shoulder, ignoring how my fingers tremble. "Now that he's gone, we can focus on what's actually important. Killing Leona."

"Indeed," Idris says, sinking down into an ornate chair. "I forgot someone monopolized your attention during the strategy meeting. I suppose you want to know the plan now."

"I—"

"Hold up, baby, we can't just gloss over this," Gideon says, trailing off. He frowns like he's hurting on my behalf and rubs his chest.

I reach for him and—

I lose control of all my bodily functions.

Not again. Not now.

I feel myself turn to leave the room, and I'm powerless to stop it. They won't know what's happening. They'll think I'm just storming off. *Shit. Please, someone question this.*

"Don't walk away when he's talking to you, Sheena. That's fucked up."

Callum sounds pissed, but I can't stop, can't even speak. I'm only two feet from the door.

"Just let her go," Idris sighs. "There is no reasoning with her right now."

"No, she doesn't get to run this time."

Callum latches onto my arm and spins me around. His mouth is opening to lay into me some more when our eyes meet.

"Oh fuck. *Fuck.*"

Callum wraps his arms around me tightly, bracing his foot against the closed door, then twists his head toward Gideon and Idris. They both spring to their feet the second they see the look on his face. I shudder internally with relief.

"Leona is here."

CHAPTER SEVENTEEN

CALLUM

I sense Sheena's terror and strengthen my grip, locking my arms around her. That witch isn't getting her hands on my girl.

"Idris," I call out. I may not know our battle strategy, but we hammered out a game plan for how to handle Leona's summoning magic after the first time she tried to force Sheena to return to her.

He gently places his hands on both sides of her face, then she slumps in my arms, unconscious. I hold her up, relieved he was able to put her to sleep so quickly.

"What's next?" I ask Idris, letting Gideon take Sheena from me. He lays her on the bed and secures her with the restraints we prepared. His movements are tender but methodical. I can see his arms shaking. I should have offered to do it so he didn't have to.

Heavy pounding rattles the exterior door. Idris disappears to answer it, then returns with his sister.

"The witch is here," Zara says.

"We are aware," Idris drawls, pointing at Sheena's unconscious form bound to the bed.

"How was I to know?" The fae queen sniffs. "I don't question what happens in your bedroom, brother, as long as you don't poke your head into mine."

Idris' skin turns faintly green, and I get the feeling Zara doesn't need to worry about her older brother looking into her personal business any time soon.

"Who let her into the realm?" I ask the queen, refocusing the conversation back where it belongs.

She shrugs. "My spies tell me it's difficult to say with any certainty."

I'm sure her spies worry about the consequences of making false reports, but there's no way she doesn't have an inkling.

"You are lying," Idris accuses her, no inflection in his voice.

Her eyes spark with anger. "Are you challenging my honor?"

I barely hold in my groan. I thought we were past their sibling rivalry, but if this is what it's like to be in the same room as Ciprian and I, I've got some apologies to make once we go home.

"I would not dream of it, dear sister. It is merely your transparency I will question until my dying breath."

Zara sighs like he spoiled her fun. "That day may come sooner than you think if the Court of Suns gets its way."

"Those traitors," Idris spits. "Making deals with a witch."

He waves his hands, and a cabinet materializes out of thin air. Idris throws open the doors to reveal row after row of gleaming swords. I scan the room with narrowed eyes. *How many damn glamours have been hanging over our heads while we slept?*

"Desperation is a tricky bedfellow for many. Even for the folk," Zara says, her voice hollow.

I watch her carefully and notice Gideon doing the same. She's been a part of every step of the planning process, but can we really trust her? I step so that I'm a barrier between her and Sheena's unconscious form. Neither fae misses the significance of my movement, but I'm not trying to be subtle. They can keep their cloak and dagger bullshit. I want Sheena and Gideon safe, and pretty much everyone else can get fucked.

"Something to say, Callum?" Idris asks.

"Since you asked, I want to know if your sister plans to fight with us or hand Sheena over the second the wind changes?"

"Such disrespect," Zara snaps, her eyes brimming with rage.

I hold my ground. Temper and arrogance aren't new to me, and they certainly aren't enough to get me to back down when Sheena's safety is at stake.

"I don't give a damn about your pride," I say, looking to where Sheena lays still on the bed. "I've trusted the wrong people with her safety before, and I won't make that mistake again."

When Zara looks at my girl, there's a curious shimmer in her eyes. "What must it be like to inspire such loyalty?" She whispers, eyes distant.

The silence that follows is so absolute that it takes on a life of its own. The queen herself is the one to break it. Zara lets out a surprisingly high-pitched giggle and removes her crown, tossing it carelessly on the velvet chase lounge.

She elbows her brother away from the cabinet and selects a wicked looking rapier with a curved blade. The hilt is ornate but worn, and she wields it with ease. When she looks up at Idris with a delighted smile, I brace myself for a blow that never comes.

"I've been looking for this sword for years, Idris. How despicable of you to stash it here."

She tests the weight, then lunges, plunging the blade deep into the upholstery of an unsuspecting chair. It glides smoothly through the fabric and stuffing, the point coming out the other side along with a cloud of feathers.

Zara's smile is chilling. I'm relieved she didn't turn the blade on me. Like she somehow senses my thoughts, the strange fae shoots me a mischievous wink.

"Come along, everyone. We have witches to kill."

After going over the battle plan, Gideon stays with Sheena while I go with the two bloodthirsty fae to the armory. They were already armed with swords, but apparently they didn't have enough blades. They've been hiding daggers in their clothes for the past five minutes. I was impressed at first, but it's starting to make me nervous.

Why do they need so many? Do they plan to throw them around like darts?

I grab a couple of blades, but honestly, I dozed off during the mandatory class on medieval weaponry at the academy. While I'm confident in my ability to defend myself, I'm usually the one who gathers intel. Gideon's the enforcer. He always has been.

"Our top priority must be the talisman," Idris says as he straps another blade to his thigh. "Once we secure the jeweled dagger, the battle will be won."

I nod, my nerves buzzing. I'll be Sheena's last line of defense if something goes wrong. *I can't let her down.*

"Once I see the signal, I'll bring Sheena out," I say. "We'll use her wishes to get the witch and deal with anyone else who refuses to surrender."

"My army will focus on the soldiers from the Court of Suns," the fae queen vows.

Zara clamps a knife between her teeth, tightening a bizarre leather corset over the top of her tunic. I'm trying not to watch too closely because I don't want her or Idris to turn me into a pincushion, but this is the weirdest lingerie I've ever seen.

Instead of whatever shit typically makes corsets hold their shape, she's using—gods help us—knives. Each blade is spaced out, a quarter of an inch between them. The queen cinches it tighter, and I wince. I've never worn anything like it, but it looks uncomfortable as fuck.

A horn sounds outside, and a violent anticipation settles over the room.

"That's my cue," I say, running my hand through my hair.

I look at Idris. We aren't exactly friends, but I don't want him dead. Hugging the fae would be weird, though, so I'm not sure what the protocol is here. If it were Ciprian, he'd crack a joke, and I'd punch him in the arm and tell him to focus.

Idris solves my dilemma by tapping his blade against my smaller weapon. "Keep her safe, Callum," he says.

"Kill Leona for her."

We exchange grim smiles, and I leave without another word. I'll swap out with Gideon, and hopefully by the end of the day, we'll be able to go home.

Weaving through the corridors, I dodge the organized chaos. The silver crackle and glow of fae magic is everywhere I look. Soldiers form up in groups, their ranking officers shouting brisk orders at them.

Some of these soldiers won't make it home tonight. I'm surprised they're willing to take that risk at only the word of their queen, so I'm on my guard for hard looks and grumbling, but many of them actually seem excited about the battle. *Don't they get sick of the fighting? Are they really this numb to death?*

There's a smaller squadron organizing near one of the massive windows. My eyes snag on a young fae staring up at the suns. A pendant hangs from a chord around his neck. He grips it between his fingers, his lips moving steadily. Even though I can't hear him, his intent is clear. The fae is praying to one of the suns, or maybe both.

The practice was commonplace generations ago, but belief in the old gods is basically dead now. Only good for a swear or two —it isn't something I've ever thought too deeply about.

Seeing the combination of old world faith and fear from a fucking kid hits me hard.

I open my senses, something I usually avoid doing in a crowd, and a wave of desires slam into me like a punch to the gut. Sexual lust is the easiest for me to make out. There's some of that even here on the edge of battle, but I also catch wisps of other wants from every warrior here. There are the longings I expect, like glory, honor, and legacy, and then there are others—softer forms of desire—for love, safety, and peace.

I close my senses and force my feet to keep moving. Knowing that we brought this battle here makes this reality harder to face.

When I pass the oversized painting of Idris, I pause. I can't help myself. *Was he ever like that young fae praying in the window?* There's a hard look in those icy blue eyes that's familiar even in canvas form, but I've seen him soften. Once for the two frightened fae women we rescued from Leona's village, then again for Sheena, when pain was stealing the life from her.

I shudder at the reminder of why this battle is necessary. Leona's ambitions are dangerous, and they won't stop with my girlfriend. We fight because we have no choice.

GIDEON

I PROWL BACK AND FORTH as I wait for Callum to come back. It feels like I swallowed lightning. My skin buzzes with excitement, nerves, and a healthy dose of dread. I've been in plenty of dangerous situations, but as I listen to the shouts coming from outside these rooms, I know nothing I've experienced compares to this.

I could die today.

Even stretched out on the bed unconscious, Sheena shows signs of strain. Her hands are clenched into fists, and there are tiny grooves carved in the skin of her forehead.

In a flash, I move to her side and unclench one pale hand until I can weave our fingers together. Feeling her reassuring heat settles something inside me. It's probably the only thing keeping me from shifting into my lion and tearing this room to shreds.

The door creaks open, and Callum appears. He takes one look at me and rushes to the bed. "How is she?"

"No change."

"And you?"

I swallow, looking up at him and shaking my head. I don't know how to answer that. Callum presses his forehead to mine and sinks both of his hands into my hair.

"No risks," he says. "Promise me?"

"But Sheena—"

"Would be devastated to lose you," he interrupts, using his grip on my curls to lift my head up. "Courage is great, but I'd rather have a long life with you both than a tragic war story."

"Okay, sure, but I'm going to do everything I can to grab that talisman."

Callum kisses me with a desperation that surprises me. It lacks his usual finesse, but he makes up for it with passion. When he pulls back, we're both a little breathless.

"Please, Gideon."

"I'll be careful," I promise, fully intending to keep it this time. I dip down to press a kiss to Sheena's cheek. Her skin is warm against my lips. It steadies me. "Watch over her."

"With my life," Callum says.

I nod, then turn to leave. Stopping at the door, I give them one last look. Callum's skin is paler than I've ever seen it, but his expression is fierce. Sheena's chest rises and falls steadily with her breathing. They're so beautiful. Even in this nightmare, they're my everything.

If this is the last time I see them . . . No. It won't be. I won't let that happen. I'll fight for them. For us. Until the day I die, I'll fight tooth, talon, and claw for our future.

The door closes with a firm thud behind me, and I leave my fear behind. I'll do more than fight for Sheena and Callum today. I'll win for them.

Stepping out onto the turret, the wind tosses my hair back as I watch the battle unfold below. The bridge is up, so no one can get to the castle on foot. Zara's soldiers line up in tight formation in the courtyard, stepping through large, swirling, silver portals. That's where the organization ends.

As soon as they step out into the fray, the disciplined orders are replaced with screams and clanging blades. Spells fly around the open field to my left, stretching all the way into the dense woods to the west. I can taste the magic in the air, the subtle flavor of fae powers mixing with the thick, earthy tang of witchcraft.

Dozens of witches fight alongside soldiers from the Court of Suns. I don't understand how Leona convinced anyone to do her dirty work, but she managed it somehow. As soon as I track her down, I'll make her regret it.

I scan the battlefield for her, snorting when I don't immediately spot anyone wearing bright pink or yellow polka dots. Leona won't be able to hide from me forever. Closing my eyes, I focus on my shift. I visualize the massive, white qamarion bird we saw in the forest, feeling my muscles and bones change. The pain is blinding but gone in a second.

When I flick my eyes open, the world around me is sharp and in crisp focus. My talons scrape against the smooth stone as I launch myself off the wall, and I feel the joy of the free fall as currents of air push at me from all sides.

I thrust my wings out wide, adjusting my metallic feathers until I'm gliding high above the ground. Being suspended in the air is amazing, but I really want to feel the grass under my paws.

Scanning the ground, I spot a group of struggling fae soldiers from the Court of Stars. Wearing silver and black, about seven or eight of them are pinned back against the moat, fighting against a much larger force. They're doing their best, but it's only a matter of time before they fall into the water or die.

Pinning my wings back, I shoot forward like a missile. It's faster than I've ever flown before, but the enemy fae in their orange armor are easy to spot. They don't identify me as a threat until it's far too late.

Just before I hit the ground, I shift into my lion form and use two of their bodies to cushion my landing. Their bones snap beneath me, and I roar with triumph. One man swings a sword at my head, but I dodge easily, tearing open his throat with my claws.

Soldier by soldier, I slash and claw my way through the group until there are none left standing. I've never killed so many. Looking down at their bodies, I feel nothing but satisfaction. Maybe I'll throw up or freak out later, but there's no time for that now.

My fae allies watch me with relieved horror. They're glad I'm on their side, but their uneasy expressions tell me they don't trust how easily I defeated their enemies. I incline my head to the group, then sprint further into the melee.

Screams, blood, magic, fear. It all blends together as I search for Leona. Every direction I turn, panicked fae fall over their feet to get away. A brave few choose to face me, and I do my best to make their deaths quick. By the time I find the first witch, my paws and mane are soaked and matted with blood.

I study the witch from a distance. She has dark hair, umber skin, and a grin on her face that doesn't belong near this much death. Even though I don't recognize her, her witch magic is unmistakable. She throws a bright green spell at a group of fae, and they fall to the ground, screaming and writhing in pain.

Anger tears through me as I creep toward her, keeping as low to the ground as I can. When I'm within range, I pounce, putting all my force into the lunge. As I'm flying through the air, the witch spots me and throws her hands up. An explosion of pain rips through my side, and green light momentarily blinds me.

I roar and knock her on her back, biting and tearing through one of her hands and pinning the other beneath my bloody paw. She screams in pain, a world of malice in her eyes as she watches me fling her severed hand to the side.

She's lucky to be alive. She wouldn't be if I didn't have questions I need answered. I shift back into a man, ignoring the burning pain on the right side of my body where her spell hit me.

"Where is Leona?" I demand.

"Fuck you, shifter," she says, spitting in my face.

I dig my fingers into the bloody stump where her right hand used to be. She screams, staring in horror at her mutilated limb. I'm surprised she hasn't passed out. Shock is probably numbing the worst of her pain.

"Let's try this again."

I push down hard on her remaining hand until I feel the bones shift under my grip. If I increase the pressure much more, things will start snapping. I know it, and from the way her eyes bulge, so does she.

"Where. Is. Leona?"

I increase the pressure bit by bit until a panicked whine slips out of her.

"In the forest to the north," the witch pants out, voice pained and angry. "She has a campsite there."

She could be lying to me. It's not like I have any definite way of knowing, but shit, I'm short on time here. *People are dying*.

"Good luck," I say to her, watching the confusion flicker in her eyes. "Maybe you'll come to in time to stop the bleeding. Maybe not. If you do survive, think about this moment the next time you consider aligning with a lunatic."

The witch opens her mouth to respond, and I ram my fist into the side of her head, leaving her in a pool of her own blood.

CHAPTER **EIGHTEEN**

IDRIS

The sounds of the wounded and dying echo like a symphony of war inside my brain. I parry, extend, lunge, and retreat—the footwork and rhythm of battle beat in my blood like a drum. None come close to wounding me.

I answer the call of my ancestors and make war in the ways I was born and bred. It's energizing, it's instinctual, and gods above and below, I've never hated anything more. Zara fights at my side, blood and dirt smeared across her cheek. If my sister loathes the bloodshed like she used to, it no longer shows.

We cut down another line of soldiers from the Court of Suns and advance. It's easier than I remembered. Are my old enemies not as mighty as the last time we clashed?

From the corner of my eye, I see a lion dart toward the woods, dripping with blood. *Gideon. Did he spot Leona?*

"What are you still doing here?" My sister snarls at me, sliding her blade across an enemy fae's throat. He clutches at the ruined skin, blood pouring out from between his fingers as the light dims from his eyes. "Go find that witch."

I open my mouth to respond, but Zara turns her back on me.

My little sister doesn't give a damn if I agree with her order or not. She flicks her wrist, hurling throwing knives from her corset one after the other. Three soldiers drop dead during the handful of seconds I waste thinking of a comeback.

"Be careful," I shout.

Zara rolls her eyes and blocks a spell with a wave of her arm. It explodes against her silver shield with a sound like breaking glass. Orange fractals of broken magic flutter to the ground harmlessly.

"Just go, Idris," she snaps.

I throw up an invisibility glamour and slink through the battle, weaving through an obstacle course of magical and physical fights.

Near the edge of the woods where I last saw Gideon, I come across a witch missing her hand. At first, I think she's dead, then I see her chest rising and falling shallowly. I shake my head. Gideon likely wanted answers, but didn't have the stomach to kill the woman after incapacitating her. Perhaps it is a noble gesture, perhaps not.

Every fae knows the more enemies you leave alive, the more chances you have to die. Since I don't want this one-armed witch to sneak up on me later and blast a hole through my spine, I ram my blade through her heart.

When the witch's chest stops moving, I pull my sword free and continue into the woods. There's a chill in the air that not even the heat of battle can drive away.

I feel the forest watching me as I dart among the trees. I leave my glamour in place as a precaution. It means I'm leaking a steady stream of magic. However, being back in my homeland gives me more to spare. It's a good feeling, but my skin prickles with awareness.

Like a pebble in my boot, the vague change in the energy of the land is impossible to ignore. It seems displeased. I just hope it doesn't start interfering with my magic the way it's disrupting the food supply.

A low growl rumbles from the brush ahead. Golden eyes shine through the dimly lit and densely packed undergrowth. The lion sniffs the air, his giant nostrils flaring, and then the growling cuts off abruptly. Thank the gods that Gideon can smell me beneath all the blood I've spilled because I get the distinct impression he was about to tear me to shreds, invisibility glamour or not.

The lion pads away, its enormous paws silently eating up the ground. I follow, carefully choosing where I place each foot. I don't want to risk my head on the minuscule chance I snap a twig and trigger the beast.

A thick, hot gust of arid wind rustles the forest, and I grind to a halt. This is Court of Stars territory—our climate is chilly on good days, but frigid on bad ones. I've never felt wind like this on my lands.

Damnation, I need to warn Gideon, but I can't risk calling out to him. He doesn't stop, even as the air ruffles his mane. I'll have to risk touching him. I'm poised to reach out when a brown bolt of light shaped like a spear pierces his shoulder.

His pained roar rips through the silent forest as witch magic shreds his skin. Gideon falls to the ground with a thud, his enormous head lolling to the side. I smell burnt flesh and will him to move. The unnatural wind ruffles his bloodstained fur, and then cuts off.

I should have called out, even if it meant revealing myself.

Dismay trickles through the cracks in my armor. Another ally lost, stolen in this never-ending series of battles. The little djinn will be devastated. Sarah and Joshua. How will I break the news to them?

My glamour slips, and I cling to it with slippery mental fingers, torn between running to Gideon's side or remaining hidden and seeing how this plays out. An icy wind—natural, this time—carries the sounds of snapping twigs and heavy breathing to me.

Someone is coming.

Their carelessness will be their downfall. Gritting my teeth, I prepare to feed them their own liver. My magic tingles along the tips of my fingers.

The witch bends down to examine the felled beast.

Before I can strike, the lion surges forward, clamping his jaws around her neck. One moment there's a witch standing there, the next a headless body is all that remains. It topples to the ground with a thump, muted by the thick leaves and lichen blanketing the forest floor. Gideon reunites the witch with her head by dropping it on her chest.

He is alive.

When Gideon sways, I can hold myself back no longer. Leaving my glamour in place, I surge to his side, bracing his enormous body with mine and using the contact to erase some of his pain. I can't heal him, but without the agony of the wound to focus on, I hope he'll be able to hold out a little longer. As the tremendous weight against my side eases, I know I've made the right call.

Three more witches arrange themselves around Leona in the clearing, casting cautious looks at Gideon. I'm relieved to see no one eying the place where I'm standing. The longer my glamour goes unnoticed, the better chance we have of getting out of this alive.

My eyes are drawn to Leona. I wrinkle my nose. The witch has dressed herself in some sort of garish, orange trouser with a striped shirt of many colors tucked into her waistband. Now that I've seen her, I wonder how she wasn't visible from miles away.

Apparently, invading a foreign realm to steal Sheena's power and autonomy has not satiated Leona's need for attention. She also had to dress like a jester. Witches and their never-ending need to be noticed.

Once I look past her horrific clothing ensemble, I spot the dagger strapped to her hip. Excitement builds low in my belly. If she's willing to put the talisman on display, Leona believes her victory is all but ensured. It's both warning and opportunity, and my mind races through ways to use her hubris to our advantage.

There will be no reasoning with her. Not today. Not tomorrow. Not ever. This fight won't end until Leona and every witch and fae she's conscripted into her plans for domination are dead.

"Gideon, dear," Leona's shrill voice calls out. "You may be standing now, but how long before blood loss brings you to your knees?"

Gideon's ferocious growl in response is truly terrifying. It shakes the ground beneath us, and two of the witches take a nervous step back, their eyes darting around. Leona smiles like his reaction was exactly what she was hoping for.

"Now, now, are you really prepared to die for a djinn? She's not even your kind. If you surrender to me, no one ever has to know." Leona's face morphs into something kind and open, but the gleam in her eyes gives her away. Cold dread dances along my nerve endings. From the sudden tension in Gideon's body, I know he feels it, too. "The enclave would be spared from any further unpleasantness, of course. Think of your parents."

Gideon tilts his head to the side like he's considering her offer, and I take stock of my magic. It's a vibrating pool, the depth both invigorating and shocking after my time away from home. Even though I've expended a lot of power already with my glamour, magic trickles in steadily and replenishes my stores thanks to my connection to these lands. I can only hope it's enough to take down a megalomaniac and her sycophants.

The longer Gideon goes without answering Leona, the more her polite, polished facade peels back, revealing the ugly, rotting layers underneath. Her foot taps, and the delicate lines bracketing her mouth twitch. I brace myself, burying one hand in the lion's coarse fur in warning.

"Enough of this, boy. Kneel before me now, willingly or by force. The choice is yours," Leona spits the words.

Gideon bristles, baring teeth coated with blood in her direction. Without another word, Leona hurls a dark green spell at him. I throw up a shield, and her magic bounces off, ricocheting directly into the young witch on her right. The woman grips her abdomen, a horrifying cross between a gurgle and a wail slipping past her lips. She sinks to the ground and goes still.

Leona doesn't spare the dead witch a glance, throwing her head back as she laughs. "I see you've brought company. Show yourself, fae," she demands.

Ignoring her command, I yank on my glamour, stretching it to include the lion as well. The witches raise their glowing hands.

Moving as one, Gideon and I lunge into the clearing.

CALLUM

ECHOES AND CLANGS. The sounds of battle outside are difficult to tune out. I crane my neck, almost sure I hear scraping coming from the right—no, the left.

My heart beats against my ribs anxiously. *Am I imagining things?*

I tighten my grip on the blade in my hand, biting down on my bottom lip until I taste blood. The pain grounds me.

A grinding whine comes from the hallway and a door slams. The urge to charge toward the noise and confront whoever made it is hard to ignore, but I can't leave Sheena unguarded. Even unconscious, her face is pinched in a frown. I'm all she has right now.

Voices ricochet off the walls. Wait. They're coming from Idris' bedroom. I twist around to face the door, and then jerk to the left when I hear a growl. *Fuck. Someone is trying to confuse me.*

I move to stand at the end of the bed where I can see both entrances to the room. Magic can be used to disorient me, but it can't change reality. I just need to keep an eye on the doors and not let anyone get between Sheena and I. The hilt of my weapon digs into my sweaty palm.

Metal scrapes against the ground.

An agonized scream.

Hissing.

I catch a ripple in the mural along the wall. While fae art is prone to moving on its own, this is new. *Tear it down. Now.* Heart racing, I start with the ripple—yanking, tugging, and scraping the illusion with everything I've got. Usually I take a slow and steady approach, but there's no time. I need to shred this false reality right fucking now.

With a violent pull, it falls down like tattered confetti in a fun house. My blood freezes in my veins. The magic was concealing four fae soldiers and a witch. We're surrounded on all sides.

Barely a foot away from the bed, a blonde witch reaches for Sheena, her eyes bright with excitement.

There's no time to think.

Digging deep inside myself, I send my magic directly into the witch's brain. It latches on like a hungry parasite and takes control of the part of her mind producing lust. She gasps and looks at me, pulling her bottom lip between her teeth.

"Go to the window," I order.

She moans and lurches clumsily toward the glass.

"Jump out."

The witch pauses for a heartbeat, then hurls herself at the thick glass. Her body slams into the window with a sickening crunch, but it doesn't break. The glass is magically reinforced.

"Again," I hiss. I don't care what shatters first: her bones or the window. "Keep trying until I tell you to stop."

Another crunch. The rhythmic thuds of her body colliding with the glass continue, only slowing as the witch's body breaks down. The remaining slivers of her illusion vibrate in time with the battering motion.

It's a distraction I can't afford, so I tune it out and focus back on the four fae soldiers. They're dressed in orange uniforms covered with those damn suns—both of which I saw way too much of during our hike.

"It's not too late to leave," I say, hoping they listen to reason. "You don't have to do the witches' dirty work."

Or die for them.

Angry shouting breaks out in fae, but I don't need a translator to get the message. The soldiers draw their weapons and fan out, surrounding me and closing in. I brace for impact.

The bed bursts into flames at my side. I flinch. The urge to pull Sheena out of the fire and run is almost overwhelming, but there's not enough heat. *Fake flames.*

I don't have the power of illusion, but fae tricks don't hold up to my family's magic. I grew up in the fucking Hall of Nightmares, and I don't need to trust my eyes to protect the woman I love. I know what's real and what's not. *I'm a Casanell, godsdammit.*

Three of the fae charge me, weapons swinging for my head.

"Back up," I snarl, shoving a tidal wave of persuasion at the group. Tendrils of magic slip beneath their skin like poison. It's more than I've ever wielded before, but my powers are eager to be used.

I twist their lust, and the charging soldiers fall to their knees. Their pitiful groans are music to my ears. Satisfaction burns low in my gut, ten times hotter than the faux flame on the bed. One soldier tears at his armor. The second falls still. The third grinds against the rough stone floor, desperate for relief from the painful urges.

I could kill them like this. Drive them out of their minds with lust.

They've already lost control of their bodies. Pushed to the edge, all it would take is one tiny shove . . . I would be justified in killing them. This is war, and they're trying to take Sheena from me.

The young soldier praying to the gods before the battle flashes through my mind, and I waiver. The fae have never known anything different. They don't deserve to pay for Leona's crimes.

I don't give myself time to second-guess my decision. I drive the flat of my blade down against each of their heads. Knocking them out might be a risky choice, but I can't stomach killing them. Not like this.

I hear a guttural hiss and spin, my stomach roiling. The fourth fae soldier has Sheena's unconscious body clutched to his chest like a human shield. He presses his sword to her throat. Orange tinted magic sizzles along the edges of his blade, and the flames on the bed die out as his attention shifts. He's a flick of the wrist away from slitting her throat.

Digging deep inside myself, I scoop another stream of magic out, ignoring how low my energy has dipped. With everything I have left, I bring a shadow to life, hurtling it at the fae.

It reaches him before he can blink, and I force it down his throat. He gurgles, losing his hold on Sheena and his sword as he claws at his neck. She slumps to the ground, and I expand the shadow until the fae's face turns blue. He falls back against the wall, eyes bulging out of their sockets.

He left me no choice.

As the life fades from his beady eyes, he reaches for Sheena, magic flickering along his palm. My pulse pounds in my ears. *Over my dead body will he put his hands on her again.*

My shadow explodes. It's like I'm watching in slow motion as his head swells and protrudes at odd angles, then pops. Blood rains down on Sheena and me, soaking everything in the room.

Bile bubbles up in my stomach as my sword slips from my fingers. With trembling hands, I drag Sheena away from the mess, wiping some of the gore off of her face. At least she's not awake to see it.

I blink. The battering sound has stopped. I force myself to look over at the witch. She's nothing more than a crumpled heap of jagged limbs now, and I grit my teeth at how thoroughly the window won that battle. The panes are covered in her blood, but there's not a single crack in the glass.

I look away, sinking down at the base of the bed with my arms around Sheena. My insides feel scraped raw. I've used too much magic. It's okay; it has to be. I have no choice but to hold on a little longer.

GIDEON

My animal wants to shred, tear, and maim, and I couldn't agree more. Stalking Leona, I take advantage of the cover Idris' invisibility glamour provides as we wait for an opening.

Leona slings a spell at the spot I was just standing two seconds ago. It hits the ground with a sizzle, scorching the waxy plants to ash.

It's hard to believe this is actually happening. Leona knew me before I could read or shift. She snuck me my first beer when I was just fourteen. Now she's trying to burn me alive. She had us fooled for so long.

Sharp pain shoots through my side. I have to end this before my blood loss wins the fight for her. Leona will be able to see through Idris' glamour eventually, especially now that she knows it's there. But it takes time and concentration to break down fae magic. If I can keep her distracted, we'll be able to take her out.

First things first, get rid of her backup. One of the two remaining witches cowers behind Leona. As soon as she glances away, I pounce, slashing my claws up her chest. Her pained wail camouflages my landing.

The gashes I opened up on her skin hurt like a bitch, but they aren't fatal. Not like the spell Leona hurls at her head. She's hoping to hit me, but I'm already out of the line of fire. The younger witch takes a direct hit to the face and crumples to the ground.

Leona shrieks with rage and throws two more spells in my direction. Too bad I'm already moving in a zigzag pattern, keeping one step ahead of her vicious attacks.

Seeing her ally become collateral damage is too much for the other witch. She takes off, running into the woods and leaving Leona alone. I let her go. She won't make it far. If the land doesn't kill her, she'll run into the wrong group of fae soon enough.

I circle Leona as Idris comes at her from the side. He hurls a dagger at her chest. I'm shocked when the blade stops an inch from her gods awful shirt. It falls to the ground, but before it lands, Idris throws three more.

Leona blocks them all, but the defense costs her. She takes her focus off of me to block the knives, and it's the window I've been waiting for. Lunging, I barrel into her, feeling her ribs crack from the impact.

My animal instinct takes over, and I tear into her flesh like a monster. By the time I'm finished, she's unrecognizable. My chest heaves violently, and I take a step back from Leona's corpse to catch my breath.

Idris pulls Sheena's dagger free from Leona's hip. He looks at me with grim satisfaction, then takes a small, round ball out of his pocket. He hurls it into the air and shoots it with a magic pulse. It explodes, painting the blue sky purple with smoke. It's the signal we agreed on to let Callum know we got the talisman.

We did it.

Relief floods my body, and I sway on my paws. There's a shocking amount of blood dripping from my shoulder. Idris looks at the wound, a flash of concern passing over his face. It doesn't last long, but I'm not a fucking idiot—he's worried about me.

"Shift back," Idris demands. "You are putting undo stress on your wounds by making your body carry such ridiculous bulk."

As usual, Idris is a bossy ass, but I listen because he's right. I force my body to change, sharp pain stabbing through me over and over until I'm kneeling naked on the chilly ground. With a groan, I climb to my feet. My movements are slow and sluggish.

When I turn to look at my shoulder, fear hits me again. Without the fur, I can see exactly how bad it is. The top half of my arm is mangled almost beyond recognition—more meat than skin. I take a deep breath. There's no point in panicking and making my blood leak faster. It probably won't kill me if we get moving right away.

Gritting my teeth against the pain, I glance back to look at the fae. "I'm bleeding out here, man. There's no point pretending me dying wouldn't upset you, so let's get going."

I'm teasing, but I don't miss his flinch. It's followed immediately by the icy, irritated look I'm so used to.

"Do not make demands, shifter." Idris' magic tingles against my bare skin as he glamours a pair of pants for me, then heads back toward the castle.

With a grin, I take off into the woods, following him and the insistent tugging on my heart. Sheena is on her way. Everyone will be fine.

CHAPTER
NINETEEN

SHEENA

I wake to a dull pain in my heart and a chilly breeze on sticky skin. Both of my eyelids feel glued shut, but I can hear all kinds of noises.

Leona came for me.

She's going to capture me again, drain me dry, and force me to hurt everyone I love. I won't be able to stop her as long as she controls my talisman.

My muscles stiffen, and I suck in a deep breath. Callum's comforting, spicy scent fills my nose, and I relax a little. He wouldn't bring me out here if the plan failed.

I pry my eyes open.

"Sheena?" Callum asks, excited.

"What did I miss?" I croak the question through parched lips and a dry throat. Callum wipes sweat from his forehead. Dried blood and new silver strands stand out among his normally dark hair. "Are you okay?"

"Don't worry about me." He forces a smile, and there are new brackets lining his mouth. "They got the talisman, sweetheart. Idris just sent up the signal."

Callum picks up the pace, and a tiny thread of hope tugs on my chest, weaving itself in right next to the unfulfilled mate bond. *Gideon.* I can feel that he's alive. I should be celebrating, but there are dead people all around me. It seems wrong to cheer in the face of so much senseless death.

An actual battle was fought here. Over me. Guilt settles low in my stomach as I take in the dead bodies stretched across the grass. They are mostly fae, but I see a few witches scattered on the ground. Leona's loyal followers. She got them killed, but I can't help feeling like my powers are to blame.

Callum watches me take everything in, but he never breaks stride. He doesn't press me to speak or offer to put me down. I hate how the fae stare as we make our way through the crowd.

Two figures break through the tree line. One glides toward us with graceful determination. The other weaves slightly in his wake. *Idris and Gideon.* I tug on Callum's sleeve, and he sets me down reluctantly. I run in a wobbly line to Gideon, stopping in horror when I see he's drenched in blood.

"You're hurt," I gasp, panicking as I reach for him.

"It's okay, baby. I'll live." Gideon wraps his arms around me, his breathing shallow and raspy. "Leona's dead. We've got the talisman."

I pull back carefully to look at Idris. He studies me with his head cocked to the side like I'm some kind of puzzle to solve. Out of the corner of my eye, I see Callum check on Gideon's shoulder, but I'm trapped by the look on Idris' face. It drags me back to that meadow . . . To a moment where I felt too much and too little at the same time. *I can't go back there. Not now. Maybe not ever.*

"You got it?" I break the silence with a tinge of desperation.

Idris inclines his head, pulling the familiar jeweled dagger from his pocket. He holds it out to me, and my breath leaves my body in a whoosh. The weapon looks the same, but I feel nothing. *Where's the bond?* Idris puts the dagger in my hand, curling my limp fingers around it.

Still nothing.

A sinking suspicion spreads in my belly, and the sickly sweet smell of witch magic sinks into my nose. We're on a battlefield surrounded by fae and witch spell residue, but this particular scent is nauseatingly familiar to me.

I prepare to sound the alarm, but my tongue sticks to the roof of my mouth. The tiny hairs on the back of my neck stand on end. When I try to cover my ears, my hands stay stubbornly still.

How is this happening? Leona is dead.

Idris narrows his eyes at my continued silence, then turns his attention to the battlefield. Internally, I'm shouting at him, begging him to notice that I'm not in control. He doesn't. Maybe he thinks I'm being standoffish after what happened in the meadow, or maybe he just doesn't care anymore.

My body lifts into the air, rotating as Leona appears—very much alive—in a cloud of green smoke. The smile on her face is sinister with a touch of mania. It's the same expression she wore when she forced me to make her creepy pastel village. Once again, I am a slave to her whimsy. Several soldiers shout and point, but it's too late.

"I wish to take all the weapons." Leona's command pierces my ears. If I could shudder, I would. Desperate, I try to wall myself off and block her will, but it's like sand slipping through my fingers.

My magic goes to work immediately. All around us, knives, daggers, spears—you name it—start flying into a pile. Soldiers duck and grunt. Screams of surprise pepper the air, but the roaring in my ears drowns them out. The stolen arsenal hovers in the air behind Leona, blanketed by a hazy purple film—my magic in action.

Idris raises his hands to hurl a spell, but Leona is too fast.

"I wish no one felt violent or talkative," she says, not even bothering to raise her voice. It doesn't matter. My magic hears her loud and clear.

I watch in horror as Idris' sneer fades to a look of slack-jawed apathy. His hands fall to his sides, and my heart sinks deeper in my chest.

"Now, dear, really. I'm all for a vacation, but you made me travel all the way to another realm to meet up with you. That's a bit much, don't you think?" Leona giggles as she goads me.

I can't answer, but she doesn't actually want me to. She has a captive audience, which is her favorite kind. The power and control—she craves it for herself and her witches. I don't know how she fooled Idris and Gideon, but we've walked into her trap. She's enjoying every minute of our helplessness.

Leona pulls on my magical tether, and I float toward her. I pass within inches of Gideon's frozen form, seeing anguish in his brown eyes. His muscles are trembling, and I feel a flicker of hope he might be able to break free of the wish. That hope quickly morphs into dread. If he does manage to snap out of it, Leona won't let him live.

My feet sink into the grass at the witch's side. With a wave of her hand, the tension in my mouth falls away.

I spit in her face. Leona isn't expecting the move, and I see her fury seconds before her hand makes contact with my face. I don't care. Seeing saliva run down her cheek is worth any slap she can send my way.

"Still no manners, I see," she says, her lips pressed thin with anger.

"You aren't welcome here, Leona." My voice doesn't tremble. It's as dead as the fae bodies that litter the ground in all directions.

"Yes, and the other supernaturals weren't welcome on Earth either, but that never stopped them from moving in and taking over." Leona looks around at the magical fae land, as beautiful as it is dangerous, with a sneer of contempt.

"What did you promise them?" I ask.

She waves her hand and grins, a row of perfect, white teeth taking over her face. "The fae are killing this land with their constant warmongering. It's early days, but I felt it the second I set foot here. They've forgotten how to hear anything but the call to battle, so the realm's magic is corrupting the food supply as a warning."

"You promised to heal the land."

"Perhaps." She shrugs.

Leona looks over at where my men are blinking slowly. I don't think they are physically stuck, but they look possessed. Knowing it's my magic that controls them plants a sick feeling in my stomach. If I have to throw up, I can at least aim at Leona this time. Vomit can't make her ugly outfit any worse.

"How are you even alive?" I ask her.

She cackles. "A simple transmutation spell. Poor Whitney. She made a convincing decoy, but she won't be joining us." Leona glances at my mate and tsks. "Talk about overkill. If only young Gideon wasn't so enthusiastic with those claws, he might have realized the truth much sooner."

Jesus, she doesn't even care that her friend is dead.

"If I go with you, will you leave everyone alone?" It's the question I have to ask, but I know better than to trust the woman in front of me. Her malicious grin tells me any deal I try to negotiate is over before it even begins.

"You grow predictable, dear," she croons.

Her eyes sweep over Callum, then Gideon, before stopping on Idris. They dart back to me, brimming with excitement.

"This is quite an assortment of young, virile lovers." She sounds hungry, and I long to lash out, but my muscles are still frozen in place. "But surely you have a favorite. If I allowed you to save just one, who would you choose?"

It's an impossible question. Leona must know that. She just doesn't care. This is a game, a diversion to feed her twisted mind before she drags me back to that pink hellscape. Even if I play her game, she's not going to leave anyone alive who might want to save me. She already made that mistake once. She won't make it again.

I roll my eyes, taking a chance.

"To pick one, I would have to care." I make my voice sound bored. "I just needed protection, and they have muscles."

"You can't expect me to believe that," Leona says, annoyance flashing in her eyes.

"You can believe what you want," I say with a shrug. "I'm the last of my kind. I have to be practical or I won't make it."

"Okay, if they're just a convenience for you . . ." Leona's lips curl up. "I wish you would kill them."

Her words hang in the air like a guillotine blade poised to drop and sever my heart from my chest. Nothing happens. I'm so relieved that the ancient, purple djinn book was right. Talisman or not, my magic can't kill directly.

If my muscles were my own, my legs would have buckled with relief. Instead, I'm still standing upright, desperately playing the part of uncaring djinn to the best of my ability. Their lives depend on it.

"You know I can't murder," I say, letting exasperation color my tone.

Leona turns to me then, her eyes narrowing as she searches my face. "That's a shame. Thankfully, I don't have the same problem."

My heart skips a beat as she calls my bluff. Leona hurls three blasts of magic at each man, and I watch in horror as they stand defenseless before her, trapped by my power and skewered by hers. I strain against her hold, but I might as well be trying to move a mountain. Leona's magic hits them one after the other, and they fall to the ground, silent and unmoving.

When the bond in my chest starts to fade, I lose my fragile hold on my composure. The pain I walled off breaks free, threatening to drown me once more. I failed them. These fucking powers have destroyed the people I love the most. Now I'm going to live the rest of my life in a cage, knowing I wasn't strong or smart enough to keep them safe.

Leona laughs, and the lock on my legs breaks. I run to

Gideon's side, dropping beside him and pressing my ear to his chest. It's so still. His larger-than-life body doesn't move. His arms don't wrap around me. Even his curls hang limp around his ears.

When I pull back, I see Callum laying in much the same way; one tattooed arm stretched out toward his best friend. His olive skin is chalky; the healthy glow I'm used to nowhere to be found. It's wrong. Everything is wrong.

All sounds fade away as I look to where Idris lays still and alone. He's only a few steps away, but my body is too heavy to stand. I crawl to him, my trembling fingers wrapping around his wrist. My other hand cups his face, and I feel his sharp cheekbone against my palm. I close my eyes, then I feel it. A thready pulse against my thumb.

Wait . . . What? Can it be?

I've never been able to grant a personal wish before, but maybe this time . . . I stare down at Idris' unmoving body and press my fingers more firmly against his wrist. There's definitely a pulse. Whatever spell she hit him with didn't kill him. I want to go back and check Callum and Gideon again, but I stop myself. If they're alive, I can't risk drawing Leona's attention.

As I push to my feet, tears spill from my eyes. I let them fall, glaring at Leona. If looks could kill, she'd be melting into a puddle of slime on the ground. But I'm not that lucky.

"So this is it?" I point to the surrounding devastation. "You fuck over the fae, kill the people I care about, and then drag me back to your creepy little village?"

Leona nods, victory and a tinge of . . . Is that unease in her eyes?

My arm twitches, then returns to my side. If the witch is trying to control me, it's not working properly. When my legs surge forward, I give in to the pull and let out a hiccupping sob.

I'm only going to get one chance.

"I'd like for you to think of that 'creepy little village' as your home. But it's your choice if you want to be difficult." Leona sniffs haughtily, but I can see her underlying relief that my body is once again following her orders.

The tugging on my legs stops as I near her. I take one more step until there's less than a foot between us. She doesn't seem to notice.

"I think you'll find, I've only begun being difficult," I hiss, grabbing for the jeweled dagger tucked into her waistband.

Gideon taught me to move fast and always take the enemy by surprise. Leona's not expecting me to move without her command. My fingers close around the hilt as her mouth opens in surprise.

"I wish—" Leona sputters.

I don't give her a chance to finish her command. Letting the pain, fear, and anger she's caused fuel me, I plunge the dagger into her chest. Leona stares down at the hilt in shock, blood drenching her striped blouse.

I'm not done.

I yank the dagger out, then slit her throat. Red liquid spurts out, and her body jerks as she chokes on her own blood. I slash at her again. Leona stumbles to her knees, clutching her neck. I step back, and she hits the ground hard. Her mouth curling into a rictus of death.

I clutch my talisman between blood-soaked fingers, my emotions threatening to overwhelm me completely. Vaguely, I hear a popping sound behind me.

"Quickly, djinn. We're running out of time."

Dazed, I turn to see Zara approaching me cautiously as a silver portal fades away behind her. Blinking my eyes rapidly, I focus on her face. She looks so much like her brother.

Idris. Idris is alive.

That thought cuts through the last of my stupor, and I rush forward, stepping to where the fae queen kneels at her brother's side.

"Wish it. Wish them better. *Now,* Zara," I demand.

"I wish for the healing of my brother, the shifter called Gideon, and the incubus demon, Callum."

For a long, horrible second, nothing happens. I squeeze the hilt of the dagger until my bones ache, then my magic stirs inside me. It's faint. All that's left are some smoky wisps, but it's enough. It has to be. I refuse to accept any other outcome. Not when we've been through so much.

Closing my eyes, I push and pull on my magic, willing it to obey Zara's request. Though the fae queen spoke the words, the wish comes from the depths of my heart.

When my toes leave the ground, I feel hope. When my eyelids snap open, I feel determination. A sharp pain spears my heart, and the mate bond roars back to full strength. I feel so much love there's no room for anything else.

Black spots dance in my vision, but nothing can tear my eyes away from watching as Callum lifts his head and Gideon's eyes snap open. By the time Idris pushes to his knees, blood is gushing from my nose. Absently, I feel the last drop of power leave my body. In its place is a hollow, cavernous hunger.

The dagger slips from my fingers, and I fall to the ground, my vision darkening as a chill racks my body.

If this is the last wish I ever grant, at least it's one I wanted.

CHAPTER **TWENTY**

CALLUM

Sheena lays still and small in the bed next to me, surrounded by cushions. Her pale skin looks ashen and lifeless. She's been given a steady drip of my blood for twenty hours, but she still hasn't woken up.

I ball my hand into a fist. If it wasn't for her shallow breathing and the pulse throbbing in her neck, I'd be freaking out. Instead, I lay here beside her, feeling like absolute shit, and waiting impatiently for the moment I can look deeply into her green eyes and tell her what a fucking idiot she is.

I've been rehearsing the lecture in my head. I'll yell at her until she promises never to risk her life for me ever again. Then I'll kiss her until she can't remember anything but the way my mouth feels against hers.

"You're obsessing again."

Gideon sounds exhausted but calm. Even though he's worried about her, he's also proud that Sheena fought for her freedom and beat Leona. I am too, but *dammit*.

"She could have died," I whisper. I don't need to keep my

voice down, but I can't stand to say those words any louder than I have to. There's too much guilt.

"But she didn't." Gideon massages his forehead and sighs. "No thanks to me."

There it is. It's been five minutes, which means he feels bad again for letting Leona fool him with a decoy. I get why he's beating himself up—honestly, I do—but if Idris couldn't sense the swap either, it must have been an incredibly strong spell.

"Dude," I groan, throwing my head back against the pillow. "If I don't get to feel guilty, neither do you."

"You aren't the one who mauled a witch so badly that we couldn't even recognize her when she died and changed back to her actual form."

"That could have happened to anyone," I say.

He grunts in response, but since my ears are mostly buried in the soft bedding, I'm not sure if it was a 'yes, you're so right' grunt or a 'fuck off, Callum' grunt.

"How much longer do you think she will be out for?" Gideon asks.

I grit my teeth. *We've been over this a dozen times.*

"You heard the fae doctor. Could be a few more minutes or a few days."

"Translation: he doesn't have a fucking clue."

Neither of us were impressed with the healer who checked Sheena over. The old fae was determined to treat Idris first until Idris literally shoved him toward my girl. Thank the gods his priorities were in order. He wouldn't be alive if it wasn't for Sheena. None of us would.

Five more minutes pass, and I circle back to my earlier impatience. I need her to wake up.

Maybe she senses my desperation, or maybe it's just time, but Sheena's hand moves in mine. I shoot up, ignoring the aches in my exhausted body.

"Sweetheart? Can you hear me?"

This isn't the first time I've tried talking to her, but the excitement in my voice makes Gideon perk up, too. He props himself up on Sheena's other side, staring into her face and watching for the tiniest of movements.

"Come on, baby," he says. "Come back to us."

Sheena's eyes flicker open, dark lashes fluttering a few times before she jolts upright. Her chest heaves as her eyes dart around the room. When she finds Gideon, she gasps, reaching out for him with one hand and pressing the other to her heart.

"You're okay," she says, her voice raspy and barely more than a whisper.

"Thanks to you, baby." Gideon's deep, rumbly voice cracks. "I love you." He presses a soft kiss to her forehead, touching her like she's made of glass and might shatter at any moment.

Sheena's face splits into a tired, relieved smile. "I love you, too." She looks at me. "Both of you." Her hand reaches up and strokes the graying hair above my ear. "Callum, you're looking . . . distinguished."

I roll my eyes. I haven't gotten around to feeding. "You mean old."

"I like it." She bites her bottom lip and winks at me.

My stomach flutters. Nope. Not getting distracted. "How are you feeling?" I ask her.

"Sleepy, but tired of sleeping if that makes sense."

She yawns, and I nod. My entire body feels like one giant bruise with the worst of the pain centered on my sternum where Leona's spell hit me. A blow like that should have been fatal, would have been, if Sheena hadn't decided to risk her life to save me. That brings me back to the conversation we need to have.

"I have some things to say to you," I begin.

"I'm listening," Sheena says. She cuddles into Gideon's side, sighing when his fingers sift through her hair.

"What you did was brave but idiotic. You can never do anything that risky again." There's heat in my voice, but she doesn't seem intimidated.

Gideon presses a firm kiss to her neck, his stubble rubbing

against her sensitive skin. Sheena squirms into the mattress, and I sense a trickle of lust in the air.

For fuck's sake.

I grab Gideon's curls, yanking his head away from her neck. Their matching looks of outrage would be hilarious if this wasn't so important to me.

"I'm trying to talk to her if you don't mind," I say.

Gideon narrows his eyes at me. "I do mind, actually."

"I was listening," Sheena insists, a giggle escaping her lips.

"You can't put yourself at risk again," I repeat. "I need you to promise me you won't." I sound more desperate than I'd like, but fucking hell, I need some assurance.

"Okay," she says with a yawn.

"I'm not kidding—wait. What did you say?" I study her face suspiciously. There's no way she just gave in so easily. Maybe I'm dreaming. I pinch my arm just in case.

Sheena grins innocently, but her eyes sparkle with mischief. "I said 'okay.' I can only assume since you're asking me never to risk myself to protect you, that you're prepared to never risk yourself for me again, too. If so, I can agree to that."

"Umm—"

"Because I know you're not telling me to stand by and watch you all die unless you're prepared to do the same thing when I'm in trouble."

"That's different," I say, kicking myself for botching this already.

"Is it? How so?"

"Dammit, Sheena," I groan. I had hours to prepare for this conversation, yet somehow I still managed to walk right into her trap. Even worse, there's no one to blame but myself.

"That's what I thought." Her voice is smug, and I grasp desperately for all my earlier, carefully thought out arguments.

"You gave too much," I say. "You're new to all this, and you pushed your limits too far. How do you think Gideon and I—or even Idris—would feel if you never woke up?"

Sheena grabs my hand and squeezes it beneath the covers. "I'm right here, Callum," she whispers, her green eyes glassy with unshed tears.

"It was too close," I say.

"I know."

I hear the fear behind her words and wrap my arms around her.

"I can't promise I won't do whatever it takes to protect you," she says softly. "I can promise to learn, though. No more denying my powers. They saved you, so they can't be all bad."

Deep in my gut, I know that's the best I'm going to get from her. Even though anxiety is still buzzing in my veins, pushing won't change Sheena's answer. Hopefully, with the talisman in her control, we won't find ourselves forced to make anymore impossible decisions any time soon. I need her too badly.

"If you're done, I'd like to kiss my mate now," Gideon growls.

He and I make eye contact over Sheena's head, then move in sync to kiss the sides of her neck. She shivers, and I feel lust running through both of them. It sinks into my skin, hitting my blood stream with the sweetest rush. It makes me realize just how hungry I am. My incubus basks in the glow, eager for me to shut up and make both of them come.

I'm on board with that too, but before we get any further into this, there's one more thing I have to say. "Sheena."

"For fuck's sake, man." Gideon lifts his head to glare at me, but this can't wait.

"Sweetheart, I love you."

Sheena's smile could melt ice. Being the one to put that expression on her face is better than any lust I've ever tasted. Nothing could top it.

"I love you too, Callum."

She cradles my jaw in her hand and presses a kiss to my lips. I lean into it, letting her erase my pain and fear one touch at a time.

IDRIS

There are many moments from my long life that I cannot forget. Kirsi's betrayal is one. The moment I limped into a portal and left my homeland behind is another. Memories that linger with me to this day because the wounds they inflicted were too deep to heal. Some days, I wonder how anyone recognizes me. I scarcely recognize myself.

I fear I've added a new traumatic memory to my scarred psyche. Sheena's collapse—after she drained everything she had to heal me—cuts my brain to ribbons every time I remember it.

Wine slides down my throat, the tart, dry tang doing nothing to quench my dark thoughts. After the royal healer examined the djinn, I retreated to my study and barricaded the door with magic. Unfortunately, the uninterrupted time to think has confirmed my fear.

I care deeply for Sheena.

Just one full cycle of her moon and not even a fraction of mine, yet in the short time I've known her, she has managed to crawl under my skin. Like an invasive insect, the little djinn has burrowed close to my heart and taken up residence there.

It's hardly a hospitable environment for someone like Sheena. She wears her loneliness and longing for love on her sleeve like a banner for all to see. She'll freeze to death or perish from neglect if I don't evict her soon. Then again, perhaps she can withstand the cold. She did turn around and barter for a portal seconds after I kissed her in the meadow.

That memory makes me smile, like every other time she's shown me a glimpse of her ruthless, conniving potential. Damnation, I knew the risk of caring for her. I swore to myself I wouldn't, but she still made it past my armor. Sheena is as much of an invader as Leona.

I swill the rest of the wine in my glass and reach for the bottle. Empty. *How could another one be empty already?*

I lumber to my feet, determined to rectify the issue, but before

I get the chance, the door clatters open. The heavy wood slams against the stone wall with a bang that I feel in the very depths of my battered soul. Zara storms in. Her arrival is an unwelcome, if not predictable, moment in a day that's veered quite extraordinarily outside of my control.

"This is pathetic," Zara says. My sister looks at me, her nose wrinkling, and takes in my empty collection of wine bottles.

"I wish to be alone," I say, an undignified hiccup escaping my mouth.

"Yes, I suspect you do, but since your djinn is not here to make it happen, you shall have to bear my presence a little longer." Zara sniffs, then scowls. "The servants were whispering about a stench, and I see they were right. I worried you might have perished after all, brother."

"Hoped, more like."

"A great victory was won, Idris. Yet you wallow?"

I turn back to the cabinet and rummage for another bottle of wine. I've already consumed all the tolerable vintages, but perhaps—

"Only Death meets you at the end of the long road. Only there will you find no battle waiting." My sister's tired voice captures my attention.

She points at the spine of one of the ancient manuscripts stored among my shelves. It's a text about life and legend, older perhaps than this castle, yet she quotes it from memory.

"You note it well." I sigh.

"It was mother's favorite."

"Perhaps she remembered that passage. In the end. Perhaps it brought her comfort."

"Fanciful nonsense." Zara snorts, blowing a wave of dust off the shelf of neglected tomes. "It is far more likely mother spent her final moments before the poison took her cursing the monster she married and the devils she birthed."

"Never you, her darling daughter," I bait Zara, but she ignores the barb.

"Your life away from here. Does it bring you happiness?"

Her change of subject startles me, my head thick from wine and unable to pivot quickly enough to match her mercurial tendencies.

"I . . . I am still alive, am I not?"

My sister's whimsy is famed across the fae realm, her moods the stuff of legends. Nevertheless, when she turns to me, angry grooves carved in her forehead, I admit I'm at a loss as to how I've offended her.

"That is not what I asked, Idris," Zara snaps, slamming her palms onto the carved wood of my desk. "I asked you if your new life brings you happiness."

"Does happiness even exist?" I sink into a chair, too weary to redirect her. As a rule, we don't talk of things like this in our family, but I'm too deep in the bottle to dodge her queries.

"I would like to think it does," Zara whispers. "I long for a day when we both wake up and see clearly. Once we have wiped the blood from our eyes."

"What would we see?" I demand, caught up in this strange conversation despite my earlier reluctance.

My sister sighs, and her eyes go unfocused and hazy as she considers. "Something or someone worth more than battle." She sucks in a breath. "Peace, happiness, or even a risk worth taking."

A chill runs down my spine. What she speaks of, it contradicts eons of fae tradition. The very idea is dangerous, especially for a queen. I open my mouth to warn her, to shout gods know what, but Zara holds up her hand, cutting me off before I can begin.

"My wish for the both of us, brother, is that we shall be smart enough to seize it."

"And what would two people such as us do with happiness?"

My sister shrugs her shoulders. It's inelegant, a gesture below her station. Our mother would surely have boxed her ears for it. For some reason, that makes me smile.

"Gods if I know, but I hope we don't muck it up." Zara lifts her chin and snaps her fingers. I watch as the familiar silvery strands of her magic consume my empty wine bottles. "And enough of the damned ice, Idris. It's time you leave the past where it belongs and look at what stands before you. Your little djinn has awoken."

With that parting shot, Zara departs the room as suddenly as she arrived, leaving me to marinate in an uncomfortable truth.

She is not my little djinn at all.

Despite that fact, I long to check the veracity of my sister's words and confirm that Sheena's recovery is progressing. I could take her pain and banish any lingering discomfort.

Something stops me from rushing to Sheena's side. I don't have a single, blasted idea what to say to her.

I return to my quarters alone.

After bathing myself in cold water, sobriety returns to my body with a violence that may do lasting damage to my internal organs. Taking the coward's route, I crawl into my large bed and pretend Sheena's not on the other side of the wall. Loneliness creeps in beside me for the first time in many years. I banish the emotion and drift off, assuring myself it's better to sleep alone than wake up to a lover wielding a knife.

In my dreams, I limp along a dusty path, worn smooth by countless travelers. To my left is Earth's moon, a waxing sliver—a solitary, luminescent slice in the sky. On my right, Sipsi and Ahnsid bob along the horizon in tandem, bright and stark.

Two realms. One road.

I lift my hand to shield my eyes from the glare and freeze. The appendage hovers in front of my eyes, foreign and grotesque, like nothing I've ever seen. Old and gnarled, I examine my hand from every angle, noting the deeply carved wrinkles and paperlike quality of my skin with morbid curiosity.

I am old. Ancient even. Seeing the signs of time is jarring enough to make me glad there's no mirror to reveal the entire picture.

I resume my walk, making good progress despite my hobbling gait. At the end of the road, I find myself standing in front of a flowering meadow, the fragrant blooms stretching as far as my failing eyes can see.

If the legends are true, Death should come to greet me soon. I cannot fathom what form my demise will take. Perhaps that's why the specter of my mortality has yet to make an appearance.

A voice calls my name. I twist toward the sound, but no one is there.

I turn back to face the meadow again, and I see Sheena, her hand outstretched, reaching for me. She calls my name, asking me to step off the path and into the blooming wildflowers with her.

A gust of wind hits me from behind, and I glance over my shoulder. Bodies are stacked on both sides of the road. They're rotting and attracting bugs. The smell makes me gag. Swords, arrows, guns—all manner of weaponry, both fae and human, litter the edges of the path.

I'm reluctant to turn my back on a potential threat, but the meadow is so beautiful, and the little djinn is waiting.

I face Sheena again. Her form seems fainter now. Is she fading away? Am I too late? I cannot let that happen.

Terror rises inside me. It's followed immediately by anger. I don't want to live a life of war. That's why I left everything I knew behind for the Earth realm. Yet, when faced with the woman I want with the full extent of the violence I left behind, my first instinct is to look back.

My withered hand reaches for her, desperate to make up for my hesitation, but my feet won't move. Enraged, I try to force my body forward. The dream wrestles control away from me. Against my will, I back away from Sheena.

My view changes, and I watch from the sky as the old man hobbles through the bodies. With each step he takes, his composure builds. His face—my face—is lined by time but unmoved by the horrors that surround him.

His implacable stoicism is the stuff of legends. It's what I've always wanted, but somehow it feels wrong, and I'm torn. In death, my path remains the same. There's no conclusion to life's battle waiting at the end of the long road. No peace.

The fae legend was wrong.

Jerking upright, I wake with a start, sweat trickling down my neck. I can still smell the sickly stench of death mixed with the sweet aroma of the meadow. It's an odious combination. My stomach turns. Still too caught up in the dream to control my body, I retch over the side of the bed.

Gods help me.

NEXT I WAKE, it's morning. I'm surprised I fell back asleep at all.

I take careful stock of my hands. There's a faint line here and there and a smattering of scars. I shudder. After that dreadful dream, I'm swearing off wine for the next decade or so.

With a flick of my wrist, my magic whisks the evidence of my weak mind and weaker stomach away. I could call for a servant, but then someone would know that the former King of Stars can no longer handle his drink. That's a familiarity I cannot allow. The thought alone makes me want to crawl back into bed.

But I cannot. I need to talk to Sheena, and I've put it off for far too long already.

Dressing myself, I glance in the mirror to confirm I look like my normal self, if a little paler than usual. Time moves differently on Earth, so I'll age quicker there than in my home realm. It's never bothered me before, since life in the fae court often ends with a sudden abridgment for most folk. Perhaps one day I'll see those wrinkled hands again, but at least I'll have time to prepare for the sight.

I knock on the door to Sheena's room. A shirtless, rumpled incubus answers. Gone are the silver streaks in his hair. Callum looks model perfect again and none too happy to see me.

"Dude, it's early," he grumbles, slumping against the frame.

Since he's clearly been fed a heaping helping of lust recently, I would think he would be in a better mood.

"I would like to speak with her."

"Well, in that case—" He yawns, and I see an unseemly number of his teeth. "You're actually late. She took off a while ago to meet with your sister."

Gideon pulls the door open wider, joining him, and I'm relieved to see the worst of his injuries have healed. The last time I saw him, there wasn't an inch of his monstrous body that wasn't dripping blood.

"Why is she meeting with Zara?" I demand. *And why was I not informed?*

Callum shrugs, and I swallow my annoyance. They claim Sheena is the love of their lives, yet it never dawns on them to ask her pertinent questions about her plans. *Do they not realize how often she schemes and plots?*

"If you happen to see her, please inform her I would like a word."

"Will do." Gideon grins, then Callum closes the door in my face.

CHAPTER TWENTY-ONE

SHEENA

Just get it over with, Sheena. I kick myself into action, clearing my throat to draw the servant's attention.

"I'd like to speak to the queen, please." I tack the last bit on as a courtesy, but the servant still scurries off with a disapproving scowl on his face. It's impossible to tell if he's offended that I'm trying to speak to his queen or just annoyed I'm talking to him at all.

I tap my foot against the shiny marble floor while I wait, blinking a few times as the polished stone shows me my own reflection. After refilling my magical well, my power crackles inside me. One strand of hair lifts on its own. *Dammit.* I tuck it behind my ear and resist the urge to scuff up the shiny floor.

Everything has changed so quickly for me. But I can't forget that it hasn't been long since I was living in a rusty, old RV, working a cash only, don't ask questions job in the middle of nowhere. Now I'm in two relationships and finally in control of my powers.

The jeweled dagger stuffed into the back of my jeans rubs against my skin uncomfortably. While the fake one turned into a simple kitchen knife as soon as Leona died, this one is authentic. It's a constant reminder of all the sacrifices made to keep me safe. I don't have to keep it on me all the time to control my magic, but after the trouble we went through to get it, I have no intention of letting it out of my sight.

The fae servant comes back, his cheeks flushed and splotchy. *What's that about?* I wasn't rude to him. He was the one who got snippy with me first. I force a smile, but his lips stay pressed in a tight line.

"The queen will see you now." He offers me an insincere half bow, gesturing with his arm for me to follow.

I trail after him down a hallway I've never seen before. Large oil paintings and intricate tapestries line the walls, each one depicting a battle scene more fucked up than the last. The fae's bloody history surrounds me on all sides like some kind of immersive museum exhibit from hell. It makes me even more nervous about the conversation I'm about to have with Zara.

I take a breath. *I'm doing this for Idris.*

The servant stops by an ornate, metallic door. It's made out of a sparkly, luminescent material I've never seen before. The craftsmanship is incredibly beautiful, which means I'll be keeping my hands to myself.

When my guide opens the door, he looks pointedly at his shoes, his face more red than any other color. "You may enter," he says.

I raise my eyebrow at him curiously, then shrug and step through the door into the most exquisite bedroom I've ever seen. My eyes eat up the decor, all silver, shimmery, and delicate. A meadow in full bloom is superimposed on one wall, but it's not a normal painting. The scene is constantly moving with plants blowing in the breeze and birds flying across the frame.

Once I peel my eyes away from the art, I notice a massive bed, piled high with plush down pillows and—*Jesus Christ*—naked women. There are so many tits I lose count. My hand comes up to stifle my shocked snort as I look away. I understand why the servant was acting so weird now.

With a glance back at the bed, I confirm that none of the ladies are the queen. One of the fae women smiles at me. I shuffle and consider bolting, but Zara appears before I can excuse myself.

"Good morning," she says, a devious grin on her face. "Sorry to keep you waiting, but I needed to freshen up." She arches one perfectly shaped eyebrow.

"I would ask if you slept well." I chuckle. "But I think I know the answer already."

Zara winks, then walks straight through the mural. I blink a few times and follow her, irritated I didn't notice the illusion among all the moving pieces. The queen tosses herself down on a settee, looking at me with her piercing eyes. Just like her brother's, they see way too much, but I'm not trying to deceive her. I just want to be taken seriously.

"Given that your bed was likely as crowded as mine this morning, I'm eager to hear what could possibly have dragged you from those comforts with such haste."

Translation: she wants to know what the hell I want, and she wants to know now. I nod, taking a seat in a comfortable looking brocade chair to her right and wincing when the dagger threatens to carve a second crack in my ass.

"Shit." I pull the blade out and place it awkwardly in my lap. The fae queen looks at me like I've just suffered a grave embarrassment and added insult to injury by forcing her to watch. "Still getting used to the damn thing," I mutter.

"You are in need of a sheath," Zara says, examining her nails. "Is this why you sought me out?"

She's laying the sarcasm on pretty thick.

I meet her eyes directly and clear my throat. "I want to heal your land."

Surprise flashes in her eyes. She blinks and it's gone, replaced by that patented fae detachment. Zara studies me for a long moment like she's working out a particularly challenging equation.

"I find myself curious to learn what such a remarkable feat would cost me," she says.

"No cost." I gulp. "Just one catch and one caveat."

"So direct," Zara purrs.

Something tells me she doesn't mean it as a compliment. I've made it this far, though. Might as well spit it out.

"My catch is that Idris stays and rules—if he wants to." The words spill out of me, and I brace for the queen's fury, but her lips curl up in a one-sided smirk instead.

"I never sought the throne, djinn." Zara leans forward, bracing her elbows on her knees, eyes glittering. She sweeps her arm toward the nearest tapestry, which depicts yet another battle. "What makes you think Idris wants anything to do with this violent mess?"

"He's homesick." I hesitate, unsure how much I should share with her. "And my caveat will make the realm a whole lot less bloody."

She narrows her eyes, watching me like a spider stalks a fly trapped in its web. "I must confess, I'm intrigued. What do you think could possibly make this land less bloody?"

"It's not actually the land that's the problem," I say, sitting up in the chair.

Zara scoffs. "In the interest of time, perhaps you'll consider bringing back that charming directness of yours."

"Okay, so the land is trying to talk to you. You've been feeding it nothing but blood; it's just returning the favor. The fighting hurts the realm, so you'll need to stop."

"This is impossible. War is part of life." Zara shoves a strand of her silky black hair behind her ear, holding her jaw at a proud angle. "Even if I wanted what you say to be true, it has always been this way."

"Has it?" I ask, eying the tapestry again. "How far back do your histories even go?"

Her brow furrows. "Most ancient texts were destroyed by raids during my grandfather's reign, but—"

"You were told it's always been this way," I interrupt, finishing her sentence and letting her think about what I'm insinuating.

Zara studies me for a full minute, then stands abruptly and begins pacing around the room. Her silence is eating me alive, but I let her circle me without breaking it. I just challenged a key tenant of her worldview. If the queen believes me, it will be because she reaches the same conclusion on her own.

Zara stops, her slippers squeaking against the floor. She whips her head around, emotion burning in her eyes as she looks at me. There's nothing composed about her expression. I feel like I'm finally seeing the woman behind the crown.

"Even if you heal the land, how could I stop the fighting?" She demands.

"I'm sure a queen is far more skilled in the art of diplomacy than I am," I say carefully. She rolls her eyes, and I smirk. "And if you wish for peace, how could it fail?"

"You plan to present my brother with his dearest dream, a fae realm at peace, then walk away from him?"

"I'm ready to go home," I tell her, a wobble creeping into my voice. "Idris deserves the chance to do the same."

"Noble words, Sheena, yet you plan to steal from him."

"That's bullshit. I'm no thief." I sit up, gripping the dagger.

She inclines her head in apology. "Perhaps I was mistaken."

The accusation pisses me off, but finding out why she made it would be like prying a brick from the middle of a wall. I'm trying to decide if it's worth the effort when she clears her throat.

"Very well. I accept both your catch and your caveat."

As we make our way outside, guilt worms its way into my chest. *Am I a coward for making this a unilateral decision?* Even if I am, I don't have the energy to argue with Callum and Gideon, and I don't think I have the courage to face Idris.

Not when I'm in love with him. After seeing him lifeless on the ground, I can't deny it anymore.

Idris doesn't want a life with me—not on Earth, as a refugee separated from his sister, his people, and his homeland. Since we met, I've watched him mourn the fae realm. If I can return it to him better than he left it, maybe that will repay him for all he's given me. Strength. Confidence. Even comfort, in his own way.

Part of me is glad this gift will mean he never forgets me. I'm selfish enough to want that.

Zara stops at the moat. Raising her hands, a wave of silver magic pushes the heavy water back to reveal a narrow bridge. She glides across it, and I rush to catch up. I'm following too closely to be polite, but I'm not about to get left behind. My talisman is amazing, but it won't make me a stronger swimmer.

Once we reach the other side, I heave a sigh of relief, glad to be back on solid ground. Zara lets the water fall back into place with great, crashing waves, and I have a sneaking suspicion that she chose the most dramatic method of travel possible.

After a short hike, we approach a field filled with neat rows of plants. A few scattered fae are working the crops, and they stop and stare in shock when they recognize the queen.

Zara waves her hand and a flickering silver portal appears. After a pointed look from her, they stumble over each other in their hurry to file through. The portal disappears, leaving the two of us alone at the edge of the field.

"That's a neat treat," I mutter.

"Perk of the job, you might say."

Zara walks onto the loosely packed dirt, her slippers leaving soft imprints in the soil. She selects a plant and yanks it up by its roots. It looks kind of like a radish, but the color isn't right. She uses magic to vanish the loose dirt, then squares her shoulders and takes a bite. There's an audible crunch and black sludge trickles out of her mouth and down her chin. She spits the piece out, wiping her mouth with the back of her hand.

"So this field is definitely affected," I joke, attempting to hide my disgust with humor. "Want to wish it all away?"

Zara frowns, showing her first reservations about the plan since we left the castle. "Are you certain you can handle the strain?" She asks. "My brother will bury a blade in my eye if something befalls you on my watch."

"He'll get over it," I grumble, pulling my dagger out. I grip it tightly between both hands, feeling my magic jump with excitement. "Let's do this."

"I wish for the fae lands to bear fruit once more and be healed of this terrible blight." Zara's eyes never leave me as she speaks, her flawless face tight with tension.

Her wish drops like a pebble above the deep well of magic within me. It hovers over the surface, waiting for my decision, and I know I could easily disregard her request if I wanted to. Sagging in relief, I run my thumb over the sparkling amethysts on the hilt of my dagger. The ability to control my magic is a remarkable gift—one we've all paid dearly for.

Blinking, I let the wish breach the surface, sending ripples out in all directions. The ripples become waves as my magic goes to work.

I close my eyes and think of Idris. The grateful shock on his face when I made him a sandwich. The flash of his icy blue eyes after I got the better of him during an argument. The tiny furrows on his brow when he took my pain away. The way he became my lifeline in Leona's basement, invading my dreams and replacing my despair with hope.

Heat spread to every inch of my skin when Idris kissed me. I've never believed in regrets before, but I'll regret not returning his kiss until the day I die. When he opened up to me about Kirsi's betrayal, he meant it as a cautionary tale, a warning against walling off my heart. But I was too focused on my own pain to listen.

Idris told me he knew the difference, and now I do, too. It's why I'm floating above this field, pouring my love for him into the land he cherishes. I'll leave a piece of myself here, the piece that will love him forever.

My bitter, guarded, argumentative fae protector. More beautiful than any man has a right to be. From his perfect eyebrows to the thick walls he maintains to keep everyone else out. I might have slithered through a crack, but I'm not stupid enough to think it's enough for either of us.

Idris will finally get to live a full lifetime in a realm at peace. His dreams will come true, and I will remember him in mine. Leaving will be agony, but I don't regret falling for him. Not now. Not ever.

I shove at my magic with everything I have. Something shoves back. I can actually taste the realm's feeling of bitter betrayal. It's an ashy copper on my tongue, but I saturate it with my magic, trying and failing to coax it back to its original form. The poison in the land doesn't want to go.

Hovering above the ground, I sense the soil beneath me as if I'm buried alive in it. Ancient. Sentient. Brimming with a foreign magic that makes every tiny hair on my body stand on end.

Clods of dirt rise to meet me in the air. They brush against the bare skin of my arms, testing my intentions. I'm an outsider here, my magic unfamiliar. I realize with a jolt that I cannot grant this wish unless the fae realm's magic allows it.

I'm no match for this level of power.

Once I accept that, I focus on my love for Idris and his love for this land. *Please.* I send that one word out, meaning it with everything I have.

There's a pause, a rumble, then magic explodes out of my every pore. I hear myself scream, and my mind goes blank. All I know is fae land as my magic goes to work.

When I finally sink back to the ground, I'm trembling with fatigue. My jaw drops as I take in the changes all around. Enormous plants have sprung up everywhere—thick, lush, and every color on the spectrum. Some of them are shades I don't even have a name for.

The cold, stoic Queen of Stars whips her head back and forth, alternating between staring at me and the bountiful crop around us.

I rub at the layer of dirt on my skin and swallow a sob before it can escape. "We have to check," I say. "Zara, did it work?"

I point to what looks like a much larger version of the original plant she tested. With trembling fingers, Zara wraps her hand around the base of the stalk. This time, she has to use both hands to pull it up. She doesn't stop to clean the dirt off. Her teeth sink into it and pink juice dribbles down her chin. I watch, amazed, as honest to god tears trickle down her cheeks.

I'm willing to bet it's against the rules to see a fae cry, but Zara doesn't even try to hide it. She rushes toward me, throwing her arms around my shoulders. Her embrace is crushing, and my eyes burn as I return the hug.

Pride swells in my chest, and I let my own tears fall, hiding my face from the fae queen. I've done what I set out to do. Even though the thought tears me apart, it's time to go home.

CHAPTER
TWENTY-TWO

GIDEON

I blink at Sheena.

"Wait, so you just fixed it?" Callum asks the question for the third time, and I barely hold back my groan.

"I don't know why you're having trouble with this," Sheena says, shooting an annoyed look at him as she stuffs clothes in her bag. "We have my talisman, I healed the land, and now we can go home."

She zips the bag shut so hard a few of the teeth jump off the track and leave a gaping hole between the sides. "Fuck," she mutters. Sheena punches the heavy-duty canvas bag viciously, letting loose a frustrated growl that sounds a lot like me. I look helplessly at Callum, who's scratching his head as he studies our girl.

"I've got it, baby," I whisper, tugging the abused bag away before she can do permanent damage. Focusing on the zipper gives me time to consider what I'm going to say next. Cal doesn't bother.

"Sorry, I am having trouble with this. You're telling me you casually healed an entire realm before breakfast, and you just want to take off?"

"I'm not waiting for a damn parade, Callum."

"Don't you think you should rest a little first?"

Sheena scrunches up her face, her hand balling into a fist. "No," she grunts. "That's why I'm actively packing. I'm ready to leave. There's no reason for us to stay here anymore." She stumbles a little over the last few words, and my fingers still on the zipper.

"Okay, I hear you, but at least tell me how Idris reacted," Callum says. "I bet he lost his fucking mind when you fixed all his problems for him."

Sheena's breath catches, and Callum takes a step closer to her.

"Sweetheart?"

She clears her throat, and I glance at her out of the corner of my eye. "He didn't say anything because I haven't talked to him."

Now we're getting somewhere.

"If you haven't told him, how do you know he's ready to go?" I ask, sliding the zipper closed and passing Sheena her bag. She hoists it over her shoulders.

When she looks up and meets my eyes, I see her pain a split second before I feel it surge along the unsealed bond. The pieces fall into place, and my heart breaks for her.

"Baby . . . are you sure?"

"This is his home." Sheena gestures at the fancy room, her movement jerky.

"He might feel differently now," Callum says, snaking his arms around Sheena's waist and resting his chin on the top of her head. "You've been through a lot together, surely you should talk to—"

"I can't." Sheena cuts him off.

The pain in her voice makes a low growl rumble out of my chest. This is bullshit. Who gives a damn if this creepy realm with its nonstop riddles and evil insects is his home? Sheena deserves better than to be passed over for some dusty ass rocks.

"You want Idris? He's yours," I insist. "I'll go grab him and drag him back with us if I have to."

She laughs, but there's no humor in the sound.

"Gideon, just because I want something doesn't mean I get to have it. I learned that a long time ago," Sheena says bitterly.

"Fuck that," I snarl. "Idris loves you."

Her bottom lip trembles, and I want to put my fist through the wall.

"You should talk to him," I say, ignoring Callum's warning look. "Or let one of us talk to him for you . . . We can't just—"

"Leave? Yes, we can, and we will. I won't put Idris in a position where he has to make a choice that would only hurt us both." Sheena pulls away from Callum, backing toward the door as she speaks. "He's been through enough pain. I can carry this alone." She stops at the door and squares her shoulders. "Are you coming, or do you two want to argue some more?"

I feel a chill in the air.

"We're with you, sweetheart. I just don't like seeing you hurt," Callum says, following after her with a sigh.

They disappear through the door, and I glance at the corner of the room and shake my head.

"Eavesdropping is rude, man."

I wait, but Idris doesn't show himself this time. I sniff again just to be sure, but my nose isn't fooled by fae glamour. Sheena might want to spare him from this choice, but it's his to make after all.

"Don't let your past fuck up your future," I say.

He doesn't respond, so I leave him to process alone, confident he'll make the right decision. *Sheena's worth it.*

Zara is pissed off. Sheena has been arguing with her for a portal back home for ages. Between my mate's nervous glances at the door and the queen's obvious stalling, I'm starting to think it would have been quicker to walk back to our realm.

Protect Idris, my ass.

She's protecting herself because she thinks she knows Idris' choice. She doesn't want to face any more rejection.

I glance at the door; he should be here by now. I swear to the gods, if he's sulking somewhere in this palace, drying his tears with silk napkins, I'm going to kick his ass.

The moment the queen finally realizes her brother won't be breaking down any doors to stop us, her lips thin. A tiny wisp of silvery magic pulses around her.

"Zara, it's okay," Sheena whispers. "Thank you for letting us stay in your home."

"I . . ." The queen sputters, at a loss for words for the first time since we met her. "I believe the gratitude is all mine." She dips her chin, the subtle bow a huge sign of respect.

Sheena's eyes well up with tears, and she throws her arms around the taller woman. "Take care of him, please."

"Idris is the strongest and most foolhardy of us all. He has no need for my protection."

"Maybe not, but your love . . . He needs that very much," Sheena insists.

"Perhaps it is not *my* love my brother has need for." Zara's voice is blank and emotionless.

I step forward. I don't give a damn who she is. She doesn't get to judge Sheena for this. Idris is the one making the worst decision of his life.

Sheena lets out a watery chuckle. "I know you don't agree with my decision. That's okay, but I'm giving him what his heart actually wants."

"No," Zara hisses. "You're running away with it clutched between your fingers, *little djinn.*" Sheena flinches at the nickname, but the queen doesn't seem to care. "You stifle your passion in the name of false mercy. Your retreat is a betrayal of every battle you fought side by side."

"That's enough." I growl deep in my throat, ready to step in if she takes it any further.

"Zara." Sheena sucks in a breath and looks down at her feet. "He deserves a life with no battles."

"You're wrong. My brother deserves a battle worth waging, not a coward's retreat."

Sheena's eyes flash, but her shoulders slump with defeat. "Retreat can be strategic," she argues.

The queen scoffs, her face twisted with frustration. "Indeed, it can, but when a cat runs from a mouse, no one praises it for its keen mind."

"I guess I'm an idiot, then." Sheena's face hardens. "Now, where's my portal, your majesty?"

Zara looks at my mate, tension radiating off her body in waves as she mutters in fae under her breath. Finally, she lifts her hands and a silver portal takes shape in the corner. "I did not seek to quarrel with you, Sheena," she admits.

"Could have fooled me," Callum grumbles.

Zara sighs heavily and touches one fingertip to the edge of the delicate crown on her head. "When you live as long as I have, you come to learn one of life's most powerful adversaries is regret."

"I get it," Sheena whispers.

"For the folk, I thank you. For my brother, I beseech you—"

"Please, Zara." Sheena's voice cracks, and I grab her hand.

I know why Zara is doing this, but she's hurting my girl. Through the bond, I can feel each word slicing her heart.

"Let's go, baby," I say, then step toward the portal.

"I wish for you to find what you're looking for, Sheena," Zara speaks softly.

I stiffen at her phrasing, reminding myself that those words can't control any of us anymore. They're just another tangled piece of symbolism in this mindfuck of a realm.

I tug us both through the portal. The palace and the queen disappear, and a heartbeat later, we appear in the woods near the compound.

By some stroke of fate, we land in the same place I ran to after arguing with dad over his inaction. Sucking in a deep breath, I smell the trees, the dirt, and a faint whiff of exhaust from the highway miles away. Tension I didn't realize my body was holding onto slips away as the familiar smell of home sinks in.

Callum comes through behind us, and we watch the portal fade away. Once the last glimmer of magic disappears, Sheena sinks to the ground, heaving sobs racking her body.

CALLUM

My eyes flutter shut as Sheena falls apart.

Gideon wraps his body around hers like he can physically keep her heart in one piece if he tries hard enough. But that's not how it works. There's nothing we can do to protect her from heartbreak, not while Sheena and Idris cling so stubbornly to their overdeveloped senses of self-preservation.

First Quaid; now Idris. Only heartless idiots could feel the way they do for Sheena and give her up.

Understanding Idris' struggle doesn't make me want to punch him any less. I swallow my anger and focus on showing Sheena that the part of her heart that belongs to me is still safe.

Sinking down on the dewy grass; I join the hug. Sheena ends up in my lap with Gideon wrapped around us both. While I won't ever use my magic to influence her emotions, I can communicate how I feel about her.

Her shoulders shake as she sobs. So I talk, keeping up a constant stream of my feelings. From the deepest moments with her to the really embarrassing shit, I tell her everything. How I felt when Leona took her, and how my stomach flip-flops sometimes when the sunlight hits her eyes. I tell her how she makes my incubus feel. Strong, unstoppable, safe . . .

It's only when Gideon chokes audibly that I realize my monologue has become graphically sexual. *Gods.* I just described how much I love the way her thigh muscles spasm around my face when she comes.

I'm supposed to be making her feel loved and valued, not like a sexual object that exists only for my gratification. Heat floods my face. If I could kick myself, I would. *Maybe Gideon will do it for me.*

There's a beat of silence, then Sheena giggles, and I sag in relief.

"Sorry about that," I groan. "My mind got away from me." I press a kiss to her damp cheek.

"You never have to apologize for that, Callum," she says. There are tears in her voice, but she seems to have a grip on her sadness.

Sitting in silence, the three of us watch our single, solitary, nameless sun dip below the horizon. It paints the sky with beautiful reds and oranges. The tears on Sheena's cheeks dry up under the final rays of the sun's light. When the sky fades to black, we stand together and walk back to the compound in the dark.

IDRIS

SHEENA WAS RIGHT to leave me behind. I was destined to disappoint her, and she was clever enough not to give me the chance. Instead, she gave me a healed homeland and a chance for the peace I've always dreamed of. It's a gift I'll never be able to repay.

I think I hate her for it.

The mirror in front of me cracks. Pieces of glass quiver in the air before falling to the floor. They shatter on impact, the shards scattering to every corner of the room. Each sliver glistens with a coating of ice, mocking me for my fallibility and sentiment.

My right eye twitches, so I force it closed. *Regain control.*

Magical outbursts are for children, not one of the most powerful fae in generations.

I swore I would not allow myself to be drawn into her orbit. Promised I would never let another woman wound me. Yet, here I am, unable to control my magic. My insides are as jagged and raw as if the mirror exploded inside me.

If I remain here, I cannot hurt her. If she remains there, I cannot be hurt.

Unless someone kills her. The very thought sends fiery rage ripping through my body. It cauterizes the gaping wound inside me. As quickly as it emerged, the feeling begins to fade, logic dampening the heat. I cling desperately to the remnants.

Gideon and Callum will love her, protect her, and care for her in a way I cannot. Letting Sheena go . . . Allowing my sister to send her home . . . It was the right decision. My brain knows it to be true, so I cannot fathom why the ache remains.

CHAPTER
TWENTY-THREE

SHEENA

How do you tell someone their mother is dead?

I watch Alina through the two-way mirror, but I can't muster up even an ounce of venom when I look at her. Blonde hair pulled back in a neat ponytail, her blue eyes are bored as she reclines on the bed in the holding room cell. She looks so much like Leona, but also somehow less.

Thankfully, Sarah volunteered to break the news to Alina. If I had to stroll into her cell and tell her I slit her mother's throat, I might also be tempted to tell her it was simultaneously one of the most horrifying and satisfying experiences of my life . . . I can't imagine that going over well.

Leaning against the other side of the mirror, I prepare to watch and listen. Killing Leona was necessary, but it's important to me that I witness the pain my actions caused. The last thing I want is to end up bitter, callous, and psychotic like Leona. No more numb for me. Some things hurt, and that's okay. I need to grow strong enough to take it.

Gideon and Callum do not agree. As I recover from everything that happened in the fae realm, they've become more protective, trying to shield me from additional hurt. They can't be logical when it comes to this situation, which is why Joshua is keeping them busy while I watch alone.

I rub my hands over my arms as Sarah opens the door to the cell.

Alina sits up straight, her boredom falling away in a flash. "This can't be good," she says, her voice coming through the speaker tinny and hollow.

Sarah lets the door close behind her and clears her throat. "Your mother . . ."

"She's dead, isn't she?"

Alina's voice has almost no inflection. It could be the speakers, but she might as well be reading a grocery list out loud.

"Yes. She's gone," Sarah says, her tone firm but gentle.

Alina's shoulders droop so slightly I might have missed it if I weren't watching her so closely. *Devastation? Relief?* Frustration sizzles inside me when I'm unable to read her.

"Thank you for letting me know," Alina says after a brief pause. "Can I go now?"

Her eyes flash as she looks at Sarah, and I cock my head to the side. She obviously wants to leave, so why bother hiding her grief when she could use it to gain Sarah's pity? What's her strategy?

"Nothing has been decided yet. This isn't as simple as just letting you go—not after what happened."

Alina accepts that with a brief nod, dropping back to sit on the edge of the bed. Sarah turns to leave, then pauses with her hand on the door.

"I am truly sorry for your loss. Leona was once a friend."

"Yeah." Alina huffs a short laugh, but there's not a drop of humor in the sound. "She was once a lot of things, wasn't she?" Her eyes go slightly unfocused before she closes them altogether.

Mine stay glued to the witch as Sarah leaves the cell, closing and locking the door behind her. I hear her join me in the observation room.

"She doesn't even seem upset," I say, pointing at Alina

through the glass. I'm not sure what kind of reaction I expected, but that was not it.

Sarah sighs and wraps one arm around my shoulder. "No. No, she doesn't, does she?"

"What will happen to her?" I ask.

Sarah squeezes my shoulder. "Well, I think for the first time in her life, Alina's future may be in her own hands. I expect she has some thinking to do, and this is the perfect time to do it."

Oddly enough, her statement applies to me as well. Alina is the one locked behind a door, but I'm also facing a future I never expected. My magic is finally under my control, and I have relationships I've literally killed for.

Twin pangs sear my chest, but I shove them down. There's no point dwelling on what ifs. I have to move on with my life, and this time around, my future is actually worth chasing.

IDRIS

Weeks pass, and I feel Sheena's absence more acutely each day. My sister and I initialize peace talks among the courts while monitoring the farms in our kingdom. The bounty is remarkable. The folk smile when they see me coming, and an infectious joy spreads across the realm.

If only it would infect me.

I play my role well, acting out the part of the wise and benevolent royal, even as my numbness loses ground to the all-consuming ache. Alone in my personal study, I can no longer support the act.

"Masochism doesn't suit you, brother."

Zara's voice pulls me from my miserable place of self-reflection. Opening my eyes, I cannot even summon the energy to give her the retort she expects. I simply close them again, tuning her out entirely.

"How long shall you be the architect of your own torment? Three more weeks? A year?" Zara circles me, her boots clacking against the polished floor. "Perhaps when she dies, her body withered by time, you shall emerge from this chrysalis of doom you have enshrined yourself in."

I flinch internally, but hold my tongue. I have nothing to say. Unfortunately, my sister is nothing if not persistent.

"There is joy in every home, warmth in every fae hearth—yet, you wallow." The noisy tread of her shoes stops, but I'm not lucky enough for her mouth to follow suit. "In truth, I should banish you."

I snort. We have not discussed whether I will assume my rightful place on the throne, and I am oddly reluctant to broach the topic. It's my birthright, but I cannot muster up even the slightest bit of enthusiasm for the role.

"Idris, the very sight of your dour, sallow complexion gives me indigestion. Yes, I shall banish you to . . . the forgotten lands."

"Whatever you will, my Queen." I incline my head mockingly, leaving my eyes closed. I don't have the energy to spar with Zara, but she will tire of toying with me eventually, then I can go back to my state of rest.

"Perhaps not the forgotten lands. That would be a waste. On the other hand, I could certainly use an emissary to the Earth realm."

"No," I hiss, my eyes snapping open against my will. The harsh light startles me, and I blink rapidly like some insipid owl from a witless children's storybook.

"You just said whatever I will, brother, and the idea has great merit for the kingdom," Zara insists. "You are the only one qualified, and given your connection to the realm, surely you have no complaints."

I glare at her, but she doesn't even do me the courtesy of scowling back. Damnation, she looks sad—an emotion she has no right to feel. Indignation bubbles up in my chest. Hot and uncontrollable, it demands retribution at once.

"You go too far, little sister."

"And you go nowhere, brother. The walls you coat in Kirsi's ice are nothing but cowardice. She betrayed you, yet you cannot leave her buried where she belongs. You are so mired in the past that you stare happiness in the face and spit on it."

"You know nothing," I seethe, shoving to my feet.

Zara studies me, her lips slightly pursed, eyes glassy with an emotion I dare not name.

"You are right." She clears her throat and lifts her chin. "I know nothing of happiness. But I like to think if it sought me out, I would have the courage to grip it with both hands and kill anyone who tried to wrench it from my grasp."

I open my mouth, but no words come out. Defeated and unspeakably exhausted, I sink back into my chair and cover my face with my hands. By the time I drop them, Zara is gone, but in her absence, I'm left with a bitter, uncomfortable truth.

I made a horrible mistake, and it might be too late to fix it.

CHAPTER TWENTY-FOUR

SHEENA

Even with my new resolve to move on, the sudden peace is jarring. I'm happy not to be running for my life for once, but the other disappointments are harder to ignore without the distraction of constant danger.

It can't hurt forever, though . . . Right?

I huff out a breath. I'd give anything to make my current task occupy more of my brainpower, but my mind keeps drifting back to memories better left alone. Physically, I'm in the fae wing of the compound, but mentally, I'm all over the damn place.

I need to face the cold, hard facts.

Idris isn't here. He's not coming back, and in his absence, there's a leadership vacuum. While some of the fae followed him home to their realm, most have made lives here and asked Joshua and Dimitri to stay.

That means the construction needs to wrap up on this wing, and I'm perfectly positioned to shave time off that process with my magic. With each beautiful space I shape, I'm able to let go of a sliver of pain.

"It's beautiful, honey," Sarah murmurs.

I force a smile. It's a pinched, pitiful expression, but she has the grace not to mention it.

Sarah has been coming over here with me every day for the past few weeks, translating my plans into verbal wishes, so I can finish the remodeling. She never pushes me to talk, and her quiet support means more to me than I'll ever be able to express.

"It's really coming together," I say, wiping my sweaty palms on the thighs of my jeans. "If only Zara could see it. She would love all the murals."

I point to the massive magical landscape sloping across the domed ceiling. It's a recreation of the meadow, complete with vibrant suns, exotic wildflowers, and the outline of a fae man in the distance.

Sarah smiles and hums in agreement, content to let me pretend this room has anything to do with the fae queen. We both know it's a love letter to the blue-eyed fae I left behind. Each room represents a moment we shared or a time Idris gave me a peek behind his walls.

"It's incredible," she says, running her finger along the leaves of one of the trees growing up and out of the wall. Part art, part living organism, it reminds me of the way nature and magic fuse together in the fae realm. "You've accomplished so much, so quickly. There's only one room left."

Her words are gentle, but they pinch my heart. A tear slips from the corner of my eye. I brush it away roughly and force another smile.

"Yep." I nod. "It will all be done tomorrow."

Sarah wraps me in a hug, and my tears soak her shirt as silent sobs rock my body. I cling to her as tightly as the vines winding down the hallway, and by the time we walk back to the shifter wing, I feel lighter.

As I close the door to my room, I hear water running in the bathroom. Smiling, I follow the sound and find Gideon kneeling by the enormous tub. He's squeezing a shocking amount of bubble bath into the already frothy water. Half a dozen candles line the lip of the tub, and—bless him—there's even a clean towel folded neatly to the side.

To my complete embarrassment, my eyes start leaking again. Gideon's eyebrows draw together, his dimples vanishing as panic transforms his welcoming smile into a look of complete horror.

I rush forward, throwing myself at him, and he catches me, letting out a tiny puff of air.

"Baby, why are you crying?"

"Because you're so sweet," I admit with a laugh, pressing a kiss to his cheek.

He grumbles under his breath, and a faint blush crawls up his neck. "You deserve it," he mutters.

I grin and start tugging on the bottom of his shirt.

"What? No, Sheena, this is your bath—"

"But what if I need help reaching my back?"

I make a half-assed attempt to reach the clasp of my bra, then pout. Gideon's lips twitch at my bad acting, but he plays along, spinning me around to make quick work of my shirt and bra. When the fabric falls to the ground, I sigh, already feeling more relaxed than I have all day.

Gideon's hands dance up my sides, stopping to cradle my breasts in each hand. My nipples stiffen as his callouses abrade the sensitive skin, and he groans.

"This was supposed to be a relaxing surprise, not some creepy come-on."

"Who said seduction isn't relaxing?" I tease him.

He pays me back by tweaking my nipples, then yanking open the button of my jeans. Our clothes go flying. Next thing I know, we're both completely naked and tumbling into the bath.

Gideon is efficient, but he's not very careful. Water sloshes over the edges of the tub, soaking the floor and extinguishing two of the candles. I grin and use my toe to turn the faucet off.

Tucking me into his chest, Gideon cradles me close in a way that takes away all the remaining tension I was holding in my body. He doesn't talk, and I savor the feeling of the mate bond vibrating between us.

If I'm honest with myself, I've hesitated to make it permanent, not because I'm unsure of Gideon or our relationship, but because I don't want him to feel my pain any more acutely than he already does. Except . . . What if he sees the delay as rejection?

"You know I want to be your mate completely, right?" I ask.

The only sign Gideon hears me is the slight stiffening of his body. The bond vibrates between us wildly like an old guitar string that's been plucked one too many times.

Nervous, I turn to face him. Gideon's warm brown eyes shine like liquid gold. Cradling his face in my hands, I bury the tips of my fingers in his soft curls and study his features. A wave of possessiveness crashes over me.

"You're mine," I tell him, surprised by how raspy my voice sounds.

Gideon squeezes my hips, and I squirm until I'm straddling his lap, bubbles bobbing all around us.

"Baby, you don't have to—"

"I want you, Gideon. I need you more than my next breath."

I shudder, remembering the moment I thought I'd lost him forever.

"When Leona . . ." My breath hitches, and a low growl rumbles up from his chest at the mention of the witch. "When I thought you were gone, I didn't regret meeting you or the pain of losing you. The only thing I wanted to erase was the time I spent holding myself back."

My eyes well up. I'm so sick of crying, but I need him to know I'm all in.

"My body, my heart . . ." I say, pressing my lips to his chest and feeling his heartbeat against my mouth. "Bond or no bond, my soul knows the truth about us. Gideon, even if the odds are stacked against us forever, I will choose you every time."

He kisses me then, and even though I'm straddling him in a bubble bath, it's not sexual. At least, not completely. From the first time Gideon kissed me, I've craved this—his focus, his care, the concentration he puts into every kiss. The way he never hides how much his desire for me consumes him.

"You know I'll have to bite you to make it permanent," Gideon says. "There's no rush on my end. I want you to be completely sure." He tightens his grip on me. "This thing between us . . . It's forever, sealed bond or not."

I snap my teeth at him as a joke and smile. "I know, and that's exactly why I'm ready."

Gideon kisses me again, and this time, I feel some of his desperation come through. He wants this a lot more than he's letting on. Realizing exactly how patient he's been makes me want him even more.

"Gideon, I love you," I whisper the words against his lips. "Give me forever."

"Fuck." He groans. "I love you too, Sheena. So fucking much."

Gideon stands, lifting me out of the water and wrapping me in a fluffy towel. His lips never leave mine as he dries me off. The intensity of our connection banishes the last remaining fear I have of sharing my full emotions through the bond.

I have nothing to hide from him.

When Gideon finally breaks the kiss, he falls to his knees, drying me so gently that my eyes threaten to slip shut. I force them to stay open. We've been waiting too long for this moment to miss even a second.

I bite back a gasp as he glides the towel into the sensitive dip at the back of my knees. Gideon grins at the sound, his dimples winking at me as he drags his lips along the soft skin of my inner thigh. The towel falls forgotten to the ground. The glide of his lips sends tingling shocks of pleasure along my skin as he maps my body with his mouth. It's unbelievably sexy and completely infuriating.

I spread my legs a little wider, hoping he gets the hint, but the soft caresses continue. When he gets to the crease of my thigh, I thread my fingers through his curly hair and pull. His golden eyes dart up to mine, teasing and burning with magic.

"What's wrong, baby?" He asks, and I shiver from the vibration of his lips.

I've never seen anything hotter than Gideon on his knees for me. I take in the view without shame, worshipping every inch of him with my eyes as light dips into the sculpted grooves of his torso. Goosebumps spread along his bunching muscles. He's as turned on by my visual exploration of his body as I am by his lips on my skin.

A strangled moan echoes around us as he licks me where I need him most. The acoustics of the bathroom amplify the obscene sound. I would be ashamed, except I'm not the one who moaned.

"You taste so fucking good." Gideon utters the words like a prayer, his voice guttural and hungry.

I suck in a heaving breath as he gives my body exactly what it wants. Not too fast, not too hard. There's no fumbling. Gideon drives me toward the edge slowly and deliberately until my legs shake and tiny, helpless whimpers fall from my mouth.

My orgasm crashes into me, consuming my entire body with waves of pleasure. Each one builds in intensity until I'm finally dragged under by the tide. Gideon scoops me up before I can melt into a puddle and collapse onto the cold tile.

"That was—" I manage.

"Just a snack." Gideon cuts me off, carrying me out of the bathroom like a bride.

He lays me on our soft bed and follows me down. I expose my neck to him, and he presses his lips to the skin immediately. When I feel the scrape of his teeth against my pulse point, my breath catches, and I brace myself for the pain.

Gideon pulls back with a grin. "Not yet. I've been waiting for this since I met you. You can wait a few more minutes."

"But why?" I whine, buzzing with anticipation as I imagine what it will feel like.

"Because I'm hungry."

With that announcement, Gideon plants my heels on either side of his collarbones, kissing first one ankle, and then the next.

"How hungry?" I ask, mesmerized by the golden glint in his eyes.

"Fucking starving."

His grumble is the last thing I hear before he falls upon me, feasting like I'm his final meal. This is completely different from the tender, gentle crescendo he orchestrated in the bathroom. This is Gideon at his most primal. Possessive, dominant, and voracious, he drives me toward the edge violently as I cling to the covers and hold on for dear life.

In seconds, I'm hovering on a dagger's edge. When he drives two fingers inside me, curling them to hit the perfect spot, I can't hold back. I shatter around him, screaming his name at a volume that will probably mortify me later.

Panting and overwhelmed, I reach for him. Gideon kisses my palm, then sucks one of my fingers into his mouth. He nips at it gently, and I show him my throat again. He chuckles, but the sound is ragged. *He's just as worked up as I am.* The knowledge settles like a soothing balm against my heated skin.

Gideon grips my waist, lifting me like a rag doll and switching our positions until I'm hovering over him on the bed. My thighs bracket his head, and his curls tickle my skin. I shiver.

"Still hungry, baby."

I'm so spent that I almost stop him. There's no way I can handle another round, but Gideon looks so desperate for me, I don't have the heart to tell him. At the first lick, I flinch, but his touch is gentle and careful.

He eases me back into the sea of sensations until I'm fully back on board and riding his face shamelessly. When his finger glides further back, I gasp. The feeling is unfamiliar, shocking even, but incredibly hot.

Gideon reads my reaction and teases me with the tip of his

finger. I jolt above him, a wild moan escaping my mouth. He's driving me crazy, and I haven't even touched him yet.

Time to change that.

I spin without warning, rotating until I have complete access to him. Gideon sucks in a breath, and I smile.

"Maybe I'm hungry too," I whisper.

Diving down, I suck as much of his dick as possible into my mouth. The movement exposes me to him even more, and I feel Gideon moan against my skin. Back and forth, we trade intimate touches until I'm grinding down on his face as he thrusts his cock roughly into my mouth.

I come again with one of Gideon's fingers buried in my ass and two in my pussy.

It's not enough. I can't wait any longer to have him.

"Gideon," I gasp, unable to articulate my thoughts.

He drags me onto his chest until we're lying with our heads at the bottom of the bed. I tuck my face into the crook of his neck and breathe him in.

"Even if we live a billion years, I'll never be able to explain how much I fucking love you," Gideon whispers the words in a husky voice. "Sometimes it keeps me up at night, looking . . ."

"Looking for what?" I ask.

"The right words."

Gideon runs his hand down my back, and I hold my breath.

"I have everything I need, but when I look at you . . ." His voice breaks, and I squeeze him a little tighter. "I look at you, baby, and my chest gets tight and heavy. My heart beats so damn hard. I swear it's trying to bust out of my chest to get closer to you. I try to tell you, but the words always slip away before I can get them out."

He growls in frustration.

"Even if I never find them," he continues. "I need you to know I'll never stop looking. For as long as I live, I'll look for the words."

"You don't have to—"

"I want to," Gideon interrupts me with a ferocity that surprises me. "I'll keep looking forever because it reminds me of how lucky I am. The gods gave me a gift I didn't even think to ask for. You're my every heartbeat, all my breaths—shit, Sheena, I can't imagine my future without you. I'll give you every word I have because you deserve them."

A hot, frantic sense of urgency swamps my heart. Gideon is mine. *My mate, my heart, my everything.* I can't wait another goddamn minute to make it permanent.

I grip Gideon's neck in my hands and meet his eyes. "Make me yours," I growl, tilting my neck back.

Gideon stops breathing, and for a long moment, he doesn't move. A slight tensing of the thick cords of muscle in his neck is the only warning I get.

His cock slides home at the same time he bites down on my neck. Intense pleasure mixes with the flash of pain, and I feel satisfaction on a soul deep level as magic flares up between us.

The bond—that electric, pulsing thread of madness inside me —vibrates wildly, expanding exponentially. I feel it transform from a single strand of pure energy into a thick, unbreakable chain. The magical tether to Gideon, the very thing that sent me packing not that long ago, settles into place in my heart. It fills a void I never knew I had.

He groans, the sound low and deep against the torn skin of my neck. We hold still and adjust to the change together. His breathing is heavy, and I feel a rush of his adoration for me shoot through the link. It settles like a warm blanket inside me, and I smile.

Gideon may keep looking for the words, but I have everything I need from him right here. I always have.

We make love slowly, trading intimate, passionate kisses. Moving as one, we share breaths and caresses.

I feel a phantom sensation that our hearts are beating in sync. *How have I ever lived without this?*

GIDEON

Never in my life have I been buried inside a woman and had to fight back tears. Until now. Gods. Fuck. Our bond is more than magic. More than fate. With her essence wrapped around my heart, nothing will ever be able to hurt me again. I feel invincible.

"Baby," I moan, grinding my body into hers.

She feels incredible like always, but it's more now. Through the bond, her pleasure becomes mine too, her love for me right there on display. I look at it greedily from every angle.

So hot. No one has ever been this lucky.

I'm starving for this unfiltered access to her heart, so I dive deeper into the bond. There's Callum. He's stamped on her heart like a tattoo, and her love for him looks like a dirty, sexy treat for me to lap up. Seeing how she feels about him is almost as much of a turn on as her love for me.

More. I want more.

Without thinking, I press further, then slam to a stop as I realize my mistake. There's more love here, but it's wilted and sore. Brown and blue like a fading bruise. I feel her pain echo in my own chest. Sheena freezes beneath me.

"Gideon," she whispers, and I know immediately she's about to apologize.

"You have nothing to be sorry for."

My words are a low rumble, and as usual, they're all wrong. Gently, I examine the hurt she's feeling and flood the bond with my love for her. I'm not trying to erase the pain, but maybe I can make her feel—

Sheena surges up and kisses me, her lips meeting mine roughly. "It's just a phase," she insists, digging her heels into my back and thrusting her hips up.

I give her what she wants. There's no point calling her out on the lie when we both sense how desperate she is to convince herself it's true.

My eyes eat her up, stopping on the drops of blood on her neck where I broke the skin. I hate seeing her hurt, but there's something about seeing my mark on her.

"This bond is such a freaky turn on." I grunt and lick a drop of sweat from the side of her neck that I didn't bite. Delicious.

"Oh yeah?" Sheena teases. "Did you unlock a new kink?"

"You're my fucking kink."

"Those words, Gideon." She gasps. "Those are pretty good."

I consider them, then shake my head. "Nowhere near good enough."

I rotate my hips, grinding and driving my cock inside her, my eyes glued to the place where we're joined.

"Your pussy is devouring my dick. Damn, Sheena. If I could only dream of this for the rest of my life, I would. You take me so fucking well."

"See? You're a poet." She laughs, but the sound fractures on a moan. "Now fuck me harder. Please. I want to feel you tomorrow, so I can remember this forever."

My mate has the best ideas. I tremble and thrust into her harder. Sheena may be laying on her back taking every inch of me and begging for more, but she's the one in control. There's nothing I won't give her if she asks.

I drive into her again and again, bringing my fingers down to play with her clit as the pressure in my heart builds right along with my orgasm. Sheena's hands fly up, and she rakes her nails down my biceps. It stings, but I grin. She can mark me however she wants. I want to feel her tomorrow, too.

"You're so perfect, baby."

I yank her legs from around my waist and plant her feet against my shoulders. I want to be careful with her, but I'm too far gone. Pinning her to the bed, I piston in and out of her, fucking into her pussy with wild abandon.

It's filthy, but the sounds she makes. Crazed. Fierce. I want more.

"Yes, Sheena. Scream for me."

And she does.

Nothing could have prepared me for how good it feels to know exactly how good I'm making her feel. When Sheena comes, I'm not surprised by the gush of liquid, but feeling her orgasm through the bond hits me like a hammer to the face. Sheena's nails dig into my arms again, and I roar like a fucking beast as I explode inside of her.

A smile splits my face as a single tear escapes my eye. *Finally.* The truth I've known since I spotted her in that bar is carved into our DNA.

Sheena May is my everything, and I'm never letting her go.

CHAPTER
TWENTY-FIVE

GIDEON

What a wonderful day.

"Would you stop grinning like that?" Callum asks. "It's godsdamned creepy."

I snort. He's pretending to be annoyed with me, but I don't buy it. He's as bad at faking his grouchy mood as I am at wiping this smile off my face. Now that he mentions it, though, my cheeks are actually starting to hurt.

"I can't help it."

I try for a growl, but the sound comes out so upbeat it's practically a chirp. Callum loses it, bracing his hands on his knees as choked laughter erupts from his mouth. A couple of fae stop in the courtyard to stare.

My eyes narrow. "I think we're losing our edge," I mutter, some of the ridiculous glee fading from my voice.

"It's not my fault," Callum wheezes and wipes a tear from the corner of his eye. "You're the one strutting around like someone's paying you to smile."

I grin, wincing at the tug on my sore facial muscles. "I feel like I won the lottery."

"Yeah, I guess you did," he agrees.

Standing in the courtyard with the late afternoon sun shining down on us, I feel my heart thud steadily in my chest. With the bond settled, I'm finally complete. Blood rushes to my face. That was unbelievably corny.

"Are you thinking about something dirty?" Cal asks.

I wasn't. But now that he brought it up . . . He snickers, and I groan.

"Shouldn't you already know if I was?"

"Not unless it gives you a boner." He licks his lips. "I'm an incubus, not a mind reader."

"Sure you are."

It's a weak ass comeback, and I don't think much of it until liquid heat rolls behind my lower abs. Arousal—sharp, teasing, and addictive—floods my body, and I growl deep in my throat.

Callum's black eyes burn with power and lust. I'm tempted to drop to my knees in the fucking courtyard and wipe that smirk off his face.

As suddenly as it came, the urge to fuck him into the dirt disappears. "You're a tease," I mutter, relieved and somewhat disappointed. I adjust myself in my pants, taking my time as I feel his eyes on me. "Stop staring."

"Or what?" Callum demands.

I haven't heard that mischievous tone from him in a long time. It's the same one he used to use when daring me to climb a big tree or sneak up on our dads in snake form. Just like when we were kids, it makes me want to do something reckless.

I glance around. A pair of shifters spar in the training circle, and there are probably half a dozen people going about their business in the courtyard. While no one is staring at us anymore, making a move would be a massive declaration.

Callum thinks I'm not ready for it, but he's wrong. I told him he's always been pack. I meant it.

Stepping forward, I bury one hand in his hair and tilt his chin up with the other. His eyelids dip partially shut as his pupils dilate.

"I think you're forgetting something," I say.

"What's that?" His attempt at a drawl comes out breathy instead.

I rub my calloused thumb against his Adam's apple. It bobs beneath my touch, and I smile. "You're mine too, Callum, and I want everyone to know."

I'm not sure which one of us erases the distance between us, but I'll remember this collision for the rest of my damn life.

Cal's soft hair clenched in my fist.

Stealing his breaths with my mouth.

He's my best friend. Claiming him like this in public shouldn't be so stupidly hot, but—*fuck*—what could be sexier than feeling horny, safe, and seen all at once?

"I'm too dehydrated to handle this kind of scare first thing in the morning." Ciprian's voice breaks us apart.

I pull back reluctantly. "Oh, you're back," I say.

"Obviously," Ciprian scoffs. "Kind of how it's now obvious to the whole compound that you're fucking my brother."

Callum stiffens at the remark as he glances around the courtyard, his lips pressed into a thin line. I step between the two brothers, ready to throw down.

"Gods, I can literally see you jumping to conclusions." Ciprian sighs. "All I meant was it's about damn time. I'm happy for you both."

He looks at the ground, embarrassed, and I scratch the back of my neck. He sounds so serious—there must be something wrong with him.

"Thank you," Callum says, staring at his brother with confusion.

Ciprian glances up, and they consider each other in silence for a ridiculously long time. I shuffle my feet. Maybe this is a reconciliation or something. Sheena would love that.

"Dude, I can't stand to look at you while you've got beard

burn all over your neck," Ciprian says with a shit-eating grin. "If I promise I've got your back, can I go?"

Callum glares at me and rubs his throat.

"He's fucking with you," I grumble. "Your neck is fine."

"No, *you're* fucking with him," Ciprian says, dodging Callum's fist. "I'm wasting my energy standing in this oppressive sunshine when there are probably cookies and definitely cold water inside."

"Was there no running water in Sin City, then?" Cal looks him over with a frown. "You do look kind of shitty."

"That was hurtful, but I'm willing to let it slide," he says. "As for what happened in Vegas, you'll have to wait like everyone else." With that, Ciprian slinks off, disappearing into the house as suddenly as he appeared.

"My brother is acting weird," Callum mutters.

I shrug. "Isn't he always?"

"Well, yeah, but . . . Damn, is he sad?"

"Maybe," I say, considering the bags under Ciprian's eyes and his wrinkled clothes. "We'll put Sheena on it."

Callum nods, his brows pulled tightly together as he latches onto something new to worry about. I smooth the furrow out with my finger, and he surprises the hell out of me by grabbing and linking my hand with his. We walk back to the shifter wing, my grin threatening to split my face once again.

CALLUM

As I sit at the table and watch my brother spin an elaborate web made entirely of surface-level bullshit, something settles in my chest. No tightness. No churning. I feel good, even while watching Ciprian talk about everything except why he looks like shit.

Sarah and Sheena are swallowing his act whole. I glance at Gideon in time to watch him roll his eyes and shovel a massive chocolate chip cookie into his mouth. I shake my head, but my lips curl up into a smile.

"So, where's the king of the fairies?" Ciprian asks.

Sheena's face falls, and I straighten up in my chair to glare at my brother. His big mouth is more of a nightmare than he is. Ciprian looks between us as an awkward silence falls over the table.

We haven't mentioned Idris. It seemed like the polite thing to do, but seeing the nervous glance Sheena tosses first at Gideon and then me, I wonder if that was a mistake. *Did we make her feel like she wasn't allowed to miss him?*

"He stayed behind in the fae realm," Sheena finally says. "With the fighting over, he needs to be there to help his sister sort everything out."

"Damned coward," Ciprian mutters, crossing his arms over his chest.

"Excuse me? I didn't quite catch that." Sheena narrows her eyes and frowns at him.

"I said he's a damned coward," Ciprian says, waving her off. "You all know he is, and if he was here, I'd say the same thing to the bastard's face."

"You shall have to thank the gods for bestowing that chance upon you." Idris steps through the doorway into the warm light of the kitchen. "Clearly, they hold you in high favor."

Sarah gasps, Gideon growls, and I notice with satisfaction that the fae looks absolutely haggard. I turn my attention to Sheena, and shit, my girl is white as a sheet. Her mouth opens and closes several times before she shoves back from the table and leaves the room without a word.

Idris watches her go, and some of his bravado seems to leave the kitchen with her. His posture, always so poised and rigid, slumps noticeably. At his side, his hands clench and unclench in an uncharacteristic show of tension. I'm not even sure he realizes he's doing it.

"Kind of creepy to just pop out of the dark like that," I mutter.

"As I was saying . . ." Ciprian nibbles on his cookie while maintaining a sinister amount of eye contact with Idris. "You're a coward."

"So I have been told." Idris' cultured drawl falls flat, and the sound of my brother chewing is loud in the tense silence that follows.

I shoot Ciprian an annoyed look, then focus back on the fae. He looks weirdly fragile. I think he's lost weight, and his eyes are sunken and hollow.

"Are you here to fix things, Idris?" Sarah asks, crossing her arms over her chest. "If not, I think you should go."

He blinks, surprised by her tone. He may have been a governing member of this enclave, but for everyone at this table, Sheena is the clear priority.

Idris dips his chin and sighs. "I intend to do my very best." He turns his piercing blue eyes on Gideon and I, but they're duller than I've ever seen them. "If I may, I would first like to have a private conversation with you two."

"You can use Joshua's study," Sarah says, nudging her son.

Gideon grunts and kicks back from the table. He has been silently seething since Idris appeared. I run my hand through my hair, then stand, leaving the fae to follow us out.

Stepping into the office, I flip on the light and wait. Whatever Idris wants to discuss with us is going to have to start with him. I'm not digging him out of the damn hole he dug for himself. He's got to do that on his own.

"I owe you both an apology." Idris wastes no time speaking up, and I have to admit, I'm stunned to hear those words come out of his mouth. "For many decades, I have let my past shape my future. Even after meeting the little djinn . . ." He begins to pace. "Especially after meeting her, I made choices based on . . . Damnation. Choices based on fear."

"You're a runner," I say. A hyper focus on self-preservation is one of the things he and Sheena have in common, but I'm surprised he's admitting it to us.

Idris pauses to glance at me and nods. "Your brother, as insufferable as he is, had the right of it. I was a coward." He trails off, but resumes his pacing.

Gideon glares at him from the corner like a lion sizing up his prey.

"You just used past tense," I say. "But nothing has changed from where I stand. You let Sheena walk away again in the kitchen, and now you're in here wasting time with us." I level him with a glare. "Idris, why are you really here?"

For the first time, his cold eyes flicker with annoyance.

"Is it not obvious? To make amends." His words are clipped like he's talking to an idiot.

I roll my eyes. "Dude, I know *why* you're here. What I want to know is why you're *here* in this room talking to me and Gideon when the women you love is somewhere else?"

Idris flinches like I hit him, but the weeks of helpless anger I felt watching Sheena grieve alone is boiling inside of me. It needs an outlet.

I advance toward him.

"She gave her life for yours, restored your kingdom to peace and prosperity, and then handed you the space to abandon her while ensuring that your people were safe and cared for here at the enclave." I point my finger at him, enjoying the way he pales at my words. "You don't deserve a single one of her tears, but she's cried herself to exhaustion over you."

"I thought it was best to let her go. I did not want to hurt her, and she had you," Idris sputters, dragging his hand over his face.

"Of course, she had me," I snap. "And as long as she can stand it, she always will. But she loves you just like she loves me and that growling menace over there."

Gideon prowls into Idris' space and stares down at him with a face made of stone. The two of them bonded while Sheena was sick and during our time in the fae realm, but there's nothing friendly about the look on Gideon's face right now.

"You were there in that room while she packed," Gideon says.

I blink. *He never mentioned that to me.*

"You let her leave, knowing how she felt and knowing it would break her heart. Explain what's different now," Gideon demands. "Or I'll toss you through the nearest wall."

Idris sucks in an uneven breath and hangs his head. "I realized Sheena is more important to me than peace. More important than my homeland. If she is willing to give me the opportunity, I will spend the rest of my life proving it."

"Good." Gideon nods. "Now, go fix it."

His head whips up. "You will allow it?"

"If you would let us get in your way, you deserve her even less than I thought," I say.

His blue eyes steel with resolve, and he nods, turning and marching from the room without another word.

"It's been weeks," I say, turning to look at Gideon. "Do you think she'll forgive him?"

"Of course." He groans. "She probably doesn't even think there's anything to forgive."

"Should we make it harder on him?"

"No point," Gideon says. "It looks like he's been beating himself up just fine."

I nod. I'm glad he looks like shit. Hopefully, Sheena doesn't forgive him the second he tracks her down and aims his mopey blue eyes her way. *Make him suffer, sweetheart.*

CHAPTER
TWENTY-SIX

SHEENA

I shove through the front door, sucking in a deep, crisp breath of pure Colorado air. Catching my toe on an uneven cobblestone, I stumble a few steps before I can regain my balance.

Idris is here.

Maybe I shouldn't have run away, but his sudden presence in Sarah's kitchen was shocking. After all my hard work putting him behind me, seeing his face again stirred up all my feelings.

Stars wink down at me. I stare up at them and feel at peace. There are more stars than I could ever count, but I have the oddest sensation that they're watching over me. I choke on a strangled chuckle. Here I am imagining the stars as guardian angels to avoid thinking about how Idris' appearance just unraveled weeks of healing.

"Care to let me in on the joke?"

I don't spin or start. Part of me knew he would find me—hoped for it with a passion that infuriates me. After everything that's happened, how can the sound of his voice still make my skin tingle?

My heart beats violently in my chest. I pray to the stars he doesn't notice the frantic thumping. I'll be damned if I give up my dignity because I'm not his dream.

"Just contemplating my place among the stars," I respond, pleased when my voice comes out even and strong.

"As legend has it, the first djinn was born of a star."

I scoff. "How could a star give birth?" As always with Idris, I find myself drawn in despite my best intentions.

"Magic, my darling."

He breathes the endearment directly in my ear, much closer than he was before. Goosebumps multiply along the sensitive skin of my neck. As much as I want to melt into him, I freeze instead.

"Did Zara send you?" I ask, stepping away to give myself room to think. Giving up ground is a sign of weakness, but as I told his sister, retreat can also be strategic.

"No." Idris sucks in a shaky breath. "I came of my own volition. After weeks mired in tedious diplomacy, I realized I had forgotten something terribly important."

Except he loves tedious diplomacy.

Like always, his words are a riddle. If he's trying to say he's here for me, then he's going to have to say it outright. I'm tired of reading what I want to be real out of interactions that tell me otherwise. *No more games.*

"The door's unlocked." I point to the fae wing. "We stowed all your things in your old room. Feel free to grab whatever you want."

"You disappoint me, darling."

His taunt lands in my gut, and I spin to face him, my hands clenched.

"Ah, there she is," Idris croons. His voice is like a caress, but I mentally bat it away.

"I came out here to be alone." I cross my arms over my chest. "I'm not interested in sifting through your verbal bullshit for gold tonight."

"Did you finally figure out there is no treasure to be had?"

Idris' face is pale in the moonlight, and he looks exhausted.

Did our separation hurt him like it hurt me? My mind is spinning with dangerous questions. If only he would just—

Absolutely fucking not, Sheena. Don't be a fool again.

"I don't want to spar with you."

"Then I suppose you have no use for me . . ."

His quip pierces my heart. Idris searches my face, but I don't want him to read me. Not anymore. *I can't do this.* I turn to leave.

"Please, do not go," Idris stammers. "Damnation, I am doing this all wrong."

Against my better judgment, I stop . . . Giving him yet another chance to bruise my heart.

"Darling, have you ever felt fear so all-encompassing you could scarcely think around the terror?"

I remain silent. He knows that I have.

"Perhaps you thought nothing could be worse, only to discover you were wrong. You become a ship without a rudder, tossed by the currents and tides, because—gods above and below —what else can you do?"

Idris paces, running his fingers through black hair that's oddly messy. It's unnerving, like having a stranger sprint past you on the sidewalk without knowing what they're running from.

"Madness would be mercy. Death, a sweet release. Work, an answer to prayers, but there is nothing to do because someone *fixed all of your damned problems for you.*"

I stare at him in shock. "Idris, I—"

"No, wait. This is all wrong." He stares at me, one arm outstretched. "Sheena, I walked the road to meet Death and saw a path to peace, but I could not take it. That is who I am, who I have always been. I will only hurt you."

Idris' blue eyes beg me to understand, but he's not making any sense.

"I don't understand you," I finally say.

It's not a lie, but it's not quite true either. This rambling speech is confusing, but I understand him enough to know what comes next. Our relationship has shaken him. With all his careful planning, he won't allow something to disrupt his equilibrium—not even me. This is the moment he leaves me behind for good.

I brace myself for goodbye, but something changes. The lost look on Idris' face turns into fierce determination, and he erases the distance between us, pressing his lips to mine.

IDRIS

SHEENA TASTES like the sweetest poison. Kissing her again is exquisite agony, but it's a pain I would gladly endure for the rest of my life if she were mine. She risked her life to give me everything I've ever wanted, then left before I could realize all I actually want is her.

She doubts me. I feel it in her hesitation and the way she trembles beneath my fingertips. I waited too long. Defeat crawls up my spine, and regret threatens to choke me. I prepare to pull back and accept my failure with grace. *If the gods will allow me just one more taste.*

Sheena makes a tiny, frustrated sound and surges forward. She wraps her arms around my neck, tugging my face tightly against hers. "Idris, I don't have a fucking clue what the goddamn fuck you're talking about." She punctuates the crass words with angry, aggressive kisses.

A shudder racks my body. Nipping at her plump lower lip, I pull back slightly. "Which part was unclear, darling?"

Sheena blinks up at me, then narrows her eyes. "How about the part with the boat or walking the path to death?" She drops her arms, but I put them back around my neck. She shakes her head. "If I didn't know better, I would think you were drunk."

"I have spent most of the day jumping through portals," I say, frowning. "You should know I would rather face the fae forest at night than travel between realms while inebriated."

"See." Sheena throws her head back, her green eyes flashing

with annoyance. "That's exactly what I'm talking about. Quit talking in riddles. Tell. Me. What. You. Mean."

The temptation to needle her is difficult to resist, but this is not the time for a battle of wits. Sheena deserves my unfiltered honesty, a gift I've given no other in all my years. It may not be the fae way, but if she wants it, she shall have it.

I clear my throat, pure terror shooting through my veins. "I mean that I am painfully, uncontrollably in love with you." I grip Sheena's face between my hands, running my thumb along her bottom lip. "I believe that the suns rise and fall each day based solely on your opinion of me. If my life is worth living without you, I refuse to see it."

I drop my forehead to hers, guiding her hand to the left side of my chest.

"What I mean, Sheena, is that my heart beats only at your pleasure. I would stake my life that there is no woman in all the realms of your equal."

I hear her quiet intake of breath, and I take both her hands in mine.

"Even knowing how you felt for me," I say. "In my cowardice, I let you leave my realm. I thought it was the lesser risk, but it was the genesis of the greatest pain of my life."

She frowns. "Idris—"

I press a finger to her lips. Even if I'm too late, I must finish. She must know the truth.

"I am trying to tell you that I am irrevocably, intimately yours, little djinn. Life with you is worth any risk. Chaos, battle—I will face it all with no complaint. For however many years I have left, I wish only to live by your side. Please, darling, tell me I am not too late."

The ferocious green of Sheena's eyes gives way to gentle lavender as her magic examines my wish. They shimmer from unshed tears in the starlight. The sight is terrifying.

"You idiot," she sobs. "That's all you ever had to say."

Sheena stands on her toes to kiss me. When our lips meet this time, I taste the salt from her tears but no poison. Under the twinkle of the mischievous night sky, I dip her backwards, devouring her mouth with all the hunger that's been building inside of me since I first laid eyes on her.

"I am sorry," I whisper.

"I know." Her hands return to my neck. "Now, shut up about it."

A shiver runs down my spine at the feeling of her nails gently scouring my skin. Hauling her back upright, I order my body to slow down. I've only just begun to court her properly. She deserves my best. I cannot rush this.

Sheena's finger runs down my chest, then she hooks it in my waistband. Her skin grazes mine, and I yearn for more. "Are you going to touch me or stand there all night thinking about it?" She demands.

"You deserve to be wooed," I insist.

"Sure," Sheena says, her eyes narrowing. "But you said you were intimately mine. Don't you think you should prove it?"

Her hand caresses the outline of my cock, the fabric of my trousers a flimsy barrier against her touch. We're outdoors. Anyone could pass by. Jealousy surges up in me when I imagine someone seeing her like this.

Snatching Sheena up in my arms, I portal us directly into the fae wing. No need to look, I know the layout like the back of my—

We slam into a tree that's growing out of the wall. I blink at my surroundings in shock. Nature surrounds me on all sides, filling me with a subtle, restorative energy.

"How did—"

"Later, Idris," she interrupts.

With surprising strength, Sheena spins us until my back is against the tree, a wicked gleam in her eyes. The thinnest branches twine around my wrists, holding me in place. I could break free, but the tree is practically dripping with her magical signature and I refuse to harm such a magnificent creation.

"May I?" Sheena's fingers pause above the fastening of my

pants, her eyes glowing purple with excitement. I nod. If she wants to amuse herself with my body, she'll hear no complaint from me.

Her fingers wrap around my length, gently tugging me free. My pants fall forgotten to my ankles.

"You broke my heart," she whispers, running her index finger along the sensitive underside of my cock. "I think you should be punished for that. Don't you?"

I nod eagerly, and when she takes me in her hand and pumps, I begin to fear for my sanity. If my little djinn wants to play games in our bed, there's nothing I would like more.

"Show me what I missed out on," I groan. "I am at your mercy, darling."

Sheena's grin flashes brightly before she remembers her role and locks her expression into a hard smirk. She sinks to her knees.

"If you beg for it," she purrs, then licks the tip of my cock. I'm thankful these branches are partially supporting me. "Maybe you'll be rewarded."

I haven't begged in decades, but I shudder and writhe as she takes me fully into her mouth and does her best to drive me mad. When I'm hovering right on the edge, she pulls back, a devious look in her eyes. I take inventory of my senses, stunned to hear the ragged sound of my own breaths.

Then, she repeats the pleasurable torment.

Again.

Again.

Again.

I lose count of the times she pulls back a fraction of a second before I reach my peak. Moaning, sweaty, and desperate, my cock throbs angrily between my legs when Sheena backs up to admire the writhing mess she's left me in.

From the sexy flush staining her pale skin to the strands of hair hanging loose around her face, the sight of her takes my breath away. Her lips are swollen and red from tormenting me with pleasure, and I close my eyes as a shudder racks my body. I don't need my vision to know those perfect lips are curved into a smirk.

"I wish to touch you," I whisper. "Please, darling, I will do anything you want."

Perhaps I can beg after all.

SHEENA

I DON'T KNOW what's come over me, but I think I could become addicted to having Idris at my mercy. Watching the poised fae squirm and beg sets me on fire.

I've never played a game like this from the position of power. I'm not sure Gideon or Callum have it in them to submit. I wouldn't have guessed Idris would be into it either, but I'm not going to waste my chance in case this is the only one I get.

His wish caresses the magic swirling in my gut, waiting for my decision. The feeling of control adds to my excitement. I'm practically buzzing with it.

I focus back on the flawless man in front of me. His lean, chiseled body is spread out like a buffet, trembling slightly under my stare. Idris looks at me . . . Fuck, he looks at me like I'm the answer to every question he's ever had.

Flashes of memory hit me. Idris falling to the ground from the force of Leona's magic. Thinking I had lost him forever. The moment I stepped through Zara's portal and left him behind. To my horror, tears well up behind my eyes.

Branches snap as Idris frees himself from the tree. He scoops me up and sinks to the floor with me cradled in his lap.

"I'm okay. I just," I sputter, wiping at my eyes angrily. *I can't believe I ruined the moment.*

"You do not have to explain, darling, but please, do not ask me to let you go."

His words make a sniffle break free.

"No, I don't want you to go."

When I look up, I see the fae wing transform into the meadow. Our meadow. The magic forming it glows silver in the dim lighting.

"Talk to me, please," Idris begs.

"I don't know," I say, another tear sliding down my cheek. "It's complicated."

"Perhaps if you just tell me what you mean." His smile is charming as he parrots my earlier words back to me.

"Dammit, I don't know. I was feeling horny," I say, feeling blood rush to my face. Idris shifts beneath me, but doesn't comment. "I wanted to let you go, so that you would touch me, but then I worried you wouldn't want to play like this again."

Idris frowns.

"Which would be fine," I rush to clarify. "Then I thought about losing you . . ."

I bury my face in his neck, embarrassed to be acting so emotional in front of him. Idris clears his throat, and I brace myself for his response.

"It may anger you to know this, but seeing how my absence pained you soothes my heart." He drops a warm kiss on my cheek. "Do not mistake that sentiment as a desire to cause you pain, but knowing that I was not alone in my agony quiets the deepest fears of my soul."

"You'll never be alone in this love, Idris," I reassure him. "I couldn't make my heart forget you. No matter how hard I tried."

"I beg you, stop trying then." His hands on my back kneed possessively, dissolving tight knots of tension I didn't even realize were there. "Now, about these games you mention . . ."

I groan, feeling my skin heat with embarrassment. A gentle tug on my hair encourages me to lift my face from Idris' neck and lock my eyes with his.

"If you want to tie me up and torment me with that tongue of yours every day for the rest of our existence, I will gladly submit.

If you long to hunt me through the forest and bend me to your every pleasure, you have only to demand I run."

Phantom silvery images appear. Two figures of us—wispy and sensual—act out Idris' words, stoking my arousal higher and higher until I'm soaking wet and throbbing. I squirm in his lap, but he's not done.

"Perhaps we encounter each other as traveling strangers. Cloaked only in shadows, you could ride me to exhaustion on a crowded train, unable to make a sound or risk giving us both away."

His words are soft and rhythmic, a hypnotic song in my ears. If I didn't feel his erection digging into my thigh, I would think he wasn't affected at all.

"Or maybe you command I carry you to this very meadow and devote myself to your pleasure until the light from both suns fades away to nothing."

His blue eyes, brutal in their intensity, pierce me.

"You may be the djinn, my darling, but I am the one who will make all your wishes come true. Any game you desire, you shall have."

I kiss him with all the pent up longing I've been carrying since we met. "The meadow one. Now," I say, choking on my emotions.

Idris groans, then strips me bare. He draws me into a sensual dance of deep, delicious kisses. I want to explore his body more, but I can't bear to pull back. Clinging to his hair, I hold his head in place so our lips never have to part.

Then, surrounded by flowers and the gentle glow of the second sunset, Idris slips inside me, his eyes never leaving mine. The feeling is pure magic.

I ride him slowly, digging my heels into the ground to give myself the leverage I need. We're not in the fae realm, but his glamour is so lifelike I can practically feel the purple grass caressing my skin.

I maintain the slow, smooth drag even as we tremble and glisten with sweat. The feeling of Idris stretching and sliding inside me is one I want to hold on to forever. I keep up the pace until my thighs burn. My next drop sends his cock pounding directly into a spot that makes me moan with delight.

The sound breaks something in both of us. Idris' hands leave my face, clamping down on my hips instead. He lifts and shoves me down repeatedly, driving into my pussy at an angle that curls my toes.

All three moons have risen now. I arch my back, desperate to feel their cool light on my body. Curling into the stretch, I keep going until my head brushes the ground. With my body bowed like the crescent moon, I'm connected to Idris at one end and the soft meadow at the other.

Idris groans at the view, and his thrusts speed up. There's an extra element of desperation driving his movements. It makes me feel powerful.

One of his hands leaves my hip and moves to where we're joined. I moan, electricity shooting through my body as he strokes me. Stretched out like I am, I'm completely at his mercy, but I trust Idris implicitly. When my orgasm finally crests, it's like waves rolling onto the shore—unstoppable and all-consuming.

"Sheena. Darling," Idris gasps, his body curling down on top of mine.

He presses a frantic kiss to my mouth, and I bury my hands in his hair as I feel his body tighten and release. He's beautiful.

When I focus back on our surroundings, the meadow is gone, and we're lying on the floor of the hallway. Thankfully, none of the folk are around.

"I see you have made some alterations to my home," Idris drawls in my ear, and my skin pebbles. "Is my bed intact?"

I shake my head, noticing the last silvery thread of his magic fade away. I reach for it, my brow furrowing with confusion. "The blue. It's gone."

Idris pushes up on his elbows, his body suddenly tense above mine. He glances around at the changes to the fae wing, then meets my eyes reluctantly.

"Fae magic is a curious thing, you know. The colors . . . . They are more symbolic than anything else. A sign of allegiance."

I frown, thinking back on all the magic I saw during our travels in the fae realm. "Your sister's magic is also silver," I say.

"Indeed. Silver is the preferred color of the Court of Stars."

"The ice. The blue—"

"Was a reminder. A warning for myself lest I forget the sting of betrayal."

"Kirsi's magic was blue." I do my best to keep my tone even. *I can't believe I didn't piece this together sooner.* Idris nods, a stubborn tilt to his chin. "But you've decided to change back to silver?"

He shakes his head, pulling me to my feet, and wrapping his hands around both my shoulders. Purple magic swirls out from his fingertips, covering my body and his before solidifying into two glamoured robes.

"Another warning?" I ask, my tone teasing as I look into his uncharacteristically nervous face.

"No, darling. Consider it a declaration."

"A declaration of what?"

"Of who I belong with."

Idris kisses me then, and I shiver with emotion. He pulls back before I've had enough of him and narrows his eyes. "Now, tell me why you remodeled my entire blasted wing but neglected to install a bed for us."

"Well, you weren't here, so it didn't seem like a priority."

Idris groans, the sound so mournful, I can't help but giggle. I'm still smiling when he scoops me up into his arms.

"Those two idiots better not monopolize you." His mutter is the last thing I hear before he portals us both straight into Gideon's bedroom.

EPILOGUE

SHEENA

A heavy, demanding knock drags me from the best night's rest I've had in weeks. Blinking to clear the sleep from my eyes, I see Callum's thick, sooty lashes flutter open irritably. A massive arm is wrapped around his waist, and messy, golden curls appear over his shoulder as Gideon lifts his head to look at the door.

For a moment, I'm too distracted by how good they look to notice the hand curled possessively around my breast or the erection digging into my lower back. My heart swells. It wasn't a dream; Idris is here.

When we came in, Gideon and Callum were already asleep—or pretending to be. Idris and I piled into the bed, and I fell asleep about fifteen seconds after my head hit the pillow.

"It's the middle of the night. Fuck off," Callum snaps as someone continues to pound on the door.

"Watch your mouth." Sarah's voice carries through the wood, and Cal pales when he realizes who he just yelled at. "I wouldn't be interrupting you if it wasn't important. You have . . . guests."

Sarah sounds worried; I sit up quickly, and the sheet falls to my waist. My skin tingles at the feeling of three sets of hungry eyes on me.

"Mom, whoever it is, can you make them go away? It's really late," Gideon says. He reaches across Callum to cup my cheek in his massive hand, then rubs his thumb across my swollen bottom lip. His dimples pop out as he grins over at me. "Your heart, baby . . ."

He doesn't have to say anything else. Since we sealed the bond, he's been able to sense my heartache. Gideon never once complained about it, but I'm sure he's relieved to feel the cracks healed by Idris' return.

"I would if I could, sweetie, but this is something Sheena needs to handle herself."

That does it. I throw the sheet fully off, crawling to the end of the bed naked to avoid stepping on anyone. I ignore the chorus of groans behind me as the guys appreciate the view.

"Sorry, Sarah. I'll be there in two minutes," I call out.

I dart into the closet to grab some clothes, roughly shoving my legs into a pair of dirty jeans and skipping a bra in favor of one of Gideon's oversized t-shirts.

When I come out of the closet, my mouth goes dry. Callum, Gideon, and Idris are all in various states of dressing, and the miles of muscled skin on display makes my brain short circuit. I want to crawl right back into the bed and never leave it, but . . . Sarah. Yes, Sarah said it was urgent.

I snap myself out of my daze, then open the door. Gideon's mom observes the parade of men behind me with a grin, but she doesn't comment. If I needed further proof that she's the best person in the universe, I get it when she presses a tumbler of coffee into my hand.

"Who's here? Is everything okay?" I ask, taking a grateful sip as I follow her to the formal living room.

Sarah stops before opening the door and pats my cheek. The gesture is reassuring, but the smile on her face is strained, and I see worry in her warm, brown eyes.

"It's okay, Sarah," I assure her, glancing at the three men behind me. "Whoever it is, we'll be okay." As I say it, I realize I actually mean it. *Together, we can handle anything.*

Sarah nods and swings the door open, revealing the tall, broad outline of a man. My heart begins to race. Dim light or not, I would recognize that silhouette anywhere. Quaid turns, and I force my body not to react.

"Sheena." My former best friend's voice is a low, familiar rumble. "I need your help."

The fucking nerve. There's no apology in the world that can heal all the hurt between us at this point. If I live ten lifetimes, I still won't be brave enough to open up the box that holds my complicated feelings for Quaid.

I open my mouth to tell him to get lost, but he steps to the side before I can speak, revealing two people I've only ever seen in a faded photograph. Quaid's parents stare back at me, and my mouth drops open in shock.

I must be dreaming. They're dead. How are they standing in front of me right now?

"We're so sorry to barge in like this, but we had to wait until it was dark to travel. My son has told me so much about you." Quaid's mother offers me a tentative smile, the lamplight glancing off her elongated canines.

Oh my god . . . They're vampires.

My hand tightens around the tumbler of coffee, and Gideon steps closer to my back.

"Please, Sheena . . ." Quaid's voice draws my attention back to him. "I was wrong about everything. We're all in danger."

AUTHOR'S NOTE

Fangs?! How did that happen? You'll find out soon.

***Lost Legacy Book 3, The Last Djinn,* is available now.**

If you enjoyed The Last Dream, please consider leaving a rating or review. These make such a difference for indie authors, and I love hearing from you!

Download Deleted Scenes, Sarah's Chocolate Chip Cookie Recipe, and receive updates on my next series by signing up for my newsletter or scanning the QR code below with your phone's camera.

ACKNOWLEDGMENTS

Wow. The response to The Last Wish blew me away, so first off, I want to thank everyone who gave a debut author a chance and invested in Sheena's story. Because of you, I get to make writing my job, and I never want to take that for granted.

In the time between publishing Lost Legacy Books 1 and 2, I've been a lot of things: elated, unhinged, and manic, to name a few. My support system strapped in for the ride, and I cannot thank them enough for bearing with my mood swings.

While The Last Wish will always hold a special place in my heart as my first published work, I would be lying if I said The Last Dream isn't my favorite so far. Writing this piece of the story was easy, which is rare for me. The words you just read poured out of me, sometimes spilling from my brain faster than I could type them.

As a result, I yapped about this plot and the characters to the people around me *insufferably* often. There's no way they weren't sick of hearing about it, but none of them told me to shut up. Gabe, Mom, Alyssa, Madeleine, Meg, Lisa, Caleb, and Thomas—I thank you for your patience.

Gabe, you're the best man I know, and you prove it day in and day out by bending over backwards to help me chase this dream. Being loved by you is turning me into a hopeless romantic, and I can't get enough of it. Callum, Gideon, and Idris have nothing on you.

For my 2nd Lieutenant and the chainsaw to my machete, thanks for continuing to fight for my books so hard. There would be zero comma continuity in this entire book if it wasn't for you.

The fact that you tolerate me sprinkling in punctuation on vibes alone is a testament to your resilience.

Momma and Alyssa, thanks for cheering me up when I was down and cheering me on when I wanted to celebrate. I can't thank either of you enough for your constant encouragement.

Gabe, Madeleine, Alyssa, Lisa, Krista, and Bethany—this book is better because you each took the time to read it and point out its flaws and strengths. Thanks to y'all, we have continuity, color consistency, and no accidental necromancy. I couldn't do it without you guys.

And for my friends from coast to coast—there are too many of you to name—dozens of you purchased my book and cracked it open, even if romance wasn't your thing. When I started this writing journey, I saw multiple warnings online: "Your friends and family won't read your book; don't be offended by that. It's just how it is . . ." Well, thank you for proving what I knew all along: my friends are top tier in every way.

Until next time! 🩶🩶🩶

ABOUT THE AUTHOR

Alana Kay is a romance author with a soft spot for imperfect heroes, tough heroines, and steamy love stories. She made her debut into paranormal romance in 2024 with her novel *The Last Wish* (Lost Legacy Book One) and completed the trilogy in February 2025. Alana Kay fell for romance novels in the early aughts after sneaking bodice rippers from her mom's dog-eared collection of paperbacks. A big believer in happy endings, she likes her love scenes on page, her adventures nonstop, and her magic off the rails. When she's not typing feverishly, she's either snuggling with her dog, cats, or husband in sunny Los Angeles or impulsively signing up for a sporting event she's not nearly athletic enough to commit to.

Author of the completed *Lost Legacy* and *Radiant Legacy* series. Stay tuned for the *Bad Bones* duet, coming early 2027.

For updates, follow @AlanaKayAuthor on social media or head over to AlanaKayAuthor.com.

ALSO BY ALANA KAY

LEGACY UNIVERSE

LOST LEGACY

The Last Wish

The Last Dream

The Last Djinn

RADIANT LEGACY

Darkest Valley

Shadow of Death

Fear No Evil

Eternal Light

www.ingramcontent.com/pod-product-compliance
Lightning Source LLC
LaVergne TN
LVHW040214110826
845146LV00005B/1289

9798991291835